UNLEASHING THE STORM

MAMA'S BROOD, BOOK TWO

SHAY RUCKER

DARK RADIANCE PRODUCTIONS

ACKNOWLEDGMENTS

First and foremost, a heartfelt thanks to everyone who read *On the Edge of Love* and loved it enough to encourage, enquire about, nudge, and for some, out and out *harangue* me into putting out book two of Mama's Brood. ALL of it worked to get us to this point, and for that I am ever grateful to you.

To Lady D, you did the heavy lifting on this one. Your feedback, the honesty of your input, and your ability to help me through doubt and uncertainty made this happen. You are invaluable. Thank you much, *beloved* (lol).

Thanks much to Zaji at www.creativeankh.com for creating a cover that embodies the energy of the novel.

And special thanks to Barb Wilson at editpartner.com, the pinch hitting MVP. You stepped in during my moment of desperation and provided on point editing at lightning speed.

Family and friends, thank you always for simply being the magnificently wise, insane, and loving people that you are.

A final thanks to the writer community I've come to know, your insights, support, advice, and knowledge have continued to inspire.

UNLEASHING THE STORM:

MAMA'S BROOD (BOOK 2)

By Shay Rucker

ig Country sat in his Papa-Bear-sized chair, naked as the day he was born. Curling and uncurling his toes in the soft fibers of the flokati rug, he reached up and adjusted the half-smoked cigar dangling from his mouth. Closing his eyes, he widened his thighs and let his head fall back against the chair's supple leather, simply wanting to relax, wanting to have an itty-bitty minuscule moment of peace in the comfort of his Tiburón beach house, but he couldn't find it.

All week he'd been running around like Marvin-the-Merry-Fucking-Mover for Sabrina and Zeus, his Ford F350 clocking hundreds of miles as he hauled furniture and boxes from Zeus's cabin and Sabrina's apartment to the garage at the base of the mountain. The hours on the road weren't the problem though; he loved driving almost as much as he loved fucking. No, something he couldn't put a finger on was barring him from his unbothered nature, and not knowing what it was pushed him farther toward the edge.

Soon enough, ol' son, you'll figure it out soon enough, he promised himself. He had a great mind and great minds figured shit out.

The gagging sound from his crotch forced him to open his eyes and look down, pulling the cigar from his mouth.

"You all right down there, darlin'?" he asked the pretty little blonde with the baby-blue eyes. She looked up at him, her pink glossy lips stretched taut over his girth. He reached down and stroked her silky strands encouragingly.

Pretty girl tried to smile, then went back to work. Her ungraceful attempts at navigating the length and thickness of his glorious manhood had him rethinking his decision to bring home a regular kind of woman—and by regular, he meant one whose skills and motivations hadn't been honed by the incentives of money and all it could provide.

Big Country flinched and grunted as a tooth caught on a ridge along his shaft.

"Shit, woman!"

"Sowwy," she mumbled while having the ever-loving grace to look both embarrassed and tickled by his reaction.

He rolled his neck to relieve the mounting tension.

Taking a slow drag on the cigar, he tamped down on a surge of impatience and watched her bob up and down a few more seconds before he concluded that, for both their sakes, it was best to give her some guidance.

"Look here, sweetness, my motto is if you ain't a pro, go slow. Learn your way around the big fella and maybe leave the deep-throating for another time."

Of course, the possibility of *another* time was a bald-faced lie. He wasn't giving this novice another opportunity to abuse Big Bubba.

"This ain't what you want, man; if you take her home you're going to regret it."

Lynx had warned him before they'd parted ways earlier tonight. Damned if his best friend didn't have a touch of psychic in him. Leaving the lounge with…with…*whatever her name was* hadn't been his smartest decision. He should've headed back to Mama's House with Lynx instead of believing an innocent face and sweet disposition would be a solution to this discontent he couldn't identify.

In his haste to return to being the easygoing man he'd struggled to be, he'd made a fool's mistake, broken his A-number one rule when he'd chosen to have a sexual encounter with a woman outside of the professional sexual services industry. Now he sat here, receiving the worst blow he had since he was a fourteen-year-old test dummy in Lucy Bell Lucree's quest to land an older wealthier boy at their high school. He'd crushed on the then-sixteen-year-old since he was twelve and had no problem being her guinea pig, and as awkward as it had been in the beginning, he'd come each and every time. Now, with each passing moment, he accepted that his chances of finding pleasure and peace between this woman's thighs were spiraling from *damn unlikely* to *a snowball's chance in hell.*

In an act of boldness, the woman on her knees tried to take him deeper and choked again. He clenched up, expecting more teeth, more pain, sighing in relief when neither came to pass. Hastily, he dislodged his dick from her mouth before she bit it clean off, and stood.

Lord, protect me from the unskilled, he thought, as a strange look settled over her face. He wondered if it was shame or sadness, but she bowed her head before he could be sure.

Well, this was a conundrum.

He scratched his left ass cheek, unaccustomed to anything other than shared orgasms during sex. Right then and there, he decided to sacrifice himself and give her a bit of pleasure. That was one rule he wouldn't break tonight. He always made sure he gave his partners their release.

"Lay back on the rug and bend your knees for me, sweetness," he instructed, grabbing the glass ashtray near the foot of the recliner and extinguishing his cigar. Placing the ashtray on the chair, he looked at…at…it started with a D but he still couldn't remember her name.

He shrugged. Wasn't like it mattered. He didn't have any intention of seeing her again, and maybe that reflected in his gaze because she seemed hesitant to do as requested.

"If you ain't the most beautiful sight a man could ever want to see, I don't know what is." He complimented her, knowing the quickest way through a woman's defenses was through her vanity.

Predictably she eased back on the rug, propped herself up on her elbows, and looked at him with uncertain anticipation.

Stepping into the space between her slightly spread legs, he gloried in her sun-kissed skin, unmarred except for the scars on her left wrist and forearm. The scarring was old, an indication of a past suffering self-expressed on her body. Maybe it had been a grab at attention, or maybe it had been an indication of something worse.

Either way, he could appreciate anybody who'd stood toe to toe with their mortality and somehow made it out alive. Near death made you appreciate living; at least that's what he'd felt when Mama and his grandparents had stepped in after his family had beaten the living shit out of him, trying to hasten his death before he was even old enough to know how to spell the word.

"Bend your knees for me, sweetness," he said and kneeled, looking at the woman's shaved pussy. *Good Lord in Heaven*, he thought as Bubba attempted to push toward the silky prize buried deep within her body. *Sorry, old son*, Big Country apologized. There was no way in hell he was going to add to the list of tonight's mistakes.

Positioning his head between her thighs, he inhaled the natural musk still able to exist despite the floral scents she tried to smother it with. He looked up beyond her abdomen and breasts to her cornflower-blue eyes. "Anything I should be worrying about, darlin'?"

It was an unusual question to have to ask. The women he had sex with were tested at regular intervals by the physicians he paid to provide him with proof of their status. The woman shook her head, blushing so red her level of embarrassment was painful. *Poor darlin'.*

"I'm not diseased. I've only been with one man, and my father is very diligent about making sure I am...not compromised," she said, avoiding his gaze as she shielded her breasts with her forearm. Her reaction to frank talk was another reason he avoided women he hadn't put a down payment on.

Big Country rubbed his brow against the soft flesh of her inner thigh, hoping to stave off the tension headache threatening to crack his head open.

He sighed.

"You're a good girl. I get that, sweetness, knew it the minute I looked into those adorable eyes."

He slowly kissed a trail up her thigh toward the base of her womanhood. "Let me give you the pleasure you deserve," he said. His gut clenched painfully as that worm of unrest moved through it, causing him to clench his teeth to fight off the reaction.

"Please, don't feel as if…"

Her words stopped when he slid his finger from the base of her opening to her swollen clit. Spreading her lips farther apart, he glided two fingers inside her tight walls, stroking in and out, pressing a little deeper each time. He groaned, feeling truly distressed over the tight ride he was denying Bubba. He plunged an additional finger inside of her and sucked her clit as if it held the key to his redemption.

The woman's high mewling cries, surging hips, trembling thighs, and gushing pussy all told him she was already on the edge of orgasm. Pushing his fingers deeper, sucking harder, cocking her thigh higher and working his hand faster, he bit back a grin and rolled his eyes as she bucked wildly and emitted some kind of high-pitched squeak-sob thing before going lax.

Had to be a record, he thought to himself as he smiled, stroking her thighs until her trembling subsided, her breathing evened. Pushing up to his knees, he gazed down at her flushed skin, glistening with sweat. With her generous, perfectly formed tits, blonde hair, and lithe body, she reminded him of a young Jeri Ryan.

She smiled up at him with her big baby blues. He'd always been a sucker for blue eyes and dimples; she didn't possess the latter but the former had factored highly in his decision to leave the lounge with her tonight. Her eyes had promised an end to the emptiness gnawing at him but in the end, only expanded it.

"That was…was…amazing."

"Always happy to please, darlin'." He smiled.

She held out her arms, encouraging him to settle on top of her body and sheathe his thickness inside the warm wet center he had a hand—and a couple of fingers—in creating. No lie, he briefly contemplated accepting what she offered; but like the wrath of God, his cell phone rang, ending his indecision.

"Sorry, sugar, but I gotta take this."

Rising to his feet, he walked to the end table beside his chair and reached for the smartest damn cell phone in creation. He looked at the display, saw it was Lynx, and grinned. It was uncanny the way his friend was always there, reaching out just before he did something that would likely get him into a world of trouble.

"Hey brother, what can I do you for?" he asked, more cheerful than the call warranted.

"Absolutely no way you can do me. Period. I'm literally shuddering in revulsion at the thought."

"Lynx…"

"Yeah, yeah, whatever, man. You need to get over to Mama's House quick. And when I say quick, I mean…" It was obvious Lynx couldn't think of a witty way to end the sentence. "Dude, you just need to get over here. Now."

Lynx disconnected the call abruptly, leaving Big Country to stare at his phone in confusion and dread. Something was going down at Mama's House and with Zeus and Sabrina in residence, there was no telling what he'd find himself walking into. Dead bodies, bloodstained walls, cleaved limbs…

He turned to the woman slowly sitting up on his expensive rug. He walked to retrieve his jeans and shirt from their pile on the floor. "Sorry, darlin', duty calls, and I must heed her cry."

"You have to leave? *Now?*" she asked, wide-eyed with disbelief and a smidge of hostility.

Another reason he only dealt with pros. No questions, no demands. You tell them you gotta go and they smiled and held the door open for you on your way out.

"Right *fucking* now," he said, tossing her peach-colored dress toward her. "Can't be helped."

He grimaced and feigned concentration as he pulled up and buttoned his jeans.

Mistakes number three, four, and five were bringing the woman to his home. He never brought women he fucked anywhere close to where he lived. Ever. This was his haven and he didn't need some woman getting any ideas about being invited back. He didn't need her believing she meant more to him than she actually did.

When they were both dressed, he walked her to the door and handed over her purse as she crossed the threshold. "Darlin,' I'm sure sorry about the abrupt end to a lovely evening," he began.

"It's okay, I'm sure we'll be seeing each other soon."

He wanted to put his head through a cinder block. Not even flames of hell licking at his balls would compel him to invite her back. Still he smiled, tipping an imaginary cowboy hat in her direction.

She laughed and did some kind of weird-assed curtsy thing before waving goodbye and trotting down the three stairs, light-footed as a doe. She got into the hybrid car she'd followed him home in and pulled out of his driveway. He didn't know how other men did it, but he knew he'd just dodged a bullet with her graceful exit.

As soon as her taillights turned the corner, Big Country went back into his house, took a quick shower, brushed his teeth, grabbed his keys, set the alarm, and made his way to his pickup parked on the street. To reward himself for getting through this clusterfuck of a night he vowed to call Sylvie with the blood-red hair, porcelain skin, and eyes so bright green they gleamed like Irish flames. Though she was pricey to keep, Sylvie had a mouth strong enough to suck the devil out of the damned.

Yes, Lord, Sylvie—above any of his other women in the area—was skilled enough to erase the memory of tonight's foolishness.

With a plan in place, Big Country sped toward Mama's House, vowing never again to break the rules he'd created to control his dealings with women.

Tonight never would have happened if he hadn't witnessed Zeus and Sabrina wallowing around in some type of shared delusion everybody in the Brood termed "a freaky love thing." Whatever it was, wouldn't likely last. He'd been a fool to believe he could find the peace they shared in the arms of a beautiful stranger.

Reaching for the half-smoked cigar in his shirt pocket, he lit it, puffing until the burn held, breathing the smoke deep into his lungs.

Slumping comfortably in his seat, he navigated his big truck along the narrow road.

No sir, he thought, Zeus and Sabrina could indulge in that happy-ever-after bullshit called love if they wanted to. He was going to continue to put his eggs in the basket reserved for straightforward, transient, noncommittal sex with a variety of well kept, highly skilled women who agreed that when a good time wasn't a good time, they'd go their separate ways.

CHAPTER 1

"Stormy, get down off that table or I'm telling your daddy!" Reign yelled over the music, laughing so hard she almost fell over. Stormy smiled down at her cousin and pulled the hem of her dress higher while rolling her hips suggestively to Muddy Waters' "Mannish Boy."

Turning slowly on the table she figure-eighted her ass defiantly in Reign's face, bringing on a wave of catcalls and laughter for the group of women celebrating with her, as well as some of the men scoping out their group from a distance.

With each undulation of her hips, Stormy wound down lower and lower until she was crouched less than a foot above the table's sturdy wooden top. She bounced up and down, attempting to put an end to the notion that a woman of nearing forty couldn't drop it like her shit wasn't pure fire. Of course, within seconds, that fire was burning its way through Stormy's thighs, making her question her ability to wind her big ass back up again. The refrain of *I'm a man*, the guttural guitar riff, the driving drum beat, had her popping her hips from left to right, rising steadily as if lifted by the hands of ancestors come down to celebrate with friends and kin during this alcohol-abundant revival.

I finally did it, she thought with a smile, moving with unadulterated pleasure.

After over fifteen years of working for the county, she'd stepped away from the job that supported her through a master's degree to her license in clinical social work, only to suck the life out of her as repayment ever since. Releasing herself from the last piece of toxicity plaguing her life, she was not only committed to being more than a silent partner in Red's Pleasure Boutique, she was striking out into the world of clinical consultation and private practice. *Finally free,* she thought as Muddy Waters declared he was "a man."

"I'm a woman!" Stormy sang loudly, overriding Muddy's gravelly tones.

The seven women surrounding her joined in, jumping up and down as if electrified by the power of her declaration. She was a fucking woman, and she was tired of feeling like she didn't matter in this world. That's what working at her old job had done, that's what years of marriage to her ex-husband had done, and she wasn't allowing that bullshit anymore.

Her group danced around the sturdy table, obviously bolted to the ground, because Stormy Redmond was nothing little or light. Standing five foot ten in her bare feet, she'd succeeded at reclaiming her curvy size-fourteen body after years of burying alive the active, vibrant woman she'd once been. Although her breasts had always been big, she'd once again had the defined curvature of her hips and ass.

Last week, even the pastor at her daddy's church had done a double take, but the sad truth was that men always looked, but they never stepped up, never engaged, allowing their gaze to pass right over her without a word.

Except for tonight.

Tonight, the men there saw her and she didn't mind being seen.

Throwing her head back, she laughed and danced until the song wound down and switched to a less energetic R&B tune. Stepping from table to chair to floor, she eyed the expanding number of men watching her group, as if dazed by the presence of women.

Before the bar had opened, Stormy, her best friend Lou, who'd come up from San Diego, her other best friend and business partner Jules, her cousin Reign, and her niece Octavia had arrived early to help the owners—Mama and Terry—move the few tables at the center of the bar to the periphery where the tables were bolted down. They'd decorated the bar in the primary colors of Jules and Stormy's sex shop: bloodred and lavender. The explosion of balloons and streamers were in opposition to the bar's dark interior.

Always aware of marketing opportunities, Jules had brought a slew of party bags—filled with items sold in their boutique—to give to the patrons of Mama's House. What none of them anticipated was the overwhelming number of men…very deadly-looking men…patronizing the bar.

Besides the women there to celebrate with Stormy, there were less than ten other women in the bar. It was an almost unheard-of ratio for the Bay Area, one that had the potential to turn their event into a wasted effort because men patronized Red's Pleasure Boutique on a limited basis. Still, Jules reminded Stormy that men had wives, sisters, mothers, and significant others who could definitely benefit from the gift bags. Already, a woman named Sabrina had taken her bag and her man through the riveted metal door that read *Employees Only* hours ago. Stormy had yet to see them return.

Hugging her cousin Reign to her side, damned near holding her up, Stormy spoke into her cousin's ear. "You know you're drunk, right?"

"I know!" Reign screamed. "Oh my God, I know!"

The normally introverted and highly anxious Reign danced off and latched onto Lou who nodded once, letting Stormy know that she'd take care of Reign. Since college, Stormy and Lou had an unspoken agreement to always watch over Reign in social settings. The one time Stormy hadn't…

Looking through the throng of dancers, Stormy located her niece Octavia—Tavi to family and friends—in the arms of a man who looked like he could be on both the FBI and DEA's most wanted lists. Maybe in his mid-twenties, he wore a beat-up black leather vest with no shirt. Tattoos ran rampant over every surface of his exposed skin, save his very hard and unfriendly face. The man looked like he was well on his way to becoming a lifer in some Aryan motorcycle gang. Stormy wasn't ready to rule out the possibility that he wasn't just because he was dancing with her brown-skinned, kinky-haired niece.

Cursing her hypervigilance, Stormy made her way over to Reign and Lou and they all began to do the bump, Lou at one hip, and Reign, who stumbled and laughed each time their hips met, at the other. Stormy watched Tavi and the ex-con press their bodies together. Her niece wrapped her arms around the Aryan's neck and his thick forearm pinned her against his body as his other hand slowly massaged Tavi's ass. Tavi said something in his ear and he grinned dangerously before dropping his head and biting her niece's collarbone. Tavi grabbed his head and pressed her mouth against his in an all-consuming kiss.

Acutely aware of the lack of intimacy in her own life, Stormy looked away.

Beyonce's "Partition" blasted around the room and her crew went wild...no, wild*er*. Hell, as hyped as they got, you would have thought the singer herself had walked into the bar. Every woman *except* Stormy had found a man to grind on. Even the bar's namesake, Mama, was moving brazenly against her co-owner's body as if she was a descendent of Salome. They had to be lovers the way Mama was tying that man up with invisible veils of seduction.

What was it about this place that stirred something wild and primal, she wondered, watching Terry's features take on a feral quality, his eyes narrowing on the much smaller woman before he threw his head back and howled like a wolf...like an actual wolf.

There were respondent howls in the crowd, and Terry hauled Mama's petite body off the ground, pressed her ass into the bar and bent her over backward, devouring her in a kiss so explicit Stormy felt her blood heat up. Mama bit Terry's lip and he yowled, attempting to pull his lip free before settling back into the kiss.

Stormy laughed at their theatrics, wiping a tear of joy and longing from the corner of her eye. *That*, she thought, *I want that*.

She hadn't been sexual with a man since she and Chad divorced three years ago, but even when their relationship was new and blossoming, it hadn't included those kinds of uninhibited intense displays of affection.

Reign stumbled over and grabbed Stormy's arm to avoiding falling on her ass.

"Oh my God, Stormy, look, *look*! There's a real-life giant over there checking you out like he's going to devour you, or…or kill you!" Reign yelled, pointing blatantly across the room—something she'd never do if she was sober. Following her cousin's wavering finger, Stormy tracked it to a massive dark-haired man who somehow managed to dwarf the doorframe he was leaning against.

Oh, good Lord, she thought. The raw power and sexuality radiating off this man made her clit throb.

She pressed her thighs tight.

The giant cocked his head to the side and listened intently to something Lynx—the Asian man she'd met earlier—said. The giant said something back, eyes never veering away from Stormy, and whatever he replied caused the Asian guy to double over in laughter. She smiled as she watched the interaction between the two men who were obviously good friends.

A hand settled against the small of Stormy's back and she turned to look up into the ocean-blue gaze of a six-foot-something chiseled piece of manhood whose touch heightened the arousal the giant had ignited. This place must circulate pheromones through the AC unit, she thought as her nipples tightened. Maybe it's just been too long, too long sampling the boutique's products, too long without the touch of a man. She'd promised Lou and Jules, her two best friends, that she wouldn't punk out, that she'd look open to looking for potential sex partners tonight. The blue-eyed man with a cup or two of melanin poured into his DNA heightened her arousal to a point where she believed she'd found one.

Tilting her head, Stormy smiled at the absolutely beautiful man with the confident hands. *God, he smells good, like crisp ocean breezes and ice,* Stormy thought as he pulled her into the circle of his arms, massaging the base of her spine, just above the curve of her ass.

"I hear you're having a bit of a celebration, love."

Oh, good Lord, he's British. She bit back a groan as she imagined her panties disintegrating under the onslaught of hot fluid flowing from the juncture of her thighs.

Oh no, she wanted to shout to Jules and Lou, I am not punking out tonight.

Wrapping her arms around the beautiful man's neck, she pulled him closer. Before this night was through, she was going to get a gift bag, take the sexy man back to her plush hotel room, and screw him mercilessly for the remainder of her celebratory weekend.

What the ever-loving hell, Big Country thought as his truck crested the top of the one-way road that led to Mama's House and he saw the number of cars parked in the gravel lot outside of the bar. The place was packed beyond anything he'd seen in all the years since Terry and Mama had it built.

Terry's Jeep was the only Brood vehicle he saw as he circled the lot, which in and of itself wasn't unusual. Most of the Brood housed their rides in the secure garage at the base of the mountain near the highway when in residence for more than a few hours. The only Brood mates not in residence were Coen and Price—they were out of the country doing contract work for another outfit based in Canada— and Juarez, whose wife and mother had barred him from returning to the mountain as long as Zeus was in residence.

If it wasn't Brood, who were all these fuckers barring him from parking outside his own goddamn home? Some of the vehicles were known to him—he'd clocked the rides of military men, a few mercs, couple of agency guys, aka government narcs, killers all—but a few of the cars he'd never seen before.

After circling one last time he headed down the other one-way dirt road they called Devil's Descent, and parked his truck at the first turnout point, about nine hundred feet down the mountain. If you weren't Brood, Devil's Descent was the only other discernible route connecting the mountain to the highway below.

Cutting the engine, Big Country hopped out of his truck, not taking kindly to having to hike up this bitch of a mountain with a flashlight, his Sig, and the custom blade Zeus, the newest member of the Brood, had gifted him with.

When he stepped on a half-buried branch, Big Country slid a good three feet back down the incline before he regained his balance. Cursing, he clenched his fists and took a deep breath as he struggled to contain his frustration. *When is this clusterfuck of a night gonna end*, he wondered as he continued up the steep climb. Though his legs didn't register any strain or fatigue, his poor heart was already racing toward a finish line that felt like death. Maybe Lynx wasn't far off when he said Big Country should stop flipping tractor tires and lifting cars and simply take a run along the beach.

He grimaced. He hated running. He hated moving fast unless his life depended on it, but when it did, he struck with the instinctual speed of a pit viper and the force of a Mack truck. Yep, just like his granddaddy used to say, *Ain't no...*

"Wouldn't go up there if I was you."

Big Country bellowed like a startled bull; some might say hollered, some might say screamed like a little bitch. Either way, his Sig and flashlight were in his hands and aimed straight and unwavering into the heart of darkness.

Otherwise known as Zeus's chest.

Big Country blinked at the sight before him.

Zeus stood half in shadow, his silver-gray eyes glinting with what *could* be called amusement, but the lack of emotion in every other aspect of the man's face defied the possibility.

With dirt-covered bare feet, Zeus stood there in low-riding jeans, sporting a healing gunshot wound, bloody scratches, and bruises on his customary bare chest.

Not one to contemplate the spiritual side of things, Big Country readily accepted that there was something downright otherworldly about Zeus. And it went beyond Zeus's relationship with his blades, or his poor social skills; hell, for truth an obsession with their weapons and a semi-antisocial disposition was par for the course for most of the Brood.

No, something about this Brood mate was just...*off*.

Big Country holstered his weapon, even though Zeus still held a blade the length and width of Big Country's forearm. Sometime over the course of the last few weeks, Big Country realized that a resting blade, one that wasn't tapping against Zeus's thigh or spinning through his fingers, was a relatively non-threatening blade.

"You lookin' to get another hole in you, cousin?" Big Country asked.

Zeus, still healing from the damage a now-dead Maxim Kragen III's men had done to him weeks ago, shrugged. "I think maybe my woman would have a problem with another hole," Zeus said. Not *'no, I don't want to be shot again'*, or *'no, I don't want you to shoot me.'*

Crazy bastard.

"There a reason you out here by yourself, Zeus, in the pitch of dark...carrying a machete?"

"I'm not by myself."

Big Country waited a moment, rubbed one hand over his jaw as he casually scanned the trees with the flashlight in the other. "Sabrina out here with you?"

"Nope. Sleeping in our room." Zeus did smile then; well, kinda. "We liked the gift bag."

Sometimes it just didn't pay to try and follow Zeus's line of thinking.

Already frustrated with everything life had thrown at him tonight, Big Country took a deep breath and stepped backward up the hill. He stilled again, reaching for his weapon as a black dagger with a beaten metal blade, red and black corded material woven over the hilt and black feathers dangling from the end, embedded in the tree trunk to Big Country's left.

Zeus was rooted in place, hadn't moved a lick except to begin circling the machete in wide arcs at his side, the indescribable yet unmistakable gleam back in his eyes.

"Who's out here with you, Zeus?" Big Country asked again, slow and measured, so there would be no room for misunderstanding.

Zeus stopped scanning the trees to his right and locked onto Big Country.

"Death," he said, then he shook his head as if to clear it. "Cizan. Cizan's out there. We're playing a game. You want to join?"

For a second, Big Country actually considered it.

There was a whole mess of aggression churning inside that needed to be released but he didn't come to the mountain for that. He was here because the man closer to him than his blood brothers had urged him to come to Mama's House. The forest surrounding the building was technically *not* where he was called to be.

Turning, Big Country headed up the steep mountainside.

"It's human chaos up there," Zeus warned. "Better to stay away."

Big Country swung around and aimed the flashlight in the place where Zeus had stood seconds before, encountering only darkness. Senses now on high alert, Big Country pushed up the hill, aware that the two men who had the least-reliable grasps on reality in the Brood were stalking through the darkness around him.

Ignoring his belabored heart, he stomped up the trail, thinking back to what Coen had said when Zeus was brought into the Brood as a substitute for Cizan. *It's like exchanging one psycho for another.*

As if Cizan heard and took issue with his thoughts, a spear adorned in the same weave of red and black sailed through the air and embedded in the ground near Big Country's feet as he crested the hill and stepped onto the parking lot.

"One day, you death-lovin' son of a bitch, me and you, we gon' go round and round," he yelled into the darkness. Thunderous laughter reverberated around the treetops, dogging Big Country's heels as he made his way over to Mama's House.

Opening the door, he was assailed by loud music and the sight of Lynx, posted in the doorway like a bouncer, grinning like he hadn't made an urgent call less than an hour before.

This night was becoming surreal, Big Country thought as he stepped into the bar, which had been transformed into some kind of nineteenth-century saloon with red and purple decorations, and a bunch of dancing women he'd never seen before.

What. The. Hell.

Mama rarely allowed outsiders to have parties in her bar, mostly 'cause the folks who gravitated there were a hair-trigger away from all-out brawling. In the interior of the building it was usually safe enough, but once you stepped outside, there were no rules, no holds barred, no guarantees of safety or survival. Zeus and Cizan were a shining example of that reality.

Nudging Lynx aside, Big Country stepped into the bar and leaned against the doorframe.

"That, my man, is the future mother of my children," Lynx said over the music.

Big Country's gaze tracked across the room to the black woman dancing on top of one of the booth tables. Damn woman was built like a brick shithouse. Her rich brown skin with red undertones reminded him of the Oklahoma soil back home. Big Country felt an unnatural urge to sow wild oats all up and through her body, and hell if she didn't move like she was the original sin that made mankind fall from God's grace. Unlike the woman he'd brought into his home earlier, this sienna-red-skinned woman had a raw sensuality that only those well versed in the sex-in-exchange-for-goods industry tended to cultivate.

When she dropped her ass low, bounced it a few inches above the table top, then wound all that gloriousness back up until she was upright and laughing with the women around the table, he knew she had to be one of his kind of woman; the kind that you paid to fuck and keep on retainer.

"I think I just came in my pants," Lynx said.

Big Country's snort of derision was more like a grunt of release as Bubba throbbed, begging to be the object she bounced her hips on top of next.

Damn if he wouldn't have his satisfaction tonight, Big Country thought, and made the mistake of looking at Lynx. The rapture on his best friend's face was different than Big Country's lustful fantasies. No, Lynx's expression spoke of infatuation and declarations of love and eventually having his heart ripped out of his chest.

Despite Big Country's attempts to educate him about the truth of women, Lynx remained an idealistic fool where they were concerned. He was like Big Country's old man in that way, glutting himself on saccharine smiles and syrupy words only to learn that what he'd been ingesting was more toxic than meth-laced arsenic. Didn't matter to him if the ol' man rotted in the hell he'd created running after Big Country's mother, but he wasn't about to let his best friend travel that same treacherous path.

His gaze hardened as the woman stepped down from the table.

She would devour Lynx.

"Son, you obviously got your balls crossed and it's made your brain addled some. It's understandable, she's a fine woman, but—"

"We're going to make beautiful crack babies."

Big Country frowned, stuck the tip of his pinky finger in his ear and wiggled it a few times before removing it. "Uhhh...say again, cousin?"

"I'm trying to create a word other than Blasian. Something that blends Korean and Black. Korack."

For the first time all week, Big Country threw his head back and laughed. "Yeah, brother, I suggest you find a different configuration."

Lynx shrugged in a *"just-sayin'"* motion.

Big Country's gaze gravitated back toward the sienna-red-skinned woman, taking in her hair, pulled back into the biggest wildest afro puff he'd ever seen on a live person and the way her halter dress hugged titties so big and full he found himself wiping the corners of his mouth. Woman had a body lush enough to nest in.

Thing was, since moving to the Bay Area over a decade ago, he'd arrived at the understanding that a large group of women partying without a man meant either they didn't fuck them, *or* they were a modern-day Nazi-feminist coven bent on magically castrating any man that stepped too close to their circle.

Given that this group was mostly women of color, he decided against the latter.

"So, why's Mama throwing this lesbian shindig, anyway?" Big Country asked, watching Sienna Red bump booties with a cute brown mouse of a woman, and a slender onyx-skinned woman who had to be at least six feet tall. The latter was dressed in a wifebeater, black jeans, and Doc Martens, which strengthened his assumption.

"If it was that kind of party, I'd wish for breasts and an inversion of my dick just so I could join in."

"Brother, that's gotta be the sickest shit I've ever heard pass your lips."

"Don't ever underestimate the power of the pussy," Lynx said matter-of-factly. "Men, greater and lesser, have done some pretty fucked-up shit to have it."

True. The male species did undeniably crazy shit just for a piece of a woman's glistening furry tail. Unfortunately, they also had to put up with a heap more to keep it. Big Country himself hadn't been exempt until he'd found some ol' time religion and baptized himself in the knowledge that the sanest relationship with a woman was one governed by money, never the delusions of the heart. When it wasn't, unfortunate incidents like earlier tonight occurred.

As their British Brood mate, London—begging to have his bridge knocked the fuck down—sidled up alongside Sienna Red and slick as you please, pulled her into a slow dance despite the song's fast tempo, Big Country concluded that, lesbian or not, the woman was a professional hitter catering to any gender willing to meet her needs.

An uncommon urge to plow through the crowd, wrap his hand around London's neck, and unleash a hail of blows that would turn the other man's too-pretty face into a bloody pulp too nauseating for any woman to look upon, gripped Big Country. Instead of descending into violence, he turned to see how Lynx was reacting to London poaching their woman.

"Do you think it's the suave, virile, biracial thing, or his British accent that has women willing to drop their panties like seeds, hoping they'll get to climb his stalk and crack open his golden eggs?"

Lynx's question was flat and reflective, with no trace of the violence Big Country was experiencing. "When I had an accent," Lynx continued, "It only got me mocked…or beat up."

Sienna Red turned into London's embrace and wrapped her arms around his neck, pressing her ample breasts into his chest. Oh yeah, this woman would gladly take his dick and his money; he just had to get over there before London or any of these other motherfuckers made her an offer she couldn't refuse.

Pushing off the doorframe, Big Country paused and looked at Lynx. "Sorry, ol' son, but this one's not the mother-of-your-children type. She's one of mine. I guarantee it."

"Nah," Lynx said, unfazed and slightly amused as his topaz eyes flicked from the woman to Big Country. "But if she's not *one of yours*, I'll take that as my cue to openly pursue her. Good luck nonetheless; I have a feeling that she will make one of us a very happy man."

Big Country frowned. He didn't want to be on the wrong end of another one of Lynx's *feelings*, but when London navigated Sienna Red closer to a shadowed area of the bar, he moved.

Standing six feet six and weighing 290 pounds of dense muscle, Big Country had a way of clearing a path without effort or intimidation. London, who just *had* to dip the woman and bring her up slowly, his rat-bastard eyes glued to Sienna Red's shifting breasts, didn't seem to notice.

Approaching her from behind, Big Country watched Sienna Red's hips move against London *way* too intimately for a man she had just met, working girl or no.

A slow tempo song came on as Big Country stopped behind the woman's thick ass. He watched London's hand ease from the small of her back toward the round of her—

Big Country grumbled a warning and London looked up, frowned, then glared, trying to back him up. Snorting, Big Country stepped to the side of the couple and placed a gentle hand on Sienna Red's shoulder.

"Hey there darlin', you mind if a big country boy has a dance with a beautiful lady?" He smiled, oozing charm.

Her breath hitched as she took in his greatness.

Scents of cinnamon and cedar ghosted her body, tantalizing his nose. He inhaled deeply. Damned woman even smelled like home; that fact alone should've made him beat a quick retreat to the woods and join Zeus and Cizan.

Instead, he continued to gaze down at her.

"Hell, woman, you're prettier than moonlight dancing through the bayou."

She smiled, a big, pretty, *dimpled* smile, and for a moment the worm of unrest eating at him for the past few weeks stilled.

"Moonlight on the bayou…sounds enchanting," she drawled, her voice easing through him like aged bourbon. He planned on getting sloppy drunk on her lovin' tonight.

Thanking London for the dance, Sienna Red took Big Country's proffered hand and stepped closer. His Brood mate smirked. Big Country pulled the woman into his arms and waved goodbye to London using his middle finger, refusing to think on the relief he felt seeing his friend walk away.

He gave Sienna Red a lopsided grin. "You may not know this, sugar, but I just saved you from a world of heartache."

"Thanks for your effort, but my heart won't ever break over something as simple as a dance…sugar."

She spoke the endearment with a half-smile that liked to ignite him on the spot. He pulled her closer, fusing their bodies so seamlessly air couldn't pass between them. Bubba lengthened against her abdomen in his own leisurely look-forward-to-getting-to-know-you dance and she didn't pull away. No, no, not his Sienna Red; like a pro, she leaned in, her hands gliding up his thick arms. She stroked his biceps and triceps before taking hold of his shoulders and squeezing, trying to figure out his worth with her hands, determining how much she could get from him, both sexually and monetarily.

Leaning down, he ran his nose up the side of her neck where her scent was strongest, more than willing to fill her lady purses until they overflowed with his bounty. He brushed his lips over the lobe of her ear, and she leaned her head to the side, granting him permission to learn what made her body hum with pleasure.

He'd never forget the words of Ms. Juno, the first woman he'd ever paid to have sex with almost two decades ago: *Any John can put money on the table, boy, but you get me off in the process and I'll always smile and make a place for you when you call. You can bank on that all day long.* And he had. He wouldn't hesitate to show Sienna Red all his assets, especially when each moment in her arms had him descending into a well of lust he hadn't been able to sample for too damned long.

Reaching through his mass of unruly hair, she stroked his nape, her fingers rose-petal soft, her caress light and soothing, yet he winced as if her nails had scraped against a raw nerve. He started to pull away, but she pressed into Bubba and undulated against him.

Big Country damned near lost the ability to stand upright. Taking a deep breath, he rested his forehead against her crown and he prayed right there, to God and the Devil, for the strength to resist bringing her legs around his hips, pushing her dress up her thighs, and taking her hard in a shadowed corner of the bar, uncaring if his ass pumped furiously for all to see.

Sienna Red raked her fingernails against his scalp and he nearly lost it and he had no fucking idea why. It wasn't like she'd reached down and tweaked his tip or sheltered his balls in her grip, but her touch had that effect just the same.

"How much you asking for, darlin'?" he managed to get out. Right then, he was willing to break another cardinal rule and have sex with a professional he hadn't had physically tested or even done a cursory background check on.

She pulled back and looked him in the eye. "I want it all, and *then*...I want some more."

Well, good Lord and goddamn.

"So, you tell me," she whispered. "How much are you willing to give?"

Yeah, *buddy*, if they had reached the point of negotiation, he'd won.

Sliding his hands lower, Big Country gripped and squeezed her ass. He hummed low in his throat. "Sweetness, I'm willing to give you damn near all I got. Money, clothes, cars. You name it and it's yours for the duration of time you allow me to make use of you."

He felt her tense, his generosity a gracious and surprising thing. Her hand slid free from his hair and stroked his jaw in a reassuring motion. Leaning in, she stretched up on her tiptoes and nuzzled his neck, her full lips so soft against his hard jaw.

Big Country couldn't maintain the gentle sway of the dance. The heel of his foot bounced spastically against the floor, as if he were a hound dog having his belly rubbed just the right way.

"Stormy, turn him loose before you hurt him!" a woman hollered out, followed by raucous laughter from the other women.

Sienna Red...no, *Stormy*...pulled away, continuing to smile. She caressed the side of his face again and he would've felt like a fucking king had her eyes not been filled with an emotion that resembled downright disappointment.

"All I really needed to know was how much of yourself you were willing to give, but based on your response, I'd say not much at all. Shame, really. I have a feeling I would have had your sexy ass speaking in tongues before I was done. Now you have a good night...*sugar*." She winked, pulled completely out of his arms, turned her back on him, and walked away.

He grinned, suppressing his fury behind a veneer of unaffected ease as he crossed his arms over his chest, and watched the sway of her luscious ass as she abandoned him. Bubba was half hard and he was ready to grab the throat of the first motherfucker foolish enough to stray within his reach. He wanted to bash in the face of every man watching her beat a sensual path away from him.

Sitting on the bar, Mama watched him like a hawk eyeing newly-emerged prey. Big Country nodded and gave her a two-fingered salute before his eyes returned to the woman who'd rejected him. Lynx had joined her and her friends, and was twerking against Stormy's groin while she laughed and pretended to smack his ass in playful domination.

Son of a bitch! This was the *very* thing he didn't want to happen.

Uncrossing his arms and shaking them out, he closed his eyes and rolled his neck and shoulders, clenching and unclenching his hands. He wasn't the kind of man that gave a damn if a woman hopped off his dick and climbed right on top of another—that's how little he was invested in *who they were as human beings*—but he drew the line at some manipulative bitch walking into *their* house trying to pit one brother against another. That shit was not going down, not today.

Opening his eyes, Big Country zeroed in on Sienna Red and watched as her friends faded away until she and Lynx were the only ones talking and dancing together. If it wasn't for the peril his friend faced, Big Country would leave and go on over to Sylvie's, where release was guaranteed. But he was stuck here, prowling the perimeter of the dance floor, waiting for the moment Sienna Red took things too far.

What he hadn't anticipated was that asshole Marine, Drake Carver, coming up behind the woman and sandwiching her between him and Lynx.

Who the *fuck* did Carver think he was?

Sienna Red smiled back at the Marine, looped one arm around his neck and the other around Lynx's midsection, and the three of them rocked to the music on the cusp of some kind of dance-floor-ménage scenario.

Big Country was well on his way to losing his shit, and it wasn't because of her; it was because he couldn't tolerate the disrespect she was showing Lynx and his puppy-dog emotions. For him, Lynx, or London to jostle around for position was one thing, but for Carver to jump the line—

Sienna Red laughed at something Lynx said and planted a lingering kiss on his jaw.

Fucking woman. Big Country's mind roared—hell, maybe he'd yelled it out loud the way folks turned toward him, looking surprised. He didn't give a damn. She needed to be set straight to rights. Women didn't come into Mama's House, *his* house, thinking they could play some bullshit game of seek-out-the-best-man-in-the-room-and-destroy-his-fucking-heart.

Plowing through the crowd, he pulled the woman from between

Lynx and Carver, and dragged her to him, intentionally crowding her space.

"You come in here trying to catch some poor bastard with the promise of your body and I get it, that's what women do. But let me tell you something, little darlin', it ain't going down that way, not tonight."

She arched her brow and smirked at him. *Smirked.* He growled and dipped his head lower, their faces so close that their heated breaths battled for dominion.

"Little man," she said, her silken lips brushing against his as she spoke. "What you're holding on to right now is a grown-ass woman. Let me tell you something about grown-ass women, because apparently you haven't had the honor of meeting one before. We don't back down from men who try to pull this caveman bullshit, so walk away like the overfed boy that you are, or limp away, these are your only options, *darlin'.* Be wise in your choice."

Big Country straightened. Who the hell did she think she was giving ultimatums to, he started to say, but then he crossed his arms over his chest, took a mental step back and tried to make sense of her, of this whole situation.

Drake Carver—son of a bitch that he was—didn't seem inclined to give him the time to do so. Sidling close to Sienna Red, Carver placed a proprietary hand on her hip as if the gesture would make Big Country tuck tail and scamper away.

"Look here, boys," Big Country called out, catching the eye of nearly every man in the place before settling his gaze back on Carver. "Let's not drag this out. This woman's off-limits from this moment on. We all got a clear understanding of my meaning, yeah?"

The meaning was that if you weren't Brood, you didn't touch her, you didn't look at her, she didn't exist in your world. Now, he and Lynx, they would have a conversation about the woman's nature soon enough, but until then, no other man or woman in Mama's House would have the right to say different.

Carver didn't remove his hand from Sienna Red's hip at Big Country's declaration, grinning as two of his Marine buddies walked up and flanked him.

"Well, well. Looks like I've got a challenge on my hands," Big Country announced.

Sienna Red rolled her eyes and motioned to the tall dark-skinned woman she and Lynx had been dancing with, then to another woman, who was already close to the entrance. "Lou, can you and Eliza pull your cars around front?" she asked.

"That what grown-ass women do, Sienna Red? Shake their asses, get men riled up, then run away without facing the consequences? If that's the case, darlin', your grown-ass ain't no different than every common-ass woman I know…at least as far as I can tell. I may be wrong." He knew he wasn't.

For a moment he sincerely believed she was going to punch him in the balls. He smirked, daring her to try it.

"Stormy!" a woman called out, and the tempest in her eyes winked out as if it never existed.

"I don't know what your issues with women are, but I'll be damned if we stay here and end up in jail or the hospital just to find out."

"Oh, you won't have to worry about jail. Up here, we got our own brand of justice."

"Come on, Stormy, the cars are out front," the sole Asian women in her group urged.

"Yeah, let's get the hell out of here before the symphony banjos and squealing pigs begins."

"Aw, darlin', only backwoods amateurs fail to cut the pig's throat before it starts to squeal. We're all professionals here. I guarantee, you wouldn't even hear death coming."

"We're leaving," she said flatly.

"I think that's best," he said, equally as flat, then looked at Carver and his crew. "You ladies won't want to be here when the blood begins flowing."

Carver drew his finger from one side of his throat to the other and pointed at Big Country.

Yeah, this stupid bastard had the good fortune of messing with him on a particularly bad night. Big Country was gonna enjoy bashing that fucker's face in.

Sienna Red and all but two of her murder of crows made their way toward the door. Turning, she eyed the one still tucked in Caleb Bailey's arms. The twenty-something woman had a problem with discernment if she thought it was safe to latch onto that devil's reject. The other remaining woman had her arms wrapped around Mama's waist, head resting in Mama's lap. Mama smiled at him and shrugged as she sat on the bar, stroking the drunken woman's hair.

Sienna Red moved toward the bar as Terry handed her the purses he'd retrieved from below.

"Octavia, Reign!" Sienna Red snapped.

"Come on, Stormy," the younger one objected. "I'm not ready to go."

Big Country was ready to intervene in the event that Caleb wasn't ready to *let* her go. The younger man was rubbing the scruff of his jaw back and forth over the crown of the young woman's head.

"Come on, Stormy," the woman holding onto Mama's waist said, lifting her head. "I'm not ready to..." Her head plopped back down. "I'm not ready to...stop drinkin'!"

Sienna Red hooked the bags over one shoulder and supported the drunken woman's weight against her other side. Big Country had already felt the strength in the woman's body, but to see her wielding it so effortlessly had Bubba pleading with him to make her to stay.

"Almaya, I'll call you about what we discussed," Sienna Red stated. Lynx strolled closer and leaned his elbows against the bar top, planting himself beside Mama's dangling legs. Sienna Red leaned toward Lynx and he bent his head, allowing her to plant a kiss against his cheek. "And you I'll see at the Boutique on Monday?"

"Absolutely," Lynx replied.

Control, son, control, Big Country cautioned himself.

Having made her way to the door, Sienna Red turned back toward the dance floor. "Tavi, do you *want* me to call my brother?"

The younger woman pulled out of Caleb's embrace and stomped all the way to and out the door. Sienna Red rolled her eyes, her gaze drifted back to him, lingered, then she turned and left the building. All the vibrant energy seeped from the bar like blood from the body of a dying man. The gnawing unrest that had been dogging Big Country's steps returned with a vengeance.

"I wanted her," a rusty voice said beside him.

Big Country looked to his left to see Caleb, with his dead-snake eyes standing there. "Hell, son, we all thought you was mute. Who knew that all you needed was the right whiff of woman to loosen your vocal cords?"

"I'm in," Caleb muttered in response. Carver and his Marine buddies grinned beside Caleb, likely believing their chances of taking him down were greater.

Blood *was* gonna flow tonight, and here he'd thought Zeus was gonna be the one responsible for it.

"Anybody else feeling froggish?" Big Country asked for good measure.

"Hell, why not. I never liked your backwater ass to begin with," Harvey Connors, the ex-DEA agent, said from the other side of the room.

"All right mate, you know the drill!" London yelled to Terry over the rising tide of voices placing bets and talking utter bullshit. "Line 'em up."

Big Country's five opponents shed their shirts and took their places in front of the bar. Terry set out six shot glasses, one in front of each man, as London leaped on top of the bar and crouched. London was a mimic—who he was changed with the situation—and with the women gone, he'd lost his spit-shined polish.

"Lads," London shouted over the voices. "We all know the rules. No weapons, and no one joins the battle after the blessed elixir has been chosen." He pointed at Big Country. "My backwater Brood mate, do you stand alone, or would you like a second at your side?"

Big Country eyed each of his five contenders, then sucked his teeth in disdain. Pulling his shirt over his head, he folded it and placed it on the bar next to Mama's thigh, placing his cigar butt on top of the shirt. "I believe I like these odds as is."

"Fair enough. And what spirit will guide you fine warriors onto the field of battle, my behemoth friend?"

"Aw son, that goes without saying." Big Country looked to Terry and tapped the bar twice.

"Firewater it is," Terry said, reaching down to retrieve a large mason jar.

"Son of a *bitch*," Carver muttered once he saw the clear liquid with the opaque briny film on top.

Terry poured equal-sized shots and Big Country was the first to down his. He imagined consuming Firewater was like ingesting blue flame, absinthe, and dry ice in one gulp.

Closing his eyes, he rode out the first hit, which was like white fire sizzling through flesh to devour what remnants of soul one might still possess. *But ohhh son…*once the fire burned through him, quiet descended as if he was the sole life form on a planet covered in snow. Numb, alone…at peace.

"You alive in there, boy?" Terry's distorted voice called to him as if he was speaking to Big Country while they were both submerged in water.

Big Country opened his eyes and the world had a glassy sheen to it. Every time he consumed Firewater, he knew he exposed himself to the danger of the phantom flame that danced just on the edge of his vision, disappearing whenever he tried to focus on it. He shook his head to clear his mind and the flame went away, only to flicker back to life.

"Be careful, boy, part of your soul walks a different plain now. Don't let it drift too far…or you'll lose it," Terry warned.

Big Country nodded, as everything around him moved slower.

Looking to the left, then to the right of him, he saw four of his challengers either on their knees or writhing on the floor. The fifth— one of Carver's Marine buddies—was on the floor, not moving at all.

Taking a deep cleansing breath, Big Country rolled his neck. "Okay, boys," he said, his voice deep and guttural. "Let's find a resolution to tonight's frustrations."

Striding to the front door, he opened it and the other four men stumbled through. He looked back and saw Mama and Lynx grin and salute one another with amber-filled shot glasses before knocking them back. Big Country frowned, turned away, and shoved into the night where vehicles were being rearranged in a circle, headlights turned toward the center where the contestants would fight.

Whatever unease Big Country felt in witnessing the exchange between Mama and Lynx disappeared the minute the ex-DEA agent's fist connected with his gut. Still half in the world of quiet and cold, he felt no pain, only the satisfaction that arose when he clenched the other man's skull and head-butted him into unconsciousness.

Big Country roared, challenging the elusive flame dancing in the distance, as well as his remaining opponents. The men came at him all at once. He dug in, enjoying the brutality of combat, feeling refreshed by it.

As he fought, he was ever present of that elusive flame flickering around in his mind, taunting him, drawing closer and cutting off every means of escape as he ducked and dodged his opponents. Then the flame exploded, consumed him, taking away the joy of battle, taking away everything except the old primal rage that burned so pure its only purpose was destruction, its only belief the sanctity of pain.

He didn't hear the other men's screams, didn't hear the sound of bones breaking, didn't taste the blood from seeping wounds. He fought well after his original challengers had fallen, working his way through every man that came within striking distance, making the world bleed copiously until Terry lifted a gun, pointed it at him, and shot.

He charged the man who had been like a father to him as the flame released its hold and slipped out of existence.

The world quieted. Cold wrapped around him, continued to numb him as vibrant green eyes twinkling with sin moved closer. He couldn't move, couldn't escape...then the scent of cinnamon and cedar overwhelmed his senses, pushing the memory away and surrounded him as he crumpled to the ground as the world went dark.

Then he was gone.

CHAPTER 2

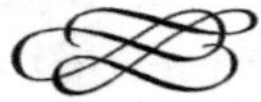

*U*nlike the anticipation that had filled Lou's SUV on the ride up to Mama's House, the atmosphere going down was tense.

Tavi hadn't spoken or looked at Stormy since slamming the door and accusing her of doing too much, of treating her like a child. Stormy pursed her lips, struggling to hold on to her temper. *Like slamming a damn door and giving me the silent treatment is the pinnacle of maturity.* Tavi was twenty-three and Stormy had no problem respecting her womanhood, but if her niece didn't have the good sense to know when her life was in jeopardy, Stormy had no problem snatching Tavi up, funky attitude or not.

Looking behind her to check on Reign, seated behind Lou on the driver's side, Stormy saw her cousin was still slumped against the door, the left side of her face plastered against the window.

"Reign baby, you okay?" Stormy asked.

Reign's eyes remained closed as she nodded, moaned, then whimpered.

"We're gonna have to pull over, Lou," Stormy said.

"All I got is trees here, Stormy, trees and unpaved road. Where the fuck am I supposed to pull over?" Lou snapped, gripping the steering wheel tighter as she focused on getting them through the pitch-black forest road in one piece.

"Reign!" Lou called out, quickly looking at Reign through the rearview mirror. "If you throw up in my car, I'll shoot you in the foot and make it look like an accident. You know I've gotten away with that shit before so don't try me."

Reign whimpered, squeezing her eyes tighter. "Don't you dare threaten me when I'm sick, Louisa *Bad* Gardener."

"Oh Lord..." Stormy fought to hold back her smile.

"This crazy heffa..." Lou muttered.

The night was *officially* a wrap when a thirty-eight-year-old woman regressed to using a name she'd coined in fourth grade to denigrate Lou, aka Louisa Gardener. The name had only ever been an insult to Reign because what normal kid cared if someone was a *bad gardener* or not.

Placing her hand over her mouth, Reign dry-heaved.

"Reign. Check it out. You fuck up my ride, put money on your *life* that—"

"Lou, you didn't even bring a gun," Stormy said.

"Well, I got a right hook that'll knock her ass out."

"Blah, blah, blah," Reign muttered.

"Okay, you bitches are way too high-strung right now," Jules muttered. "Have you all seriously forgotten how great tonight was?"

Stormy took a deep breath and sent Lou a *chill-the-hell-out* look. Lou mumbled something about putting them *all* out.

"We're almost to the highway, Reign," Stormy said. "We'll stop, and you'll feel better, I promise."

As soon as the SUV broke through the coverage of trees and hit asphalt, Lou made a hard right and pulled the vehicle to a stop along the shoulder. Stormy unbuckled her seat belt, hopped out of the car and darted around to open Reign's door. She practically dragged her cousin around to the dirt- and foliage-covered ground along the passenger side of the car to give Reign a little privacy to empty her stomach, but Reign didn't throw up. Instead, she stood hunched over gripping one hand over her mouth and the other over her stomach.

"All right, Reign, I'm going to need you to get over your aversion. You'll feel better, Ladybug, I promise."

"But it's so disgusting…" Reign mumbled behind her hand, eyes pleading.

Stormy stepped behind Reign and gathered her thick hair, pressed straight for tonight's celebration, into her hands. The rear passenger side window rolled down and Stormy turned to see Tavi leaning from behind Jules, armed with water and mints.

Stormy winked at her and turned back to plait Reign's hair.

"Reign, you remember when we were in sixth grade and Cesar Hernandez came over to our lunch table trying to impress Lou?"

"Oh no, Stormy—" Reign begged, clutching her mouth again.

"You remember him drinking the carton of milk and making it come out of his nose? Too bad he had a cold, right? Remember how the snot and milk splattered all over the table? Remember how you—"

Reign spewed the contents of her stomach in much the same way she had as a kid, this time sobbing as she did so. When she was emptied, and the retching quieted, Tavi handed Stormy the bottle of water. Stormy had Reign rinse and spit, then directed her to swallow a few sips of the water. After giving her two mints, Stormy smoothed her cousin's damp hair back, kissing her temple. "Did you have a good time tonight, Ladybug?"

"Best time ever," Reign said, smiling weakly.

Squeezing her cousin's shoulder, Stormy steered Reign back around to her seat and helped strap her in. Reign belched loudly and began to laugh-cry as they all burst out laughing.

"You're all certifiable," Stormy murmured as she smiled, shaking her head as she closed Reign's door. Moving toward the rear of the vehicle, she stopped beside the taillight, the fine hairs covering her body on alert. Straining to hear over the low music and muted conversation inside the car, Stormy scanned the shadowed trees on the opposite side of the highway. Higher up from the tree line, something pale floated, shifted, then it was gone.

That wasn't her imagination. Someone—or something—was out there, watching.

"Stormy, stop daydreaming about that big burly-assed mothafucka and get in the car!" Lou yelled out her window.

Laughter erupted inside the car.

Rounding the back of the SUV, Stormy slid into the passenger seat and snapped her seatbelt into place. Eyeing the tree line across the highway, she decided that whatever was out there wasn't her mystery to solve.

Steering the car back onto the asphalt, Lou headed down the smooth blacktopped road.

Jules leaned into the space between the two front seats. "I gotta say, Stormy, you surprised me. You had men hanging on you like tinsel on a tree. The scent of your cooch had men ready to fight."

"To the death, if I judged Cowboy Big Dick correctly." Lou sucked her teeth. "Y'all know I was scoping his shit out, right? Middle of the thigh, bitches, middle of the *goddamn* thigh." She looked over at Stormy. "What did I tell you? Didn't I say that when the Stormy *I* grew up with was ready to break free of that bullshit trap Chad constructed for you, life would be worth living again, didn't I say that?"

She had, and finally, life was.

It was glorious dancing on top of that table, in those men's arms. She'd felt sexy for the first time in God knew how long, and the southern giant with the moss-green eyes which turned emerald in anger, his soft hair as unruly as his attitude, had made her feel the sexiest.

A good night could have been spectacular if he hadn't exposed the underbelly of contempt he seemed to have for women. And the man's willingness to commit violence with almost no provocation meant anyone in a relationship with him was at high risk for getting her ass beat on a daily basis.

"And just so you know, Stormy, I'm going to need a sample of your vaginal fluids so I can patent that shit and sell it in Red's for, like, a gazillion dollars an ounce," Jules announced.

"Uhahh!" Tavi yelled from the very back of the SUV.

"That's so disgusting," Reign muttered.

"Jules, you need to learn to watch what you say. For Christ's sake, there's a child in the back seat," Lou said.

"I am grown!" Tavi snapped.

"I was talking about Reign," Lou countered.

There was a pause. Then they all burst out laughing.

"Screw you, Lou," Reign snorted in her laughter.

"Well, I don't think *anybody* should be discussing screwing in front of Stormy. I thought she was going to bone every man she danced with right there on the dance floor. Especially the humongoid dude." Jules was an athletic Japanese-American woman, but at five feet three, anyone over five feet ten was big.

"He was really intense," Reign said.

He was an asshole.

"He thought I was a prostitute," she muttered.

"Wait, wait, what? He offered to pay *you* for sex?" Tavi asked. "First, nasty. Second, did he at least offer you a decent amount?"

"What the hell is wrong with these millennials?" Stormy asked the other women in the car who were all nearing forty. "You know how many times it has literally pained me that I didn't smother her in her infancy?"

"Yeah, yeah, like I haven't heard that before. Come on, how much we talking?"

"Money, clothes, cars." She shrugged. "He told me to name it and he'd give it to me."

Blessed silence reigned in the car for a full two minutes.

"You have lost your goddamn mind," Lou said. "Did you see his big fine ass? You should have been paying him to knock the cobwebs off your old-assed cooch."

"You should've taken it back to God and asked for another one years ago…or at least a refund," Tavi chimed in, her words petty payback from being denied the Aryan biker.

"He called me a *hooker*."

He hadn't actually, but he'd assumed, which was close enough.

"You've been called worse, usually by me!" Jules yelled in her ear. True. Tires squealed as Lou hugged a corner too fast.

"You're getting as bad as Reign, putting too much on minor shit, Stormy," Lou said. "You didn't have to marry the man or take his money; all you had to do was allow him to fuck you bowlegged, that was it."

The city of Marin sparkled against the dark horizon, still miles away. At least the celebration wasn't completely a bust, Stormy thought, soon they would be in their own luxury hotel rooms overlooking the ocean for the rest of the weekend.

"Tonight was a good night though, right, guys?" Reign whispered as they sped down the road.

"Tonight was a good night," they echoed back.

∼

Delilah rested her forehead on the bedroom wall, flattening her hands over her lower abdomen.

Her womb still felt heavy, ripe, ready to release with ecstasy again, and again, and again. Groaning, she slid her hand down her bare pubis. Widening her stance, she parted her lower lips, dipped her fingers into her liquid center just as he did. Lucas Beaumont, otherwise known as Big Country, had opened her to possibilities she never believed existed. He was her pleasure and her salvation.

Her smile turned wicked as she worked her fingers in and out, rolling her hips in a rhythm she'd learned with him. Cupping her breast with her free hand, she massaged, tugged her nipple, pushed her fingers harder and faster into her sex until for the second time in her life, she orgasmed, sobbing and weakened, yet it still wasn't as powerful as the completion he had given her. She could only be completed by him, could only be freed by him.

As her body calmed, she turned and faced the shadowed guest room she'd claimed in the worn Victorian. Crossing over to the second-story window, she peered out, unconcerned with her nakedness as the house was tucked back from the main street, too enshrouded by trees and tall shrubbery to expose her to would-be prying eyes.

Unlike Lucas Beaumont's modern home with its wall of windows offering an unobstructed view of the bay, this secluded home was ideal for formulating plans and determining how those plans would impact the bond she'd already formed with the lovely Mr. Beaumont. The man was delicious, strong and imposing, gentle and charming, *and funny*... God, who knew that laughter could be so filled with joy? Her father, the Good Shepherd, preached that laughter was an undisciplined act and therefore a punishable offense against God. He taught that emotions were best used to connect to those in need of God's salvation.

Delilah had initially discovered Lucas as he packed up the apartment of Sabrina Samora, one of the two people she was ordered to eliminate for killing the son of a wealthy patron of the Shepherd's Keep, the religious order run by her father. The intense and unexpected attraction she'd felt for Lucas couldn't be described as anything other than divine intervention, and tonight, in less than two hours of his presence, she knew God had set Lucas Beaumont upon her path. He was meant to be her gift, her means of freedom, her future.

And once she sent the killers of Maxim Kragen III to hell, Lucas would be her reward.

With him, she would no longer need to return to her father's deadly flock. She could have a full life with Lucas, one where she'd be cherished, one where she'd have explosive orgasms, and if the Shepherd should attempt to bring her back into the fold, Lucas had the size and strength to defeat him.

Delilah nodded, pleased with this unexpected blessing.

The sun wouldn't be up for another two hours, but she was still too restless to sleep. It was midday in Ireland, a good time to contact the Shepherd's warrior Caine, who kept vigil in the town bordering the Shepherd's lands. She would relay her progress and the news that she was close to finding the man and woman who had taken a very costly life. She smirked; she would, of course, not divulge her plans to leave their order. Not yet.

Leaving her bedroom, she passed the room of the elderly home-owners and headed to the small home-office downstairs where their bodies were securely wrapped in black plastic and duct tape. She would bury them in the backyard later tonight instead of taking food to Cornelius, the acolyte who'd accompanied her to the States to demonstrate his worth to the Shepherd. Suffering was a part of an acolyte's' training; therefore, Delilah felt no urgency to lessen his. Cornelius was weak and needed to become strong and she would do her part to assist him on his journey.

Sitting at the office desk, Delilah opened her laptop and experienced a moment of panic when she saw that the tracking device she'd placed on Lucas's truck wasn't emitting a signal. Then she remembered that when he was on the mountain he frequently visited, the signal always died. She prayed that was the case, that he was on the mountain. She couldn't lose Lucas Beaumont. He was her only chance at happiness, the only person with the strength to turn the Shepherd away.

She took a deep breath and closed her eyes.

Shutting down all emotions, she reached for the burner phone and dialed the number that would connect her to Ireland. To allay her concerns regarding Lucas's whereabouts, perhaps she would seek Cornelius out and learn if he'd witnessed Lucas's truck go up the mountain while he kept watch.

Zeus growled, burying his face in Sabrina's chaotic hair to escape the bright light. No matter where she ended up falling asleep, she was always naked on top of him when he woke, her soft kiss pulling him from darkness to initiate their daily ritual of wake-up sex. This morning she had her back to him, her ass pressed into his groin, her shoulder blades stabbing his chest, her head nestled between his neck and shoulder.

Zeus listened, eyes closed, as her thumbs touched rapidly over the surface of her cell phone. Stroking his nose against her jaw, he reached down and began to massage her warm abdomen. The feel of her, her unique scent, the knowledge that she was his to keep, were a comforting lullaby guiding him back toward sleep.

"Why did you tell Brianna that you would teach her to *hunt* once she moved in with us?" Sabrina asked casually.

Casual was good. Casual meant she was pissed, but was willing to have a *rational conversation.*

"Straddle your feet on the outside of my thighs," he directed.

If she wasn't going to allow him to go back to sleep, they would begin their wake-up ritual, and her asking him obvious questions wasn't part of it. Unless she was begging, demanding release, or he was muttering inarticulate sounds as he exploded inside of her, conversation wasn't a part of that ritual.

She slid her bare feet up his legs, stopping when she reached his knees. Zeus opened his eyes to slits, grumbling low in his throat as he waited for her to place them outside his knees and grant him full access. Sabina tilted her head to the side, challenging him with her eyes as she shined the phone's illuminated screen into his face.

"Really?" she said, arching her brow.

He shifted the angle of his caress, moving his hand down her stomach toward her manicured pubic area. Her hips jerked in anticipation as his fingers slid through the cropped hairs as his other hand palmed her left breast, squeezing as he dragged his fingernail over her nipple.

His mouth cocked up on one side when her breath hitched.

"Brianna and I already came to an agreement," he told her.

Sabrina frowned, about to say something combative. She was disrupting their morning ritual.

"Place your feet on the outside of my knees, Sabrina," he repeated.

She didn't. "I'm more than willing when you ask, Zeus, but you ordered me, *again.*"

He ground his teeth…*again*, annoyed with being told there was a fucking difference.

Sighing heavily, she rested her head against his shoulder, apparently contrite for all the disruptions to their ritual because she placed a foot on the outside of each knee. Zeus relaxed into the pillow and he widened his thighs, pushing her feet farther apart, knowing the limits of her almost limitless flexibility. Splitting her outer lips, he speared two fingers beyond the rim of her opening.

"Zeus..." she mumbled, finally speaking in the tone he wanted to hear. The phone fell to the bed, and their sublevel bedroom beneath Mama's House was engulfed in darkness.

Zeus's dick butted up against his fingers, rising like a golden obelisk between the juncture of her thighs. Sabrina reached down, stroking the swollen head before removing his hand from her opening and grinding the length of him against her sex, clit to ass, gyrating her hips as she worked his dick like a gearshift. Zeus caught her rhythm and thrust his hips in sync with hers.

He grunted, sack already drawing tight.

Sabrina lifted her back from his chest and rose up on her knees, placing the head of his penis just inside the rim of her opening. She tried to ease her way down his length for a leisurely fuck, but he wasn't in the mood, not after being forced to disrupt their morning ritual. He gripped her hips and surged up, slamming into her pussy over and over until she gripped his thighs, surged up, slammed down, and took control, riding him backward as if she was a trick rider.

Their pace grew frantic. Zeus gripped her hips tighter, went in a little harder, faster, his cock expanding inside her constricting walls. He gritted his teeth, grinding down on pure ecstasy as Sabrina stiffened and cried out, the torrent of rippling waves against his sensitive flesh forced an eruption of heated fluid to spew inside her womb.

Once she stopped bucking against him, riding her second wave, Sabrina fell backward onto Zeus's chest and nestled her head back into the crook of his neck. He used the hand not coated in her juices to smooth her hair back from her face while she caught her breath.

"You don't have to worry," he said. "Unlike you, the kid's picking up what I'm teaching quickly."

He stroked the baby-soft hair at her temple. Now that their ritual was complete, he could engage in her rational discussion.

"First, you're a terrible teacher," she said. He snorted, remembering her lessons while they were at his cabin. "And second…"

She felt around on the mattress, and the blinding light of her cell phone found him again. She scrolled up the stream of texts with Mrs. Jace, their niece Brianna's current guardian.

The two women had been in constant contact after Sabrina had opened the package Mrs. Jace had sent on behalf of Sabrina's deceased sister; the package that contained information about Sabrina's deceased sister and the niece she never knew she had, a niece who Mrs. Jace now needed Sabrina to assume caring for. Though the Jaces had raised Brianna since birth, they were elderly and now needed to attend to their own health.

"Mrs. Jace found Brianna on the computer researching different kinds of knives last night."

Zeus was pleased. "She was doing the homework I gave her, then."

Sabrina rolled off him, sitting on the edge of the bed and switched on the bedside lamp. He grunted and flung his forearm over his eyes, not ready to have this conversation after all.

"Brianna is a child. You can't expose her to that kind of violence."

He didn't bother to correct the misperception. He wasn't exposing Brianna to violence at all; he was giving her knowledge, teaching her a spiritual trade. If violence one day happened, it was his job to make sure she knew the steps she could take to deal with it.

Shifting his arm to reach beneath the pillow, Zeus freed the blade resting there, pointed its tip to the light brown ceiling, and began rolling it through his fingers.

"There are tribes in Africa and New Guinea, indigenous tribes in the Americas, where kids learn to hunt at a young age, sometimes land animals, fish, insects, to help sustain—"

"And I'm talking about twenty-first century urban America, not some National Geographic documentary!" she snapped.

But she was the *rational* one. He snorted.

She reached back and smacked him on the thigh. He gestured for the black blade on the table, and she handed it to him.

"Did you hear what happened with that Billy Lancaster kid?" he asked, twisting blades through the fingers of each hand. Sabrina pushed off the bed as his blades spun through his fingers in steady motion. Zeus swung his legs around and sat up, planting his feet on the floor. "I teach her, and kids think twice about going after her or her friends," he said, referring to Brianna bloodying this Billy Lancaster's nose for picking on her smaller, quieter friend.

Sabrina paced in front of him. "Yet *another* reason I had to reassure Mrs. Jace. She said Brianna's always been bossy, and I'll admit that may be hereditary—" *No shit.* "—but Mrs. Jace says it's rare for Bree to put her hands on someone else because she's always eaten up with guilt afterwards."

He'd cure the kid of that. If a situation required violence for it to be resolved, then guilt was both unnecessary and without purpose.

"This rational discussion over her training is pointless. She's already pledged herself; she's going to be bound to the blade spirits."

The feeling he'd learned to recognize as pride stirred deep. Brianna's training was a divine responsibility, one he never thought he'd be gifted with.

A number of emotions crossed Sabrina's face as she paced, then her features relaxed as she seemed to resolve something within herself.

"Okay." She nodded. "Okay. This just means I need to monitor the correspondence between you two until she's with us. If she continues to behave the way she is, Zeus, the Jaces may decide they want to contest putting her in our care."

The blades ceased all movement. Brianna was now theirs. Her mother had planned for it to be so. It was bad enough he and Sabrina had to wait these few weeks to heal to Mama's satisfaction before they retrieved Brianna; now Sabrina was saying he could possibly have to fight the kid's guardians for the right to her?

He smiled, the blades whirled through his fingers at an accelerated rate.

"Zeus!" Sabrina called out.

His focus shifted from images the blade spirits shared on how to resolve the potential threat, to Sabrina's very real and naked body standing directly in front of him.

"Baby, you're doing it again," she said.

Like the apt student he was learning to become, he lifted the other side of his mouth in what Sabrina and the rest of the Brood termed "a normal smile."

"Better?" he asked, blades humming in pleasure as he spun them about intoxicatingly.

"Better." She frowned and walked toward the bathroom on the other side of the room. "But don't think you're fooling anybody," she tossed back. "I'll be monitoring your communications with Bree from here on out."

His smile disappeared as the bathroom door shut.

Sabrina was concerned. He got it. His woman wanted family, she wanted normal, she believed having her niece with them would erase the years of loss, loneliness, and violence she'd endured. She believed that with the death of Kragen—the man who'd abducted her, attempted to rape her, played center stage in her recent bout of night-mares—the threat was gone.

Zeus knew it wasn't.

Maxim Kragen III was dead, killed by Zeus's very own ax-wielding hand. The blood-letting he'd been responsible for on Basir's estate that night was...deeply satisfying. That the Brood had exposed yet another sex-trafficking ring linked to the Consortium was even more so.

None of it meant the group would stop their abuse and exploitation. Fuckers like that just didn't react that way. They simply disappeared from view, so they could quietly change the discourse associated with them until their crimes were transformed into things of fiction.

But once the members felt safe, confident that their money, assets, and reputations were secure, they'd resurface and seek revenge for the loss of Kragen. Once they found out that Kragen had fathered a child with Sabrina's sister, the Consortium would come after his new family. He knew this.

So, yeah, Brianna would learn the skills needed to survive, and eventually she would learn to kill, but for both her and Sabrina's sake, he didn't want that to be anytime soon. He needed his family happy. Safe.

But as a predator of predators, he knew time was not on their side.

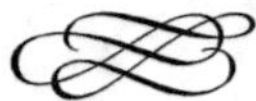

CHAPTER 3

*B*ig Country twirled around in Stormy's office chair, stopping after the second rotation to prop his size fourteens on top of her sleek desk. Yeah, she'd paid a pretty penny outfitting her office, but neither she nor her little business partner had the sense God gave a duck when it came to installing a decent security system. Might as well post a *Please Enter* sign on the front door. Ironic given the nature of their services, inviting in any thief bent on dicks and vibrators and shit he was too tired to guess the purpose of.

Lacing his fingers behind his head, he reclined as far back as the space would allow and looked up at the tray ceiling painted a slightly darker cream than the walls. Sienna Red had done well, taking her dog and pony show solo. Why work for a bureaucracy when you could get folks to shell out fat checks for an hour-long mind-fucking, *then* guide them downstairs to purchase whatever they needed for the kind of fucking you could actually take pleasure in.

He snorted.

Fish, fuck, fight, be a technical wizard, and lift heavy shit; those were the activities he used to stay balanced. Fuck therapy—he'd been forced to try it long ago and no one could ever force him to drink that particular brand of Kool-Aid ever again. Just because his regular stress relievers weren't working right now, that he'd had his first episode in a long time, didn't mean he needed therapy.

What he needed was to end this infatuation Lynx had for Stormy Redmond. Once she was set straight about what her relationship with Lynx *wasn't* going to be, he was sure everything would ease back to normal.

Settling deeper in the chair, he closed his eyes, basking in the sunlight shining from the window behind him. Images of him and Stormy—or just images of Stormy—bombarded him, as they were wont to do, whenever his mind wasn't focused on a task. Prior to meeting her, he'd been plagued by disrupted sleep, sexual dissatisfaction, and a potentially deadly agitation, the kind that led to his berserker-like episode two days ago, but right here, right now, surrounded by everything that was hers, he was so content he could barely stay awake.

Maybe it was his snoring, maybe it was the sound of keys hitting the floor and a door banging shut that woke him, but either way he kept his eyes shut and listened as heels *click-clacked* against the hardwood floors downstairs. A woman cursed as she tapped in the alarm code—a code that no longer worked since he'd deactivated the system. He smirked when she strung together a thread of creatively linked curses. The echo of footsteps climbing the stairs, moving toward his location filled him with a God-awful sense of anticipation.

As the woman got closer to the door with the engraved plaque **Stormy Redmond, LCSW**, he struggled to hold on to his relaxed demeanor.

All movement ceased at the threshold of the open office door.

Hearing the sharp intake of breath, Big Country opened one eye and let his head loll toward the stunned woman gaping at him.

"Hey there, darlin'," he said, voice gritty from sleep. "Sounds like you wasn't expecting company."

Wide-eyed, Sienna Red stood there taking in the devastating masculinity that was him. Her mouth moved but no sound came out.

"I know," he said, stretching. "I have that effect."

She swooped into the office like a banshee, raining down a bevy of slaps to his head and shoulders. "Get…outta…my…damn…chair!" she snapped, punctuating each word with a smack.

He ducked and dodged, tumbled to the floor and crawled to the far side of the room, laughing as he scampered backward on his hands, feet, and ass, until his back hit the far-right wall. He grinned like a fool as he reached up and rubbed the spot on his head that still stung from her hand-whooping.

"Hell, woman, if I'd of known you was into the old slap-and-tickle I'd a worn my special jeans; you know, the kind with the ass hanging out." He didn't have no booty pants, but he'd buy a pair in ten shades of sexy if she was willing to bend him over her knee and allow him to do the same after.

"Mr. Big Country, you have exactly twenty seconds to get the hell out of my place of business before I call the police," she said as she unsnapped her bag; damn thing was too big to be called a purse.

Big Country rested his head against the wall and gazed at her. Lord, if this woman wasn't made for loving on, he'd never met one who was. It had been less than forty-eight hours since he'd seen her, but he'd swear on the souls of his grands that she'd become more beautiful in that time.

"Darlin', I can't say I'm inclined to leave anytime soon. Not when the sight of you alone makes me feel all warm and tingly inside."

Sienna Red placed her bag on the desk, smoothed her dress down the back of her thighs, and sat in her recently vacated chair.

"In my experience, Wide Earth, warm and tingly inside is usually a sign of infection. Maybe you should get tested for an STD. If you're available between the hours of six and nine tonight, the mobile clinic will be out in front of Red's to provide free testing." She smiled. "And given your penchant for offering money to strangers in exchange for sexual favors, I encourage you to be there."

He flinched dramatically and placed his hand over his heart. "Ouch, woman! A man makes one wrong assumption…."

"Bullshit, Hulking Mountain…and just to warn you, you've got less than ten seconds."

"Well then, let's get down to business," he said, dropping the jovial attitude. "If nothing else, I truly do believe you got a keen mind, and because of that, I know you're more likely to be swayed toward logic sooner than the average woman."

He drew up his knees and rested his elbows on them. "Now, Lynx has called you over five times since you left Mama's House and I know y'all have talked well over thirty minutes on some of those occasions, which kind of makes sense; Lynx can be chatty. What he can also be is vulnerable to falling for the wrong kind of women. I'm here to tell you, Stormy Redmond, you're absolutely the wrong kind."

She didn't react negatively to his opening salvo. No, she was cool as an icicle in a snowstorm, that's why he flinched at her calm words.

"So, are you two fucking? You here to stake your claim on his very beautifully formed ass?"

Lynx did have a beautifully formed ass, but the idea of… His throat tightened, bile surging up from his gut at the idea of boundaries being violated. Lynx was like a brother to him. He clenched and unclenched his hands, fighting off the cold by moving blood forcefully through his veins. Calming his body's reaction, he took a deep breath and gazed back up at Stormy; the calculation in her gaze told him she was looking for a reaction.

"That right there, darlin'," he said with dead-eyed calm. "That little mind-fucking game you just played is the very reason I won't let you have him." He spread his hands wide and smiled. "But I didn't come armed without a bit of incentive, Sienna Red. I know how scary it must be to strike out on your own after fifteen years of working at the same job. I mean, you make decent money as a partner in Red's and got a decent retirement package, but let's face it, nothing you own is really safe when you make enemies out of folks like me, not even that big house you won in the divorce settlement with your ex. And why exactly is he still depositing money in your account after all this time? For the life of me, I can't figure that one out. No matter. Ultimately, I want you to understand how essential it is for you to turn Lynx away when he comes visiting today; gently, mind you—don't need to be unnecessarily cruel."

He'd thrown down his gauntlet. Hard. Now all he needed to do was watch her fold.

Time passed slowly as Stormy Redmond sat there observing, silent. He knew this game, that was the only reason he resisted the urge to do anything but stare back. Thing was, his Grams once told him *if you threaten all a person holds dear and they don't bat an eye, something is real wrong with them.* He was starting to get that feeling about Sienna Red. Then she averted her eyes and with a slight tremble in her hand, began to rifle through her bag.

"Mighty River—," He narrowed his gaze, ground down on his molars. "You just can't seem to stop insulting and threatening me. You come in here, inform me that you've violated my personal space *on multiple levels*, just so I will stay away from the most kind, fun, and sexy man I have met in years? Do you know how unhinged you sound?"

He nodded, understanding that his actions went beyond what may seem rational to her, but the situation more than warranted it. "Except for the sexy part, sounds like you got a real good handle on the situation, sweetness."

When she stood, pulled a taser out of her bag, and pointed at his groin, he conceded that he *might have* overlooked some pertinent information about her mental health when he executed his search. The women he usually interacted with always put their financial well-being over everything else.

Big Country wanted to rub a weary hand over his face but was wary of moving. With the high voltage in that particular brand of taser she could burn a hole through his balls, and turn Big Bubba into a grotesque stain in his pants.

He never should've printed the photo of her dancing on that table Saturday night. Never should've taped it on the wall near his computer monitor. It distracted him from the important things, *she* distracted him.

And what the hell kind of woman walked around with something like that in her big-ass bag in the first place?

"You keep underestimating me, Tall Tree—"

"Look here, woman, I'm about good and goddamn tired of you intentionally mangling my handle. Now, if you're so hell-bent on using a name, have the grace to call me by my given name. Call me Lucas." He took a deep breath and held it, wanting to get back to the issue at hand. "Now be reasonable, darlin'. The last thing you want for this place is to have a mangled dick lawsuit attached to it. That's gonna affect your bottom line in a real bad way, plus, no crazy person in their right mind is gonna wanna open up to a woman who electrocutes innocent, well-meaning, virile good ol' boys whose only aim is to give a spot of life-changing advice."

She had the gall to turn her lip up in contempt as if he weren't acting from the kindness of his heart. "You don't scare me, Lucas..." She waved the taser, urging him to complete the sentence.

"Beaumont."

"Lucas Beaumont. In my line of work, I've had my life threatened by people who seem a bit more depraved than you." She held up her weapon. "Hence this."

"I hear ya, Stormy, I do. Just last night I told my buddy: *'Buddy, one day real soon now, running a dick emporium is gonna be the most dangerous job in the world, worse than any battlefield we've ever fought on.'* He didn't pay me no never mind but after I tell him about this here—," he said, waving his hand between the two of them, "—he's gonna think I'm a fucking prophet."

She aimed the taser as if preparing to shoot it.

Instinct and lightning reflexes had Big Country covering Bubba with both hands and clamping his thighs together.

Stormy pursed her lips, turning her head to the side as if he couldn't see that she was trying not to laugh at him. "Look here, woman, that shit ain't funny."

"Oh, but it is," she said. The smile she flashed at him was blatant and undisguised, her dimples so tempting he had to press down on Big Bubba to stop him from making himself a bigger target. "Who would've imagined that the big dangerous country stalker-boy would be so delicate and trembly when his itty-bitty man parts were threatened?" she said, resting the taser gun on her desk.

A few things became clear to Big Country real quick. One: she wasn't going to shoot him, didn't even seem to *want* to shoot him anymore so he spread his thighs as wide as flexibility would allow and adjusted his crotch, daring her. Two: he was gonna have to fight to regain the intimidation factor...if he ever had it. And three...well, three he could rectify right now.

Planting his hands on the floor, he stood and unbuckled and unzipped his pants, pulling them down far enough for Bubba to spring out and wave about in a friendly *hey, how do.* Bracketing his hands on either side of his pelvis, Big Country showcased Bubba for Stormy's viewing pleasure.

"I'm called Big Country because everything about me is big, sweetness. Big mouth, big ego, big bank account, big intellect, and most important, Big Bubba." Her eyes were heavy on his crotch, lips slightly parted in what he liked to imagine was unrestrained awe. "Now if *nothing* else happens this morning I want you to give my friend his due. He works hard for his lovin' and deserves respect... and as you can see, he ain't nowhere near itty-bitty."

Stormy contemplated Bubba for a few seconds before storing the taser back in her bag. In a few strides she was a hairbreadth away from him, her scent pressing him farther into the wall.

Shocking the sweet Jesus out of him, Sienna Red reached out, took hold of Bubba and squeezed so hard he thought the head would pop off.

Goddamn, she is strong, he thought, scrunching his eyes shut and banging the back of his head against the wall from the pleasure-pain of it all.

"Nice to meet you in the flesh, Bubba," she said, releasing his dick and giving it a conciliatory pat before grabbing Big Country by the top of his open pants and pulling him toward her office door.

"Now that we're all on friendly terms, I'm going to need you to go downstairs and fix the security system before Jules arrives to open the boutique."

Big Country allowed her to push him out into the hall mainly because...well, he just liked the feel of her manhandling him.

When she winked, shot him that mocking fucking smile, and slammed the door in his face, he just stood there, bemused. Bubba deflated. Scrubbing his hands over his face, he tried to figure out exactly where the hell he'd lost the high ground.

Reaching for Bubba, he leaned over and examined him, checking to see if Stormy left bruises before gently tucking his friend back inside his pants and zipping them up. "I gotta say, as somebody who does security for a living, y'all got a shitty system anyhow," he said loudly. "You keep skimping on security and you may not like what you find in your office next."

"Just fix it!" Stormy yelled through the door. "Tick-tock, cowboy."

"I ain't a'scared of you, woman," he called out. "Despite your manly hands and kung fu grip."

Her laughter mocked him all the way down the hall.

It's all right, ol' son; you retreat for now, nothing wrong with retreating, just gives you time and a better vantage point for planning the next attack.

Confident in his ability to come up with a more effective plan, Big Country popped his cigar in his mouth, jogged down the stairs, and began reconnecting, rerouting, and recalibrating the entire security system. When he was done, though, the system—along with the tiny camera he'd installed above her office door—was completely in his control.

Big Country was about to yell that he was leaving when his phone rang. Unclipping it from his belt, he looked at the display, saw it was Zeus, and frowned.

"Zeus?"

Silence stretched over the line. Big Country looked at the display again to make sure the call hadn't disconnected.

"Got a job for you." Zeus finally spoke.

After so many weeks of stagnation, Big Country wanted to whoop with pleasure. A little action was just what he needed to distract himself from Sienna Red and the trouble she represented. It niggled to leave without knowing what threat made her carry a taser gun, but she was tough and capable; she didn't need his protection.

Plus, he wasn't into playing hero without being paid to do so, and the saving grace behind all of this, if there was a job, Lynx wouldn't be able to slink down here this afternoon and destroy the inroads Big Country had made.

"On my way," he informed Zeus as he headed out the front door, making sure that it locked behind him.

This is ridiculous, Stormy thought, shutting off her computer and standing so violently the chair banged against the wall behind her. The man had left the building *hours ago,* yet she hadn't been able to complete one goddamn sentence on the flyer for the two-day instructional she and Jules were co-facilitating next month.

In a perfect world—a Lucas Beaumont-free world—she would've been downstairs by now cutting it up with Jules on the sales floor. After that, she would've met with Lynx and spent the remainder of the first day of her sabbatical enjoying this new phase of her life. Instead, she had to contend with the horse-dicked country stalker who'd broken into her business and hacked into her personal information... and that bastard had intentionally provoked her, had goaded her, not knowing that her first nature was to push back when pushed. She grinned. The man had nearly jumped out of his skin when she'd grabbed—

She fell back into the chair mortified.

Lord, she had grabbed that man's naked penis.

What the hell had she been thinking?

She hadn't, she hadn't been thinking, she'd been reacting, and that was not okay; that was the response she'd spent too many years tempering and transforming into calm practicality. She couldn't let him come in here and steal that away; she'd wasted too much time thinking about him as it was.

For a moment, she'd actually thought she was having a psychotic break when she'd walked into her office and saw him lounging in her desk chair. All weekend her mind had been cannibalized by memories: of him pressing into her body, of his voice whispering in her ear and rolling like thunder through her body, of the strength in his hands as he gripped her ass, of his scent infused into her skin tormenting her until she'd washed it away. She took a deep breath and groaned. His scent was more than a memory now, it was everywhere, like he had come in and sprayed all over her freaking office.

Pressing her fists into her temples, she pounded lightly.

Memories of Lucas fueled every orgasm she'd had this weekend, but having seen the beauty of Bubba, its length, its thickness, having felt its throbbing power, she knew, *knew*, she was going to use that moment to feed her orgasms for weeks to come.

Groaning, she stood, abandoning the project, and headed down to the boutique where Jules stood at the checkout counter hunched over a magazine. Stopping opposite her, Stormy wasn't surprised to see that it was a French adult magazine—*cultural porn*, Jules liked to call it.

"Anything interesting?"

"Sexy women, creative French shit," Jules said, looking up at her. "Mostly I just like perving over the sexies. Finish the flyer?"

"Question should be, have I *started* the flyer."

"Dude," Jules frowned, straightening to her full five feet three inches of height. "What have you been doing up there, sampling the product?"

There was nothing in the boutique she wanted to sample as much as she wanted to feel Bubba again. Not even Jules' favorite—Dave-the-double-sided-dildo—compared. She imagined Bubba would be like Benadryl for her pussy; one dose and she would be out. It was unfortunate that Bubba was attached to a bigger dick than he was.

Jules snapped her fingers in Stormy's face.

Somewhere between everyone parting ways last night and coming to work this morning, Jules had dyed her hair again. The upper layer of her asymmetrical page cut was a rainbow kaleidoscope of lavender, pink, and red while the lower layer remained silky black. Jules wore her black plastic horn-rimmed glasses with gold rhinestones, a cream peasant blouse, brown leggings, and five-inch black matte platform boots that reminded Stormy of something Lurch from the Addams Family would wear.

Generally, people couldn't reconcile the many faces of Jules, but at thirty-eight years old, her friend hadn't lost her passion for helping people live in their own truth because she had fought so hard to stand in hers. Stormy loved that about her.

"No, I haven't been sampling the product…you wish. But because you're slightly more levelheaded than Lou, and a licensed psychologist to boot—I'm going to really need you to remember that last part—I'd like to run something past you and get your feedback."

"Okay, shoot," Jules said, shutting the magazine and pushing it to the side.

Lou was usually the first person Stormy shared confidences with. It was a habit forged by fire, stone, and decades of trust. But Lou was opinionated and sometimes forgot to pull her punches. With all the emotional turmoil Stormy was experiencing, she would flash if she heard "stop punking out" one more goddamn time.

"Say there's this hot guy…or girl…that you can't get out of your mind…"

"Country Boy?"

"We're not talking about me, we're talking about you in a hypothetical situation."

Jules nodded. "Oh yeah, okay."

"All right, so say this person pulls some real stalker shit and breaks into your space—"

"But the guy is hot, right? I mean, didn't you say he was hot?"

Stormy closed her eyes momentarily. "I'm gonna need you to focus."

"Dude, I'm like a laser with my focus, please continue."

"So the person breaks into your space, threatens you, and shows you his junk."

Jules perked up. "His junk? As in his dick?" Stormy nodded. "Is the dick spectacular?"

"Yes, very."

"This is getting hot."

Stormy lifted her eyebrow.

"Focused," Jules assured her.

"So, to prove that you're not intimidated, you grab his junk—"

"Are you intimidated, though…I mean, am *I* intimidated?"

"No."

"Turned on?"

"Yeah, but that's not the point."

"What's the point, then?" Jules practically shouted.

"What would you do if the guy comes back?"

Jules shrugged. "Fuck him."

"You're absolutely no help."

Stormy thought the elements of danger would garner a more thoughtful reaction.

"What are you doing?" she asked as Jules pulled out her phone and began tapping the screen.

"Did the guy from the bar break into your place and threaten you?"

"No, he broke into the boutique and threatened me."

That made Jules pause. "Should I call the police?"

"Well…"

"Of course I shouldn't. If you wanted the police called, they would have been here hours ago." Jules continued tapping, then held the phone to her ear. Stormy could hear the phone ringing on the other side.

"Who are you calling?"

Jules grinned. "The one person who said something would happen and that I should call her when it did because you would be too chick-enshit to do it." She hit the speaker button and placed the phone on the counter.

"What up?" Lou answered after the second ring.

"Mangy bitches," Stormy mumbled, irritated that they'd conspired behind her back.

"She grabbed his dick!" Jules said, using the counter as leverage as she jumped up and down. "She said it was a *very* spectacular dick."

"Did they have sex?"

"No, we didn't have sex, I don't know that man!"

"Still punki—"

"I swear to God I will snap this phone as if it's your neck," Stormy finally yelled.

"Hey…hey there, sister," Jules soothed, grabbing her phone and holding it close to her breasts. Jules continued to eye Stormy warily as she returned the phone to a few inches from her mouth. "She says he broke into the boutique, threatened her, and wiggled his dick in her face."

"I did not say that," Stormy said, weary of the conversation.

"For real though, is he dangerous?" Lou asked.

"She didn't call the police…or her daddy, or her brother."

"So dangerous in ways that she likes. How'd he get in?"

Jules looked at her.

"The security system was down when I got here but the alarm hadn't gone off. Nothing was broken or jimmied open. He said the system was crap, then I made him fix it before he left."

"Ed warned you guys that you should have gotten a better system."

Ed was Lou's husband. He was a physical therapist, and like all men, he liked to believe he knew everything about everything when it came to repairs and electrical systems. Didn't matter that Lou was a licensed master electrician and plumber. Stormy would take her advice before Ed's, even if he happened to be right about the security system.

"Getting back to the question on the table…" Jules said. "What do you think she should do if he comes back, Lou? I said 'fuck him' because she obviously wants to, but she didn't like that response. And I'll say this, then let it go." She looked intently at Stormy. "This is a new phase of your evolution, remember? Stormy, you know so much about intimacy and the value of touch, but you've stopped experiencing both in your own life. The antebellum Okie is the first man you've reacted so strongly to in all the years we've known each other. When the Asian boy comes today, find out if the big guy is someone sane enough to share orgasms with, then move on when you're ready, simple as that."

"And let me hit you with a piece of truth that I've been holding onto because until this weekend, I didn't think you were ready to hear it," Lou added. The silence that filled the line made Stormy's stomach knot up. "You need to set yourself free, Stormy, all the way free, simple as that. For years you've smothered the wild child I miss and love to within an inch of your life. Because of the incident in college where Reign was assaulted, you enjoying yourself at a frat party doesn't equate to you being responsible for what happened; you didn't do anything wrong." Stormy tried to blink back the tears gathering in her eyes. "You need to let that big country boy fuck you until you are filled up. You need to let go of whatever it is that has you staying connected to Chaduwo's shady ass, and you need to live out loud so that we can be mangy bitches running wild together again."

Stormy laughed as she wiped the tears gathering at the corner of her eye. Their words were said in love, yet they were ripping her apart, and it hurt, her past decisions still hurt, but she was no longer willing to continue playing the sacrificial lamb to appease her guilt.

The front door chimed, signaling someone was entering the shop.

"Okay, Oprah moment over, customer in route!" Jules said, moving from behind the counter. "Bye Lou."

"Bye mangy bitch, bye Stormy."

"Bye woman; call me when you get home."

"Sho' 'nuff."

Stormy turned to face the customer who'd ended their conversation, and found a slender young woman aimed straight for her, stopping well inside her personal boundaries.

"Why are you crying?" the woman demanded.

Hearing the barely perceptible lilt in the woman's voice, Stormy reminded herself that people from different cultures had different understandings about personal space. She couldn't shove the woman away despite instinct urging her to do so. This was her sole place of business now, and her income could rise or fall based on how she conducted herself.

Smiling, she took a step back, patting the damp skin beneath her eyes.

"The beauty of Red's Boutique is that when you're here you'll get everything you need...even when it hurts." She winked, glancing over at the cat-o'-nine-tails. "I'm Stormy and this is Jules; we're the owners of this lascivious place. How can I help you?"

The woman's gaze flickered toward Jules, took in her multihued hair, titanium septum piercing, diamond stud near the right of her mouth, and dismissed her, shifting her sky-blue eyes back toward Stormy. The intensity of the woman's focus went beyond the awkward avoidance she normally saw with people who had never been inside a sex shop. This woman was interested in something, but Stormy doubted it had anything to do with their merchandise.

"Can I offer you some tea?" she asked. "Maybe water with a twist of lemon?"

The woman looked around the room, reddening when her gaze landed on the assortment of dildos toward the back of the store.

"I prefer tea," she informed Stormy as her eyes shifted around the room, turning curious when she looked up toward the second level.

"I'll be right back." Stormy stepped away from the younger woman.

"No, no," Jules motioned for Stormy to stay. "I'll get the tea."

Walking across the sales floor to the curtained archway that led to the salon/reading room, Jules ducked out of view only to peek her head out and mouth *what the fuck* as she pointed at the customer and circled her finger near her temple. Jules might have a doctorate in psychology, but she didn't have the temperament or the empathy to be a therapist. That's why she had opened Red's Boutique.

Grinning, Jules disappeared behind the curtain, forcing Stormy to turn back to their customer. "You'll like this week's selection of tea. Twig tea, very soothing." Stormy smiled at the young blonde. *Maybe it'll loosen you the hell up*, she thought, then chastised herself. She usually wasn't reactionary or quick to judgment. It was Lucas's fault. Every irritating experience she'd had since Friday night was his fault. Before him, she was known for patience that rivaled Job's.

"I've never been inside a place of deviance. Do you provide men with sex upstairs; is this also a place of prostitution?" The woman narrowed her gaze on Stormy. "My father teaches that all houses of ill repute and those that dwell within them should be cleansed by fire."

The woman smiled, her left cheek dimpling. "Lucky for us, he doesn't know I'm here."

Did this bitch just try to insult me and threaten my livelihood, Stormy wondered, not falling for the woman's smile or the teasing toward the end.

"Your father sounds like a bit of a zealot but lucky for you, you've found a place that doesn't censure judgmental men prone to arson. Too many women are taught that celebrating their bodies and sensuality is somehow a bad thing; that our bodies are secondary to, if not made solely for, a man's needs. At Red's Boutique, we nurture a woman's desire to celebrate her sexuality, to know it, to own it. Never believe anyone who would shame you into believing you're wrong or evil for worshiping that which the Creator has blessed you with... father or not."

The woman's regard turned speculative. "I do need to be more skilled, more confident in my ability to give pleasure."

"Well I'm happy that you chose Red's to start your journey. We provide books, toys, tutorials, games, whatever you need. I'm sure we can assist you or point you in the direction of someone who can, Ms...I'm sorry, I didn't ask your name."

For a moment, Stormy thought the woman was going to slap her for asking and walk out the front door. An air of superiority thickened around the woman and she stood taller. "Delilah, my father named me Delilah."

Okay.

"Well, honey, there is power of biblical proportions in that name. We've got to help you master the skills to live up to it, huh? Did you want to take some time to look around or is there a specific area of interest I can help you with?"

Delilah tilted her head to the side, contemplating the question...or simply contemplating Stormy?

The younger woman was definitely odd.

Dressed in a lemon-yellow sundress, with gold gladiator sandals, and a cream clutch pressed into the front of her thighs, there was nothing in Delilah's appearance that was overtly off-putting. She had a striking beauty accentuated with a simple coating of mango-pink lip gloss, but beneath it all there was a not-quite-rightness.

Glancing toward the curtained salon opening, Stormy cursed Jules; she was intentionally avoiding this customer. Jules' aversion to overly entitled people, a bias reinforced by years in her doctoral program, didn't usually get in the way of business.

"This is so demeaning," Delilah finally said, letting out a huffing breath.

"It doesn't have to be. There's nothing you can ask or say that someone hasn't already come in and asked or said before."

The death grip Delilah had on her bag was painful to witness.

"My boyfriend is a strong man, a good man. He wants to get married."

"Do you want to marry him?"

"He is God's gift to me, he loves me fiercely. He would defend me against the world, of *course* I want to marry him."

"Well…I can only hope that I'll be so lucky one day. Good men like that are hard to find."

"I had never imagined that the level of pleasure he showed me during our first time together could even exist," Delilah said almost boastfully, like her man was the only man in the world who knew how to make a woman come. "I want to learn how to please him as much as he pleases me. I tried to take him into my mouth, but he's so…big… I believe I caused him pain."

Ooooh, bad head. For some men, that was an offense worse than death. Delilah's man sounded like a good guy, though; someone she obviously adored.

"Well, my young temptress," Stormy said conspiratorially, linking her arm through Delilah's. "I do believe you've come to the right place."

She proceeded to show Delilah books and videos covering every-thing from human development to women's sexual revolution to oral copulation and role-playing. She recommended a couple of games that explored sensual touch and getting to know your lover's body and needs as well as your own.

"You know of many ways to seduce, Stormy. I'm not fully convinced that you are not a whore."

"Delilah, let me tell you something," Stormy said, not caring about the big sale they were about to make. Sometimes you just had to stop being polite.

Jules rushed back into the main room, carrying a cup of steaming tea on a saucer just as Delilah took her armful of items toward the register.

"What, did you have to go to Japan to snap each twig individually?" Stormy muttered as Jules passed her.

"Whatever do you mean?" Jules blinked innocently.

"Mangy bitch," Stormy said as she took the saucer. "Delilah, I'll just put this in a to-go cup, get you on your way, I know a woman like you has a busy schedule. And in apology for not honoring your time, Jules will throw in two handfuls of our most popular ribbed, extra-large condoms for free."

"Yeah, that'll show me." Jules snorted as she crossed over to the other side of the counter and rang Delilah up. "Sorry about the delay," Stormy heard Jules mumble. "Technical difficulties."

"Apologies are unnecessary, I didn't have very high expectations. Tell me, do men come here to buy all the things you offer here? My fiancé was in the area earlier; maybe he came in to buy me something?"

"I've been here since opening, no men have stopped by," Jules said. Unlike Stormy, Jules' responses didn't welcome conversation. The younger woman left with her purchases by the time Stormy reentered the room with the to-go tea.

"Next time I see that crazy woman coming I'm shutting this bitch down for the day," Jules stated, drinking Delilah's tea.

For the next two hours, Stormy and Jules stayed busy with an afternoon rush. At three-thirty on the dot, Lynx walked into the boutique wearing black sunglasses, a fitted black T-shirt, a worn brown leather vest, and black jeans. Stormy shook her head; he looked sexy and utterly stealth.

The four regulars laughing with Jules quieted, smiles turning predatory, as they noticed the younger man walk in.

"Ladies," Lynx greeted, shedding his glasses, amber eyes smoldering with sexual promise.

The man was a menace. With the grace of a predatory big cat and the playfulness of a tabby, Lynx was all trouble. Despite what Lucas said, the only person who needed to be protected around Lynx was whatever woman he felt like toying with. And Stormy included herself among them. He had been relentless in his campaign to have Stormy give Lucas another chance.

"Hey Asian boy, when we partying again?" Jules called out.

"I'm only a phone call away from my family Jules. You can come up the mountain or I can go down on you…my bad, I meant come down to you."

Jules laughed, and Stormy would have, too, if she hadn't had to move fast to intercept Lynx before the four regulars—deemed regulars because they wore shit out and needed to constantly replenish their supply—dragged Lynx behind the salon curtain and showed him what it really meant to be wild.

"Gwen, I will drop-kick you. Don't play with me," Stormy threatened, pushing Lynx behind her as she held out her arm keeping the stout fifty-six-year-old white woman with two adult kids and four male *friends* away.

Stormy navigated Lynx toward the stairs, keeping her body between his and theirs. The myth about a woman's diminished sex drive in older years obviously came from someone who had no real knowledge of older women's needs.

"No!" Stormy barked out, holding her finger up at Gwen as if the woman was a rambunctious pit bull.

Gwen rolled her eyes and she and the other three regulars fell back. "You can't keep him up there forever, Stormy."

"Oh, but she can, 'cause I can last just that long with the right motivation. You ladies good at motivating?" Lynx asked.

"Get yo' tight ass upstairs before they wear you out," Stormy snapped, fully intending to have Lynx leave through the door at the end of the upstairs hallway, leading to the back stairs her clients would use when she began seeing them in her office.

"Did you see that opening move?" Lynx asked as he walked into her office. "How I wowed them in their tracks with my Asian persuasion? Practiced that move for weeks."

"You are such an idiot."

"No, that's how I lull women into a sense of safety. When they're all 'oh my God, you're so funny, such a good guy I feel like I can share everything with you,' I show them the bad and get all the good lovin'."

"You're as bad as Lucas," she said, sitting down in one of the plush wingback chairs near the wall to the left of her desk. She could see it, why Lucas was so protective of Lynx. Though she had no doubt Lynx was more than capable of taking care of himself, there was an impishness to him that pulled for her to watch over him.

Wondering around her office, Lynx looked out the window to the right of the room, the one behind her desk. He picked up knick-knacks, examined artwork. He explored her office like a curious cat in a new environment.

"So, how'd you discover the big guy's real name?" he finally spoke, sitting on the edge of her desk and squeezing her stress ball in his hands.

"He told me this morning…after he'd broken in here to let me know he'd hacked my personal information and could basically cause me problems if I continued to have anything to do with you. All weekend you've been trying to convince me that he's a good guy, but in truth he's a bully and an asshole."

"But that's the best part, it's only with you!" Lynx said, tossing the ball in the air. "I can't believe he broke in here. Wait until I tell Mama." Something about the plaque above her door caught his eye, he tilted his head and gazed at it silently.

"It's in recognition of my volunteer service for a nonprofit working with sexually exploited minors."

The hooded sidelong glance he cast at her made her uneasy. Why had he looked like that? Her soul rebelled at the idea that he would abuse children, but her mind saw too much in this life, knew how ugliness hid itself. And why hadn't she noticed the shadow in his gaze before?

Because he's so easy to talk to, she thought, too fun-loving.

"What was that look, Lynx? Do you feel some kind of way about kids and sex?"

And this time she watched him, watched him close.

He watched her closer, then shrugged.

"You're one woman. You should have a team at your back when you disrupt the money of people in that line of business."

"I got a team. It's called Desert Eagle featuring .44 Mag. Today I pulled my taser, but your boy Lucas will find that out if he keeps messing with me."

"You pulled a taser…on Lucas?" Lynx laughed so hard, his lightness returning as he was consumed by laughter, bending over and nearly rolling off the desk onto the floor. She laughed too, remembering Lucas's reaction.

"Yeah, you need to be watched," Lynx said, wiping at his eyes as he stood back up. "I'm not one for playing matchmaker, but me and Mama think you'd be good for the big guy. You have the fire to take him on, and you're smart, and you care about people."

"Didn't hear the part about the breaking in and the threatening, did you?"

He waved his hand dismissively. "He has a small problem with boundaries and limits. He's very free that way."

"He thought I was a prostitute."

"He *wanted* you to be a prostitute so he could justify having you," Lynx clarified. "Big Country doesn't do relationships, he has contractual agreements revolving around sex in exchange for financial support and no drama. You're right, though, there's only a few women he values, but he's got his reasons for that. I don't think you're a fool, Stormy, I just think you'd be good together even if for a short period of time. Plus—," he smiled wide, "—you didn't call the police, that's got to mean something."

She thought about her conversation with Jules and Lou earlier, thought about the ways she still allowed Chaduwo in her life, and shook her head. "I'm not looking for a relationship."

"Most excellent. Big Country's not either!"

She groaned. Was the universe conspiring against her?

"Tell you what, you give him a chance and I promise you won't regret it. I got a good feeling about you." His cell phone buzzed and he pulled it from the interior of his vest pocket. He smiled, fingers moving quickly over the screen.

Putting the phone away, he looked at her and walked toward the door. "Sorry about that, I gotta get back to the mountain. Sabrina asked if you can make her a fun bag and Mama says she'll call tomorrow. And just so you know, Stormy, when I have a feeling, people do well to pay attention."

She didn't respond. It wasn't that she disregarded Lynx's feelings, it was that her own took precedence. Right then, those feelings were warning her that Lucas, Lynx, their friends, could tear her life into pieces.

CHAPTER 4

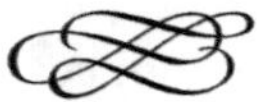

ig Country stood on one side of Zeus, Cizan on the other.
The Brood mates looked down, faces emptied of emotion, arms crossed over their chests as they watched their young trainee glare at them from the laptop's monitor. Her thin arms were crossed over her chest in imitation of their body language, save for the scowl of disgust curling her lips.

"Is this all you got?" Brianna challenged.

Zeus lowered his head like a wolf sizing up its pray.

The female bucked at them. "What?" she shouted, throwing up her hands.

Big Country reared back and made a show of holding his arms in surrender. "Damn girl, you just gave me chills." He smiled, then stroked his jaw. "Okay, I'll give ya 'bout a seven out of ten."

Zeus and Cizan nodded in agreement.

"Why just seven? I didn't back down!"

"You were the first to break silence, little one," Cizan said, tone both gentle and severe. "Never be the first to break silence in a stare down."

"He's right, sweet pea," Big Country added. "In a real battle of wills, posturing implies you got nothing but some last-ditch effort to goad your enemy into reacting. Any seasoned fighter will see it as weakness. Silence can be powerful," Big Country said.

Cizan placed a finger over his lips. "Shhhhh."

"Then boom!" Big Country struck out, pulling his fist back jackhammer fast. "You bring the *motherfucking* thunder."

Brianna laughed, jumping up and down. "Boom! I bring the *motherfu—*"

"Hey!"

Brianna's hand flew to cover her mouth and Big Country flinched at the sound of Sabrina's voice as if she'd physically knocked him upside the head.

Righting himself, he made a slashing motion across his neck and coughed, "Abort, abort." Turning, he faced Sabrina who dominated the door that led down to the sublevel. Mama stepped from behind her and dread coalesced in his stomach. Cizan moved closer to the table and smoothly shut the laptop, hiding it inside the folds of his leather coat.

"So, here's the thing, I...we...Zeus called *me—*" he began, ignoring all his training in the name of self-preservation. Zeus's mercurial eyes flicked toward him, silently condemning him as a rat-ass snitch and Big Country was totally okay with that. Matter of fact, he didn't give a damn; Mama was mean when she was mad, and Sabrina was fast claiming a part of his heart that he didn't want to see hurt with disappointment.

"If this is you-all's idea of being responsible uncles, maybe I'll take you over to my cousin Debra Ann's to work with her bad assed kids. They would love your self-defense lessons."

Zeus grunted.

Big Country nodded; he wasn't going anywhere near those heathens. *And* when they weren't on assignment, these women weren't the boss of them. Practicing what he preached, Big Country drew up to his full height, crossed his arms over his chest again and widened his stance. "Now look here, ladies—"

Sabrina cut him with a look so sharp he fought the impulse to touch his cheek to see if it was bleeding. Taking a step back, he nodded to Zeus. "This is all you, cousin."

Sabrina, looking like an older version of Brianna, glared up at Zeus.

"Zeus."

"Woman."

Cizan eased toward the front door, away from the brewing conflict.

"Don't even think about it," Mama warned. Big Country grinned when the personification of death detoured and settled in the shadows against the wall, trying to hide from Mama's gaze.

"We talked about the need to wait on teaching Brianna any more of your lessons." Sabrina said.

"We talked about it."

"Yet here you are, and bringing them in on it, no less."

Zeus's blade-less hand began to dance at his side.

"She's ours, though," Zeus said calmly. "Our responsibility, ours to keep, ours to protect?"

The question took a little air out of Sabrina's impassioned sails.

"She's absolutely ours," she said, as she closed her eyes and massaged her temple. "For better or worse."

Zeus approached Sabrina, stopping so close that he had to be sucking all the breathable air out of her lungs. That uneasy gnawing churned through Big Country's gut again. The intensity of emotion these two shared should have made his skin crawl with horror; instead, the gnawing wanted to be filled with what they shared instead of rejecting it.

"Trust," Zeus declared.

And with that one word, all the fear and tension vanished from Sabrina's body. She reached between them and rested her hand over Zeus's heart.

"With my life, big man. With the life of our girl."

Zeus threw a look of raw pleasure Big Country's way. "Woman's brain. Sometimes you have to cut through to the heart of a matter to make them see reason."

Big Country blinked twice. Zeus was now schooling *him* on women? *In what fucking life…?*

"Okay, fascinating as all this domestic bliss bullshit is, I got a woman off-mountain who ain't worried about heart or reason, just all of this well-endowed sexiness," he said, motioning toward his groin and grinning as Sabrina pretended to retch.

Zeus pressed his lips against Sabrina's forehead, his steely gaze flickering toward Big Country again. "Maybe you should stop and say hello to the saint on the side of the road. Think he's getting lonely."

Big Country looked to Sabrina but she shrugged, shaking her head. Sabrina had a knack for deciphering the leaps in logic sometimes required to follow Zeus's train of thought. Over the weeks, Big Country had learned not to dismiss what Zeus said out of hand, no matter how bizarre it sounded at first reckoning. Where most folks got from point A to point B in a reasonably linear fashion, Zeus's thought process could make you to work like hell to link his meaning to your reality.

"Look here, cousin," Big Country began, feeling around his pockets for his keys. He wasn't of a mind to sort out riddles when there was a house full of people who could do that. The woman who'd laid waste to his damn-near infinite amount of good sense was down in the real world waiting for him to come unravel all her mysteries so he could use her vulnerabilities as he saw fit. He wasn't giving that up to say hey to nobody. "I'm gonna pass on that invite and head on home, but y'all make do without me, yeah."

"Why are you rushing off the mountain so much lately? Don't tell me it's because of one of those no-account women who don't know nothing but laying up on their asses all day waiting for you to come and fu–"

"Mama!" he shouted, covering his ears and backing toward the door. Lord Jesus, his poor mind couldn't handle her thinking about him and his women. She despised them on a level that wasn't healthy, believing they were taking advantage of him when everyone else knew he held all the advantages in his unions.

'Course she cared so much because he was her favorite. She'd saved him when he was barely out of kindergarten, so her mothering tendency was stronger than with the others. In general, he didn't mind, but Mama was mean, and bad things tended to befall people who threatened her Brood.

"Big Country, if there's someone out there dogging my mountain, saint or not, I want to know what his purpose is." Mama said.

"There's likely nobody out there! Don't act like y'all don't know this," he said, turning to glare at Zeus. The bastard smirked at him, rubbing his jaw against Sabrina's temple. Blue flame tried to spark into existence as Zeus held onto Sabrina while keeping him from the tempting threat he knew actually existed.

Taking a deep breath, Big Country cracked his neck left, then right, and exhaled. Reaching for his cigar, he funneled his anger away from the cold spark by adopting an easygoing smile. He had to smile, he had to be calm, he didn't want to be the one to unleash a chain of events that wouldn't leave the bar standing or the Brood intact.

Mama must have sensed his struggle because she held his gaze and made her way to him, linking her arm through his as she guided him toward the front door. This woman knew him better than anyone, was more of a Mama than his own sadistic bitch of a…

Steady, ol' son, the past is dead and buried, yeah.

Breathing in Mama's scent grounded him. Mama knew his demons and the effort it took to rein them in. He leaned down and placed a kiss on the crown of her head.

"I know you're anxious to be away," she said, patting his forearm. "Just do a feeble old woman this one favor before you go."

He snorted. At fifty-eight, Mama's unlined face, radiant brown skin, and agile body made her look only a handful of years older than his thirty-six. Yeah, she was feeble as a velociraptor.

"All I need is a level mind to accompany Zeus and Cizan."

Cizan groaned, none too happy about being included in this

excursion that was no doubt their punishment for being a part of Zeus's lesson. But Mama was right; if there was even a small possibility of a threat, they had to root it out. "Just make sure that if there's a person down there, those two don't kill him before we learn what his business here is," Mama whispered once they'd reached the parking lot. Mama slid her arm free of his and headed back into the bar, retrieving both Cizan and Zeus and leaving them on the gravel lot right beside him.

"Now you boys have fun," she called out, joining Sabrina at the front door, waving them off before slamming it shut.

"Always sayin' I'm rude," Zeus said, looking toward the closed door. "That was rude."

"You brought it on yourself," Big Country muttered as he hit the key fob and headed to his truck.

Zeus looked from the truck to Big Country then shifted his gaze toward the forest.

"You head down the mountain on foot if you want to, I'll be damned if I follow your spry ass down the mountain only to have to walk back up this hefty bitch."

Cizan must have felt the same because he walked to the truck and got in the passenger seat.

Zeus shed his shirt, pulling a Bowie from the small of his back before the shirt hit the ground. He cocked an eyebrow at Big Country in challenge.

"First to the road wins?" Big Country asked, grinning. Zeus didn't respond, simply sprinted from the parking area and tore down the mountain ignoring the trail.

"Son of a—" Big Country ran for the truck and leaped in. He gunned the engine, tires spitting dirt and gravel as he sped onto Devil's Descent, slowing only to wrestle his beast of a truck down the winding narrow trail, riding that motherfucker like a rollercoaster to reach the highway before Zeus. Laughing wildly, he swerved to avoid a massive tree that would've put him and Cizan in traction for months.

The shot of adrenaline that followed gave him a moment of crystal clarity. He'd been handling the situation with Lynx and Stormy all wrong. Enticing her with material things, trying to scare her off with threats...that put the onus of responsibility on her. It was Lynx's desire he had to kill and the only surefire way to do that was to have sex with her first.

Hitting a curve too fast, he fought to not flip his truck, riding on the two left wheels while Cizan braced one hand against the roof and the other against the passenger side door as his side of the truck floated off the ground.

"*Yeah, cousin!*" Big Country hollered. "I'm fixin' to bring enough thunder to quiet this motherfuckin' storm for the rest of her days."

The truck dropped down on all four tires and Big Country gunned the engine, trying to make up for lost time.

"You do realize it's not raining?" Cizan said, peering at him with his ghostly white eye.

"Not *yet*." He grinned.

But by the time Bubba was done, he'd make Stormy rain her loving down on a scale of biblical proportions.

It was growing dark.

He hated the darkness of this place, but he hated the cold it brought more. It wasn't the relentless penetrating cold of Ireland, but he was never exposed to the cold for hours on end there as he was here unless he was being punished.

Perched high above the road, he was forced to watch the day draw to a close, to watch shadows merge to form the skin through which darkness clawed, spreading its despair over the earth. Reaching for the large ornate cross dangling from his neck, he squeezed, praying for God to deliver him from this creeping darkness, to find him worthy enough for warmth, for salvation.

His only response was silence. God was forever silent to his requests. It was a hardship he must endure until he was worthy, as the Good Shepherd taught, but he prayed that this sojourn would soon end. He was dirty and starving and dreadfully tired...

He was not like his brothers. He wasn't strong of mind or body. When he was on the receiving end of discipline, he had not become honed and hardened and focused on the divine lesson, he became a sniveling heap of flesh, huddled in pain, begging for mercy.

Tightening his fingers around the cross until his knuckles showed white, bones threatening to break through parchment-like skin growing thinner by the day. He closed his eyes and begged forgiveness. He was chosen and therefore it was an honor to be given this divine duty; he would not fail because of his undisciplined thoughts.

This is sacrifice, he could hear the Shepherd intone severely: *With sacrifice comes the greatest of God's gifts.*

Hearing the echo of a large engine, he looked up and scanned the road. Maybe she was coming back for him. His heart raced at the possibility. He was wrong to have believed that Delilah would allow him to die up here like the vermin that inhabited the woods. He was always so wrong, but one day he would be right, do right.

Cocking his head to the side, he closed his eyes and listened.

Something was definitely coming.

As the roar of the engine grew louder, he determined that the vehicle moving toward his location was more powerful than the car Delilah drove. In his role as watcher, he had begun to learn the difference between trucks and smaller cars. Big engines from less powerful ones.

A truck burst onto the road from the opposite side, surprising him. The vehicle's tires squealed against the asphalt as it made a tight turn and came to a stop, straddling both lanes as it idled. He knew this truck; it was the most familiar thing he recognized since coming to this place. The driver was a big man, bigger than any he'd ever seen.

Cornelius became light-headed, believing he would faint from fear but he remained alert and aware as floodlights on the truck's roof lit up the road. The driver angled a massive light toward his side of the road, searching. Somehow the driver knew he was here. Maybe he should walk down and greet the driver, embrace his destiny.

A hand flattened over his forehead, jerking it back as a metal colder than ice pressed against his jugular. Heat now radiated behind Cornelius but did nothing to thaw the terror that had encased his mind. Legs sprouted from each side of Cornelius's hips as large booted feet planted themselves near his knees.

"Yell out."

"Wha…what?" Cornelius tried to turn his head to see which of hell's creatures had materialized behind him, but the knife and hand kept his head facing forward.

"I won. Yell out."

"I don't—"

The knife bit deeper into his neck and a thin trickle of blood snaked down his throat.

"Help!" he yelled, hoping this time to reach the ears of God.

The bright light found him, and the truck was pulled over to his side of the road. The driver who stepped out was a modern-day Goliath. He heard another door open and shut, but didn't see anyone else exit the truck. The Goliath stomped up the incline, stopping less than ten feet away.

"Well I'll be damned." Incredulity etched over the Goliath's face as he cautiously drew closer.

"Like I said, a saint." The man behind Cornelius spoke. "Wonder if he can save your soul."

"Not even a saint has the power to save a thing that don't exist." Another voice spoke from the darkness.

Chills raced through Cornelius as he searched for the thing that sounded like some dead and buried apparition that had clawed its way from unconsecrated soil to walk among men.

Follow the trail of Fallen feathers and you will eventually find the nest of evil, the Shepherd had said. Cornelius began to pray fervently.

"Hey, hey, cut that shit out, son, you're giving me a fucking migraine with that foolishness," the Goliath ordered.

Cornelius ceased praying out loud, but continued the prayers that were already having an effect on the Goliath.

The hand on Cornelius's forehead pressed his head back further and the knife bit deeper. "He said *hush*," the man behind him said.

Demon, Cornelius thought, only demons had the power of knowing a man's mind. The trembling that overtook his body had nothing to do with cold and everything to do with mortal fear. Dear God, he didn't want to die, he didn't want to—

"Help!" he yelled out to God again.

The Goliath's shadow shifted, detaching from the Goliath and coalescing into the very visage of death. The left side of the creature's face was scarred and covered with a black tattoo that resembled some kind of bird. The entity's right pupil was black as tar, but the left was opaque white, as if blind…or seeing into the realm of damned.

The creature was equal parts beautiful and grotesque.

Crouching before him, it bared its teeth in a grim smile as its black hair cascaded over its face like a heavy black shroud obscuring its features. It extended its right arm and beckoned toward Cornelius, a tattoo of a skeletal hand overlaid the flesh.

"Come with me if you want to live," it said, peering at Cornelius through the shroud, its grin widening like a serpent.

Cornelius seized the instant the being touched his shoulder. In his fear, he voided his bladder a split second before he fainted.

"You are one sadistic bastard," Big Country said, shaking his head.

"That shit was priceless," Cizan smirked.

What was priceless was the look of disgust on Zeus's face as he held his hands up in seeming surrender, angling his blade toward the saint's temple.

"He's touching me," Zeus muttered, looking at Big Country as if it was his fault.

"Well you've got a good two seconds before that piss spreading over his robe touches you, too, cousin," Big Country said.

In one swift motion, Zeus leaped up into a crouch and the saint's unsupported body fell to the ground, head colliding so hard against the earth it recoiled and hit a second time. Scrawny son of a bitch wasn't getting an ounce of Big Country's sympathy; he was the motherfucker who'd ruined any notion of being able to go home and watch today's video feed of Stormy, maybe rubbing one off as he and Bubba fantasized over just how sweet her pussy would be.

Standing, Zeus sheathed his blade and jogged down the hill, silently crossing in front of the truck's headlights and disappearing into the woods on the other side, leaving Big Country and Cizan to do the quick work of searching the saint's brown robe and funky-assed pale body. They found nothing but a large cheap-looking gold cross with what looked to be a rod overlaying a staff in a circular enclosure at its center.

Rolling the unconscious man in the green tarp from the back of his truck, they carried him down the hill and tossed him in the truck's bed. Climbing into the cab, Big Country took five minutes to rub hand sanitizer over their hands and arms and then started the engine, looking to the area where they had found the saint.

"So, tell me this, cousin, why camp out right *across* the road that leads up to Mama's House? Why not just mosey over to our side of the mountain and learn all he could up close and personal?" Big Country asked.

"Maybe he knows just how securely it's monitored."

Big Country had created a custom program for Mama's House, utilizing code that recognized heat signatures, motion patterns, and weight distribution, to identify just about every species of land animal in northern California. He had a canopy of sensors imbedded in the trees from the mountain top on down to the lower perimeter beginning at the highway.

Through Gambit—the computer system he created for the Brood—they could track movement on the mountain and be alerted to any unauthorized or suspicious activity. They were their own emergency broadcast system, and with the sensors and camera's they could easily track the intruder's location and direction.

"If he knows about our security—" Cizan began.

"He knows too damn much," Big Country muttered, heading back up the mountain at a more sedate and contemplative pace.

Mama and Terry joined them outside when they came to a stop, watching silently as Big Country and Cizan unloaded their tarp-enshrouded burden.

"The saint?" Mama asked, walking with them toward the small building to the left of the bar.

"Cloak, cowl, cross, stench of unsatisfied misery." He nodded once. "Appears that way."

Mama unlocked the metal door to the holding cell. It was about 400 square feet, with six beds in the main room, each bed with a manacle that attached to the concrete wall. The place was created for any poor bastard visiting Mama's House, unwilling to go gently into the night.

Tonight, it would be the resting place for saints.

Carrying the body into the locker-room-style shower area adjoining the main room, they rolled out the tarp, dumping the saint on the polished concrete floor. Knowing where Big Country's personal boundaries lay, Terry and Cizan unrobed the saint and held him under a spray of water, eventually having to wash him because the man never roused to consciousness. Once dried, they placed him in bed and Mama covered him before ushering everyone outside the building and locking it.

"He'll hold for the night," Mama said, reaching up to pull Big Country down so she could plant a kiss on his cheek. "Thank you for staying, Lucas. Go home and take care of your lady business; we won't talk to him until the morning."

"Since I ain't one for looking a gift horse in the mouth, I'm gon' take my leave and bid y'all a hasty *au revoir*."

By the time he made it to his truck and turned the ignition Zeus crested the plateau, looking none the worse for wear. Guiding his truck toward Devil's Descent, Big Country leaned halfway out the window, grinning at Zeus as he tipped an imaginary cowboy hat, and was on his way.

He was finally getting off the mountain to indulge in some Class A-felony stalker-type shit. *Yes Lord,* before the night was through he'd make a certain Ms. Stormy Redmond agree that orgasming beneath him over and over until she could no longer feel her legs was the most prudent decision she would ever make in this life.

CHAPTER 5

*A*fter scrubbing off whatever contamination the pissy saint exposed him to, Big Country slid on a pair of blue cotton boxers and headed to the kitchen. Pulling a couple of beers from the fridge, he walked through the living room where he had done a Mama-style deep cleaning over the weekend, removing any physical trace of the blonde he'd brought there. He couldn't recall anything about the woman other than she was pretty; his mind had effectively done its own deep cleaning, erasing everything except an embarrassing regret for bringing her home in the first place.

Entering a code into the panel along the back wall of the living-room, he stepped into his war room, his beach house home office which housed a bank of computers and monitors. Placing the beers on the L-shaped wall-facing desk, he fired up his system and moved through the gauntlet of security measures he'd put in place. After completing a system check, he leaned back in his chair and gazed up at the five-by-eight still photo of a dancing Stormy placed on the wall behind one of the monitors.

"And just why're you making it so hard to get *you* out the picture, beautiful?"

She smiled at him from the photo, her lips, her eyes, her body preserved in a state of seduction.

He grunted, rubbing a hand over his chest to ease the sudden tightness. Maybe it was time for a checkup. Between his squirrelly gut, the constriction in his chest, his inability to sleep more than two hours a night for the past two weeks, his inability to settle his mind… and to top it off, he had had a full-blown episode Friday night after managing that condition for years.

Reaching for his keyboard and settling it on his lap, he reluctantly accepted that he might well have some kind of undiagnosed disease, one that destroyed his coping mechanisms and made him do stupid shit.

Stupid shit like accessing the video feed from Red's Boutique to spy on a woman who had the gall to desire his best friend over him, *him*, a man who was told he knew he was made for lovin' on since he was old enough to pee straight. Taking another swig from his beer, he swallowed down the bitter bile at the back of his throat and used two of his four monitors to bring up the video from the four cameras within the boutique, plus the one he'd planted in Stormy's office. He began his viewing pleasure at the moment she'd walked into the building this morning.

"My god, woman, there ought to be a damn law against hiding the glory of your body inside clothes. Wish I had some popcorn," he muttered, too engrossed to actually get up and get it. Emptying his first bottle of beer and reaching for the other, he laughed at all the action that went down between them in that office.

He felt a deep soul-abiding satisfaction at seeing her unravel when she was in her office alone. He'd gotten under all that lovely sienna-red skin all right, and she didn't like it one bit. "That's good fo' ya," he taunted as she fled the office. At least he wasn't the only one being tormented.

The audio had been off-line, and he'd left it that way thinking it was taking things too far to listen in on what was said but now, he was real curious to know what made her tear up when she was downstairs talking to her partner and whoever else they called on the phone. He wondered if he should go back and—

"What the ever-loving fuck." He sat up abruptly, nearly dropping the keyboard to the floor. It was what's-her-name, the bad decision, the blonde from the other night. What the fuck was she doing there? No, it didn't matter; whatever it was bode ill for him, and he didn't need Lynx's fucking feelings or Cizan's mystical eye to know that shit.

He watched Stormy walk the woman around while her friend hid out in the other room, listening to what was said on the other side of the heavy red curtain. He zoomed in on the blonde. Something about her made the beer burn like acid in his gut.

He sighed when the blonde left the store with bags in both hands. Maybe it was a coincidence but since he didn't believe in coincidences, he hacked into the store's purchasing information while simultaneously fast-forwarding the feed until Stormy and her partner started cutting it up with three matronly women.

His phone rang.

He didn't recognize the number but answered, distracted and disturbed when one of the older women started doing a nasty dance with a large purple dildo. *Jesus*, when did matrons start acting this raunchy in public? The sex shops he'd visited for mostly male customers were a damn sight more subdued. Seeing shit like this would scar a lesser man.

"There's the voice I've been yearning to hear all weekend."

"Who is this?" he asked, forgetting there was someone on the line.

"Oh, my love, is my voice so very forgettable then?"

"Look, if this is Harper, your contract won't be up for renegotiation until next week so don't call back until then—or we can end this agreement right here and now."

"You're quite the intimidating negotiator, but no, my love, this is not business, this is your destiny… Well, Delilah actually, but…" Her laugh held a touch of irony before she quieted. "I've missed you."

It was *her*…on *his* fucking phone.

He shut down the connection to the security feed and brought up his tracking program, running a trace on the phone he also hoped to get the account information on. The last thing he wanted was to find out Delilah was at his front door, wanting to show him how she'd used some book-learning to master the art of giving a damn blowjob.

"Hey darling, how'd you get this number anyways?" he asked.

Shit, she was using a burner phone, so there was no identifying information for him to access.

"My big strong lover, are you tormented by demons that have consumed the beautiful memories of us?" Her words were gentle, but the caustic tone underlying them didn't escape his awareness. "You gave me your number in the event that we were separated when I followed you home from the pub?"

He groaned away from the phone. Well, he remembered now. Lynx had *warned* him but no, he just had to—

"I didn't want another day to go by without telling you how wonderful you made me feel," she said, sounding sincere.

He didn't buy it. Some of his earliest memories were of Belle Mère shifting into whatever skin she needed to manipulate the old man. Most women were treacherous, and most men were too blinded by sex and emotion to care.

His monitor flashed her location. She was calling from San Francisco. *Got you.*

Digging deeper, he learned that the owners of the house were not named Delilah, nor was the place a rental. *Who are you, darlin'?*

"And being a woman of resource, I learned a number of ways to make all our nights together as memorable as our first. Can I come over?"

Hell, no. Fuck, no.

He might be a lot of things but he wasn't stupid; far from it.

"Delilah darlin', you know them memory demons you mentioned are really doing a number on me, sugar, because for the life of me I can't remember your last name."

The Brood had enemies and he had to find out if Delilah was a threat to the team at large or just a crazy stalker who didn't know how to say thank-you-and-goodbye after one little interlude.

He looked at the picture of Stormy, whose smile seemed to mock him now. *I am not unaware of the irony of the situation, Sienna Red.*

"What's more important is the name that we will one day share."

Okay, time to stop this bullshit in its tracks with some real *meeting-Jesus-by-the-sea* kinda talk.

"Delilah, I'm not about to sit here and make 'tend that what happened on my living-room floor was more than two adults sharing pleasure and I suggest you don't, either." He rubbed his fingers over his forehead. He never should have played fast and loose with an innocent, he thought, digging deeper into the house owner's info to see if she was a family member of the owners. "Darlin', I'm glad I gave you some happiness but understand this—if you try to make a relationship where there ain't none, you'll just be courtin' a world of heartache. Trust me, sugar, there ain't nothing a good woman like you could have with a man like me."

He braced himself for the desperate histrionics he witnessed every time his crazy-ass Belle Mère didn't get what she wanted, but the other end of the line stayed quiet. Eerily so. Almost like she was on the other end silently screaming...or plotting.

He didn't know if she was hurt by his words, but he was fully prepared to wait her out. Even if she was putting on an act to get close to him, he doubted she was skilled enough to bring him or the Brood down.

Still, it was the hidden, the unknown, that sometimes posed the biggest threats.

He rubbed the bottom of the empty beer bottle over his forehead.

"You are a good man. I don't doubt it for one minute," Delilah said, her voice so soft and certain he wanted to believe it, but he knew his rot ran deeper than the eye could see. "It's your weakness as a man that makes you want to push me away. Whatever your fears, we will overcome them. Together."

"Damn it, Delilah—"

"Goodnight my love," she said, disconnecting the call before he could say another word. *Scratch everything,* that woman was industrial-grade crazy, innocence be damned.

Standing, he rolled his shoulders, breathed deeply, and cracked his neck left, then right, rolling his shoulders three times more before sitting down in front of the monitor, prepared to find out all he could about Delilah no-last-name-given.

An hour and a half later, he hadn't found anything. He'd discovered a lot about the people whose house she was living in. The older retired couple were good folks, by first reckoning. They were devoted to their faith, their five children, and their eight grandchildren. Financially they lived within their means and had no outstanding debt. More importantly, they didn't have any relatives named Delilah. He'd checked two generations before them and after.

At least he knew where Delilah was. Maybe he'd have one of his Brood mates go to the house and investigate tomorrow, maybe even bring back her fingerprints so he could run them. He'd do it himself but thought it best to stay as far from the woman as possible.

It was after two in the morning when he turned off his computer, secured his house, and went to his bedroom to lay down. An hour later, he was no closer to sleep. He couldn't corral his thoughts. Delilah was an irritant he didn't need; his inability to keep calm, the struggle he was having managing his episodes was a danger to everything he held dear, and Stormy...his thoughts and needs always circled back to Stormy.

And that was a reality that couldn't be borne.

Rising from his bed he adjusted his boxers, laced on his gray steel-toed Doc Marten ankle boots, pulled on his Sooners baseball cap, and grabbed his gun and his keys as he headed out the front door. In less than an hour, he was parked in front of Stormy's house. The Alameda neighborhood was quiet, dark and quiet. He rubbed his hands over his face, eyes burning with fatigue even if his body refused to relax.

He'd thought life would return to normal after he, Lynx, and Zeus returned from dealing with Sabrina's ex in Florida. However, bearing witness to Zeus and Sabrina sacrificing themselves for each other, seeing them survive being beaten bloody for each other, watching them heal and love on each other...that shit was messing him up in a way he couldn't have foreseen. His grands, the love they had for each other was rock-solid, unflinching. Mama and Terry, their long-burning passion, fierce devotion to each other, unstoppable, but those two unions were aberrations of past generations. Nothing he'd witnessed in his own generation seemed to come close to those couples. Until Zeus met Sabrina, and he hadn't been right since. Now things left buried if not forgotten, were intruding into his reality, feeding a malignancy inside of him powerful enough to destroy the perfect life he created from the inside out.

Stepping out of his truck, cold air hit Big Country like his daddy would on those nights when Belle Mère abandoned their family for livelier times—hard and without remorse. Now, like then, Big Country shook it off, fought his way through it, as he made his way to Stormy's front door.

Stormy snapped awake on the brink of orgasm, remnants of the dream surrounding her. She still felt a half-mad Lucas gripping the back of her neck, pinning her on her hands and knees. Still felt him ramming her from behind in bone-jarring thrusts as a storm raged around them. She still felt her hands digging into earth that oozed like rusted blood through her fingers as she screamed out...

Trembling, she sat up and wiped sweat from her face. Her whole body was drenched in it, her sleep shirt and sheets were soaked with it.

Jesus, she couldn't take this much longer, it was like her libido was raging over being ignored for so long. Lucas had riled it up with words of bayou's in the moonlight and it hadn't been acting right since. Shoving the covers off her, she pushed them aside and perched on the edge of the bed as she peeled off her nightshirt and panties.

Sudden banging at her front door made her startle. It was so forceful she was afraid the double doors would break off their hinges. Cursing, she reached for her knee-length teal robe and wrapped it around her body, tying the belt around her waist as she marched downstairs knowing, *knowing*, no one except cops or inbred country boys banged on residential doors in the dead of the night like that.

Bare feet slapping against the cherry-oak floor, she stopped to disarm the alarm, stepped toward the front door and looked through the peephole before cracking the door open. Lucas used his massive body to push through to her foyer, holding a gun in one hand and keys in the other. He was wearing a pair of dark blue boxers, a beat-up baseball cap over his wild hair, a pair of camel-colored suede boots… and a weary smile, nothing more.

Her nipples hardened painfully.

"Sienna Red, as I live and breathe," he uttered as he kicked the door shut and locked it.

"Stormy. It's Stormy," she snapped, trying to hide that she was a jittery shaking mess on the inside. "Use it."

"Oh, I'm gonna use it good and well, darlin'."

She crossed her arms under her breasts, looking away from the temptation trapped in the crystallized green of his eyes and looked down at his gun. "So what, is this supposed to be payback for this morning?"

"I understand how you could draw that conclusion, but naw, that's not me at all, I'm not a violent man, I'm a shy fella." She pursed her lips in disbelief. "No, I'm serious now, I'm shy. Get all tongue-tied and start twitching at the very idea of talking to a beautiful woman such as yourself."

"I distinctly remember you holding me in your arms and serenading me with blatant lies Friday night, so you can take that shy bullsh—"

"It's a different kind of shy! It ain't as obvious because I'm so big… and manly."

"You're such an idiot," she muttered as she smiled. She couldn't help it.

His gazed lingering on her unbound breasts. "Biggest idiot I know."

The way her heart quickened, the way her clit fired shots of pleasure through to her womb, readying itself, made her the biggest idiot *she* knew. "Why are you here, Lucas?"

"Can't sleep," he groused, tossing his keys and hat onto the entryway table beside the door, rubbing a hand over his face.

"So what am I supposed to do, sing you a lullaby?"

He shook his head, his gaze turning roguish. "I'd rather be rocked to sleep."

Stormy took a step back but couldn't escape his touch as he grabbed her upper arm. He turned off the foyer light and dragged her up the stairs, seemingly guided by the second-floor illumination from her bedroom. Lucas released her arm as he stepped into the room, toeing off his boots before walking over to place his phone and gun on the end table next to her bed.

He took in the bottle of wine—minus any wine glasses—beside the items he placed on the nightstand. His gaze travelled to the overflow of laundry in the wicker basket near the en suite bathroom door and the garments she'd just discarded on the floor. The rest of her house was immaculate, but her bedroom was her haven and never really prepared for company.

Sadly, her dad and brother were the most likely to be found here when they wanted to avoid their wives, lounging on the bed beside her as they all watched sports or action movies on the big screen.

Lucas propelled himself backward and landed in the center of her bed, bouncing on it experimentally.

"What kind of mattress is this, sweetness—Posturepedic, Pillow Top? You must sleep like the dead on this thing." He pushed back the covers and shifted and started to climb beneath them. "What the...*ewwww*, wet spot."

He shot her a strange look. Heat exploded over the surface of her skin.

"What you been up here doin' in this bed, Sienna Red?"

Having dreams of you pounding into me like a bull. That's what she *wasn't* going to say. "I was having a nightmare."

He pressed his nose to sheets and breathed in. "Your nightmares smell lovely, darlin'," he said, propping himself up on his elbows and gazing at her knowingly. "Like you...and sex."

"Well I guess I just smell like sex when I sleep then, Lucas," she snapped.

He watched her as if wicked scenes were playing out in his mind. Her womb grew heavy, yet felt oh so empty…

She looked away as he pushed the covers farther back and slipped between them.

"What are you doing?" *And why the hell was she letting him do it?*

"I sure hope I don't feel nothin' from the dick emporium pushin' against my backside," he mumbled. "That could be awkward for both of us."

"You need to leave. It is three o'clock in the morning—"

"Fully aware of the time, darlin'," he said, patting the mattress. "Climb on in and rock me to sleep so we can get some shut-eye, okay? I got a busy day tomorrow."

Watching him there, his head cushioned on her pillow, his eyelids half closed, his left hand resting on his thigh, thumb lazily stroking the side of Bubba—who was pushing against the thin material encasing him and threatening to break free—she couldn't deny how much she wanted him inside her, wanted to feel the press of his massive body against hers.

It had been years since she'd slept with a man, but oh, the things she'd learned since divorcing Chaduwo. Being a partial owner of Red's had provided benefits that had nothing to do with IRAs or a 401(k).

Lowering her head, she unknotted the belt and let her robe fall open, exposing a strip of flesh that extended from cleavage to her pubic area. His eyes locked on the latter as his hips jerked up, causing him to fist his dick as if holding Bubba back.

"So you like it wild?" he asked, taking in the triangle between her thighs. "Or is it just that there was no one to showcase her for?"

She let the robe puddle at her feet. "A little of both."

"Aw, Stormy, aw, Stormy…" he muttered, rising to his feet. "Come here and let me play in all that wildness. And if you can handle that little bit of roughhousing, well then maybe I'll unleash the fiend, see if you can survive his predilections."

She didn't trust the shadow reflecting from the depths of his hard green eyes, and he must have seen her flash of indecision. His hand shot out, shackled around her upper arm and pulled her against him. He slid his hand over her shoulder until he gripped the back of her neck, his thumb stroking her jaw. "Now now, ain't no cause for distress at this stage." He pressed a kiss against her temple. "But I am gonna make her cry, Stormy, I'm gonna make her weep real hard, darlin'."

Stormy swallowed. She was actually trembling, and she couldn't determine if it was from fear or lust. Lucas's left hand kneaded her hip, digging deep into the flesh, loosening the tension there before moving to cup a heavy breast. His fingers gentled, working relentlessly for a response she struggled to suppress, feeling stripped bare as he held her gaze.

She wasn't ready...she thought she was, but she wasn't ready for him, wasn't ready for—

He pinched her nipple and she cried out. Contractions deep inside her womb shook her, caused her pelvis to bump against his hip, seeking, needing. His fingers stroked her body, creating a heat that cried for her to devour him, to consume his life-giving seed until she'd glutted herself into a sex coma.

"You got protection?" His voice was gravelly, as if something wild spoke through him. And she liked it. Liked the danger reverberating within it, the power.

"Always," she muttered, feeling utterly exposed and unprotected as she retrieved a handful of condoms from her nightstand and tossed them on the bed.

Reaching up, she exercised her own power, gripped the hair resting against the back of his neck and pulled it to the left exposing the cord of tendon. She bit down, holding and sucking as if she were a bitch and this was her favorite bone.

He growled, maybe moaned, she wasn't sure.

Fanning the fingers of her other hand against his thigh, she drew her nails up over his skin until she reached the mound of his ass and dug in, just to give a little pain, just to let him know *he* wasn't safe.

Though he might dominate her physically, he was by no means protected.

The world shifted and she was no longer on her feet but flying through the air.

He'd lifted her off her feet and threw her like it was nothing. Like her five feet ten, 170-pound frame was no more than a sixteen-pound shotput.

Lucas dragged his feet against her carpeted floor like he was a bull about to charge and Stormy laughed and used the bed's bounce to propel herself to a standing position inches from the bed's edge. She spread her feet apart and placed her hands on her hips in a Wonder Woman stance. Lucas's grin was demented as he watched her soft parts—breast, ass, and thighs—go from jiggle to stillness. His muscles bunched and she knew he was about to launch himself at her.

"Stop!" she ordered, holding one hand out. His eyes snapped to hers and narrowed; the raw hunger in them nearly put her on her back with her legs spread wide for his pleasure.

"Now," she said, dropping her arm to her side. "Walk to me *slowly* —" she gripped the underside of one breast and held it up in offering, "—and tell me how I taste."

He closed his eyes and shook his head. "Stormy darlin', I don't think you want to play this game. It won't end well for you, I promise."

Arching a brow, Stormy stroked a thumb over her distended nipple, pussy releasing a gush of warm liquid that could very well be dripping down onto her sheets. "Do it now Lucas, or the offer is rescinded."

He moved so fast she cried out in surprise when his lips wrapped around her breast, sucking it in, thumb and all. Her vaginal muscles contracted and released in sync with each tug from his mouth, her pelvis working, seeking an end to the pressure growing and expanding inside, something to fill the emptiness…

Oh God!

She placed her hands on his shoulders, shaking, as Lucas's fingers slid up her thigh pausing as he felt the glistening liquid flowing from her center.

"Aw sweet Jesus," he murmured burying his face between her breasts. "Aw fuck darlin'...fuck!"

As if compelled to do something he didn't want to do, three fingers plunged inside of her as far as they could go without fisting her. He was relentless, and she bore down on him, rode his hand as his fingers sought, pressing up against—

She seized. Threw her head back and screamed out as if her orgasm was primal energy shooting from her body to the heavens.

"Shit," she whispered wrapping her arms around Lucas, trembling, unsteady. "Shit, shit, shit," she mumbled in his hair.

Lucas eased her down onto the bed, laying her on her back as he straightened her legs and rested her ankles on each of his shoulders. Spent, Stormy swept strands of hair off her forehead and the side of her face.

"You sure were talking some big shit there, Stormy," he said low and slow, staring down at her exposed sex. He moved closer so that his legs touched the edge of the mattress. Bubba, thick and imposing, now posed a credible threat to her internal organs. "Thought you was in charge with all that commanding and demanding, huh?"

His big hands squeezed her thighs as if testing their durability.

"Lucas..." she muttered as she attempted to rise up on her elbows.

"Don't move, darlin'," Lucas warned. That damned southern charm oozing from his words would have eased her, but the smile ghosting his lips seemed altogether unholy.

Lord, what had she done?

"Lucas..." she began again, lying absolutely still as Bubba danced between her spread legs, menacing her poor pussy.

Stormy swallowed as her gaze searched the ceiling. Despite the rivulets of sweat rolling off her body, her mouth was dry.

Feeling her legs shift, she looked back to see Lucas lowering his body down between her thighs, her knees now bent over his shoulders. Her feet resting against his densely muscled back were still decadently wide apart.

"You gonna tell me how to taste you now, too?" Lucas asked. "You gonna tell me to put my tongue here?" he asked, pushing two fingers inside her again.

Stormy's back bowed off the bed and she cried out.

"I'm sorry, darlin', was that a yes or no?"

She didn't know…she didn't… "What was the question?" she asked, out of breath.

"You done giving orders, Sienna Red?" Lucas asked, removing his fingers, the walls of her vagina clutching, trying to pull them back inside.

"Fuck me, Lucas," she demanded.

Lucas shook his head as if she'd said something disappointing.

Had she? She tried to scramble up—

"Don't. Move," he warned. He didn't shout, actually spoke softly, but the wildness in his gaze was made her afraid despite her pulsating arousal. "I just need a little peace, Stormy. Can you give me that? Just a little peace?" he asked, massaging her clit.

Her hips undulated in rhythm with his hand. His pace increased, pushing her hips to move faster. Free hand clamping down on her breast, he squeezed and she squeezed the other, crying out as he twisted her nipple. The jab of pain made the need grow twofold, her body arched, only her head touched the bed as she was suspended there like a bridge.

"Yeah, I'm gonna take what you're offering, darlin'," Lucas said, releasing Stormy's breast. She felt crushed by the loss.

Lucas guided her hips back onto the bed and withdrew his hand. Tears of frustration and loss stung her eyes.

Releasing himself from the cradle of her legs he kneeled on the floor and placed her feet on the bed so wide there was nothing of her he couldn't see. The muscles of her groin ached, ligaments and muscles not quite ready to be stretched so wide.

He raised a brow, the not-quite-smile on his lips seemed to mock her as his hand moved out of sight, either putting the condom on or slowly stroking Bubba or both.

"Gotta say, darlin', I'm in a bit of a bind here. Bubba's hungry, but so am I. Who you reckon I should feed first?"

"Me," she said. "I'm starving, Lucas. Feed me."

The muscles in his jaw ticked. Whatever he was fighting she didn't know, but she had to come again. Her orgasms were usually shallow things that quickly left her, but the last stoked something deeper and she needed more.

Continuing to stimulate her breast, she guided her other hand down her pelvis to touch the slippery—

Lucas's hand wrapped around her wrist and forced it back onto the bed.

"I'm trying to be nice here, but you keep interfering and I promise you I'll stop trying." Stormy raised her head, looking down the length of her body which terminated at Lucas, larger-than-life Lucas, hot-as-hell Lucas.

"Is that how it works with your other women, Lucas? You pay them, and they give you whatever you want, do whatever you say?"

She wrenched her hand free and gasped as she touched herself, briefly shutting her eyes as she fingered her clit. The overly sensitized bud caused a lightning bolt of pleasure to shimmer through her blood.

Opening her eyes, she looked into Lucas's fevered gaze and smiled, taunting him, teaching him as she fingered herself. "This pussy is mine. I touch her when she wants to be touched and I make her come when she wants to come. If you don't like that, then you can go crawl into the bed of one of your paid women while I get myself off and go back to sleep."

His body seemed to exhale, losing all tension, his face losing all emotion.

Stormy felt a moment of regret. *Her mouth, her fucking mouth,* she thought, but the part of her that fought to breathe was ruthless in its disregard.

If Lucas couldn't handle who she was, he wasn't worth mourning over.

Lucas lowered his head and she could no longer see his eyes

behind the waves of thick brown hair flowing forward and obscuring his features, but he nodded slowly, contemplative.

"I try so hard, so hard to be nice. Can't say I never tried."

Fine hairs rose in a warning all over Stormy's body. Not one to ignore a credible threat, she scrambled back toward the center of the bed on heels and elbows as he propelled his bulk forward, planting his hands above her shoulders, caging her. The front of his thighs pressed into the back of hers, she could feel the weight of Bubba on her stomach, felt him slide down until his large bulbous head pushed just inside her opening, stretching her further than she could imagine. He was too much. He had barely entered her and already he was too much.

"This pussy is yours, yeah?" he asked, still hidden behind the mantle of sable hair. "Let's see if I can change that, darlin'."

Stormy reached up, desperately shifting the hair back from his face, needing to see him, needing to see what burned deep inside his eyes before he—

Bubba surged, tunneling through her like a freight train on a collision course with the farthest reaches of her womb.

She screamed but all she heard was Lucas's grunt as he plunged into her. The thick length of him splitting her at the seams was too much…too much.

Lucas grabbed her hips, as he began to pull out of her. "Yours, Stormy? Was that what you were telling me, darlin'?"

The pressure, the slightly burning sensation began to recede as he gazed down at her.

The air caught in her lungs escaped and she gulped it back as if starved for breath.

Lucas drew out of her until Bubba's head rested just inside her opening. He propelled his hips forward, impaling her again, but this time he didn't stop at just one stroke. He pounded into her again and again, his fingers digging into her hips as he pistoned up and down, Bubba's head ramming into the wall of her womb until she feared it would be bruised or ruptured.

She held on to Lucas's hair, crying out as the next orgasm detonated, held on as Lucas dipped his head and his lips found hers, mouth greedy in its destruction of her. But she held on because that was all he was allowing her to do, hold the pieces of him. His hair, his tongue, his dick, while denying her the ability to hold onto her sanity.

"Yours, Stormy?"

He shifted the trajectory of his thrusts and hit that spot that made her body shatter, made it levitate, made her have an honest-to-goodness out-of-body experience as the orgasms deepened, grew faster, mounting one after the other, wave after wave setting her adrift as her mind struggled to process what was happening to her.

"Yours, Stormy?" Lucas demanded again.

She nodded, tears streaming into her ears.

Lucas's pace increased, a hard, impossible, bone-crushing rhythm. And she screamed as the orgasm wouldn't abate, mounted, her pussy contracting and releasing around his dick in desperation.

"Whose?"

"Yours," she yelled out again and again, as he slammed into her.

Wrapping her arms around her shoulders she held him tight to her, held on to him until he finally let go, Bubba swelling, fusing against every part of her that he touched as he drenched the condom in liquid heat while Lucas's roar filled her bedroom walls before he went lax, the weight of him pressing her deliciously into the bed.

Stormy closed her eyes and relaxed her hold on him.

"For right now...yours," she mumbled before passing out, praying that her neighbors hadn't called 911.

Lucas felt as powerless as a newborn babe.

It was as if the weight of the world had ground his flesh into extinction, only to remold him into a man content, a well-rested, well-loved-on man who didn't need to exist beyond now, beyond Stormy's warm bed.

Stormy.

He opened his eyes and his other senses engaged. It was an odd feeling to not wake up vigilant and partly aware of everything around him. It was downright disconcerting to know that Stormy had left the bed and he'd slept on, none the wiser. She could have shot him with his own gun and he never would have seen it coming, just been a bloody mess on her indecently comfortable bed.

Rolling onto his side, he wrapped his arms around the pillow cushioning his head and listened as Stormy showered behind the closed door of the bathroom. Bubba didn't even stir as he imagined her rubbing foamy white soap over all her soft cinnamon skin…

What the *fuck!* Sitting up, he pushed the covers down to see if Bubba was still there.

Oh, thank you, Jesus, he thought, heaving out a sigh when he saw a still-condom-wrapped Bubba sleeping peacefully against his thigh. Carefully he took the condom off, knotted it, and flung it into the trash basket on his side of the bed. Standing, he walked over to his boxers and put them back on and looked around the room, trying to figure out if he should wash up with Stormy or just leave. For all intents and purposes, he should leave. Lynx wouldn't have anything to do with Stormy now, and there was never a time that he'd joined a woman in the bathroom unless they were having sex there.

Dragging his hand over his jaw, he felt two days of growth covering it. He may have rubbed the inside of Stormy's thighs raw. He smiled.

A phone rang on the table on the other side of the bed, and he lunged over to pick it up, not ready for Stormy to be drawn back into the bedroom before he'd made his decision.

An image of a manicured dark-skinned man wearing an expensive charcoal suit and dove-gray dress shirt smiled from the display. Big Country hit the *decline* button. That slick fucker had better lose Stormy's number or he'd wind up losing half the teeth in from his Colgate smile.

The phone buzzed twice, and Big Country read the incoming text.

Chad: Pulling up to the house. Will b @ the door in a sec.

Oh, the hell, Big Country thought, leaping off the bed and quietly making his way downstairs before the doorbell alerted Stormy to her ex's presence.

Dressed in nothing but boxer shorts and his God-given strength of will, he unlocked the front door and flung it wide. Crossing his arms over his chest, he assumed his wide-footed stance, and stared at the approaching man in much the same way they'd taught little Bree to do the day before. Keeping his face neutral, despite the desire to smile in derision, he saw the little prick's sure-footed steps falter when he gazed up from his phone and saw Big Country filling the doorway.

Yeah, this slick pretty fucker was gon' have to go.

In the time that it took him to get down the stairs and to the door, Big Country had decided he didn't want to end his time with Stormy, and he sure as shit didn't want another man stepping in to derail his attempt to negotiate a mutually pleasurable agreement between them over the short- or long-term use of her body.

"I'm sorry." The other man frowned, looking around him as if making sure he was at the right house. "And you are?" he asked with slight disdain in his refined, slightly accented English.

Big Country cocked his head to the side and looked at Chad as if he was something peculiar. As if good looks, expensive clothes, and articulate speech were the most unusual things in the world.

"You have exactly two seconds to tell me where my wife is before I call the police."

Awww, little fucker. Big Country smiled, more than ready to follow Zeus's example of eliminating exes. He'd never been so inclined, but for the first time, he could understand the lure of staking one's claim. He wouldn't, but he'd be damned if he was going to allow a man—one who didn't have the good sense to know that divorce meant a woman was no longer your woman—to do so.

"Your wife should be at home with your two children, but in the event that she's not, I promise you Alma is not here, Chad," Stormy said from the top of her stairwell.

Big Country turned to see her walk down the stairs as she put on a pair of dangly silver earrings. Her hair had been tamed into two neat thick French braids that reached to her breasts. She was barefoot and wore a teal sleeveless T-shirt that showcased her magnificent breasts, and a pair of gray yoga pants that hugged onto all that ass and thigh. If more women were built like her, yoga would become his choice of recreation.

Bubba was spent, but Big Country could feel him stir in greeting. "Well shit, shug, ain't you the finest sight for these tired eyes."

She smiled at him in playful seduction.

The bastard ex, Chad, took Big Country's moment of distraction and slipped past him into the foyer.

"Lucas Beaumont, I'd like to introduce you to my ex-husband of *many* years, Chaduwo Akombi."

"I could give a flying fuck what this little fucker's name is. He needs to get gone."

"Wow, Sinclair, is this the caliber of man you're forced to accept these days?"

Big Country sucked his teeth and rocked back on his heels. "Look here, cousin, you got a good twenty seconds to turn around, get in your sleek little car and move on to your next destination. If you're here any time after that, I can't guarantee you'll be leaving as pretty as you walked in."

The other man laughed and looked around. "Am I being punked? Is this some kind of joke, Sinclair, because—"

"Why does he keep calling you by your middle name?" Big Country asked.

"Because he doesn't believe the name my parents gave me at birth is respectable enough."

Was that the reason she demanded Big Country use her name instead of the handle that fell from his lips like a prayer? Calling her Sienna Red was not a denial or a rejection of her, but his special handle; just for *her*. Almost all the Brood had a handle...not that she was Brood.

"Bet your parents didn't think highly of him disparaging your name."

Stormy's eyes widened as if he'd verbalized a well-kept secret.

"Darlin', back where I'm from, storms are a living force. When they hit, some people would go quiet and stay prayed up as the world raged around them, some went wild...*storm-drunk,* we called it, and some... some folks just sat in appreciation and wonder at the beauty of life. Stormy..." Her name fell from his mouth reverently. "It's a beautiful name, darlin', and you'd be all kinds of right to cut loose any man fool enough not to see that."

"Cut *me* loose?" Chad said incredulously. "She was desperate to save our marriage, but back then she didn't want to do what it took to make me *want* to stay. It's only recently that she's begun to present herself in a way that a man would even look at her twice. If she had kept herself up in the first place I wouldn't have had to give up on—"

The flame sparked and Big Country's reaction was instinctual. He struck out, slamming his fist into the other man's chest. Chad stumbled back, lost his footing, and landed at Stormy's feet, giving Big Country a soul-abiding satisfaction...until Stormy gasped.

Shit. He was supposed to be trying to get her to say yes to a contractual relationship with him.

In an attempt to salvage the situation, Big Country bent down and grabbed Chad by the collar, helping him back to his feet as he covertly choked the little pissant. "Sorry about that, cousin, sorry, I got this medical condition, see..."

"Call the police." Chad croaked out the order to Stormy as he wrenched himself free of Big Country's hand. "I'll have you charged with assault and then sue your inbred ass for every wooden nickel you have in your possession."

"No. You won't." Stormy countered. "You came to *my* home after I expressly told you not to...and I have the texts from yesterday to prove it. For all intents and purposes, Chad, you entered my home without permission, verbally disrespected me, and Lucas simply did what any good man would and moved to protect me from harm."

"I have never laid a finger on you—"

"Which is very different from not harming me now isn't it, counselor?"

"Harmed," Chad muttered, tucking his shirt more securely beneath his belt before flinging his arms wide. "Look at this house, Sinclair, look at all that you have! A graduate degree, a life where you are respected, you are retired *and* about to have your own practice, you know how to carry yourself in all arenas. You've finally returned to the beauty I once desired. How is any of that harm? I taught you to be better, Sinclair, to want more, achieve higher. Without me you wouldn't have developed into more than the crass college sophomore from West Oakland on a fast track to single motherhood and subsidized housing after screwing some frat boy who wouldn't remember your name the second after he finished with you."

Well now, Big Country thought, keeping his head down, crossing his arms over his chest, and focusing on his overly large feet. This was a peculiar kind of situation he never aspired to find himself in. On the one hand, he wanted to put his fist so far down Chad's throat until it came out the other end, smelling like the ass Stormy's ex was. On the other hand, some sixth sense told him to shut the hell up, do nothing, and wait.

He chose the latter.

"Muthafucka, please," Stormy said calmly and turned a tight smile to Big Country. "As you can see, Chad likes to believe the great lie that he created me. It was a kind of unspoken agreement between us; I pretend his great lie of creation was truth, and somehow our lives, our relationship would be stronger for it. I feed his belief that he is the end-all and be-all, then he is no longer insignificant. And as for me, I got to have a safe place to hide away the pieces of me that I no longer wanted…but then, of course, that wasn't enough, I was no longer enough, and *poof*, Chad went on to create another life. Another wife." She stepped closer to Chad and smoothed out his lapels. "And yet here he is, still demanding that I worship him. How ridiculously selfish is that, Lucas?"

She turned away from Chad and walked to within kissing distance of Lucas. "The truth is, I *was* wild and irresponsible, and someone I love almost got hurt because of it, but he did not make me. My grades have never dipped below a B since I started receiving grades in elementary. My parents are solidly middle-class and have owned their own home the entirety of my life. I have always had a good heart, put myself out there for others when I damned sure should have known better. For me, having stuff has never been a priority." She smiled and shook her head. "Chad could never understand that. But, as my grandmother used to say, being smart doesn't save you from being a fool."

Could be it was the intimacy in their nearness, or the way Stormy's nipples pebbled as she gazed up at Big Country, but it was obvious to Lucas that Chad just realized the almost naked man in Stormy's house was her lover…and oh son, the man looked madder than a rattler with his tail cut off, realizing it could no longer claim it was a rattler.

"Chad didn't make me, Lucas," Stormy said, drawing Big Country's gaze back to her lips. "He just gave me the means to unmake myself. But a woman can only hide from who she is for so long. Luckily—or maybe unluckily for you—you've pushed your way into my life just as I'm reemerging. I'm giving myself a month to play; it can be with you or with somebody else."

"But not Lynx—he won't touch you now," Big Country said.

"But wasn't that your purpose? Make me untouchable by touching me first?"

"Hell yes," he said unapologetically, then looked at Chad. "And definitely it can't be him."

"Shit, no, not him," she said, sounding like him.

Big Country threw his head back and laughed, pulling her flush against him. "I'm game, darlin', but we got to be clear on the rules, got to negotiate what's acceptable and what's out of bounds."

"Yeah, yeah, I heard about your little contracts," she said as she pulled away and smacked him on the ass.

Chad looked both confused and disgusted. Big Country winked at him and Stormy walked toward the open front door, both he and Chad watching the mesmerizing sway of her ass.

"Are you so desperate, then?" Chad said when she turned to look back at him. "Please tell me you haven't been reduced to having rela-tionships with ignorant hicks?"

"Well, what you see as a reduction I see as a robust gain, of epic proportions," Stormy said.

"At *least* nine inches of proportions," Big Country confirmed.

With a swing of her arm, she motioned her ex out the door. "Now run along before I call your actual wife."

Big Country almost felt sorry for the other man. He'd always thought conflicts with women meant tears and high drama, but Stormy was all calm words and smiles. If he were on Chad's end of things he'd choose the histrionics hands down, made it easier to walk away knowing you'd made the right choice, instead Chad would walk away looking like an ass.

Chad eyeballed Big Country and he must have determined something in his mind, because he smirked and walked toward the front door.

"This won't last," Chad informed Stormy. "You think you can reinvent yourself, recapture your youth; you'll be forty in a few months." He rolled his eyes. "Please feel free to contact me again after you find yourself alone and coming to terms with just how old and tired you really are, Sinclair."

Fucker's time has just expired, Big Country thought, lunging forward.

"No," Stormy said, blocking Big Country's path, holding out her arm to keep him at bay. "Goodbye, Chaduwo."

The man quickly exited Stormy's home.

Denied an outlet for the rush of violence that threatened to overtake him, Big Country paced the entryway, watching as Stormy closed the door and leaned her back against it. She looked drained of all the vibrancy and life he'd come to associate with her and that little fucker was the one that took it away.

He'd *destroy* that little shit, make him hurt, make him bleed, then he'd kill him. His body grew colder as his anger burned brighter. He'd make Chad pay, *make'em all pay, make'em all hurt, kill them all…*

"My first point of negotiation: while you're with me, you can't be with any of your other women."

As if a lodestone had been tethered to his balls, he dropped back into his body, and his rage dissipated under the calm reflection of her words.

"Are you fucking Chad? Is that why he's giving you money, that's why he acting like your pussy is his?"

She stood up straight and pushed off the door, the glow returning to her sienna-red skin.

"This pussy knocked your big ass out," she said. "So, if you want to continue to enjoy her, you need to fix your tone. And as for the money, that's what Chad's guilt looks like, that's what his unwillingness to let go looks like. Fuck Chad."

"All right, sweetness, all right. We're in agreement on the first point, while we're together, we're together. No others for *either* of us." He headed toward the stairs. "Get whatever you need for the day 'cause you're coming with me." She looked ready to object. "While you're with me, you're with me," he reiterated. "And bring paper and pen, we'll bang out the rest of the contract on the road."

"Hey, you drink coffee?" she called up to him.

He turned at the top of stairwell and smiled at the sight of her, at the realization that he was rested, that the gnawing worm had quieted for the first time in weeks. He understood now, with all the activity, he hadn't attended to his sexual appetites and the undischarged semen had started to sour in his sacks and rot his relaxed disposition. All this time he'd just needed to have some life-affirming sex.

Stormy smiled up at him challengingly, waiting for a response.

She was damned beautiful, this woman.

"Prettier than moonlight on the bayou," he muttered to himself.

"Black." He called down. "With a touch of cinnamon."

Tck...tck...tck...

The rusted brass minute hand of the cathedral's clock ground to a halt, but everything inside the rehabilitated ruin was already still and suspended in cold. With its gray-brown stone and wood visage, the Shepherd's Keep did not favor softness. In all his years of living here, it had never been a real home, yet it was the only home he had. It was such a grim and ominous place that even its spires pointed accusingly at the sky, the very dormitory of heaven. A storm was brewing there, one that couldn't be seen, only felt and heard.

Tck, tck, tck...

His hands began to tremble.

The clock hadn't moved from the witching hour, yet he heard it, he heard the ticking. Spinning around, he watched in horror as the Shepherd's Keep crumbled around him, the gray day shifting into the blackest of nights. He was cold and alone in a dark forest, demons surrounding him, laughing at him, mocking him. He was powerless in their presence. He was *always* so powerless.

Falling to his knees, he was ready to accept the fate of the damned; but one of the Good Shepherd's many teachings arose from memory: *When will you learn, Cornelius, you must stand with a warrior's focus and fortitude against evil lest you be consumed by it.*

He didn't want to be consumed; he no longer wanted to be afraid. He needed to be seen as worthy in the eyes of the Shepherd and by proxy, the eyes of God.

"You are the holy redeemer of faith, the mouthpiece of the Lord's will on earth. You are His sword and our salvation. Good Shepherd of the wayward flock, continue to guide the unholy, for it is your will and your vision that lead the wicked into the blessed eternity of the Lord's Grace..."

He continued the oft-recited mantra of the Shepherd's flock until his fear subsided and he was cocooned in the peace and solitude of salvation.

Tck, tck, tck...

No!

Terror jolted him into wakefulness. Chest heaving, he opened his eyes to find himself looking up toward a concrete ceiling in a deeply shadowed room. Sitting up slowly, he looked down the length of his blanket-covered body and beheld an angel of the fairest skin with waves of silken ebony hair perched at the foot of his bed. She gazed at him through soulful eyes and a beauty so haunting his heart constricted.

"Fallen," he whispered.

The fallen angel's eyebrow rose and she snorted in disgust before lowering her gaze, continuing to reassemble the gun that lay in fragments at the foot of the bed.

Tck, tck, tck. The metallic sound rang out within the cell, her hands sure in their accuracy and speed as she assembled, dismantled, and reassembled the weapon again and again.

Cornelius admired her skill, her precision. It reminded him of the passion the Good Shepherd had long ago forbade him to practice at the Keep. There had been many beatings to curtail his obsession, but it had never been completely extinguished. Delilah had promised that if their sojourn to this wretched place was successful she might allow him one indulgence before returning to the Shepherd's Keep.

"Where I'm from in Ireland, guns are not allowed," he informed her, stopping her before she began breaking the gun down again.

"*Mar sin, ta tu as an oilean?*" she asked, focused on the metal pieces. Her voice wasn't as delicate as her form, it was melodic but raspy as if rarely used.

"Yes, Ireland is my home," he responded. "But I wasn't born there. You are from Ireland?"

She had no trace of the Emerald Isle in her English.

Cornelius propped a pillow between his back and the cold cinder wall, fascinated with the beauty of the fallen angel. Unlike many of his brothers, he'd never risen high enough in rank to be allowed to interact with females. Before his sojourn, he'd only heard of the Shepherd's child Delilah, he'd never encountered demons and especially never dreamed of meeting a fallen angel.

She placed the gun on top of the mattress. "What's your name, saint?"

Cornelius smiled. He was far from a saint but was honored to be thought of as such. Even the demons had believed him a greater man than he was. Perhaps this journey had already elevated his place in the order.

He observed her more carefully, paying attention to the inked discolorations creeping up her neck from beneath the formfitting long-sleeved black cotton top. She also wore thick fuzzy pink socks and blue jeans that fit her like a serpent's skin. He didn't allow his eyes to linger on her well-formed breasts or shapely thighs; instead he focused on the tattooed skeletal hand superimposed over her right hand. He thought of the long-haired demon with a similar tattoo and pressed into the wall, drawing his knees toward his chest.

"Your name," the fallen demanded, aiming the gun toward his head. Though he knew it wasn't loaded, he felt fear. Fear for his soul.

"Cornelius Shepherdson."

Though she was fallen, the female was small, no more than five feet three, with an almost childlike form if one ignored her noticeable curves. His brothers would never be so cowed, even if the gun pointed at them was loaded and cocked to fire.

"Cen fath a bhfuil tu anseo?"

Why *was* he here?

One must follow the trail of fallen feathers to locate the nest of evil, the Shepherd had instructed. But he hadn't told Cornelius what to do once the nest was located, so he spoke the words written upon his heart. "I am here to save you, to cleanse you of your sins so that you can be made anew through God's grace."

The fallen lunged and smashed the empty gun against the side of his face. He felt a second blow, and squeezed his eyes shut from the pain, raising his arms as he attempted to shield himself from more violence. The high-pitched ringing in his ears almost obscured the sound of a door banging open, of a commotion. Her weight was lifted from his body and Cornelius lay there stunned.

When he dared to open his eyes, he found the woman standing docilely—save the banked hatred in her gaze—between the demon with the white eye and scarred, tattooed face, and a man twirling a blade at alarming speed. Cornelius suspected that the latter was the demon who'd pressed the knife into his neck the night before.

An older black woman about the same height as the fallen, and a sable-haired Native American man walked from the sun-dappled outdoors into the interior of the cinder block building. An Asian man stepped between the older couple and came to a stop, eyeing the towering demons with wary exasperation. They eyed him back with disinterest.

"The fuck?" the Asian man said, watching blood seep from Cornelius' temple. Cornelius flinched, the foul language assaulting his sensibilities as surely as the fallen woman had assaulted him physically.

The Asian swung his gaze back toward the silent trio. "*Bride* as the interrogator? Really? She's, like, less communicative than the two of you combined…and less patient."

The demons remained silent, which was unnerving.

"She did okay," the Native American man said. There were more cultures in this room than Cornelius had interacted with in his entire life. "She would have done better had he not spoken of saving her."

The Asian rolled his eyes. "He's a saint, he's supposed to say that shit."

"Except with Bride," the knife-wielding demon said; the other snorted beside him.

The little black woman advanced and the demons made space for her, allowing her to wrap an arm around the fallen's shoulder and press a kiss to her temple. "Randy must be rubbing off on you, little Falcon. Soon he'll have you saying 'please' and 'thank you.'"

The blade stilled, and the two demons looked at each other before turning to leave.

The Native American checked his phone and turned to follow them out, looking severely at the Asian and the black woman. "Big Country's on his way up the mountain with Stormy. You two ought to leave well enough alone before it bites you in the ass."

"Please. We got this." The Asian smirked, heading out the building behind him.

"You look half-starved, so I'll bring you to the main building to eat soon. There's some clothes and house shoes under your bed, and bathrooms through there." She pointed to the left. "We have more questions and for your own safety I want you to answer them and answer them honestly."

"It is a sin to lie."

The black woman's eyes narrowed. And then she smiled.

Cornelius's soul shuddered. *Mother of Demons* slithered through his throbbing head. He was in the nest of evil. He must persevere, take the time to discover his purpose as neither he nor the Shepherd were unable to do at the Keep, and allow the Lord to work through him.

His stomach growled, and he turned crimson with shame. He would fortify his body and soul against the unholy tempest to come.

"Breakfast will be served soon." The black woman said and left with the fallen, who turned and cast her evil gaze upon him as she shut the door.

God preserve me, he prayed as he pushed the covers back and rose from the bed.

CHAPTER 6

*B*ig Country drove toward the mountain in the same boots, boxers, and baseball cap he'd arrived at Stormy's house in because one, he wanted everyone to know he'd been balls-deep inside Stormy this morning, and two, with the interruption of fuck-boy Chad, he and Stormy hadn't had a chance to say a proper good morning.

They'd remedied that by good-morning-ing each other all over her kitchen.

"Okay, so we agree to item one: during our time together we're exclusive, no sex with outside individuals until we end things."

Chewing on the end of his cigar, he glanced at her and nodded. She reclined in the passenger seat of his truck, her bare feet propped against his dashboard, bent knees cradling the tablet in her lap.

"And when the contract ends it ends; no blame or drama, Stormy, we just wish each other well and go our separate ways," he added, and she typed that in.

"Also, I have a few toys from Red's I want to experiment with so if I want to play, you at least have to try it…" She slanted a look at him from under her long eyelashes. "You being a *Sex God* and all."

"I said what I said!" he shouted, causing her to crack up. His smile

111

didn't come close to expressing the joy he felt inside at seeing her laugh so hard. "Fine, I'll play your dick emporium games." Though a straight-up hard fuck was all he really required.

She typed in their second item, wiping a tear from the corner of her eye.

"Third item," she said. "There will be no monetary exchange for our time together. If either of us is inclined to get the other a trinket, it can't be over fifty dollars."

He rolled his eyes but agreed to the third item, knowing full well it was encoded in a woman's DNA to want to have the finer things. Some women just had to feel a man was fully committed before hitting 'em up for the expensive stuff. He'd be paying for something big by the end of their time together, but he wouldn't bow out on that one point when he knew it was bound to happen. He wouldn't hold her limited understanding of her nature against her.

Stormy gnawed on her bottom lip. "The final issue for me is that we have to agree to have fun. If it's no longer fun, if it causes us pain and unhappiness to be together, we agree to end it. And we should assess how things are going in, like, two weeks."

Big Country nodded, feeling as if they had come up with a workable agreement. Usually he laid out the terms and the women agreed, so in essence, this was the first real negotiation that had actually taken place.

"Two more things on my end, darlin'," he said. The two issues usually didn't need to be stated explicitly because his liaisons were never more than sex. "First, we got to be who we are, accept each other for who we are. No trying to change each other; I'm set in my ways. No trying to change ourselves thinking it's gon' make the other happy." He'd heard how much it cost her to bury her nature for Chad, and he didn't want an imitation of Stormy—he wanted the woman sitting right here beside him.

She nodded as if impressed, then typed the item into the tablet.

"Very good, Big Lug. I wholeheartedly agree to that point."

He ignored the misuse of his handle.

"*Secondly*," he said, a point also for her benefit. "And *the* most important of everything we've agreed upon today: no falling in love."

Her eyes got owlish and she blinked at him, a smile blooming on her face in Grinch-like increments. The way she collapsed into full-on, indelicate, snort-filled laughter was neither amusing nor attractive.

He dragged a hand over his jaw and clenched the steering wheel. Eventually, her conniption abated, and she recovered enough of her composure to speak.

"Yeah Lucas, you don't *neeeevvver* have to worry about that. You're the jump-off, my friend; love is not a possibility, on that much we can both completely agree."

Directing his gaze back to the road, he forced himself to relax. He didn't want or need her love, but the depths of her mirth, her conviction that she could *neeevvver* fall in love with him rankled.

All women loved him; they couldn't help themselves. Stormy would love him, too, if that's what he'd wanted. But it wasn't. He side-eyed her as she happily added his final item to their contract.

You've negotiated good terms, ol' son. That was all that really mattered.

Zeus stood in the shadows watching and listening as Sabrina and Mama talked and smiled and laughed about Brianna. While conversing, they folded a cream-colored sheet into thirds and placed it on the bar's wooden surface.

He grunted. His woman had no problem helping Mama around the house but every morning when he reminded her that their bed needed to be made before they left the room, she'd either smirk at him and leave, ignore him and leave, or call back over her shoulder, "*Man, I'm not thinking about that bed,*" and leave.

She had a bitter disdain for making beds but had no problem sleeping in them, reading in them, or fucking in them. He didn't understand it.

Lowering himself into the booth seat, he never took his eyes off her. It wasn't just because he liked to see her body in motion, or because he liked the expressions that flittered across her face...*she had so many emotions*. It definitely wasn't because he was saving every part of her to memory for those moments when they weren't together, or because his blade spirits were mesmerized by her. They worshiped her.

No, Zeus watched Sabrina because he was strategizing, trying to figure out the best way to make her comply with his request because his last tactic—*not* reminding her to make the bed—hadn't been successful. Beds needed to be made after rising, that's what the nuns at the orphanage had taught and that's what he believed, not because the nuns were always right, but because a made bed brought order to the day and order helped combat the chaos of humanity. He didn't understand why she didn't just take his word for it.

As Sabrina and Mama straightened the sheet over the bar, the rest of the Brood-in-residence brought up large aluminum pans of steaming food from downstairs because they couldn't take the saint below to eat. He frowned as he gazed at all the food. His woman had helped Mama cook breakfast this morning and Sabrina hated cooking almost as much as she hated making beds.

That's how he knew he just had to find the right motivation with her.

As the pans were placed on the covered bar top, Mama ducked beneath it and brought out dishes and utensils. Zeus's stomach rumbled at the late morning meal. He'd been up for hours contemplating the saint before he and Cizan had come up with the plan of having Bride interrogate him. They were both from Ireland, and it made perfect sense until Bride snapped. She'd been doing better since she'd been staying off and on with Sabrina's best friend Randy.

Though the saint appeared weak and harmless, Zeus had lived with nuns and priest most of his childhood. He knew what could exist beneath the adornments of faith and holy attire and he didn't trust it. He'd wait, see if Big Country had any luck in finding out why the saint was here, and if not, he'd let his blades garner whatever information human conversation could not.

Standing, Zeus made his way to the end of the line, waiting as the others made their plates and sat at the tables pushed together to create one long communal table. Like most of the men, Zeus took two plates and piled them with food. There were scrambled eggs in one pan, grits in another, sausage patties, hot links, country-fried potatoes, two pans of homemade biscuits, and a smaller tin that held gravy heavy with shrimp and garlic to spread over their grits or biscuits. Zeus and Sabrina preferred butter and Blackburn syrup on their biscuits. The biscuits were the best he'd ever had, and they came from a recipe Mama learned from Big Country.

He needed Sabrina to learn how to make them once he got her to learn to make the bed.

If the mercenary group hadn't taken it upon themselves to rescue her from the warehouse that life-changing night, neither she nor Zeus would be struggling with being a part of a larger collective.

Zeus waited until Sabrina finished making her plate and guided her to the booth behind the table where Mama, Terry, Bride, London, and Cizan sat. Just as Sabrina was getting used to the large amounts of food Mama prepared when there was a large gathering of Brood-in-residence, Zeus was growing more accustomed to not eating alone. He liked it here, liked that he could have his woman, dance with his blades, stalk the mountain, and still get fed. He liked that Mama treated his woman like hers because Sabrina enjoyed it. For her happiness, he was willing to share her.

When Lynx nodded at something Mama said, rose from the table, and left the building without his plates in hand, Zeus stilled. The second the front door shut, everyone at the table except Mama shifted away from the food on their plates and ate the food off Lynx's plate. Zeus even found himself walking over to snatch up an abandoned biscuit before walking back to the booth.

"You know you all are wrong," Sabrina said, shaking her head.

She still hadn't gotten used to it, but it made sense to Zeus. He believed that at some point everyone in this room had to fight for scraps to survive. Just because they could have most anything they wanted now didn't mean they no longer had to protect what they valued; they still had to watch over what was theirs or risk losing it because those who hungered were always watching and waiting.

"It's a family tradition, Sabrina," Terry said, winking at Mama.

Only smears of gravy were left on Lynx's plates before everyone went back to their own food, their banter louder than the blues playing in the background.

Lynx had the saint at his side when he returned, gray sweats hung loosely over the saint's gaunt frame and bruises mottled his pale face. The man was lucky his face wasn't riddled with bullet holes; Bride had a quick trigger reflex. Her obsession with guns just didn't seem natural.

Head bowed, the saint's lips moved in what looked to be fervent prayer as Lynx escorted him to a solitary table toward the back of the room. Lynx shook his head when he walked past the communal table and saw the condition of his plate. Lynx was the only one to lose his food since Zeus had been recovering on the mountain, yet he seemed surprised each time it happened. Zeus didn't believe he ever had to fight to survive for his meals.

After blessing his food, the young saint opened his eyes and ate like a starved man. The man had been on the other side of the mountain for days and had chosen to starve instead of hunt in a forest rich with game and edible plants. He'd deserved his hunger.

Sabrina placed a hand on Zeus's thigh and whispered, "Maybe we should have said grace?"

"You are my grace, and I say your name daily."

Sabrina's eyes softened and she pressed a lingering kiss on his shoulder before returning to her food.

Zeus continued to watch the saint, continued to watch the Brood joke and tease each other though he sensed their attention never strayed from the terrified man. The rumble of an engine, doors slamming shut, heavy feet stomping up the front porch put him on alert.

The room went silent as the front door flung open and Big Country stepped through with keys in one hand, a gun in the other, and wrinkled boxers as his only attempt at modesty. The sex witch who'd handed out the gift bags the night of that party was abandoned in the doorway as Big Country headed straight for the food and grabbed three plates.

"I tell y'all what," Big Country said. "If I'da walked in this som'bitch and all my biscuits was gone, I'd of knocked this fucker off its foundation. Every last one of y'all would have enjoyed your last meal, that much I guarantee."

Mama rose from her seat, wiped her hands and mouth with a napkin, and headed over to the sex-witch pinching Big Country on his arm as she moved past him. "Boy, don't think I'd let you tear up my house again just because you didn't get a biscuit," Mama said as she pulled the sex witch fully into the bar and hugged her. "It's good to have you back Stormy."

"Good to see you again, Almaya, even though everyplace this one goes, he's threatening something or someone."

"All I'm sayin' is these biscuits come from my grandmère's recipe. If they're made and I don't get any, her spirit calls out for vengeance and I can't be responsible for what happens. I'd mourn y'alls passing, though."

Not waiting for his woman, Big Country sat at the table with the saint. "How you doin' cousin? You sleep well, you ain't got a concussion or nothing 'cause you was out cold when I left." Big Country's words never paused as he consumed half a plate of biscuits. "What I'm trying to figure out is how you get that shiner—wasn't there last night when I left you."

The saint's eyes darted and retreated from Bride. "There was a misunderstanding of intent," the saint said.

"Yeah," Lynx said between bites. "Bride misunderstood that an offer to have her sins cleansed wasn't a plea for her to smash the hell out of his face with a gun."

Big Country shrugged. "Women, huh, who can ever guess how they'll react to an act of random kindness?"

Mama guided Stormy over to the communal table, but Big

Country pulled out a seat for her on the other side of him. Mama sat her there instead.

"Those two shared a gift bag," Zeus assured Sabrina, watching the way Big Country ate with one hand and massaged the inside of Stormy's thigh with the other.

Big Country joked with the saint, and the man lost his pensiveness, even smiled as he quietly engaged with Big Country and Stormy as if the rest of the Brood had faded out of existence.

To have to talk or listen to someone he didn't give a shit about seemed like it would be exhausting, Zeus thought, but the more Big Country and the sex witch engaged with the saint, the more he shared about how he'd come to be dropped off on the side of the highway and instructed to watch the road that led to Mama's House.

"It must have been you out there the night of my party," Stormy said. "I knew something was out there, but then you seemed to disappear."

"I saw you," the saint said, rattling off the make and model of the vehicle Stormy rode in as well as the vehicle's license plate number. Stormy confirmed that the information was one hundred percent accurate.

The saint proudly informed Big Country that in the near two weeks he'd been watching the road he'd remembered each car that had gone up the mountain, detailing the number of vehicles and the number of times they returned. He stated that he could describe each car and its corresponding license plate number. He also reported that on those occasions where he could make out the people inside the vehicles, he could give a detailed description of them as well.

Zeus's fingers moved rhythmically, phantom blade twirling through them.

Big Country held out his hand and shook the saint's when they locked grips.

"Boy, I tell you what, you got a fine mind when it comes to remembering. Yeah, I bet where you come from they put that God-given gift to good use."

The saint seemed to shrink into himself and resumed eating. The sex witch—Stormy—held Big Country's gaze, silently communicating with him in the same way Sabrina did with him.

Stormy nodded in understanding at the saint. "It hurts when people who say they love you don't care about what makes you extraordinary. It's worse when they make you feel like crap for not being who they want you to be."

Zeus felt a sharp pain in his gut as if her words had pierced him. Every eye in the room was glued to Big Country's woman, Stormy. "Well, I for one am honored to have seen a glimpse of how brilliant your mind is. My name is Stormy, Stormy Redmond."

Unshed tears filled the saint's eyes and Zeus saw how vulnerable the younger man was, if he could be brought to tears by a few kind words.

"I'm Cornelius Shepherdson, and I am blessed to meet you, Stormy."

Big Country reached out, gently freed Stormy's hand from Cornelius' and held on to it. His smile held but his eyes had gone flat. Zeus understood the reaction. Other men didn't get to touch the softness of your woman's skin while looking at them like they were an answer to a prayer. That path lead to mortal wounds...or the loss of a hand, at the least.

"I reckon it ain't often you see a lot of beautiful women, being in the saint business, but trust me, cousin, unless you've been raised to navigate the treacherous winds and waters of womanhood, it's best that you abdicate those blessings to men who know of such things backward and forth and from the inside out." Big Country cast a triumphant glance at Lynx and London.

"I don't understand," Cornelius replied to Big Country.

"That's because he's part idiot," Stormy said, snatching her hand away. "Don't bother trying to understand the ramblings of idiots."

Zeus snorted and gathered his and Sabrina's plates. He had a feeling Big Country would end up paying more for Stormy than he could afford.

Ignoring the humor from the main table, Big Country leaned closer to the saint.

"What made you choose to camp out on our mountain?"

"I did not choose, the Shepherd chooses, and I obeyed. This is my sojourn, my time of learning God's purpose for my life and fulfilling it."

"How old are you, cousin? Finding one's life purpose sounds like a whole lot of pressure for someone so young."

"I'm twenty-three. All the brothers at the Shephard's Keep have long since found their path. It is what's required to ascend in the order." The saint's eyes roamed over Big Country. "Um, pray forgive my curiosity, but what happened to your clothes?"

"I run hot, cousin," he said, looking at Stormy's breasts. "I run real hot. You done eating?" Big Country asked as he stood. Cornelius nodded, folding his napkin in his plate. "Good enough, Cornelius, Stormy and I'll see you back to your room so you don't have to worry about these heathens bothering you."

The saint looked at Zeus, Bride, and Cizan, then stood. He nodded to Mama. "Thank you for the meal."

Mama smiled as she also stood, escorting them to the front door. "I'm glad you enjoyed it, Cornelius. Trust me, while you're here I'll make it my purpose to feed you well."

"Thank you," he said before exiting the bar, Stormy following close behind. Big Country threw a sober look at the Brood before closing the door.

The saint was a watcher like Zeus, but he did more than watch, he remembered everything he seemed to pay attention to. He remembered faces, he'd remember all their faces if his words were true. He would know Sabrina's face and be able to place it if someone asked him to. And someone would eventually ask.

Standing close to Sabrina, Zeus's blades twirled through his fingers at a dangerous speed. He nodded to no one in particular, playing out possible scenarios to their conclusion before he spoke.

"The only way that man leaves this mountain will be by way of death."

The grim faces of the Brood told him that they had already come to the same conclusion.

~

Her heart raced but her breaths were calculated, steady in preparation, as she walked up the stairs, step by agonizing step. Perhaps she was imagining an indiscretion where there was none.

She was too quick to judgment at times, a consequence of being a tool of God, but her ability to discern where others lacked was a skill she'd mastered. To deal with their sickening weaknesses and idiotic choices had been an asset to her survival. This skill would be less necessary in her role as Lucas's wife, but as she reached the second floor of the house, she determined that she may have to adapt the skill for her new life, if only to protect her relationship with Lucas.

She prayed he had not made an idiotic choice, but the constriction around her heart warned her otherwise, warned her that indeed he had. Why else come to this house, *Stormy's* house, during the darkest of night and stay well beyond the sun's rising?

She wanted to scream at the interference of the devil in her plans, but she would not give into the theatrics of emotion; she would not judge him poorly without proof.

Lucas, beloved, please tell me you were not that weak, tell me you did not climb into her bed for a brief moment of pleasure when I would give you a lifetime of peace and happiness.

Entering the bedroom, she placed a hand over her stomach to settle the roiling disgust at the sight of the large bed in disarray, bedcovers on the floor, sheets bunched and disheveled, the stench of sex ripe in the air. The pain of betrayal was acute, worse than anything she'd felt since coming to live with her father. It wasn't only Lucas's betrayal, it was also the whore's, the one who had pretended to be her friend, pretended she hadn't known about the love between Delilah and Lucas.

Lucas was *hers*. He was her gift, her salvation, and she would not lose him to some undeserving *slut* who had no understanding of the plan God had for her and Lucas's future. Delilah knew herself to be better than any woman who spread her legs for base pleasure, but one who peddled sex could do nothing but betray by sex.

Pivoting, she rushed out of the bedroom and back down the stairs, heading toward the kitchen. Stepping into it, she looked around and wanted to scream with rage. *It wasn't fair!* Who was Stormy to have this beautiful home, to have this life of safety and prosperity, and still not be satisfied, still attempt to steal the *one* blessing Delilah had been granted after a lifetime of duty.

She'd had to first fight to live and when that was constant, she had to fight to learn and survive her father's teachings and use them, along with her mind and body. She was the Good Shepherd's most trusted weapon in the battle against man's evil, and she had killed, brought many men down for not being more.

Still, Lucas had been more, had given her more. She would fight for him, fight for their new life, for love, and in that process, Delilah would send Stormy Redmond back to hell before allowing the other woman to destroy those newfound possibilities.

Delilah closed her eyes, took a breath, settled, and opened them again, thanking God.

For too long, the Good Shepherd had ruled her. With Lucas, God had given her a choice, a man who had the strength of Samson, one who could destroy that which she could not. It was not too late. She could save him, and in turn, he would save her from a life choice that she never truly made but had come to accept.

She searched the kitchen, opening cupboards until she found a bottle of vodka and grabbed it, heading back upstairs. She opened the heavy curtains in the whore's bedroom to banish the darkness and began to recite a passage from *the exorcism of water* as she opened the bottle and flicked her wrist, dousing the bed with the clear liquid.

"Through the power of our Lord Jesus Christ, who will come to judge the living and the dead and the world by fire. Through the power of our Lord Jesus Christ, who will come to judge the living and the dead and the world by fire. Through the..."

She continued to recite the words as she placed the bottle on the dresser and reached inside her purse and pulled out the small box of matches she used to light the candles in her room that staved off the evil lurking in the dark. Striking a match, she tossed it into the center of the bed, feeling only peace and purpose as she watched the flames slowly spread.

Without looking back, she walked out of a house that would never be hers and slid into the rental car. She would return to the house she'd usurped, gather her belongings, and if needs be, drive up to the mountain to retrieve the man who was her gift from God.

As she drove down the tree-lined street in the serene neighborhood she saw one older woman scrutinizing her from a porch two houses down. She heard the echo of sirens from a distance, but she wasn't concerned. The black wig and large sunglasses that hid most of her face would render any description of her useless. The long black coat she wore hid her body, as the blank expression she wore as she passed the old woman hid her unspeakable need for vengeance.

Stormy sat on the cot beside Lucas, struggling to understand what was going on with the people on this mountain. Lucas's fingers edged beneath the waistband of her yoga pants as they sat opposite the young religious man gazing at them.

Lucas was going to hell, she thought as his fingers wiggled like insistent little serpents beneath the material and stroked the upper region of her ass. She arched her back to dislodge his hand but succeeded only in giving him more access.

Yep, he was going to hell and he was taking her with him, she thought as his nimble fingers slid along the crack of her ass toward—

"Oh!" she cried out as a finger dipped. "I'm going to need you to stop!" She rounded on Lucas before turning back to Cornelius's confused gaze, hoping she hadn't outwardly exposed her growing arousal before she'd cried out. Lucas's finger stilled along the seam of her ass, and Stormy released a pent-up breath of relief.

Crossing his legs at the knee, Lucas pressed against her side as if attempting to block her from Cornelius's view while he continued his easygoing chat, commanding all of Cornelius's attention as if she had never uttered a word.

Trying to stay relaxed, Stormy lowered her head and closed her eyes before Cornelius could see them rolling toward the back of her head. Lucas's finger had begun to massage. She heard and felt the vibration of Lucas chuckling beside her as he made her aware of sexual nerve endings she never knew existed there.

He was the devil.

"I am so going to pay you back," she muttered. "I swear to G—"

"Now don't blaspheme in front of a man of God, darlin', don't want to endanger your immortal soul, do you?"

Stormy's daddy had long ago taught her that sometimes a woman had to deal with sneaky people directly. Lucas thought she would quietly allow him to torment her with his covert finger-fucking, believing she would be too embarrassed to expose what was going on to a man of the cloth. He obviously had a lot to learn about her.

"Lucas, if you don't remove your hand from beneath my pants I will find a hammer and smash every knuckle on every finger of your wandering hand."

"Aw, come on, woman, how you gonna just put my lovin' out in the streets like that?" he grumbled, dislodging his finger from her flesh.

She stood as Lucas snatched his hand away, heading to the front door of this isolated little jail. "Pray for him, Cornelius, I have a feeling you may be the closest thing he will get to salvation in this lifetime."

"That I can always do, Ms. Redmond."

"Saint, if you got a mainline to the Lord, I suggest you pray for me and Stormy both because we're going to be raising some hell in the month to come."

Stormy was ready to tell Lucas exactly where to shove his prayers, when she saw Cornelius nervously stroke the cross he'd donned, along with his brown robe, upon returning to the concrete room. He seemed to find comfort in the motion which meant Lucas's antics had made Cornelius uncomfortable.

"Cornelius, do you remember the license plate of the person who brought you to the forest, maybe the make and model of the car? With that, we might be able to get you back to where you belong," she asked, hoping to put him at ease.

"I must find my own path, and until then I cannot belong anywhere," Cornelius said, then rattled off the license plate number and color of the Prius that had dropped him on the side of the road.

Lucas frowned and stared at Cornelius intently. "And the driver's name?"

Cornelius continued to be preoccupied with the cross. "I only know her as the unseen one."

Lucas's frown turned into a full-blown predatory scowl. "Describe her."

"I can't, Lucas, she is unseen. Thank you for visiting me. I hope to see you again soon," he said softly, and lay down on his cot, curling up and closing his eyes.

"Is there anything you need?" Stormy asked, feeling sorry for the younger man. He seemed so lost.

"A Bible, please."

She looked up at Lucas, who drew a hand over his jaw and shrugged. "I'll ask Mama, she's the only one likely to have one," he said and rose up to accompany Stormy out of the building.

"What's going on here, Lucas?" she asked, once the door was shut and locked.

"Trying to figure it out, darlin', trying to figure it out," he muttered.

She tried to read his expression, but his face was emotionless, his voice flat.

That first night at the bar, even at the boutique, she'd seen him seamlessly morph from seductive and jovial to flat and threatening with little warning. She'd seen the same thing with Lynx at Red's. Lucas's tendency to turn his emotions on and off like a faucet reminded her of Chad, and it didn't bode well for building a trusting relationship. Unlike with Chad, she reminded herself, she wasn't trying to build a relationship with Lucas; their time together was finite which meant she didn't have to ignore her concerns about a possibly innocent man being unfairly imprisoned.

"Why is Cornelius being detained in there? If he's done something wrong, shouldn't you all call the police?"

"Nope," he said, reaching for her hand and steering her back toward the bar. "On the mountain we have our own system of justice. Police literally have no jurisdiction here and that's the truth. Until we know why Cornelius is staking out our home, holding him ain't illegal, it's a matter of life-and-death."

"Yes, but how could he possibly be a threat? I mean, he's a freaking sai–"

He pulled her into his arms and kissed her. "Come on, darlin' let's do a little of our own freaking…go find a sturdy tree and see if we can address more burning issues."

"Man, didn't I tell you to go to the clinic to get that condition checked out?" Stormy snapped.

Lucas's bark of laughter was shocking in its suddenness and intensity. It filled her with the most exquisite feeling. If she wasn't careful, she'd become obsessed with trying to keep him laughing. "And you need to go put some clothes on," she groused, annoyed by how easily he was slipping into her affections.

His arm tightened around her waist and he lifted her, walking toward the side of Mama's House, where he undoubtedly intended to *freak* her against the side of the building.

At that moment, Mama and Terry emerged from the building, their somber gazes zeroing in on them, killing Stormy's arousal and stopping Lucas where he stood. Sabrina and her boyfriend Zeus lingered in the door's opening, looking as curious as she felt.

"What's happened now?" Lucas asked, lowering her.

"Where's your phone, son?" Terry asked, stepping down onto the graveled lot.

"My phone, what does my—?"

"It's in the truck, both our phones are in the truck," Stormy said. Lucas had barely put the truck in park when he'd made the mad dash to get inside Mama's House for breakfast.

"There a reason you askin', Terry?" Lucas asked.

"Merlee. She's been calling you," Mama said as she walked to stand beside Terry. "Seems there's a problem out at your grandparents' farmhouse."

Lucas shot toward the truck with a speed that shouldn't have been possible with his size and the instability of the ground, but he was inside the truck well before Stormy wondered who Merlee was. She definitely meant more to him than the four women he'd called during their drive, informing them that he was enacting his "no-contact" clause.

Stormy had a feeling he had no such clause with this Merlee woman. Was she the one who got away, the one he loved but couldn't have, a childhood crush who possessed his heart and made all others settle for having contracted bits of his time and body?

Stop, she commanded herself as she watched Lucas rifle through the truck until he found his mobile. He walked back toward Terry and Mama as he made the call.

"Merlee darlin', what's going on?" he asked, putting the phone on speaker as he motioned for Stormy.

She hesitated to join the small group, glanced over her shoulder at the concrete building. It wasn't her nature to shy away from danger but she was cautious; protecting others was almost biologically driven, even when she failed.

Would she be failing Cornelius if she left him here unprotected?

Unlike the night of her party, when she might have been a little too high on life, a little too preoccupied with sensation to reflect on who these people were, walking into Mama's House today felt like stepping through a field of electrified air where predatory intent was a force hovering over each inhabitant. And Lucas was a part of them.

He held her gaze, waiting for her, then his gaze narrowed.

It had been her choice to come up here with him, but she thought she was choosing sex and adventure. The man ready to knock the world on its ass over a woman named Merlee implied that it was going to be more than sex and adventure, Cornelius inside the concrete building meant it would be more, and the group inside *Mama's House,* definitely meant more. She wasn't choosing more at this stage of her life, she reminded herself, just a month of unentangled sex. *That was it.*

"I'm sorry, Lucas, I didn't want to drag you into this. I should've listened, but I thought…" The woman couldn't seem to go on. Her voice was strong, but it was filled with shame.

Stormy may not have wanted to join the group, but she was propelled by her fearsome curiosity.

"Just tell me you're all right, Merlee girl, let me know you're safe, darlin'."

"I'm safe, Lucas," Merlee said. The unspoken *for now* hovered like a phantom.

"Merlee, it's Mama again—"

"Hey Mama."

"Lucas didn't get your messages so he doesn't know what's happening there."

"Somebody better tell me something soon or I'ma lose what little patience I'm holding on to," Lucas demanded.

"Lucas, I need you to stay calm," Merlee pleaded.

Lucas closed his eyes, cracked his neck, and relaxed his shoulders. He opened his eyes and smiled down at the phone, his whole vibe mellowing as he rubbed his free hand over his chest. Though he projected ease, Stormy didn't believe it for a minute.

"Come on now, Merlee girl, I've eaten three plates of Mama's cooking and ain't had my midday nap yet, so if you're safe, ain't much gonna get my pressure up today. Now, what's going on?"

Leaning closer, Stormy peered at the phone's screen. The woman Lucas was video-calling was strikingly beautiful. Like…gorgeous. Thick long sable hair, catlike hazel eyes, defined cheekbones, and lips that appeared plush and full.

"PaPere and Belle Mère are here at the farm," Merlee said, her gaze avoiding the screen, avoiding Lucas. "They said it would just be them, said they'd only need to stay a week until their new place was ready, said they had nowhere else to go. They brought Armand and Thibideux and it's been over a month, and now PaPere is saying he's not leaving because the farmhouse is his birthright."

Merlee looked back at the screen. "I wouldn't bother you but Belle Mère and Thibideux are causing problems in town. Armand tries to do what he can, but the three others are treating our grands' home like a squat house. I have a business to run and folks are reluctant to bring their animals to the farmhouse clinic because of them. I tried talking to PaPere alone. I told him it was time for them to leave willingly or I'd have the police escort them out. He said he'd burn it all down before he left and didn't care if me and 'every fucking animal here burned with it'."

Whatever that emotion she'd felt earlier slunk away in shame as Stormy realized that Merlee was Lucas's sister. She could see the similarities clearly without *the emotion that shall not be named* distorting her perception.

"The old man threatened you," Lucas reflected quietly. And despite his soft smile, violence was a kinetic energy that seeped through his projected calm. "And Thibideux...he out of prison then, yeah?" There was a distinctive shift in his accent; still country but the inflections more Acadian, reminding Stormy of the bayous and moonlight he'd mentioned the first night they met.

What the hell was going on?

"He's been paroled," Merlee replied.

"And the sheriff hasn't arrested them for the trouble they're causing?"

Traveling across state lines was a parole violation, but since none of this was her business Stormy remained quiet.

"Sheriff Anderson? Really? Even if he had a notion, Belle Mère's already worked her way into his pants, PaPere holds the proof, and Belle Mère threatened to destroy the Sheriff's good name if he interferes in our family business. That woman, Lucas...I *never* should have let them come."

"Don't worry yourself, Merlee girl. I'll be out on the earliest flight to Tulsa International."

"It's no rush, Garret is insisting that I stay with him and Doc Travis is offering to let me work out of his veterinary hospital in town. You know he's been trying to get me to buy him out so he can retire. I'll use his space for now, but the county fair is coming up in three weeks, and I can't afford to be away from the farm then. Armand and my farmhand William can manage the in-house animals and my gardens, but I need to be back at the house before the fair gets underway."

"You will," Lucas said. "Stay with the runt of a fiancé and don't go out to the farm, darlin', I'll call you before I board the plane. And Merlee, tell Garret that if he tries anything of a sexual nature with you while you're in his house, I'll castrate him."

"I'll do no such 'a thing, big brother, because what you're threatening to cut off is actually mine and I'm not parting with it."

Every part of Lucas's flesh not contained by boxers and boots flushed red. "Boy yeah, I'll be making you a widow before you become a bride."

Merlee's laugh was as loud and bodacious as her brother's.

Despite how easy he was with his sister, Stormy couldn't shake the feeling of dread settling in her gut.

"Lucas?" Merlee said.

"Yeah, shug?"

"Thank you."

"You're my blood, Merlee-girl; above all others I'll kill for your well-being or die trying."

"Well let's just make sure it never comes to that, Big Luc," Merlee said.

Lucas groaned and rolled his eyes at the endearment. "See you soon, darlin'," he said before disconnecting the call.

"I'll call Edgar, see if he can fly you out to Oklahoma so you won't have to deal with the worries of commercial," Terry informed Lucas.

"I'd rather ride the skies bareback on a drunken dragon," Lucas said.

"I don't understand why the two of you can't just get along," Terry said, walking toward the bar. "I'll see about booking a flight."

"If I could get a ride back to my house on your way to the airport, I'd appreciate it," Stormy said to Lucas, sad that their time had come to such an abrupt end.

"I got you, Stormy," Lynx called out as he lugged a large green duffle bag over his shoulder and flipped it onto the porch as he came to a stop. "I got your to-go bag from your room, Big Country, I'll drop you at the airport, then Stormy Redmond, of Red's Pleasure Boutique, can spend the rest of the day in the city playing tourists with me. You game, Stormy?"

"Absolutely—"

"Not," Lucas jumped in. "She's coming with me."

Noooo. No, I am not, she thought.

She felt for Lucas and Merlee, she did—but getting involved in family conflict was not how she intended to spend her sabbatical.

"Lucas, you go take care of your family's situation and call me when you get back to town," Stormy said, trying to be encouraging and helpful when part of her, the shallow selfish part, simply wanted to go back to her bed so they could lose themselves in each other again. She stepped closer when Lucas failed to responded to her. Instead, he stared at the phone in his hand as if there was more to be communicated through the blank screen.

Lynx looked at Mama and she nodded, expression flat, eyes focusing on Lucas. The dread in Stormy's gut spread, left her feeling both tense and jittery as a dump of adrenaline burned through her bloodstream, demanding she do something as her mind coached herself to be still, be calm, wait.

"Big Country, son, it's time to get dressed…" Mama said. "Time to go help Merlee."

The phone fell from Lucas's fingers, his arms lax at his side as he looked down at the small device on the ground.

"He threatened her, Mama, threatened to hurt Merlee." He looked at the petite older woman. "He was going to hurt the baby."

Lynx stepped forward, catching Lucas's attention. "But Merlee's fine, big guy, she's okay."

"Sabrina, go get Terry, tell him to bring a dose, he'll know what I mean," Mama said.

Sabrina looked at Zeus and went inside the bar as the other Brood members exited the house and walked onto the gravel, spreading out around Lucas. Only Zeus, who looked mildly curious, took one step down from porch to the top stair and watched.

Lucas's gaze shifted toward Stormy and what she saw made her retreat back a couple of steps.

"Don't run."

She stilled, barely recognizing that the guttural voice commanding her was Lucas's.

"Lucas—" Mama called out to him.

"They were gonna hurt the baby," he said, still looking at Stormy, but she knew he wasn't seeing her. "She's just a *bébé*, ain't strong like me, can't let 'em hurt her, no."

"She's safe," Mama said.

"Can't let them hurt…"

"*You're* safe, Lucas," Stormy urged.

"No, I ain't safe, *chi*, I ain't safe," he said, his focus on something beyond the present moment, something Stormy's heart wanted him to turn away from.

"Stormy, step away," Lynx said softly, moving toward her.

Lucas's face contorted and became inhuman as he rushed Lynx, spearing him in the midsection with his shoulder, continuing to charge until he slammed into the wooden post on the side of the porch, shaking the whole structure. Lynx brought his elbows down close to Lucas's neck and the bigger man momentarily dropped to one knee, shaking his head before reaching up to grab Lynx by the throat and shirt. Roaring as he stood, Lucas pressed Lynx over his head and flipped him. Lynx flew through the air and landed on his back.

The rest of the Brood descended on Lucas, their goal seemed more to subdue than to injure, but in the melee, punches and kicks landed between them over and over again, brutal blows that made Stormy cry out and move toward the brawl, only to be restrained by Mama's strong grip. Lucas became more enraged at Stormy's cry.

Zeus hopped down to the ground, approaching Lucas from behind. "I get this game now, I'll play along."

Zeus went low, striking Lucas in the back of the knee, causing it to buckle, and Bride, who sat on Lucas's shoulders squeezing his neck with her thighs, leaped off before he hit the ground. The Brood struggled to keep him pinned down, and Zeus—who was holding onto Lucas's legs—was flung around as if wrestling with two powerful anacondas.

Terry ran from the bar, Sabrina froze just outside the door as she took in the scene. Dropping to his knees, Terry stuck a syringe into Lucas's shoulder, and Stormy watched as his eyes found hers and the bright flame behind his green eyes dimmed as Terry injected him with something that leashed his fit of rage, rendering him unconscious.

"And *I'm* supposed to be the crazy one?" Zeus asked as he squatted beside Lucas's body.

Stormy felt her own rage building and shook off Mama's hand. Pushing through the Brood she sat on the graveled earth and placed Lucas's head on her lower thigh, stroking his wild head in an attempt to comfort him in a way that she didn't know how to just moments before.

Terry assessed her so long and hard, she wondered if she would end up in the cell beside Cornelius.

"You've stumbled on a fine mess, haven't you?" he said, his eyes crinkling at the corners as he offered her a smile. "It's only going to get messier for you, my dear. I received some unsettling news."

CHAPTER 7

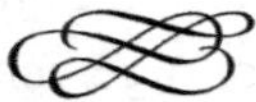

Something jarred Big Country to wakefulness.

He didn't outwardly acknowledge his return to consciousness, allowing his mind time to get back online. Flashes of memory showed him what had transpired, and he was ashamed. Images of Lynx being slammed into the porch post, attacking the Brood, Stormy crying out...

Each time he felt the cold creep through him, each time he wasn't able to stop the numbness or escape the blue flame, he hated it; hated what he became, hated that yet again he'd proved himself powerless to control his reaction.

He'd had an episode. He'd had *another* goddamn episode, he thought, gritting his teeth. As big and strong as he was, even after all this time he hadn't proved strong enough to defeat the most hated part of himself.

Shifting his weight, attempting to turn away from ugly realities, he focused on the things his senses picked up. By the shape and feel of the surface beneath him, he knew he was in his favorite recliner, which meant he was in Mama's living-room.

Another jarring impact shook his chair and he almost broke the pretense of unconscious and threw the pillow beneath his head, knowing the only person who made a habit of kicking his chair did it to irritate him, wake him, or both.

"Lynx, if you don't leave him alone…." Mama threatened.

"What?" Lynx said, "I wasn't doing anything."

He always tells that lie.

"Daddy," he heard Stormy say. "I know what I *should've* done. I made a mistake…"

"How many times have I told you to set your alarm, how many times have I *told* you that safety is never guaranteed, that you can only minimize risk. Your whole house could've burned down."

Wait, what the hell did her daddy say about Stormy's house burning down?

And why the hell is Stormy in Mama's living room in the first place?

Opening his eyes, the first person Big Country saw was Lynx lounging beside him in an identical recliner. A long ice pack was placed between Lynx's spine and the back of the recliner. Lynx tilted his head up in silent greeting, silent forgiveness, then nodded toward the center of the room where Stormy was talking on her mobile phone.

Jesus, she is a beautiful woman.

He flinched as the memory of her screaming out rattled around in his head. He clenched his fists and jaw to control his body's response to her panicked desperation.

Relax son, breathe, his granddaddy used to guide him, splaying his hand over Big Country's chest, teaching him how to ground his emotions when he was a boy seething with a well-cultivated rage.

Big Country inhaled deeply.

Control this shit, ol' son, here and now; Stormy's seen too much already.

Which begged the question, why was she down in the sublevels of *Mama's House* where only Brood was allowed in the first place? Whatever she might be, Stormy wasn't Brood.

Mama never should've allowed her and her friends to party on their mountain, he thought, his shame turning into justifiable anger. He hadn't had an episode in over two years, and now here she was with a ringside seat to the worst of him, no doubt anticipating the opportunity to use what she saw against him.

He lowered his gaze, not ready to reveal his suspicion that these episodes were somehow her fault, and noticed the dust and debris covering his relatively unmarred flesh. It was a wonder that in his rages, his body didn't register pain or sustain signs of any except the most severe injuries. In comparison, there were a number of bruises and contusions covering his Brood mates.

They got hurt protecting him from himself.

If this shit kept on, he'd have to step away. He couldn't let his lack of control put them at risk.

"Daddy, look, I'll go back to my house as soon as—"

"No. Hell no, you come home. Your brother is already at your house dealing with the situation, he'll keep us updated. And if the investigators want to talk to you they'll do it here, where I can make sure you're safe, I'll be damned if my baby girl—"

"Arthur, give me the phone," a woman demanded impatiently.

"All I'm saying, Reesy, is that if Detective Tracy doesn't have a suspect in custody by weeks end, me and my boys will get it done ourselves."

"You and your law enforcement boys' old asses are retired. Leave the investigating to the ones paid to do it."

"How bad is the damage, Ma?"

Stormy's mother summed up the situation with a precision that made Big Country wonder if she was also a retired cop.

Aside from the first story window that had been broken into, the damage was exclusive to Stormy's bedroom where a bottle of vodka was poured on the bed as an accelerant. There was some damage, but the fire never spread beyond the bedroom due to the vigilance of Stormy's neighbor.

"Mrs. Yin called the police the moment she saw the woman disappear into your back yard," Stormy's mother said. "Not long after, she said she saw smoke coming from an upstairs window, and by the time the cops and fire department got there, Mrs. Yin was ready with the time the woman arrived and left, the make, model, and license plate number of the car, and a detailed description of the woman. I told your daddy the best security system your block has is Mrs. Yin."

"Lucky for you, beds aren't as easy to burn as people think," her father said.

"It just doesn't make any sense," Stormy muttered in confusion.

Big Country lowered the leg extension on the recliner, planted his dirty feet on the floor, and leaned forward, placing his forearms on his knees as he watched her. "Oh, it makes some sense, darlin'. Think, where have you heard that car described?"

Stormy looked at him and it was as if her eyes were seeing him for the first time. Maybe she was fighting to reconcile the man she invited inside her body with the man she'd watched him become.

"Is that the white boy Mrs. Yin saw strolling out of your house in nothing but his raggedy draws this morning?"

"Daddy."

"Arthur." Stormy and her mother spoke at the same time.

"Look here, cousin, ain't nothing I own raggedy. I got too much money and too much of my grand's home training *not* to be meticulous with the things I own," Big Country said. "But that's neither here or there, because I suspect what me and your daughter did in that bed just hours before is the reason it was set fire to."

Neither of her parents responded immediately, so he took the opportunity to recount his first-time meeting with Delilah and each exchange they'd had, glossing over his moment of what passed for intimacy at his house.

"You're the fiancé!"

"Come on now, darlin', that don't even sound right," Big Country said.

"You're right, it's ridiculous, but she believed it enough to try and burn down my house, to spy on me at my place of business," Stormy said, telling them about her interaction with Delilah at Red's the day before.

"At least we got video from the boutique to give to the investigators," Big Country said.

"Um...the video erases after twenty-four hours."

"But I fixed it," Big Country said slyly. "Remember?"

Terry, who had been sitting at the bank of computers on the step-down level adjoining the living room, pushed back from the computer system and joined them. "I'm sorry to complicate your life more, Stormy, but I just learned that the car Mrs. Yin saw driving away from your house belonged to an elderly couple in San Francisco. They were found murdered and freshly buried in their backyard. Their estimated time of death predates even your meeting with this Delilah, Big Country."

Terry sat on the loveseat beside Mama. "This woman is more than a happenstance bar hookup, she's a skilled murderer or associates with people who are, and I don't believe you or Stormy are her end game."

"The car Mrs. Yin saw was a 2013 Toyota Prius—" Stormy said, looking at Big Country, no doubt thinking of the conversation they had with the saint.

"Delilah is the one who dropped Cornelius off on the side of the mountain," Big Country said, standing. "That weak little fucker knows what's going on, and it's time for me and him to have a real come-to-Jesus moment."

Zeus and Bride also stood, heading toward the heavy steel door that led to the hallway and stairs connecting to the bar.

"No," Mama said, and all eyes turned to her. She looked at Big Country first. "You have business at home. That takes precedence."

Until that very moment he'd forgotten all about Merlee and those fuckers nesting in his grands' home.

"I purchased two tickets to Oklahoma. Which of the Brood do you want to go with you?" Terry asked.

Big Country didn't want any of the Brood to go to Oklahoma with him, didn't want anyone to witness the rotted skeletons that would claw their way through his family's seedy closets, and expose their depravity to the light of day. His family's ugliness was one he'd keep his Brood mates away from as long as he could.

"Her," he said, nodding toward Stormy. "She goes. We got a contract."

The red undertones in Stormy's brown skin deepened as all eyes swung toward her. The Brood knew the only contracts he made with women were the ones for money and goods in exchange for fucking.

"It's not what you think," Stormy said.

It wasn't, but it was a contract just the same.

Lucas recited the terms of their contract word for word. "Now, did y'all hear the part about us not leaving each other's side for the next month?"

"But we didn't say anything about leaving the state," Stormy argued.

"If you wanted that stipulation added, you should've negotiated it into the contract."

"Reesy, you hear this shit?" he heard Stormy's father say.

"Look, actually I don't mind going with you, we can drive wherever you want." Stormy shook her head. "But me and planes, Lucas—"

"Hey, not a problem, darlin'; we also said we'd cut bait if either of us wanted to."

He wasn't going to beg her. He preferred to go alone anyhow; hell, it was probably for the best. Merlee's security was his priority, not some woman looking for an excuse to tuck tail and run from the beast she'd seen that had emerged from him.

"Tell him to come to the phone," Stormy's mother said.

Stormy didn't tell him shit, only glared at him, likely mad that he'd called her on her bullshit excuse. She didn't fear a fucking plane, she feared him and didn't have the balls to say it.

Big Country walked over and took the phone from her hand.

Stormy's mother was a classic red-bone, with skin a few shades lighter than Stormy's, but eyes, lips, and nose a near-perfect match to her daughter's.

"Well, hell." Her mother blinked. "Mrs. Yin wasn't exaggerating when she said you were the biggest sexiest man to walk through my daughter's door she'd ever seen. I have to admit, she was right on both counts."

Big Country smiled. Mothers loved him.

"Give me the damn phone," Stormy's father snapped before his face dominated the screen. His mocha skin, the sculpted angles of his face; they were also Stormy.

"Boy, go put some damn clothes on. What kind of grown man walks around in public damn near naked Reesy, huh? That's the kind of country shit your people are good for."

"You better watch it," Stormy's mother warned.

"Am I lying?" he said smugly. "Now Stormy, you know I'm not one to meddle in your sex life, I'm glad you finally got one, but all this talk of contracts reminds me too much of Chad. This family ain't putting up with another Chad…and this one's ass too big to fight so I probably will have to end up shooting him."

"Daddy."

"Arthur." Stormy and her mother said in unison again.

Mama stood, stepped to Big Country's other side and angled the phone toward her. "Lieutenant Redmond, I'm Almaya Hendricks, most folks know me as Mama. Big Country is one of my Brood; you may have heard of us." Stormy's father didn't seem impressed. "Until we can understand this situation with Delilah, I believe it's safer if Stormy goes to Oklahoma with Big Country. Delilah and whoever she's working with won't know where they are, and Big Country knows how to protect her; it's what my Brood does."

Stormy's father regarded Big Country silently and Big Country let him.

Stormy ignored the stare down, grabbed his jaw and turned his head, forcing him to look at her. "You don't understand, me and airplanes—"

Her daddy chuckled and the fine hairs on Big Country's ass bristled. "No, baby girl, they say he can keep you safe, you get on the plane with the man. If nothing else, we'll really see if his constitution is better than your weak-assed ex."

"Had a feeling you'd choose Stormy. I got a commercial flight for both of you leaving out of San Francisco in a little over three hours, enough time to take Stormy to buy a few items and make your flight, which arrives in Oklahoma late tonight. I've reserved a rental truck for you at the airport," Terry said. "Merlee has rooms prepared for you at her fiancé's house. The return trip will leave tomorrow evening, enough time for you to visit with your sister once your other family is cleared out. When you get back to the mountain, we'll deal with the Delilah situation."

Big Country nodded.

"Call us when you get there, Stormy, let us know how the flight goes."

Stormy gave him a sideways look. "All right, Ma, I'll call you guys when we settle in. Bye, Daddy."

The call ended, and Big Country could see Stormy was struggling with her decision to go. He understood, he truly did—the contract didn't say anything about her walking into a shit storm without a raincoat and that's exactly what she'd be doing. If he could, he'd keep her as far away from him and his family as possible. He liked his world compartmentalized into the part for his women and the other part for everything else. Stormy was already blurring those boundaries but he'd take her, he had to; if she didn't go, Mama would send someone else, and Mama was right, Stormy would be safer with him than staying at her house or with her parents.

"Look here, darlin', just so we understand each other, this ain't some invitation to get in my head. None of that psychoanalyzing shit. We hold to the original contract, treat this family meeting as a part of the fucking adventure and move on, yeah?"

"Did no one ever teach you the graces, mate?" London asked as he entered the living room from the hidden wall panel that led to the second of four sublevels.

Big Country shook his head. The whole of the Brood seemed hell-bent on exposing their secrets to a woman who wouldn't even be in their lives a month from now. "Stormy, a woman of intellect, power, and beauty, is not to be treated as one of your basic conveniences." London walked over and pulled Stormy against him, looping his arm over her shoulder. "He truly doesn't deserve you, love; you should be with me. Take me to your boutique so I can play with the enticing wonders you have there." London's gaze didn't stray from her breasts.

Stormy had the gall to laugh over London's innuendo as if he'd said something funny. That shit wasn't funny, it was just the accent that made it seem that way. London was, in truth, more mercenary in his treatment of women than Big Country ever was.

"You're breaking my heart over here, Stormy. Yep, I am literally bleeding out," Lynx said, holding his hand over his heart.

"Enjoy your trip to the afterlife, mate," London called out. "We'll grieve your passing in very physical and sweaty ways. In your honor, of course."

Big Country took a deep breath, closed his eyes and cracked his neck.

"London. Son. I will fuck you up. I will fuck you the *fuck* up if you don't back off that woman." He uttered the warning as heat leached from his body, the familiar cold replacing it.

This wasn't supposed to happen; he'd never had more than one episode in a day, to say nothing of one within an hour of another. He was half afraid to open his eyes for fear that the elusive blue flame would be dancing somewhere close, waiting to steal his control again.

He bit back a growl.

He never lost control over a fucking woman, whereas they ripped lives apart and celebrated as they did it. Hate and disgust churned inside him as cold promised to harden all feeling and shatter the world into shards of violence that brought respite.

Two warm hands wrapped around his left fist.

The contact hit him like a bolt of lightning, welded the chasm between his mind and body back into one seamless being. Warmth rushed back into the room, and he inhaled, Stormy's cinnamon and cedar scent washing the bitter taste of jealousy from his tongue.

When he opened his eyes, no flame flittered on the outskirts of his vision. There was only Stormy pressing into his side as she held his hand. No flame, only her heat, her scent, her sienna red skin touching his.

"You flirting with other men, Stormy Sinclair Redmond, that ain't part of the contract," he said, voice rough and strained.

"Well, if you wanted that stipulation added, you should have negotiated it in the contract huh?" She smirked, tossing his words in his face.

Cute, real cute—but he'd let her have her moment of glory only because she was right. Problem was, before now it had never been a stipulation he needed to add.

He didn't *get* jealous.

Pulling away from her, he looked around the room, not surprised to see Zeus twirling his blades through his fingers, Terry standing with his hand behind his back where Big Country knew a tranq gun was at the ready. London had relocated to the heavily plated rein-forced steel door still sealed shut and was leaning against it with his arms and ankles leisurely crossed as he winked at Stormy. *Shit-starting bastard.*

What made him pause was seeing Mama and Lynx look at each other, then at him, as if they were cats that ate the proverbial canary. Usually they were the first ones to be at his side, trying to pull him back from the chasm.

They are really starting to weird me out.

Choosing to ignore them all, to ignore what could've just gone down, he walked to the wall panel, opened it, and left the room.

Less than thirty minutes later, he'd showered and dressed, reclaiming his normal levity as he put his weaponless to-go bag in his truck and helped Stormy step back up into the passenger seat before completing his goodbyes.

Lifting Mama off her feet, Big Country wrapped her in a bear hug and held on.

"You sure you don't need me to come with you?" Mama asked anxiously. "I've dealt with your family before. I'll gladly do it again."

He rested his head against the side of her neck and closed his eyes for a moment before setting her back down on her feet. "I'm a big boy now, Mama, I'll deal with this situation just fine."

"Well…call me if you need me. You know I'll come running."

"You always have, and I'll cherish you for it always." He kissed her on the forehead and placed her back on her feet.

Terry joined them and wrapped an arm around Mama's shoulder, extending his free hand. They clasped each other by the forearm and held on.

"Don't let them pull you off your path, son. You've become more than they ever wanted you to dream of being. Guard your heart and soul," Terry said, eyes flicking toward the truck. Big Country took in Terry's words as if they were his lifeline. "…And if push comes to shove, Almaya's right, call us and we'll come, and by the time we're done with those bastards the world will forgot they ever walked upon it."

Big Country grinned and wondered just how Mama had made a good man like Terry go so bad. He knew it was her doing.

Walking to his truck he hopped in, turned the ignition, and rolled down his window, hanging halfway out the truck as he backed it up, grinning like he was on his way to his first rodeo. "Y'all don't let Bride practice no more of her interrogation skills. We'll need the saint to find out who Delilah is and whoever she's working for."

"Dude, we got this," Lynx called out. "Just take care of my woman out there in Hicksville USA."

His woman. Big Country lifted his arm and gave Lynx the finger until he was out of sight and heading down the narrow dirt road. He looked over at Stormy. "You ready for this, darlin'?"

She cocked a brow and looked him up and down. "Question is…are you?"

He winked at her; he liked that she hadn't folded and run, but she still wasn't ready.

She hadn't been prepared for this. Her emotions were making her reckless…and there were repercussions.

Time was running out. She could feel that window of freedom shrinking on a cellular level and wanted to be on the other side before it disappeared. She didn't want this life the Good Shepherd had chosen for her anymore; she wanted Lucas, wanted all the reckless emotions he made her feel: love, happiness, desire. They were her reward for enduring.

She checked the time on the gold watch encircling her wrist. With its shiny diamonds at the twelfth, third, sixth, and ninth hours, the beautiful piece of jewelry was a gift from the dead elderly couple's locked cache of valuables.

She ran her finger over the face of the watch which clearly denoted the lateness of the Patron's emissary. She had been forced to sit on the cold metal bench and wait for over ten minutes for the information that would provide her with the answers needed to secure her future.

She didn't like waiting. It didn't matter that the California sun was warm upon her skin, or that the trees surrounding the paved park trail rustled gently with the passing breeze. The rippling waves on the surface of the manmade lake did not inspire her toward tranquility. Time was running out. Soon she'd have to act, either with or without the information the Patron's emissary provided.

When a man in a business suit came around the curve of the trail carrying a suitcase, she knew it was God's blessing for her patience. Standing, she tightened the belt of the cream-colored mid-calf trench coat and smoothed her hands down her thighs, sliding them inside the deep coat pockets. Before she could offer a greeting, he sat down on the bench and made a show of unlocking the leather briefcase.

She smiled and sat beside him, placing her purse on the outside of her right thigh while crossing her legs at the ankles.

"Mr. Kragen is not pleased with the attention you're receiving. This priest of yours—"

"Shepherd," she corrected. "The Good Shepherd. You will respect his calling."

He barely schooled his impatience…with her…was he not the one who'd been over ten minutes late?

She continued to smile kindly.

"Your Shephard assured Mr. Kragen that you were one of the most discreet and efficient members of his little order of altar boys. I must say, in light of recent events, I'd say that description was a vast over-exaggeration."

He pulled an envelope from his briefcase and placed it on the lid. "You've killed two people who bear no resemblance to Sabrina Samora or Zeus."

"They were old. The Lord decreed it was their time, otherwise they would be alive."

"They have family with a long history in the city calling for justice, and guess who was seen driving in their car?"

"I'm sorry," she said. "You've confused the purpose of this meeting. You are here to give me the information I've requested, and I am here to graciously receive it."

She held out her hand and he placed the envelope in it.

"Mr. Kragen is concerned. Nothing you've requested moves us closer to the whereabouts of his son's killers. And if you think your father's acolyte has learned anything, we'll never know because he is no longer where you left him. Perhaps he's also lost faith in your ability to complete this assignment."

Cornelius would have died perched above the road before he willingly left. If he was gone then someone took him, and it was undoubtedly the people who lived on that signal-killing mountain. The tracker she'd put on Lucas's truck always died when he turned onto the path heading there. This morning he'd left the whore's house and gone to that mountain, only to leave again a few hours later.

The last time she checked, the tracker's signal was steady indicating Lucas's truck hadn't moved from the location. Delilah had discarded the elderly couples' car and taken a cab to within a mile of the signal, giving her ample time to approach while devising two courses of escape should one be warranted.

A hundred feet from the signal, Delilah hadn't been able to locate the truck, but the signal was strong, it had been right…there…emitting from a fire hydrant. She'd known it was a trap when she saw two individuals less than fifty feet from the hydrant who had appeared casual yet hyperaware of everyone moving about.

The whore had tried to set her up, to taunt her with the fact that, though Delilah had attempted to burn her house down, she hadn't succeeded. Now the whore believed she had Lucas and there was no course of action Delilah could take without a tracker.

"I'm sure you're right," Delilah told the Patron's man as she opened the envelope. "Cornelius was constantly disciplined for losing faith. I, on the other hand, am ever committed. The woman you see before you isn't the woman they are looking for and in a very short time, this woman will be forever gone. Unfortunately, I find myself without a car and I don't see any keys in this envelope."

"I've advised Mr. Kragen to limit contact with you until you've proven you are capable of completing this job. This will be our last interaction until that time. In the two weeks you've been here, Ms. Shephardssin, this Lucas Beaumont hasn't led to the capture of the murderers. My advice: cut bait, lady, that particular lead is dead."

The man's phone rang, and he answered, which gave her time to skim over the latest information on Lucas. There was so much she wanted to know about him, needed to know.

"I'll inform her," The man beside her said before disconnecting his call. "It appears that your man in the photos was flagged at SFO waiting to board a plane to Oklahoma with a female companion. I was right, you've done nothing but waste time; time your father has been very generously compensated for. When I return to Mr. Kragen's office, I'll recommend that he terminate the contract with your father's order. There is no benefit to us if his son's killers continue to live free while you indulge your infatuation with the oversized mammoth in the photos."

His gaze slid over her, as the weight of his derision and sexual interest weighed heavily upon her. It was a look Delilah was all too familiar with—one that gave her a measure of advantage, as simple men were easily led by greedy pleasures. Today would be the last day she tolerated their disrespect. She no longer had to, her commitment to Lucas freed her from that obligation.

Leaning closer to the man, she placed her hand, exquisite with the addition of the watch, on his knee while resting her chin on his shoulder, stroking the damp hairs at the nape of his neck. *Disgusting pig.*

Pulling away slightly she lowered her gaze and touched her tongue to her bottom lip before looking up again and smiling.

"I'm appallingly bad at this hunting people down thing, aren't I? You're right, you know, I'm out of my depth. The assignments I usually handle have more to do with pleasure, not all this running around and trying to strategize. I'm sorry to have caused Mr. Kragen —and by extension, you—any dissatisfaction."

With a flick of her wrist she released the short blade hidden inside the sleeve of her jacket and angled it millimeters away from the area of his neck she'd just stroked. "Let me make it up to you," she whispered, leaning in again, her other hand caressing from knee to thigh to groin, nudging his unimpressive erection as she skimmed her hand over his chest.

Placing an open-mouthed kiss against his jaw, her fingers inched up his throat, fingertips brushing back and forth over his weak chin before she pushed it back savagely, thrusting the blade through the back of his neck just as ferociously. His only reaction was a widening of his eyes before his body went slack.

Allowing his head to loll back, she rested it upon the bench.

There was blood, that was to be expected, but she liked that particular kill spot precisely because it wasn't a bloody mess. Picking through his pockets, she took his wallet and the meaningless wedding ring on his finger and placed them inside the briefcase along with her knife and the manila envelope.

"You would have ended my contract? Well, I have terminated your contract with your life, I hope you can appreciate just how effective I can be at my job with the right motivation."

She arranged his non-functioning limbs so that he appeared at rest on the bench after a hard day of work. "Please enjoy the blessings of this beautiful place before you descend to hell. Perhaps Mr. Kragen's son has prepared a place for you at the devil's table," she said, standing.

"Now I must be off, I have to find the ones responsible for the death of the Patron's son *after* I find and save my beloved. I have new priorities, you see." She took the man's phone and cut off his thumb.

Cleaning his blood off her hand, she used the same handkerchief to wrap the severed digit and placed it inside her coat pocket. "May the Shephard's blessings be upon you," she said to the Patron's man before lifting his briefcase.

Her father's teaching of having something beautiful in one hand while wielding something deadly in the other had always resonated with her. Walking in the direction the dead emissary had come, she again felt as if God had placed her feet on her true path.

All she had to do now was follow it to its destined end.

CHAPTER 8

*S*tormy walked down the concourse alone, clutching her oversized purse tightly to her side. *What was she even doing here*, she thought, turning to look behind her before she scanned the bustling area, wondering if Delilah was out there waiting to throw some mixture of hot piss and acid on her.

It didn't help that Lucas had been escorted from the security checkpoint by four angry-looking TSA agents earlier, grinningly assuring her that everything was all right.

Deep in her heart, she believed that he'd had at least one concealed weapon on him. He'd complained too much about having to store his shotgun in the thick metal lockbox embedded into the back of his truck. He'd said that if it wasn't for his electronic gear, he'd be naked walking into the airport, but he'd said it with that shit-eating grin, and now he was gone. Any minute airport security could swarm her in full riot gear, guns and batons drawn, looking for the slightest reason to violate her rights and lock her away in some undisclosed detention site where she'd never be seen by her loved ones again.

So why aren't you taking your black ass home Stormy?

The answer correlated directly to the way Lucas Beaumont made her feel, like every part of her was pure lusciousness he couldn't stop himself from playing in. That, combined with the simple freedom of just being herself, was too hard to walk away from. It was insane, but this was the time to allow for a bit of insanity; almost thirty days of it to be exact.

She just hoped Lucas returned, prayed to her ancestors that he wasn't somewhere decimating the place. Under normal circumstances he seemed like the most laid-back person, but when triggered, she'd seen what he could do, knew that he'd had a dissociative episode, believed she was capable of intervening if she saw him begin to check out. She'd worked with the most wounded and dangerous parts of folks for most of her career. The fact that Lucas's violence resided within a body the size of a small mountain did give her pause, but in the end, it was Terry's subtle reassurance that his special syringes would be available to her once they reached Oklahoma in a few hours, and Mama not-so-subtly guilt-tripping her about what could happen to Lucas if Stormy wasn't there that kept her feet moving forward.

Approaching her boarding gate, she saw a group of empty seats along the windowed wall and sat, dropping her large bag into the chair to her right. The suited man and expensively dressed woman further down the row seemed to hold a certain contempt for her purse, if their frowns were any indication. She stared them down until they turned away, and was in no way ashamed that her purse nearly filled the entire seat bottom. She had stuff she needed to have close at hand if—

She startled violently, clasping a hand over her mouth to cut off the scream that escaped when Lucas plopped down in the empty chair on her left. The whole room seemed to turn toward them with expressions of surprise and concern.

"Sorry y'all, little woman's got a fear of flying, makes her a bit twitchy, yeah."

"God, I hope we don't have to sit next to them on the plane," Stormy heard the woman who'd thrown disparaging looks at her bag whisper loudly.

Instead of glaring down the row again, she glared at Lucas. He was to blame for her agitation as well as the little flutter in her chest when she saw the twinkle in his emerald eyes. He enjoyed the fact that he'd scared her.

"I'm not a little woman, Big Bunion," she mumbled. "But compared to you, I guess mature oak trees look like twigs."

He leaned over, his large body crowding her back against the chair, his lips stopping millimeters from her ear as his hand slid from her outer to inner thigh, his fingers digging into the meaty flesh near the juncture. "Darlin', as long as you remember that I wield the hardest, most satisfying wood both sides of the Mississippi, I don't care what names you call me."

A shallow orgasm rippled up her vaginal walls. It was becoming a common response to his touch, the confident way he moved, the sexy drawl that sometimes veered toward bayou twang when he wasn't more mindful.

She crossed her legs, trapping his fingers within the seam.

"You don't know who you're messing with, do you, Lucas Beaumont? You'll learn, and I have a feeling it's gonna be the hard way."

His fingers pressed deeper. "The hardest."

She smiled. She loved flexing her sexual power with him, loved that he wasn't repelled or intimidated by it.

"I got a feeling we may be joining the mile-high club tonight darlin'."

"What makes you think I'm not already a member?"

He pulled back and frowned. "Chad...was it fucking *Chad*? I should've popped that little fucker's chest wide open when I had the chance—"

"It wasn't Chad."

"Wasn't Chad...then who the hell had you up here...?" He ended in a huff of confusion.

She struggled to hold back a smile. "A little spring break wildness. You know, back in the day it was way easier to join that club than it is today."

Sitting back, he faced forward, planted his feet wide apart and he stared off in contemplation.

"Well I'll tell you what, when we hit altitude, I'm laying you out, right there in the main aisle, so *everybody* can see, and you know what I'm bringing?" She shook her head, though he wasn't even looking at her. "The thunder. I'm bringing the *mutherfuckin'* thunder, have you coming so hard everyone on the ground will think it's raining manna from heaven." She burst out laughing. "I ain't lyin', wait and see."

The overhead speaker announced that the flight would begin boarding, and the bottom nearly dropped out of Stormy's stomach as people began forming a line at the ticket stand.

"Flying really ain't that bad, sweetness, you gotta relax, ya know?" He sat up straight, pressed his thumbs against the pointer fingers of each hand as if doing a yoga pose. *"Breeeathe…"* he intoned, closing his eyes momentarily before turning to her and smirking. "Time for the healer to heal herself."

"Wow, you're really going to mock me like that, right to my face?"

"All right in here," he said, circling his open hand inches from her nose.

She laughed. "Okay…okay, Lucas, you'll see. Like my auntie Lettie always says, some people won't believe fat meat is greasy until reality sizzles through that ass. You'll see."

She reached for her bag and stood but Lucas pulled her down into his lap, circling his arms around her like a vise. "Don't worry, Sienna Red. I promised your folks that I'd keep you safe, didn't I?"

She rested her forehead against his temple. "Yes, you did." She lifted her head and freed an arm from his hold, draping it across his shoulder and stroking the back of his neck. His left foot began to bounce just like it had that first night they'd met.

"I will be all right on the plane. You know why?"

"Why?"

"Because I'm touched by a Goddess. Right here," she said, pointing to the small circle of waxy skin at the hollow of her throat.

"Um hum, and just how does that kind of thing happen?" he asked, barely opening his eyes as he leaned in to kiss the mark.

Stormy looked over at the line of people boarding the plane; she had time to help him understand.

"When my mom was eight-and-a-half-months pregnant with me

she had a dream, woke up in the middle of the night knowing she had to get home, her *childhood* home, to have me. Daddy thought she'd lost her mind because she tore through the house pulling things from closets and drawers to put in her suitcase. Daddy said when he tried to stop her, she threw his department-issued gun at his head and he knew she was serious—Ma was afraid of guns back then. Anyway, Daddy took my brother across town to stay with my aunt, and when he got back home he tried to book a flight out but no airline would allow my mom on the plane two weeks from her due date. So, they packed up the El Dorado and headed down to Tarahouchy, Louisiana."

"Now *that's* a country-assed name."

He didn't know the half of it. Her father's family had lived in the Bay Area for three generations; he was urban through and through. But her mother's people…

"Daddy says the moment they crossed the border into Louisiana the weather turned from *can't-catch-a-cloud-in-the -sky* to *Armageddon-in-the-form-of-a-storm*. For an hour there was nonstop thunder and lightning, wind so strong they felt the car pushed across the flooding road. Ma didn't even know she was in labor until she felt a strong urge to push. Her water had broken sometime during the storm, but it was so humid and she was so afraid, she didn't even notice."

Lucas's knee had calmed and there were only a handful of people left to be checked in.

"We should head to the gate."

He held her tighter, watching her intently. "Go 'head on, woman, what happens next?"

She smiled.

"Daddy went into cop mode—his focus goes laser sharp and he's all action. He laid my mom down on the front seat and they brought me into the world. My dad swears on a stack of Bibles, my Ma on the souls of her ancestors, that the moment I inhaled my first breath the storm dissipated, and they say my first cry sounded exactly like the wail of the storm. My mother believes the storm breathed life into me, so they named me Stormy Sinclair Redmond."

Lucas eased her off his lap, grabbed her purse and hand, and walked them toward the gate.

"Just so I'm clear, what you're telling me is that you were born some kind of weather witch?"

"No, what I'm trying to tell you is that I have no problem flying, I love being in the sky, even when it's turbulent, but others, maybe not so much."

They boarded and took their seats immediately after entering the plane. It was the first time Stormy had ever sat in first class. Sitting next to the window seat, she sank into its buttery softness, practically feeling privilege drape over her shoulders like a mantle. "Order me a double shot of bourbon, will you? It usually makes the flight easier."

He shook his head. "Nope, I want to experience your not-afraid-to-fly terror just so I can tease you later, and when I've got my ammunition, I'll get you that bourbon."

He was so condescending. She smirked and shrugged.

"Buckle up," he said, pointing her at her seat belt.

"Yeah, you do the same. I'm anticipating a bumpy ride."

He looked around her and peered at the sky through the small window.

"Blue skies as far as the eye can see." He smiled.

Big Country gripped both armrests as his stomach dropped toward his clenched asshole. The plane had to have plummeted a good twenty feet before it leveled off, swaying sickly toward the left and overcorrecting toward the right. The storm had gathered slowly as they'd ascended, clear skies darkening, gray clouds hemorrhaging water. They couldn't seem to escape the effects of the storm despite the steady climb.

The plane dropped again, people screamed, a baby cried.

Like everyone except for the woman beside him, Big Country had his oxygen mask perched over his mouth and nose.

Stormy turned to him, her brown eyes wild and radiant.

"It's like riding a wave of energy."

No, *fuck no,* it wasn't, he wanted to yell, but the plane shuddered, he reached out, pressing his hand against the seat in front of him to steady himself.

Stormy turned back to the window, touching her palm to it. The power that churned outside, terrifying everyone else, was alive within her, and she looked at peace. For a heart-stopping moment, he felt it, felt her spirit alive in him, felt connected, felt her peace. He peered over her shoulder, and damned if he didn't see what looked like wisps of vapor reaching toward her, winks of light flashing inside.

He blinked twice and faced forward.

Maybe he wasn't getting enough oxygen to the brain…or maybe she *was* a weather witch.

Either way, truth rolled through his awareness like thunder; the peace he'd sought for so many weeks, that sense of connection, it was there when Stormy was around, his soul felt it, felt settled. He liked the feeling, liked having her, didn't want either taken away from him any time soon.

He tensed at his train of thought. That thinking was probably how every man in creation foolishly began relinquishing their control to something they would eventually get around to calling love. He wasn't falling for it, refused to lose his God-given good sense to have her destroy his life in ways only a woman could.

The plane's engine vibrated as if it was about to drop out.

"All right now," he said commandingly. "You've had your fun time in the sky, now tell the storm goodbye so everyone can get to where they're going in one piece."

She rounded on him as if she was going to rip off his oxygen mask and punch him in the face. "I'm not doing anything, this doesn't happen every time…it's just been so long," she said, as if all hell breaking loose had no effect on her. "Plus, the time for intervention would have been before the plane took off. All we can do now is ride it out."

Soon after her words, the pilot came on the intercom and informed them that they were making an emergency landing in Albuquerque, New Mexico. The closer they got to the ground, the more the storm abated.

By the time they touched down and taxied into the terminal the sky was baby blue, the sunshine bright and optimistic.

Inside, the plane reeked of vomit and sweat and a fair number of other odors Big Country didn't want to contemplate. Unbuckling his seatbelt, he leaped up despite a flight attendant directing him to stay seated.

"Darlin', if that door ain't open by the time I find my shit, I will rip a hole through that motherfucker and dare you sons of bitches to charge me for it."

There was a smattering of applause. Others also prepared to depart, the flight staff too harried to do anything but work to get the cabin door open.

Stormy looked embarrassed as she reached for her purse beneath the seat and stood to exit. "Sorry about that, I didn't know it was going to be so bad for everyone," she said to the confused flight attendant. Lucas ushered her out of the plane ahead of him.

"I just wanted to feel what it was like to be in the heart of the storm again," she said.

"And get your revenge on me."

"No, I wanted to share it with you."

He refused to be warmed by the notion. Instead, he pulled her into the circle of his arm as they navigated the crowded airport.

There was a spot of blood on the back of her hand. It was a perfect circle, the undried center still glistened with dying energy. Delilah released the steering wheel and brought her hand to her mouth, sucked until she removed the spot.

Wasn't there scripture about feasting on the flesh of one's enemies, she wondered opening the folder on Lucas. If so, she would gorge herself on Stormy Redmond's flesh and dance on her dead remains once she'd won Lucas. It was infuriating that the whore had used the pretense of helping to undermine her relationship with Lucas. That level of subterfuge was masterful, and Delilah hadn't seen it coming. She'd never been in love before, nor had she had enough dealings with other women to know that they were truly as deceitful as the Good Shepherd warned.

Men are simple servants of the Lord, daughter, but every woman in creation, including you, bears the taint of the unclean, and it is only through my guidance that you are saved—so hold close to me, do not stray and you will one day have a place at my side in the halls of heaven.

She no longer wanted nor needed a place in heaven with the Good Shepherd, not when she could have a place on earth with the man God intended her to have.

Reading through the information on Lucas, she saw that he had wealth on top of handsomeness and was trained to kill and protect...*like her*, he was trained to kill and protect.

She smiled. She'd had no reason to protect anything but the Shepherd's interest before, but now she would protect Lucas, their love and their future, and that unequivocally meant severing the binds Stormy Redmond was attempting to use to tether Lucas's soul.

Looking at her watch, she determined she had time to make one phone call before checking in at the airport. She believed Stormy was forcing Lucas to take her to his family's home; the whore would know that a potential wife must be accepted and approved of by a man's family.

If one wins over the family, one wins the man.

Delilah planned to win it all.

She would show Lucas's only sister—she flipped through the pages —Merlee, *what a silly name*, she would show Merlee that the mud-colored whore was no more than a disciple of evil who would tear through Lucas's life until he was a husk of a man with no chance at redemption.

Picking up the dead man's phone and retrieving his severed thumb, Delilah placed the digit on the button and unlocked his phone. Dialing the number she'd memorized minutes after Lucas had given it to her, she waited for his voicemail. Lucas rarely answered his phone, perhaps the whore kept it from him.

"Hello?"

Her heart soared, a rush of satisfaction she hadn't experienced since being in his arms overcame her. "My beloved…"

"Delilah darlin', is that you?"

It's me, she thought, *it will always be me.*

"Darlin', if you're there let me know, I've been awful worried about you."

She nodded and smiled.

He was worried about her; no person in existence had ever worried about her well-being, not even the ones who'd left her in the care of her father a lifetime ago. "I'm here, beloved, I'm here."

"That's good to know, sweetness, but I gotta say, I'm feeling some kind of way about not knowing where you are, especially after you took so many steps to know where I was at all times. That wasn't real fair, I had to balance things out."

"I understand, my love. I believe I saw your friends looking for me when I went to find you. I'm sure you can understand when I say I wasn't feeling particularly social."

"Understood. I don't particularly like socializing with those pushy bastards either."

"And what about the whore of deceit and illusions—do you like socializing with her?"

Delilah heard a movement on the other side of the line.

"Wouldn't say *like,* darlin', more like forced to, now that you've gone and set fire to her house."

Delilah shrugged. "It's her destiny to burn in hell. I was only giving her a glimpse of what awaits her in the afterlife. Is she with you?"

"I'm sure she's around, but I had to get away to speak to you in private, I miss hearing your voice, darlin'. Didn't want any distractions, you know?"

"I know, my love, I know. Forces are working hard to keep us apart but trust me, the clarity I bring will destroy any spell that witch has bound you in."

Movement proceeded her beloved's voice again. When he spoke he sounded winded, pained.

She had to get to him; he was fighting for their love but wasn't strong enough to break the whore's hold on him. "Tell me where you are, beloved, I will come to you," she said, attempting to compel him.

"No, I need you safe and out of harm's way, darlin', go to the place I left the tracker and my friends will find you. They'll bring you up the mountain, protect you like they're protecting your friend Cornelius. He was awful alone, you know, half-starved and scared when we found him."

"He's an idiot," she snapped, reined in her temper and decided to take a gamble. "Besides, how can I be sure your friends Zeus and Sabrina won't kill me in my sleep if I go up there?"

"Because Mama won't let them. She's real protective of those in her care. I'm sure she'd take real good care of a woman as devoted to me as you are."

"Yes, well, I beg to differ, Almaya Hendricks is no better than the two murderers she's harboring. You really do have to make much better choices in the company you keep, my love."

"Don't I know it," he muttered.

She looked at her watch. "Fight, beloved, tell the whore she cannot have you and fight until we are able to see each other again."

She disconnected the call, leaving the thumb and phone under the seat before sanitizing the car and abandoning it. She now had less than an hour to get to the airport terminal. She'd have to rush to catch her flight, but she knew God would ensure that she was on it, she had a man and a future to save. She would not fail at either, at any cost.

Hopefully, that idiot acolyte Cornelius wouldn't fail either.

Lucas refused to board the connecting flight to Oklahoma, even after she'd promised the trip would be better if she had a couple of drinks or took a sleeping pill before takeoff. He didn't budge but continued to silently side-eye her, acting as if she posed some kind of credible threat all the way to the car rental agency and out to the rental truck.

Even though Lucas hadn't criticized her explicitly, she felt that old tension rise, the one that came from feeling as if she had failed in some way, had done something unforgivably wrong. She felt the need to push aside the elation she'd experienced and put him in a better mood.

She refused.

Lucas would come to his own conclusions, she thought, climbing into yet another oversized truck. He'd either continue to have an attitude and end their contract or embrace the spirit of adventure they'd developed. Either way, her journey would continue, with or without him.

Relaxing into the seat was akin to relaxing into her life right now. She watched Lucas sync his phone to the truck's audio system, lifted a brow at him as twangy country music filled the interior. The look he threw back at her dared her to say something. When she didn't, he navigated the truck out of the lot and eventually onto the highway.

Idiot didn't even know she loved this band.

They rode for an hour in silence before Lucas pulled into a truck stop, filled the tank and loaded up on enough snacks to fill a full-sized grocery bag. As he reached for his phone, Stormy sat in confusion as he called to reserve a cottage for the night at some place called Golden Trails Luxury Resort.

"Why are we stopping for the night? I thought we only had a couple of hours before we were at your sister's fiancé's house."

"It's late, I'm hungry, and I got to blow off some steam—you all right with that?" he gritted out. "I already texted Merlee, she'll be expecting us tomorrow afternoon."

Placing the overflowing grocery bag between them, he was all frowns as he started the engine.

"You are moody as hell," she muttered, seeing how he ran hot and cold, open then remote.

He shut off the engine. "Excuse me, darlin', I didn't quite catch that."

"Oh, you heard me."

A look that bordered on disgust passed over his face, but she didn't care. Backing down and acquiescing, tiptoeing around a man's feelings, getting along for the sake of getting along…that was a thing of the past. She didn't care how big and bad and dangerous he could be, she was here for adventure and support with no obligation to navigate his emotions. They even had a contract that said as much.

"Just like a woman," Lucas practically growled. The level of resentment directed at her was out of proportion with anything she had said or done. "Something doesn't go as planned and you wanna say I'm the one with the problem, yeah? I'm the one who should lay down like some docile bitch and just let you have your way…because your pussy rains manna from heaven?"

He snorted. "Get the fuck outta here with that shit. I don't get down on my knees for nobody. No woman will ever make a necklace out of my balls and parade around for everyone to see and judge me a fool. That ain't the kind of time we go'n have on this here trip. You think because we fuck so well together, I'll lose all good sense? I've been fucking since I was a kid, I know that shit well, so don't ever think you got the magic pussy that's gonna control *any* fucking thing I do."

He literally stopped her breath.

The vitriol he'd just heaved on her, the sheer maliciousness—hatefulness—of it, made her want to annihilate him, to literally tear him apart and leave him dying at her feet, alone, terrified, in pain, and without hope. The urge for violence nearly overwhelmed her, pushed to be set free with a primal scream. She clenched her jaw to keep it at bay, clenched her hands to stop herself from lunging for his throat and trying to rip his spinal cord free from his body.

Her thoughts and emotions were terrifying. And then she knew, she *knew* that the most visceral experience of rage she'd ever experienced in her thirty-nine years wasn't even hers, it was a projection of Lucas's rage.

Closing her eyes, she took deep breaths and let the chaotic emotions rush through her like water through a rain stick. Imagined nullifying it into the earth, knowing that whatever Lucas had been through in his life, it had overwhelmed his mind and nearly ripped his soul from his body.

Shit. As awful as it felt to be the one he shitted on, the ugliness he'd spewed was actually better than him disconnecting from it, from himself. She had been dishonest with him as well as herself when she agreed to not psychoanalyze. She was who she was; all her years of training and experience, that couldn't be undone, but what she intended to do with her knowledge, with his pain, was to allow him to continue managing it in the best way he could. She'd moved beyond sacrificing herself for the well-being of others. That was a slow death she would not endure again.

Opening her eyes, she turned and looked at him.

He was larger-than-life in his anger, yet she saw his spirit, saw that at his core, he was a caring man, relatively speaking.

Leaning over, she placed a hand on his knee, felt his muscles tense. "Did it make you feel better, talking to me like I'm the most disgusting piece of shit to ever roll into your life...because I called you *moody*? You are moody, Lucas, moody as hell and you know it, but that's neither here nor there. What just came out of your mouth has nothing to do with me and everything to do with you, and *I* know that. I also know I didn't deserve *any* of it. Our contract is officially over...which is probably a relief for you. I'll keep my promise to Mama, though, I'm with you until the situation with your family is resolved and after that our journey ends."

Sitting back in her seat, she pulled her phone from her purse and texted her aunt Letty in Louisiana to let her know she'd be visiting in a couple of days. She smiled at her aunt's response, aware that Lucas hadn't moved an inch in the moments following her words. It wasn't until his own phone rang that his body reanimate. She looked over at him as he reached toward his phone, saw that his eyes had been locked on her before he looked at the screen. He frowned, hitting speaker.

"Hello?" he answered, voice rough and impatient.

"My beloved...."

Reaching for his backpack, Lucas pulled out a laptop and spoke with Delilah as if he cared about her while motioning Stormy to stay quiet. She watched him retrieve information on the number and location Delilah called from, did a background check on the owner of the phone, and uttered a muted curse when he linked the phone's owner to some organization called the Consortium.

Her sense of adventure restored, Stormy had no problem remaining silent until Delilah began referring to her as all kinds of whores. On the heels of Lucas's verbal battering, it was too much. She opened her mouth to respond and Lucas's hand fastened over it, covering half her face. She bit him, and he snatched his hand away, but she remained silent, understanding that Delilah was more than the strange and awkward woman she met at the boutique; she was certifiable, dangerous, and without remorse.

After his call with Delilah, Lucas called the information back to Terry, who said he would be sending two Brood members to the location Delilah called from.

"Fucking women," Lucas muttered, disconnecting from Terry and storing his electronics in his backpack.

"Actually, I think you and Delilah would be perfect together," Stormy said, smiling at him with faux humor. "Beloved."

He glared at her, reached out to start the truck, and pulled onto the highway without a word.

They sped down Highway 40 in virtual silence, but the quiet didn't put Big Country less on edge. On the contrary, despite the comfort of being on the road and passing familiar scenery, he felt on the verge of chewing off his own tongue.

Stormy Redmond was a cold piece of work. She had the gall to munch on his snacks, sing along to his music, tap her pretty feet on the dashboard as she let her hand dance through the air outside the open window.

Yeah, she was having a good old time, just not with him.

"Oh my God," she shouted, sitting up in her seat and pointing.

He jumped, body gearing up for battle. They'd crossed the border into Texas over fifty miles ago so there was no telling what kind of good-old-boy trouble they were likely to run into. "It's an armadillo, a live one, and oh my God it's huge! Usually they're just dead husks on the side of the road when I've seen them before."

He didn't respond, and good thing, because when they'd gone too far for her to see it any longer, she relaxed back into her seat, rested her elbow on the arm rest and let her fingers play through the wind again, humming along to his *Rising Appalachia* album.

Soon they'd be on the other side of Amarillo in the small town of Yulee, where they could register at the main building before heading to the luxury cottage a mile away. He'd often stopped at this resort during his biannual trips back home. Hopefully Stormy wouldn't think he'd booked the place to impress her, which he had. She'd obviously wanted to be done with him and their adventure, so now, impressing her was the last thing on his mind. The sooner he took care of his folks, the sooner him and Stormy could part ways.

That was the best outcome he could ever hope to envision.

He expected that any minute now, Stormy would make some demand, or attempt some manipulation. He expected some kind of meltdown, but unlike him, she was having a good time with her own fucking company. He ran his fingers through his hair in frustration. He wasn't used to this shit! Why didn't she just act like a normal woman, why didn't she do something, so he could justify his earlier tirade? Hell, she had him over here acting like *he* was the irrational woman and that wasn't him…at least, it hadn't been until her.

He rubbed his forehead. The tongue-lashing he gave her had nothing to do with an episode, he'd been fully in control of his mind, if not his emotions. None of it made sense…

Then his stomach rumbled. *Of course*, he was just hungry! He was hungry and…*and* he needed sex; it usually smoothed out the rough edges when he was out of sorts, and this trip had put him so out he almost forgot what it meant to be sorted.

He eased back in his seat. Get some food and some sex, and life would be right as rain. *Yeah boy*, he thought. They'd check in, store their gear, and head over to Teats and Meat for dinner, and for him, a bit of entertainment of a sexual nature. Stormy sure as shit wasn't going to give him what he needed tonight, or ever.

He rubbed at the sudden sharp pain in his chest following the thought. Maybe he was sick. He'd have to go to the doctor when he got back to California for real.

Once they'd checked into the resort's main hotel, they drove up a slight incline along the tree-lined road before parking in the space in front of cottage 151. Handing Stormy her card key, he retrieved their belongings as she bounded up the five stairs and entered the one-bedroom unit.

"This place is awesome," Stormy said, wandering back into the living room as he made his way inside.

She opened cabinets, turned her eyes on the gas stove, drew her hand along the marble counter top of the kitchen island, darted to the sliding doors along the back wall of the living-room. "There's a river and a trail right off the back patio… I never thought I'd love to hear myself say this, but maybe me and my girls should come back here for a Texas vacation."

This woman had the unmitigated gall to want to bring other folks to *his* spot, a spot he'd only wanted to share with her.

"Get your purse if you're coming with me," he snapped. "I'm getting hungry, and trust me darlin', you won't like me when I'm hungry."

"I don't like you now," she said, retrieving her luggage and going into the bathroom. He clenched and unclenched his fists and rolled his neck to ease the stress that had nothing to do with an episode and everything to do with his growing frustration. When he heard the shower turn on, he sat down on the couch and let his head fall into his hands, using the time to quiet his mind and emotions.

In less than fifteen minutes, Stormy exited the bathroom wearing a short red dress that clung to every hip, dip, and curve her body possessed. The V-neck displayed way more cleavage than he was comfortable with her sharing. Walking right past him in golden sandals, she picked his truck keys off the table and walked outside.

"Move your ass, Lucas, you're not the only one hungry already!"

A long horn blow was followed by two shorter bursts. He gritted his teeth and fair shook with the need to drag her ass back in here and fuck her into submission, fuck them both back to a place of languid serenity. But that wasn't going to happen; his reckless mouth had seen to that.

Slamming the cabin door, he stomped to the truck and tried to pretend calm, tried to pretend he wasn't fazed by the shift in their dynamic, especially when Stormy sincerely seemed to be lighter, more vibrant, now that their contract had ended.

Maybe that was her goal once she'd seen what lived inside him; maybe she'd looked for a way out of their contract, and like a fool, his temper had provided her one.

Arriving at Teats and Meat, Big Country felt well on his way to coming back to himself when he opened the door to the building and was assailed by loud music and a packed house. Closing the door behind Stormy, he placed a hand on her lower back and navigated her through the entryway with two decorative slot machines, a totem pole, and a steer head above swinging saloon doors.

The building dated back to the town's inception over one hundred and fifty years ago, but about three decades past, Claudius Felton and his wife Missy Ann expanded the existing saloon to include a restaurant, dance floor, and a small stage for whatever entertainment they had for the night.

"Oh good Lord," Stormy muttered as she eyed the staff moving about the place. Teats Tuesday was in full effect, which meant the male and female waiters were all topless, glittery silver star pasties covering their areolas and nipples.

Big Country grinned as he led Stormy to the bar, folks parting to let them pass freely. It was a privilege of his size. People didn't always comprehend how massive he was, but up close all illusions were shattered.

A few feet from the bar, Big Country barked like a slavering wolf, catching the attention of the bartender and startling the people around him. "Who dat at the bar scaring the pretty ladies away?" he called out.

Claudius Lee grinned, resting his gnarled hands on his hips. "Big Country Beaumont—boy, where you been? We was expecting you to come through two months ago."

Big Country reached across the bar and shook the old man's hand. "I got caught up in some Brood business, you know how it is."

"Still messing around with Almaya and her crazy-assed Choctaw, huh?" Claude groused. "You're too damn smart for it, is all I'm saying. Those two will get the lot of you killed one day."

"We all got to go sometime."

"Ain't that the ever-loving truth," Claude said, flexing gnarled fingers that looked a little more arthritic than the last time Big Country was here. Shifting his attention to Stormy—more accurately Stormy's breasts—Claude smiled. "You know, darlin', you ever want a job away from this meathead, just call old Claude here. I cain't pay you as much as he does, but I can surely save you from losing your heart to a man who ain't interested in finding it."

Big Country tensed, remembering Stormy's reaction when he'd mistaken her for a pro. Instead of laying into ol' Claude, she leaned into the bar, the motion causing her cleavage to bulge from the neck line of her dress, and Claude's eyes did much the same.

Big Country didn't blame Claude; he didn't. Stormy's breasts were large and magnificent, sculpted by a generous God, a gift to mankind; but even knowing that, Big Country wanted to blacken the eye of every man looking Stormy's way.

There are bare titties on display all over the place, Big Country thought, *and you sons of bitches better find them or I'll pluck your eyeballs right out of your worthless skulls and pop them like grapes*. He tried to transmit the thoughts through his glare, and sure enough, many heads turned elsewhere.

"…I see all these women looking at him like he is the second coming," Stormy said. "But our business is just the job—"

The hell…

"—and we part ways the moment it's done."

Damn right we do, he thought savagely.

"My name's Stormy, and I'm what you call an *Honorary Brood Mate*, in for the job and then back to my life."

What was she playing at? It was as if she was auditioning for some deadly assassin role in a D-list espionage movie.

"And what's your specialty, beautiful?" Claude asked, flashing the dimple in his weathered cheek. "Poison, guns, explosives?"

"None of the above," she said, leaning in more. As if her body were magnetic, Claude leaned toward her. "My job is to simply devour men's souls."

Big Country rolled his eyes and spoke in a flat emotionless voice. "Speaking of eating, what do I have to do to get some food around here?"

Claude pulled back from Stormy and waved one of the waitresses over. "All your regulars?" Claude asked.

Big Country nodded.

"And what about you, temptress?"

"Whatever you think will satisfy me," Stormy said.

"Oh, for fuck's sake," Big Country said, pulling Stormy away from the bar and escorting her up to the private booth upstairs, overlooking the small stage and dance floor from a shadowed corner.

They virtually ignored each other, listening to the DJ-delivered music and watching the dancers below until their meal came. The ate in silence, which was just fine by him; the less they said to each other the less chance there was for things going sideways again. The last thing he needed was for her to adventure her way downstairs and slide up to one of those good old boys whose eyes kept straying to her curves, to her lips. He took a deep breath and sat back, wiping his mouth with the linen napkin.

He didn't need to have an episode in Claude's place of business, but any one of these motherfuckers try to do more than look, he'd light this bitch up, tear it down to its very foundation…so it was best that they continue to quietly ignore each other, best that—

Stormy scooted out of the booth and stood.

Reflexively, he grabbed her wrist when she came around to his side.

"What you doing, Sienna Red?" he asked, holding on, looking down at the table, trying to stay grounded. He would not lose his shit again because of her...but it felt like he was losing his shit again, because of her.

"Let go of me. Now." She snatched her arm back and he released it. The fire in Stormy's eyes was raw and true, no more of that polite-stranger act, no more of that treating-him-like-he-didn't-exist bull-shit. He leaned back, feeling inexplicably at ease.

Stormy saw his reaction and composed herself. "I have to go to the bathroom. Is that okay with you?"

He nodded and watched her leave.

What kind of craziness was it that had him wanting drama from her when it was a quality that he'd steered clear of in women. Those early years with Belle Mère had taught him well and taught him early. He knocked back the last of his whiskey to calm the bile rising in his gut. He hated thinking about the insanity of his parents.

"Hey lover boy, I've missed you."

Big Country looked to his right to see Angel enter the VIP section. She was one of the few waitresses here who offered additional services for a fee.

"I must be in heaven because God has sent me his beautiful Angel."

She laughed, pulling a chair from the table opposite his booth and directed him to sit in it. He hesitated, believing Stormy would lose her shit if she found him up here getting the kind of lap dance that always gave Bubba a decent release.

But he and Stormy didn't have a contract anymore, she was here to do a job, ain't that what she said?

Grinning, he rose and sat in the seat, widening his thighs. He watched as Angel leaned over the rail and motioned to the DJ. The music shifted, and she turned back to him, rolling hips clad in tight glittery silver hot pants. The anticipation he felt had nothing to do with Angel and everything to do with Stormy's return.

Even Bubba, who usually perked up the minute Lucas laid eyes on

Angel's slim body, was patently uninterested and unresponsive. Angel danced in front of him, Bubba slept, not waking up when Angel's tits were nearly touching Lucas's lips, didn't even stir when Angel turned and ground her ass against him.

Big Country was in the process of pushing her off of him when Stormy walked over to them, lifting a brow at the sight of Angel on his lap. Shrugging, she dragged another chair from the empty table and placed it beside Lucas's. She sat, reached over and pulled his piece of cigar from his shirt pocket and placed it between her lips, then smiled up at Angel.

"Well, aren't you the prettiest thing in Texas I've seen all day," Stormy drawled. "If I'da known Claude had such hands-on entertainment, I'da made sure Lucas brought you to us sooner."

Big Country looked at Stormy as if she'd lost her mind. *What the fuck was she playing at*, he thought, frowning, when she reached over and pulled his wallet from his pocket and put $50 on the booth table. *What the fuck?*

Angel shifted from Big Country and gave her full attention to Stormy, dancing in front of her before backing her ass up and wiggling it against Stormy's lap. Pressing her back into Stormy's front, Angel reached around and gripped the back of Stormy's head, turning to expose the side of her neck and placing a kiss there. The softness, the true desire Lucas saw in Angel's eyes, made him wonder for the first time if she really even liked men. He'd never cared before; a lap dance was a lap dance and getting head was getting head.

"Place another hundred on the table and you can take me home for the night, beautiful. I'll make you feel things this one never dreamed of," Angel said, waving a dismissive hand toward him.

"Get out," Big Country said, standing. "Get the *fuck* out, you traitorous cow, grinding your ass on my woman like you ain't got no home training. What's wrong with you?" He pulled Stormy from under Angel and placed her behind him. "Go on now," he said, motioning Angel toward the exit.

Bemused, Angel snatched the money off the table and left, but not before turning to blow Stormy a kiss.

"Get!" Big Country shouted over Angel's laughter.

"So, it was fine for you to have your fun but not me?" Stormy asked calmly, but there was fire in her eyes. His emotions were too volatile to argue with her right now.

Peeling $150 from his wallet, he left the money beside his empty platter, grabbed Stormy's forearm and pulled her back downstairs and through the dancing crowd, ignoring her struggles to break free.

A shaggy-haired blond man latched onto Stormy's waist and tried to pull her into a slow dance.

The level of pure disrespect he was facing tonight was out of control.

Lucas yanked Stormy behind him and crowded the other man's space.

"Motherfucker, do you see me? Do I look like I'm somebody to be fucked with right now?"

"This ain't about you. Looks like the lady's not ready to leave, looks like she wants to be shown a good time and you ain't the man she wants to have it with."

Big Country's hand shot out and wrapped around the man's throat, lifting him until the tips of his toes scraped the floor.

"Let him down, son. Wes is drunk, he don't mean no harm," Claude called out from the edge of the dance floor, a shotgun cradled in his arms. A few of the locals stood behind him and looked ready for a fight.

This was Texas, after all.

"If another motherfucker tries to get between me and this woman, Claude, I will level this bitch to its foundation, burying all these sons of bitches in the rubble."

"Fair enough," Claude replied.

The man he had by the throat went lax and Big Country let his unconscious body fall to the floor.

Stormy tried to push Big Country out of the way, but he didn't move, not till she was rushing toward the exit without him.

CHAPTER 9

*T*hunder rolled overhead.

The smattering of people milling in the front of the building didn't stop Big Country from spotting Stormy immediately, her red dress a flame, a beacon engulfed by darkness as she moved farther away from him. His truck was parked in the remotest part of the parking lot. Cursing the distance between them, he knew he had to get to her before she reached the truck. She had his keys and she'd leave him stranded out here without looking back.

Hearing the chirp of the remote, seeing the flash of the truck's lights, Big Country sprinted forward, furious that she'd forced him to chase after her ass, furious that he wanted her to stay. He spun her around just as she lifted her hand toward the handle.

The slap that flowed like a choreographed ending to his action landed solidly against his cheek, freezing him where he stood.

A jagged fissure of lightning cracked the dark sky open, unleashing a torrent of water.

"*Don't* touch me!" Stormy shouted over the downpour. "I am sick of you touching me like you own me!"

She'd hit him.

She'd. Fucking. Hit. Him.

"Maybe we should make a contract about you keeping your hands to yourself, but we can't do that, can we; not when the contract man always breaks his own agreements. Why create another contract with you, your fucking liar!" she shrieked, rainwater streaming down her face, saturating her body, transforming her dress into a crimson stain upon her skin.

"*I'm* a liar?" he asked.

She retreated until her back collided with the truck.

"Thing is, darlin', I was *always* a man of my word, *stayed* in control of my goddamn emotions until you." He grabbed her again, forced her around and pressed the front of her body into the truck. He stepped forward and molded himself along the length of her backside.

"It's you," he growled, grinding his dick into her ass. His vision blurred as rain slid into his eyes.

Pinning her hips with his pelvis, he kicked her ankles, pushing them wider but not too wide, just far enough apart for him to access the parts of her he didn't have rights to anymore. "It's you," he muttered again, unzipping his jeans, and shoving the material of her dress up over her ass.

She didn't have on any panties, not even a damn G-string.

There would be no barriers between them.

Working Bubba loose, Big Country slid his dick between the silken juncture of Stormy's thighs. The combination of rainwater and warm liquid gushing from her core turned Bubba slippery as an eel.

"It's *always* fucking you," he muttered pumping his hips into the narrow seam.

"Lucas—"

"No."

The time for words was done.

Gripping her hair, he forced her head back, kissed her as if the air she breathed was the only oxygen his lungs could survive on. He kissed her savagely, consuming her, as he pumped his hips, his tip colliding with her engorged clit over and over. She arched back, pushing her ass deeper into his groin, demanding more.

"You feel this shit, right, Stormy?" he growled, letting her ride

Bubba's length, quickening the slide until her whimpers became moans. "Don't want my touch, though, huh? Want me to stop, that's what ya say?"

She tried to shake her head, but he tightened his grip.

"Who's the fucking liar now?" he asked, adjusting Bubba so that the tip breached Stormy's vagina. She made a needy sound, a confused unfulfilled sound, trying to push Bubba deeper.

Big Country withdrew until he was almost outside of her, smacked the side of her ass and let the sting linger before he surged into her, lifting her off her feet and made the truck rock with the power of his thrust. Stormy screamed, thunder took the sound and rolled it across the heavens.

Big Country rested his forehead against the nape of Stormy's neck as her pussy squeezed on Bubba, milking him of the seed that could fertilize her womb, and he wanted to see that, wanted to see her body swell and ripen as it provided the nutrients to make his seed grow strong inside her.

There were no barriers between them.

The realization hit him like a fentanyl high, and he thrust harder, unrepentant in his addiction. He craved Stormy Redmond, longed for her fucking pussy even though he was still deep inside it.

Stormy's head fell forward onto the truck.

She was panting as if she'd been running from him her whole life, as if every step meant to distance herself from him led them right to this moment.

Even though rain and wind whipped around them, it felt as if they'd shifted beyond time and space, inhabited a place where they were one consciousness, one light merging, expanding, then contracting down to a pure sensation of pleasure, and he had to be deeper, feel every part of her, wanted the deepest parts of her to feel him. He needed her to know him, crave every fiber of his being, good, bad, and one day, maybe even the ugly.

Stroking her abdomen, he slipped his hand up and sank his fingers into her breast, her heart hammering inside his palm.

Using the strength of his body to suspend Stormy off the ground, impaled on Bubba, he placed his hands outside of hers, gripped the truck, and thrust deeper. Stormy's shout was rough and guttural, but his sienna-red woman didn't tell him to stop, didn't tell him to be gentle, didn't relent, she arched, signaling it was okay to go deeper still. Bubba swelled and lengthened at the challenge, stretching his skin as if ready to break through it, transforming into something only Stormy's pussy had the power to command.

Big Country pounded into her then, Bubba's head colliding into the furthest boundaries of Stormy's womb. She was sobbing now, begging, and he retreated but he couldn't take pity.

He reached down and angled her body just right, jackhammered into her, pulling back until his tip just barely breached her nether lips and surged back into her, Bubba hitting a spot that made her wail and buck as her body imploded in orgasm. Her words turned to desperate mutterings, but he didn't relent, he fucked her hard and fast, balls drawing tighter each time he came into contact with that inner barrier. He shouted into the storm as he burst inside of Stormy, pounding his seed into her womb until he was too weak to do anything beyond breathe and stand upright, the truck supporting them both.

He gave her all he knew how to give and didn't fear that he'd have nothing left of himself. For the first time he understood that giving didn't always mean losing.

Unwilling to retreat from her body, Big Country stayed locked inside her, at peace in the heavy rain. Stormy rested her head on his forearm, covered his hands with hers and held on, too. He felt her smile against his arm.

"I'm going to lose my license fucking around with you."

Looking over the truck's edge, he saw that the weather had chased everyone inside the shelter of the building, so her license was safe for the moment.

"Well I've lost my ever-loving mind fucking around with you, so darlin, I think we're pretty much even."

She chuckled, leaned her head back and kissed him, then shimmied down his body until her feet rested on solid ground. Pulling out of her completely, he eased her dress down her hips and walked her around to the passenger side of the truck. Lifting her into the cab, he couldn't avoid the temptation to smack her on the ass.

He walked to the driver's side of the truck feeling light on his feet. The worm of discontent dogging him for weeks was gone and his old spirit had returned. Peeling his shirt over his head and stepping out of his jeans, he tossed them into the back of the truck and got into the cab.

"What exactly do you have against wearing clothes?" Stormy asked as he reached for the ignition.

"Not a thing, darlin', it's my nature. If there's nothing else I've learned, you gotta live as free as you can as often as you can."

She rested her head on the back of the seat and watched him, smiled, and closed her eyes. By God, she was beautiful.

"Don't drift off just yet."

Her eyes fluttered open and he tapped the steering-wheel, found himself uttering words he never thought he'd say.

"I know our contract has ended, and you'd be right to not enter into another with me because I'm clear, I would break that bitch, too...no doubt. But I want to propose something else, something downright foolish."

"Like?"

"Like we agree that life is what it is between us until we decided it ain't. No contracts, no stipulations, just us."

Her eyes turned all soft and smiley, and his chest tightened from the impact of it.

She nodded, leaned toward him, and sealed their fates with a kiss.

Driving back to the cottage, Big Country looked out along the long dark road they were traveling and couldn't immediately recall a time he'd felt more at ease.

Stormy awoke when Lucas lifted her from the truck.

Half-opening her eyes, she rested her head on his shoulder as he carried her into the house. This felt good, felt right, like they were meant to move through this moment in life together, no matter where they ended up.

Once he'd navigated her inside the entryway, Lucas sat her on her feet and kissed her back to wakefulness, laughing softly when she reached for the band of his underwear. He secured her arms at her side and turned her in the direction of the bedroom.

"Go on, take your shower while I call and check in with Merlee."

Stormy looked toward the bedroom. Darkness and shadows coalesced beyond the open double doors, rooting her to the spot.

Delilah had broken into her home and tried to burn it down because she'd believed Stormy an obstacle to happiness with Lucas. Delilah had also inhabited the home of the elderly couple she'd killed and buried in their own yard. It wasn't just paranoia that had Stormy imagining the woman inside the dark room, waiting to gut her or cut her throat.

"Um, shouldn't you secure the perimeter or something like that?" she asked Lucas. "Make sure no one—Delilah, for instance—is in the house waiting to kill us?"

"I don't know where you get this *us* from. I'm her beloved; it's your ass she's trying to take out."

"Fuck off," Stormy muttered, watching shadows shift in the bedroom. "But for real, Lucas…"

He laughed.

"We're good, darlin', see that device on the table?" She'd seen the matte black cylinder in the jumble of electronics he'd pulled from his backpack earlier. "That there is a Big Luc customization. It scans, monitors, and records heat signatures as well as atmospheric changes in a specified area. If someone would've entered the cottage without this on them—" he held up his cell phone. "—a few things would have happened. One, my phone would've alerted me. I could have hit this button and the cylinder would've released a gas that knocked our uninvited guest unconscious. With this button I could have sent an alert to the nearest police station. I don't usually include the police in my business, though," he said, winking at her.

"You think you're pretty smart, huh?"

"Darlin', I'm a damn genius, and that's the truth."

"All right, Mr. Modest, if you're so smart, why didn't you know Delilah was tracking you?"

"Real talk? Arrogance…and distraction. If I hadn't been distracted I'd have checked my truck's data systems and known it was there, but honestly, I'm of a mind that if a motherfucker wants to find me, all they got to do is come get me. And if their asses end up dead or in traction, well that ain't my problem, is it?"

"Well, it kind of is—"

"Not. My. Problem."

"Whatever, man, I don't know if I completely buy into your southern menace persona."

"Have you *seen* me, darlin'? I destroy shit without even trying, and that's not including when I'm in a berserker rage."

She patted his thigh indulgently and walked toward the bedroom. If he wanted to describe his dissociative episodes in mythological terms, it wasn't her place to tell him different, until he asked.

"Oh, and just so you know…" She paused in the act of closing the bedroom doors. "I know you're incredibly intelligent, but the next time you plant a camera in my office to spy on me, I suggest you don't allow Lynx to come snooping around afterward. He's very curious and way too obvious when he sees something of interest."

Lucas groaned and ran his hands over his head. "Lynx is my brother and I'd surrender my life for him, I would, but he's got to learn how to keep his shit together around beautiful women or he's gonna find himself caught up in something he can't get out of."

"Says the man who's so adept at handling women he doesn't have one chasing him down, huh, *beloved*."

"All right now, don't make me come over there and put that smart mouth of yours to better use."

"Yeah, yeah, call Merlee and afterward I'll show you just how useful my mouth can be."

"Aw hell," he said, nearly dropping his phone in his rush to make the call. "You're gonna mess around with Bubba and lose a tonsil tonight."

Stormy laughed and closed the door to give him some privacy.

After Stormy took her shower, she was sat on the bed lotioning her feet and ankles when Lucas walked out of the bathroom naked, toweling his head dry. Snapping the lid of the lotion closed, she reached over and placed it on the nightstand intentionally giving Lucas a glimpse of her ass in the sheer peach bikini panties.

"Brick shit house," Lucas marveled.

She glanced over her shoulder and saw Bubba pointing at her as if to say *right there, I want to go right there.*

"Lucas, you okay?"

"Hell, no, I ain't. Matter of fact, I'm in a whole heap of pain, and it's your job to ease it."

"Is that right?"

"I'm thinking it ain't wrong."

"Well, if you're laying this responsibility at my feet, you'll have to follow my course of treatment without question. Are you willing to do that?"

He grinned. "I don't know, am I going to need a safe word or something?"

She shook her head. "Nope, I'll keep you safe. All you have to do is give me complete control. You tell me to stop and I'll stop but…your pain won't go away. And stopping mid-treatment will be torture, so be sure before you accept my help."

She was asking for a lot; the one thing he refused to trust a woman with was his carefully constructed control.

Lucas's eyes hardened, bitterness flashing within the green depths. She'd taken a gamble, hoped he'd trust her with some small piece of him. It was disappointing, but at some point you had to accept when a person couldn't give you what they didn't have or want to give.

Lucas rolled his neck, rubbed his hand back and forth over his abdomen as if trying to soothe it.

"All right, Sienna Red, you think you can take the reins on this bull, then I'm perfectly willing to let you try."

Yes, Stormy shouted in her head. She walked over to him, as close as she could get without touching, maintaining an outer display of calm seduction.

"Close your eyes," she directed.

Lucas squinted at her, but he did as requested, and lowered his lids, long tangled lashes fanned out over his deeply tanned skin. Stormy brushed her thumbs over his closed eyes and kissed the center of his chest.

She'd asked for a gift and he'd overcome his fears and biases to give it to her. Now it was her turn to be as courageous, allow herself to explore desire in a way that she had never been permitted to do before.

She caressed his unlined forehead; this man wasn't much for worrying. Tangling her fingers in his damp hair, she pulled his head down and stood on her toe tips, touching her lips to his, simply feeling their warmth, their softness.

He growled, opening to consume her. She pulled away.

"No. Only if I tell you."

His brow furled, but he took a deep breath, then nodded, acquiescing.

She resumed her exploration.

Lucas truly was large all over. She caressed the deep cut and bulk of his muscles, skimmed her fingers over his waist, dug her nails into his ass cheeks, recalling when he'd toyed with hers back in the cell with Cornelius, remembering her vow to pay him back.

Dipping her tongue into the hollow of his throat, she sucked gently, pulled back when his body coiled to strike. She maneuvered him around so that the back of his knees pressed against the foot of the bed.

"Open your eyes."

He did. Her breath caught. Fire was alive in his green gaze.

"Lie back on the bed and grip the headboard. Don't let go until I say."

His expression was both curious and suspicious, but he crept backward on the bed and held firm to the ornately sculpted wooden rail that ran horizontal in the center of the headboard. She walked to the side of the bed and sifted through her luggage until she found the items she sought.

"Spread your legs a little wider for me," she said as she lined the items beside his hip.

"Hold on now, what the hell is all that?"

Lucas eyed the narrow four-inch black silicone device that had a subtle corkscrew design. There were three distinctive nobs that got successively bigger toward the base. After the largest bulge—which really wasn't that large—the device narrowed and smoothed out, ending where the on/off switch was centered. Stormy placed a tube of lubricant beside the vibrating butt plug and reached for one of the pillows near Lucas's head.

"Lift your hips for me."

He shook his head, eyes wide, staring at the vibrator, then at her, in horror.

"Don't you trust me?" she asked, stroking Bubba as she awaited Lucas's answer.

"Come on, ol' son," he muttered, shutting his eyes. "This cain't be no worse than being stabbed or shot or bitten by red ants. Don't *let* this woman send you running scared now."

Despite his words, he remained frozen in place.

When his hips eventually rose, she placed the pillow beneath them.

"How brave you are. I promise you, Big Country Beaumont, you'll enjoy this."

She crawled onto the bed and settled in between his legs. "Now bend your knees for me."

On each side of her his legs stayed straight, rigid, thigh muscles taut and corded.

"Trust me, Lucas."

He let out an agonized breath. "I can't believe I'm doing this shit," he muttered, his feet sliding back toward his hips until his knees pointed toward the ceiling. With his thighs so wide apart, all his business was spread out before her.

She reached for the plug.

"Wait! Wait, woman…I just…I want you to think about this—"

Stormy pursed her lips to hold in her laughter.

Picking up the lubricant, she coated the butt plug's surface and pressed the button, bringing the small device to life. The panicked look on Lucas's face was priceless.

He squeezed his eyes shut. "Aw Jesus, *Jesus*…" The Lord's name careened into a high-pitched plea.

Stormy doubled over in laughter. "Oh, come on, you big baby! You'll barely feel it, it's so small."

"It's virgin territory, woman!" he said, eyes desperate. "Promise me, promise you'll be gentle, darlin'… go slow, don't…don't rush it."

Stormy wiped a tear from the corner of her eye. "*Lucas,*" she said, attempting sternness.

When he calmed, she trailed the device from the back of his knee, along his inner thigh, and closer to its destination. "You must have done some kind of anal play in the past."

"Not to me. I've done it to them, but not…tell them I'm sorry, oh Lord, I don't know how folks do this shit."

"You'll soon find out."

He squeezed his eyes shut, pelvis jerking as she slid the vibrator down Bubba's engorged length and over his balls.

"Oh no, no, no, no, no…" Lucas chanted.

She paused in the act of spreading more lube over his opening. "You want me to stop?"

He nodded, then shook his head, clenching his jaw and expelling breaths as if preparing to give birth. He looked at her and gripped the headboard so hard she swore she heard it splinter, then he nodded again.

"Okay, I'm ready."

Stormy rose to her knees and placed her free hand on Lucas's chest while the other navigated the vibrating tip just inside Lucas's body. She bent forward and kissed him deeply, distracting him from the shallow invasion. When his body took the first ball fully inside, he groaned and bucked. She let him get used to the feeling, working her mouth down his neck and chest, sucking his nipples, grazing them with her teeth as Bubba nestled between her breast, oozing with pleasure.

Lucas's arms grew slack.

"Do not let go," she warned, lifting her head, looking pointedly at his hands.

He tightened his grip, rivulets of sweat rolling from his forehead to the pillow, his face a portrait of rapturous agony.

"See?" she murmured. "It's so much better than you ever could have imagined."

Before he could respond, verbally or physically, she scooted backwards, sliding her hand from his chest down to Bubba's base which she circled with her palm and fingers and squeezed tightly.

Lucas made a strangled sound as she eased the second, slightly larger ball inside of him. "It's okay," she said, tightening her grip on his base to stop him from coming until she wanted him to. "Only one more."

She took Bubba in her mouth and eased the last ball into his rectum and Lucas seized.

"Whoo Lord!" he shouted, as the vibrations and her ability to give steady, enthusiastic, meticulous head overcame him. The intense sensations and his inability to come made him beg and buck, his hips bowing, surging, but she didn't relent. She didn't have to deep-throat Bubba or swallow him whole, she just sucked harder, faster, consuming all she could of him.

"Mon Dieu..." Lucas gasped, and continued to utter other words she couldn't decipher.

When he began yelling so loud she feared the police would break down the front door, she slid him from her mouth and while holding a very angry-looking Bubba by his base, climbed on top of him.

She sank down and worked her hips, rolling them, riding him hard, and when Lucas's eyes rolled toward the back of his head, she released Bubba and allowed Lucas to let go of the headboard. In one smooth motion, he had her on her back, her knees draped over his shoulders, ankles around her ears as he pounded into her, in revenge or punishment, she didn't know, didn't care, it felt so damn good she could barely gather the breath to cry out as he battered her pussy, shouting as he came and came and came.

His heated seed flooded her, and in symbiotic response her body convulsed, pussy clenching in continuous contraction, greedily consuming him as the rolling orgasm left her too weak to do anything but sink into the mattress. Lucas collapsed beside her, unconscious.

That was amazing, Stormy thought and closed her eyes, ready to follow Lucas into sleep. The buzzing vibrator forced her to sit up and ease the device from Lucas's body.

With the last vestiges of her energy, she went to the bathroom, cleaned up their toy, wet a towel and went back into the bedroom to take care of Lucas before taking another shower. Stormy took two Motrin, turned out the lights and slipped beneath the covers, pulling them over a still-unresponsive Lucas. She kissed his temple.

This had been a crazy day, but it ended better than she ever could have imagined.

She closed her eyes, but thoughts of Lucas confronting his family in a few hours snapped them back open. She had no doubt of the violence and suffering he'd endure. She prayed for his protection. He'd given her his trust tonight and she had no intention of betraying it, not when he needed her most.

Cornelius woke violently, for no apparent reason. He hadn't had a nightmare. It was quiet inside his room, equally as quiet outside. The Lord's light hadn't broken the oppressive darkness of night, yet it soon would; he knew it would.

Rising from his bed, he walked past the rows of empty cots to the window on the far wall and looked up. There were no stars shining down from above; if there were, he couldn't see them through the trees. The dark heavens offered no relief from the confusion residing in his soul. He had no place to turn, no means to draw clarity as he struggled with so many conflicting thoughts and experiences.

The men and women on this mountain had not visited upon him

the levels of physical punishment the Shepherd and his warriors had subjected Cornelius to—in the name of discipline and obedience. The people here had not shamed him for being weak. Outside the singular incident of violence from the hands of the dark-haired fallen, he was treated with kindness, with some measure of respect. Even the ones he believed to be possessed remained watchful, but they kept their distance. The power of God's grace surely surrounded him, but it didn't make his purpose here clearer.

The older woman, Mama, kept him filled with food that satisfied the depths of his soul. The Native American man spoke with him long into the night, fascinated by Cornelius' stories of his home, his life, the spiritual teachings of the Shepherd.

Wouldn't it be a boon if he could convert Terry, train him to understand the Shepherd's teachings of God, transform a heathen into a soldier of the Lord? Did he have the power to persuade a man of intelligence into becoming a member of the shepherd's flock? Terry seemed as wise as the Shepherd, he even displayed some measure of control over the possessed ones, and most importantly, he helped Cornelius to not feel as afraid or judged as Cornelius always had been at the Keep.

Lynx—*what a strange name, but he was Asian after all*—Lynx was very kind. He made Cornelius laugh, brought a lightness and joy to his heart. He also supplied Cornelius with DVDs depicting various stories of faith and devotion, but none quite encompassed the beliefs and rituals of the Shepherd's order. Cornelius had not realized how small his worldview had been until coming here.

Delivered to the Shepherd's Order at a young age, Cornelius had strategically erased the feelings of terror and grief he'd felt when separated from his family. He'd buried the memories of his parent's house in upstate New York, buried the love, the happiness; it all had to be stripped away in order to survive at the Shepherd's Keep.

The longer he was here on this mountain, the more his childhood memories returned, making him want a life without the Shepherd, without the order. The memories made him feel so vulnerable, so confused over his path. If he hadn't had them, he wouldn't be so conflicted, but he was remembering a happier time, a different life, and yes, without question, there was darkness here, but there was also life and light. Spirit was alive here—he could *feel* it—and a part of him wanted to stay, wanted to live among them. In time, perhaps he could even expel the demons influencing the fallen ones, help them see that they could be far more powerful in the light of the Lord than in the shadows of evil.

Cornelius was giddy with all the possibilities this new life could bring. Yes, the Shepherd would seek to return him to the order, but Mama and Terry would defend his right to be here, and if the Shepherd would not see reason—for he was not often a reasonable man—the fallen could be used to fight on his behalf.

Kneeling onto the hard floor, Cornelius laced his fingers together and closed his eyes. He had to be clear that this path was not of his ego's making, that it wasn't a decision built on cowardice and fear as many of his past decisions had been.

Though God was often silent when Cornelius sought his guidance, the Shepherd taught that one must always pray for direction; *for without prayer the act will not be based on the will of God, but on the will of man.*

Cornelius prayed for God to show him the way. Prayed that he bestow upon him the clarity to recognize the truth of all things and the courage to do what he must.

"I know I have been unworthy of your favor, my Lord, but this time I pray that—"

There was a whisper of movement across the room and Cornelius was immobilized by fear. He was loath to open his eyes, he wouldn't, he didn't like seeing what came for him in the dark hours, it was never good, and prayers had never saved him.

But this was a new life, could be a new beginning.

Courage, he admonished himself, *you walk in God's love, courage is all that is required of you.*

He opened his eyes and he felt a moment of embarrassment. There were no monsters ready to drag him from his cot and tear his flesh apart. This was Mama's House, not the Shepherd's Keep.

Courage.

But he would not look left or right, could not look across the room where the sound originated. Instead he raised his arms up toward the heavens and began to pray in earnest.

"...be strong in the Lord, and in the power of his might. Put on the whole armor of God, that ye may be able to stand against the wiles of the devil—"

"For we wrestle not against flesh and blood, but against principalities, against powers, against the rulers of the darkness of this world, against spiritual wickedness in high places. Ephesians 6:10-12," an angelic voice called out, speaking with a conviction and clarity stronger than his own.

Was she mocking him, revealing to God and the darkness his weaknesses, his unworthiness?

Soft orange light sprung to life.

A diminutive figure crouched in the corner near the door, her back to the wall, her feet planted wide apart. Between her thighs she gripped the neck of a half-empty bottle of brown liquor. The flickering flame of the lighter made the tattoos on her body appear to shift, as if coming to life, and still she remained a vision of beauty, one who watched him silently as she slid up the wall, her resentment striking him as if it were a physical force.

She swung the hand holding the lighter wide and used the other to place the bottle against her lips, swallowing twice before extending the liquor to him in offering.

"This answers prayers quicker, saint. Suggest you call on it when all else fails."

She placed the bottle next to her feet, appearing more fragile than a demon had a right to be. She extinguished the flame, dousing her vulnerability inside the shadows.

The faintest rays of the Lord's light had made their way to him. He gave a silent prayer of thanks.

His path was clear now. It terrified him, but he was clear.

"The others don't know how easily lies fall from the mouths of men of god, but I know, I *remember,*" the female fallen said. "You hurt them, you betray them, you die. I promise you."

She opened the door and walked through the opening. Before she could shut it, Cornelius called out, "Please, can I have my robes brought to me? Can you ask Mama? Please."

The fallen shut the door without responding.

Cornelius stood up. Outside the window, the vibrant colors of dawn filtered through tree branches and leaves.

His purpose was clear now. It was time to do what was needed and embrace his future.

CHAPTER 10

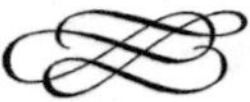

*E*very part of her ached, but not the part she'd taken the pain pills for.

No, that part felt wonderful, well-loved, *juicy,* even.

Stormy stretched and turned to face the man snoring beside her. He was in the exact position he'd collapsed last night, and if he didn't sound like an industrial-sized leaf-blower she would've believed he was dead.

Detangling herself from the sheets, she scooted off the bed and eased down on the floor on all fours. Quietly digging through her luggage, she pulled out a pair of yoga pants and a sports bra and tiptoed to the front room to dress, then grabbed her phone and earbuds and walked outside into the late morning sun.

It was already hot and humid, so temperatures would likely reach the high nineties before they made it to Oklahoma. She hadn't planned on it, but nature provided her the perfect conditions for some hot yoga.

Opening the *Downtempo* folder in her music app, she hit play and started with a sun salutation, flowed from warrior one, to warrior two, to inverted triangle. By the time she worked her way into downward dog for the third time of completing the series, the poses and heat had loosened her muscles to near-liquid fluidity.

Breathing deeper into downward dog, she barely registered the click behind her. Opening her eyes, she looked under her arm and saw Lucas, totally naked, as he stood with his arms braced on each side of the doorframe, face obscured by unruly hair. She could see glimpses of emerald through the dark strands, and knew he was staring at her ass.

Stormy rose out of the pose and paused her music.

This man is standing out here buck-naked, she thought without surprise, because that was just him, raw and unconcerned.

"Morning, Lucas."

He remained quiet so long she wondered if he'd fallen back asleep.

"Lucas, are you awake?"

He rested his forehead on his forearm and peered down at her. "Humph?"

"You okay?"

He shook his head. "My boy won't wake up...I think you broke him, Stormy, he always wakes up with the sun, but look at him now."

She looked at Bubba, who hung low and heavy against Lucas's thigh.

"Um...he had a hard night, Lucas, he's tired, it's okay if he rests."

"My grand used to say, you break it you buy it. If Bubba is broke, you gon' have a limp-dicked man at your side for the rest of your days."

"Bubba's fine, he just—"

"Oh, my Lord," a woman's voice gasped. Stormy turned to see two older white women bring their power walk to a complete stop in front of their cottage and stare at Lucas...well, Bubba mostly.

Lucas flicked his hand in lazy greeting. "Hey there, y'all."

"In the house, Lucas, *in the damn house,*" Stormy said, attempting to block him from sight as she propelled him inside the house and shut the door.

~

Big Country stumbled back into the cottage. In his half-dead state, he could barely keep himself upright when Stormy charged at him. He'd never felt like this after sex, not even when he'd binge-fucked multiple women in one night's time. No, this morning he felt wrung out and lethargic, like he'd truly been drugged—had to crawl out of bed before he could walk kind of drugged, five shots of firewater kind of drugged, Bubba flopping around senseless in his hand as he tried to shake him awake kind of drugged.

Of course, the moment Stormy slammed into him, Bubba acted like a pitiful puppy and lifted his head to get her attention. Lucas was too exhausted to be relieved. Through hooded eyes he watched as Stormy pressed against him, looking worried as she stroked his hair out of his face.

"What's going on, Lucas, are you all right?"

Like she wasn't the succubus that had leached a decade's worth of life from his soul, he thought, pressing his cheek deeper into her touch. He had to be a fool 'cause he was ready to give her another decade to have one more hit, to feel her essence moving inside of him, providing a salve to places he believed long past healed. One more fix and he'd be ready to let her go without reluctance or remorse.

Yeah, that shit wasn't happening.

"Why were you out there with your titties in full bloom and your ass all..." He spread out his hands, making an air mold of her ass. "I tell you what, if those women had been men gawking at you like that, some shit would'a went down. I ain't in the mood, Stormy—"

"Lucas, there were no men."

"–You gon' mess around and get someone killed, and I mean 'ain't-eligible-for-resurrection-or-even-zombie-status' level dead."

"Baby, I think you need to go lay back down"

He pulled her in the circle of his arms and held her. "Only if you come with me."

She wrapped her arms around his waist and laid her head against his chest.

Giving and receiving comfort from women he was sexually inti-mate with had never been allowed, but it didn't feel sickening or wrong, it felt damned right, none of that crazy shit that defined his parent's relationship, but something like what Terry had with Mama, what Zeus had with Sabrina. Maybe this was the woman he was supposed to have something with.

He was about to say something to that effect when his phone rang from the bedroom. The ringtone identified the caller as Merlee.

Big Country pulled out of Stormy's arms and went to the bedroom, tensing the moment he answered and heard his baby sister crying.

"Shug, tell me what's wrong."

He heard the fiancé murmur something in the background.

"It's okay," Merlee assured the fiancé. "I need to be the one to tell him."

Tell me what? What does she need to tell me, and why the fuck is it making her cry?

He should've driven directly to Oklahoma. It was selfish, a betrayal of his duty to protect the only blood kin whose *job* it was for him to protect, and why, just to have another night with Stormy?

"Talk to me, Merlee."

"I got a call from Armand early this morning telling me to come to the farm. He said that Will had gotten on PaPere's bad side and was hurt. We went to the farm..." Big Country closed his eyes. "And Armand took us to the shed and Lucas, Will was beaten half to death."

The line became muffled and the next voice Big Country heard was the fiancé's.

"I called 911 before the rest of the family were up. The ambulance took Will to ER and we're here with him now."

"Is the old man in jail?"

The fiancé's silence told Big Country all he needed to know. His father was still out there free to destroy at will, as was the one that had to be responsible for orchestrating the violence.

"That *bitch*," he said, feeling only disgust for the woman who birthed him. "Sheriff Anderson won't move against the old man, not as long as Belle Mère's got him by the balls; that's how she and the old man get away with all the shit they've done since I was a kid, threats, violence, blackmail."

"I should never have left Will there on his own," Merlee said, back on speaker.

"No more tears, Merlee-girl, this ain't your fault. I'll be there in a few hours, you hold out till then?"

"But if he dies, Luc…"

"No, darlin', he'll be okay. You still trust me to make this right, don't you?"

"Yes."

"Good, that's good. I'll see y'all soon…and Merlee, don't go back out to the farm. If you see those bastards on the street, in town, you move in the opposite direction, yeah?"

Big Country dropped the phone when she disconnected the call and closed his eyes, shaking from the effort to contain his rage. This was his fault. All the damage his folks caused, all the pain and suffering people endured because of them…

He balled his hands into fists. He'd lived with their shit, knew what they were, and his only response in all these years was to pretend that time would somehow nullify their evil. But they were still hurting people—and choosing to ignore their existence as long as they stayed out of his world wasn't working, not when they'd crossed the only line his grands had drawn in the sand. That line? They stay away from him and stay away from Merlee.

All this was on him. He killed bad people for a living, but he never put those motherfuckers down, and that was on him.

He roared in fury but unleashing the emotion didn't lessen it, only brought Stormy running into the room as coldness swiftly crept over his body, numbing him, shutting down pathways that kept him connected to this world.

The blue flame sparked to life just outside the periphery of his consciousness, doing to his mind what the cold did to his body, destroyed all the fail-safes that kept his beast caged, and when that flame landed, he'd be gone.

"Stay with me, Lucas, in this moment. Feel me. I'm here, I'll fight for you, I'll protect you…but you have to stay."

He didn't want to hurt his sienna-red woman, but the cold and flame had protected him so long, *so long*, before he even understood why he needed them to.

"I'm not asking you to silence the rage, Lucas. I'm not asking you to stop acknowledging the pain, it was real, and it was wrong, and you didn't deserve it. All I'm asking is for you to stay here now, for you to be in the driver's seat, put that other part in the seat beside you so it can see you handling what comes without him. And me, I'll be sitting in the back seat, along for the ride, but just chilling."

He opened one eye, frowned at her.

"Hey." She smiled up at him. "I'm here. Know that. Know that it's me holding you, it's my voice filling your ears. It's me reminding you to breathe. Breathe, Lucas."

He breathed, and her scent invaded him, pushed back against the cold, triggered images of her in laughter, of her loving on him, of her cursing him out, of her at peace in a raging storm.

Another image sprang to life, one of her in her yoga outfit dead at his feet.

With no one here to stop it, the thing inside him would leave her beaten and bloody, and it would be at his own hands. If he hurt someone he cared for, he'd be as bad as his folks. And he'd already hurt Stormy on the road coming here, betrayed her with his words just as certainly as her ex had back at her house.

He couldn't betray Stormy again; he couldn't.

"Trust me just one more time, Lucas, trust me like I trust you and we'll get through this together. I promise."

Together.

All his life he'd fought this battle alone, fought the ugliness and shame alone, and here she was promising that he didn't have to anymore, that she would have his back, and he believed her…at least, he wanted to believe her.

"I got you, big man. When you need me, I'll always have you."

He shook harder than he had when the flame and cold first came into his life, shook harder than when his ol' man and older brothers had beaten him near-senseless, harder than that moment Mama had jumped out of her still-moving car, brandished her guns when she saw him on the ground and started firing, harder than when she took him and Merlee away forever.

Part of him died that day, but that dead part always resurrected itself, always fought to live, raging over the truth; his family had tried to destroy him when no one was looking. They would've killed him to protect their secrets. And after a lifetime of shutting it all down, he felt it, all of it, and Stormy held onto him as emotions that were never allowed to be, flowed free.

He lifted Stormy off her feet and held on to her; let her comfort him when for so long he believed that he didn't deserve comfort, believed that in some way, shape, or form, it was his fault that the ones who were supposed to love him, didn't, that he was to blame for everything they'd done, even when Mama, Terry, his rational mind, tried to help him see none of it was true.

Stormy held him until the beast inside was lulled back to the depths.

"I warned her...I should've prepared her better. She wasn't raised with them, the grands wouldn't allow her to even talk to them, so she didn't know... I should've prepared her better."

"Is Merlee okay?"

He nodded.

"Then that's all that matters right now. What happened?"

He set her on her feet, but wasn't ready to turn her loose.

"My younger brother called Merlee, told her he'd found her foreman beaten and unconscious near the chicken coop. Told her to come get Will and take him to the hospital before he died. She and the fiancé went to the farm and Armand helped them tend to Will until emergency services arrived." He took another breath. "They shouldn't have had to go to the farm at all, Stormy. I should've been there. I should've been there to fix this before anyone got hurt."

"I hear you, but Merlee and her fiancé are safe, and Armand made sure Will got to the hospital where he's recovering. Are your parents in jail?"

He snorted. "Hell no."

"Good. That means you have time to do what you came to do." She patted his ass. "Let's get packed and hit the road."

She tried to move around him, but he held her in place.

"Hey, back at that truck stop…I was all kinds of wrong. I've never spoken to another human being like that and I'm ashamed I started with you." He lowered his head, making sure he held her gaze. "I promise you, I'd cut out my own tongue before I speak to you like that again."

She was quiet for a while, then a little smile formed along the edges of her mouth. He exhaled.

"Don't worry, if it happened again I'd rip it out for you." She spread her fingers as if they were claws and placed her nails around his larynx. "You don't know how close you came."

"Darlin', I'm always close to coming when I'm around you."

She shook her head. "Yep, I stepped right into that one."

∾

This is it, Delilah thought as she stood at the front door, waiting for someone to answer.

She hadn't rushed to Lucas's sister's home immediately upon arriving to Oklahoma, and that was a testament to her faith and patience. She wanted to see him; more importantly, needed to free him,

Still, instinct—honed by years of discipline and training—cautioned her to take the time to get to know her surroundings, mingle with the residents of the small town, and learn what she could about the legacy of the family she would soon join.

What she learned so far confirmed that she'd chosen well. The Beaumonts had been a staple in the community for over five decades. Between Lucas's grandparents and now his sister, who temporarily

197

resided and conducted business on the family farm lands, Delilah would be marrying into a respected family.

Based on the stories from both the proprietor of the clothing boutique she visited and the owners of the bed and breakfast she'd stayed in the night before, Lucas himself was a town treasure. When she had asked about the remaining members of her beloved's family, people were more guarded, only offering that his parents and brothers weren't a part of the community but were in town visiting. Lucas must have brought them here so the whore could weasel her way into their good graces.

She knocked on the door again, smothering her growing impatience. If the whore was inside manipulating Lucas's family as she'd manipulated him, Delilah would need to impress them with her beauty and wit, show them that the whore wasn't worthy of Lucas, nor the right to continue his bloodline.

The acres of fertile farmland, the regal bearing of the farmhouse— it all supported the rightness of her place here. Of course, she could only stay when the weather was tolerable; the midday heat and humidity was suffocating.

Despite the rusted tan truck in the yard, she acknowledged that there was a chance no one was home. She debated returning to her air-conditioned rental car, but knocked again, this time more insistently, attempting to maintain composure.

She'd purchased today's outfit because of its daring style; the skirt ended two inches above the knee, and the neckline of the sage silk blouse displayed her delicate cleavage. She was sure it would be enough to entice Lucas back to her.

Jesus Christ, she thought, wiping her brow, *this heat is boiling me alive.* The silk would wilt upon her frame before Lucas or his family even got a chance to see it.

She prepared to return to the car, but a crash echoed inside the house, heavy feet stomped toward the door. With a swiftness and violence that caused her to reach for the gun in her purse, the front door swung open and a filthy bear of a man filled the space.

Her initial impression was that he indulged in more than one deadly sin. His eyes were mean; angry red blood vessels surrounded the murky green irises. He wore a stained white T-shirt and wrinkled black boxers, both looking as if he'd pulled them from the bottom of a dirty laundry bin. His height was nearly that of her beloved's, and his body was thickly muscled like her beloved's but with a dense layer of flesh that spoke of unchecked indulgence.

This could be Lucas's future if I abandoned him to the machinations of the whore, she thought. The level of physical wreckage she witnessed in this man could only come from the destruction of spirit.

She could not allow Lucas to exist in this particular circle of hell. She would not.

"Whatcha say now, out heah tryin' to bust ma do'! Told y'all I don't know nothing 'bout who whooped on that old man, so less ya got dat warrant and a mind to come up missing, you best go 'head on."

Delilah blinked, worked to filter the man's words, to ascribe them meaning as he looked her up and down. The haze of anger surrounding him receded, only to be replaced by the pungent sent of lust. Her body reacted as if worms crawled over her.

Then he smiled.

That was her beloved's smile, that was the way her beloved's eyes had danced with humor and light the night they'd first lain together. The semblance stayed her desire to strike out in preemptive violence. This man was clearly an older member of her beloved's family. Perhaps it was best for everyone involved if she offered her hand in peace and healing instead of using it to end his life. Perhaps she could even forge a new path for this man, as God in his grace had forged for her.

"I believe there's been a misunderstanding, sir. My name is Delilah Shepherdssin, and I'm here to meet my fiancé."

"Yeah chi, and who's ya man?"

"Lucas, Lucas Beaumont."

"Julian, who's that at the door asking about my *beau bébé?*" a woman called out.

"*Une belle fille,*" the man said in a guttural form of French.

Delilah offered a shallow curtsy of thanks, though she was beyond being impressed with men who thought her beautiful. The only man's opinion that mattered was Lucas's.

A woman wearing an indecently short champagne-colored slip with cream lace edging at the bottom, pushed past the large man as if he were an overgrown pup. Placing her back to the man's chest, she curved a hand over her hip. Her long nails looked as if they'd been painted with someone's blood. The possessiveness in the woman's stance, the jealousy lurking in her vibrant green gaze, dared Delilah to challenge her place in the older man's affections.

Poisonous creature, Delilah thought.

At five feet eight, the older woman was slightly taller than Delilah and had long sable hair—dyed, no doubt—that flowed in waves over her shoulders and down her back. Like the whore, the woman had an earthy quality, *tainted* earth. Something about the woman was repulsive.

"You tryin' to step out on me, Julian? Got you a new young t'ing, yeah?" The woman asked in a voice as thick and rich as chocolate molasses. "You here trying to put a shine on my old penny, aim to put him in ya pocket and steal him away from me?"

Oh, good Lord, Delilah thought, *what level of hell have I descended to?*

In lieu of a verbal response Delilah gave the woman a bland smile and tried to look beyond the pair, hoping to see some sign of Lucas in the house's messy interior.

"Don't fret ya'self, dawlin', this here's li'l Luc's woman. Seems we finally gave that boy good reason to come see 'bout the ones gave him life."

"That right?" the woman asked Delilah. "You my boy's woman?"

"His fiancée," Delilah corrected.

"Well, ain't you the lucky one?" The woman smiled. Delilah knew she was being mocked. She didn't like these people. At all. But the possibility of getting them to intercede on her behalf kept her there, standing in seething undercurrents she didn't yet understand.

"I'm very lucky. Lucas is the best man I know."

"Yeah, he was my best boy, but they took him from me, denied his mama the right to see him grow, and that wasn't right, all those years denied me, my boy…"

Julian wrapped a thick arm around the woman's chest and held her. The woman, Lucas's mother, swiped at the tears that spilled down her tanned checks. Her grief seemed real, it clung to her as oppressively as the humidity clung to Delilah's skin.

"Don't fret ya'self, Emilia, you'll see the boy in due time."

"But has he forgiven us, Julian?" Emilia looked at Delilah. "You his woman, you tell me, has he forgiven us?"

Delilah assessed the pair and found it easy to imagine them as horrible parents undeserving of a child as precious as Lucas. Still, she wouldn't convey those sentiments, not when there was the slightest chance she could use them in the fight against the whore.

"Lucas is a good man with a good heart. In time, I believe he can forgive you for any hurt you've caused. We've spoken about the importance of family at length and I know with a little more guidance, I can persuade him to accept you back into his life. I think in the end, it's something he already wants…but he's stubborn," she said with a humorous groan.

"It comes to him good and honest," Julian said. "By way of the blood, ya see."

"Why isn't my boy here with you now?" Emilia asked, suspicion replacing her moment of vulnerability. She was the one to be watchful of, the stronger of the two.

Delilah now understood that women were far more complicated, more discerning than the men she'd encountered. But Lucas was this woman's vulnerability and Delilah had no qualms exploiting that knowledge.

"Quite honestly, Lucas isn't here yet because of my stupidity. A woman I trusted, a woman I considered my friend, used me to get to him. I hadn't realized how she'd manipulated us until I told Lucas it was time to come home and heal the past. She seduced him away from me, knowing that if she keeps him away from those who love him she can control Lucas. I can't allow that to happen. I love Lucas more than any person in this world and I won't see him destroyed by Stormy."

She wiped a tear from her eye and lifted her head in determination. "I believe he will do the right thing. I believe he will come here because he believes in our love. He believes in the future of our family."

The animosity that both parents had greeted her with shifted to Stormy, the woman who could disrupt their happy reunion.

Got you, Delilah thought, fighting the desire to smile in triumph.

Emilia pulled away from Julian and hugged Delilah. "All will be fine, chi, all will be just fine, nothing to be upset about, no." She guided Delilah toward the house's interior. "Come on inside now and let us get to know each other and come up with a special homecoming for our boy."

Delilah allowed Emilia to pull her into the house.

Her misgivings about the couple intensified the moment the door shut behind them.

～

"It was a bad idea bringing you down here," Lucas muttered.

Stormy shifted in her seat, placing her back against the door and her bare feet into Lucas's lap. He'd been tense since they'd crossed the state line into Oklahoma and now that they were on the outskirts of his hometown, he seemed to reach a breaking point.

Stormy wiggled her toes, demanding attention, and Lucas moved his right hand from the steering wheel to her feet, massaging one foot, then the other. As intended, the small rhythmic motion settled him, allowed him to release kinetic energy without leaving the confines of the truck.

"If things go south, call Mama, she knows how to handle bad situations. The Brood'll get you out fast if you call her."

Stormy didn't plan on calling. She knew how to handle bad situations, too.

"And if I…lose control…you get the hell out, Stormy, you get the hell out and you don't come back."

She wasn't abandoning him, but she wouldn't tell him that either; it would only agitate him more and Lucas didn't need to reunite with his parents already on the edge of losing himself. He needed to stay present, to resolve the current situation for Merlee, and maybe, if he was ready, to address what lay between him and his parents from the past.

She planned on being there—for all of it.

"Are we within the city limit?" Stormy asked, watching trees and grassland give way to single-structure homes on large acres of land.

"Yep, welcome to Wexford, Oklahoma."

The deeper they drove into town, the more the city of Wexford took shape.

Two-story buildings distinguished mostly by the shade of brick and the storefronts specific décor, lined the street. There was a step between the road and the sidewalk, and the parking in front of the buildings slanted at an angle. The metal street lamps that ran the length of the road were painted dark blue and ornately designed, harkened back to a bygone era of gas-lit lamps. American flags waved from the second-story mounts on each building. Stormy wasn't surprised by the number of Confederate flags she saw mounted as well.

Although they were in the downtown area, the place wasn't bustling, it was more of a meandering flow of mostly white people walking down the street in T-shirts, jeans, cut-off shorts, and pastel or patterned summer dresses. This place was way more Mayberry than the towns her family lived in Louisiana.

Lucas made a couple of turns and the people-scape changed. Darker shades of folks, mostly black and Latino, added depth to the town's cultural tapestry. Though their numbers were smaller, Stormy breathed easier knowing she wasn't the only one, that she had people to stand with if a race-war broke out while she was down here.

She laughed a little. Who was she kidding, if a race-war broke out she was sticking to the massive brawler who made men crumble like blue cheese with one punch.

"I know you're not laughing at the grandeur of my hometown."

"*Never*. I'm simply considering the possibility that we've gone over a hundred and fifty years in the past and I'll find myself having to fight my way to freedom."

"Nah, you're firmly in present-day Wexford, but given why we're here, you may still have to fight your way out of here."

"You know, sometimes you take the fun right out of living," she said in a dry monotone.

Lucas grinned and winked at her.

"I ain't always gonna bring you fun, but you can guarantee I will always bring…" He looked at her expectantly. She refused to say it.

Lucas continued. "I will always bring the *motherfuckin'*…"

"*Thunder.* Whatever, man," she said, waving her hand dismissively.

He laughed from his gut and she fell in love with him a little. As large as he was physically, Lucas's spirit glowed around him like a supernova, inextinguishable within the darkness that sometimes overwhelmed him. When the power of it touched her, it did powerful things to her heart.

The scenery outside shifted again and they drove through a residential area. The houses were a mixture of styles, mostly ranch and colonials on big lots with grass and trees. Lucas slowed down and parked the truck near a soft yellow two-story colonial with cream columns and piping, a wraparound porch, and beautiful ancient trees sitting on the opposite side of the horseshoe-shaped driveway.

"Is this your grandparents' farmhouse?"

"Darlin', we're still in town. The farmhouse is about seven miles outside of town…in the country…on an actual *farm.*"

"Oh, fuck off." She nudged the inside of his thigh with her heel before sitting upright in her seat. "And don't get all bold now that you're back home."

"I *stay* bold, woman, and again, this is not my home, this is the fiancé's home."

"Oh yes, the man that you sister will marry and spend the rest of her life with."

He opened the door and stepped out, muttering *not if I have anything to do with it.*

Stormy slipped on her shoes and opened the door, stepping onto the metal step before hopping down to the ground.

Was it a rule in the older brother handbook that said they had to dislike any man their younger sisters fell in love with? In the case of Chad, her brother genuinely never liked him, but Stormy couldn't tell if Lucas was pretending not to like Merlee's fiancé or if he genuinely didn't like him.

The front door of the house flew open as they walked up the paved driveway, and a tall rawboned woman in T-shirt and jeans ran out in her bare feet. From nearly seven feet away, the younger woman launched herself in the air and Lucas plucked her out of it and spun her as if she was weightless.

Lucas's sister sobbed, wrapping her arms around his neck and holding on as if she never should have let him go the last time they'd seen each other. The embrace reflected love, but there was also grief and fear in Merlee's eyes. There was also the unspoken commitment that these two would always be there for each other…no matter what. It was the nature of the *what* they were facing that concerned Stormy.

"Look at you, Luc," Merlee said when Lucas lowered her to the ground. She stepped back and took him in. "You're practically skinny!"

"Been doing yoga," Lucas boasted, side-eyeing Stormy, daring her to say different. He was so brazen with his lies.

"Thanks for getting him back home in one piece," Merlee said, surprising Stormy when she pulled her into a quick strong hug. "Mama didn't exaggerate when she said how damn gorgeous you are. When she said you may be the one woman that could bring my brother to heel I didn't believe her; now I'm beginning to wonder."

"We're just good friends sharing an adventure," Stormy said, though her face felt heated.

"Mama's got stars in her eyes because of Zeus and Sabrina, and it's made her loopy," Lucas added.

Merlee pulled a cell phone from her back pocket. Her green eyes had the same teasingly mischievous gleam that Lucas's had but with none of the shadows. "Bet you won't say that to Mama's face."

"And you'd win. Don't mean I'm too scared to say it now."

Merlee laughed and pulled him in for another hug.

"Y'all come on in. Garret's out back frying up some catfish but everything else is done, so we'll be sitting down to eat once you get settled."

A wave of nostalgia hit Stormy the moment she walked into the house and the scent of food welcomed them. It reminded her of the times she and her family had gone back to Louisiana. No matter the time of day or night they arrived, there was always a meal warming on the stove for them, there was always a tumble of folks coming out to greet them despite their state of wakefulness or dress.

In that moment she knew the next leg of this journey would be to her birth state and her own family less than four hours away.

"How's Will?" Lucas asked as Merlee led them to the kitchen, toward the left of the house.

"Doc Grove said he should heal up just fine as long as he doesn't give himself a coronary over missing the county fair."

"Tell him I'm here and he'll stop worrying. He knows I'll take care of everything that needs to be done," Lucas said.

"The prodigal son returns."

Stormy and Lucas turned to see a man entering the house from the back. Merlee's infamous fiancé stepped through the French doors holding a large pan of fried fish. He had a slim athletic build and was about the same height as Merlee, maybe six feet. With sandy blond hair and blue eyes sheltered by black plastic-framed glasses, Merlee's fiancé looked like a sexy nerd.

Placing the pan on the huge marble-topped island, he extended a hand to Stormy, then pulled her in for a gentle hug. Stormy liked him instantly. He had kind eyes which filled with mischief when he pulled away and settled his arm around her shoulder. "If you ever think of leaving me, Merlee Jean, don't, 'cause I got the woman I'll replace you with right here. Welcome to my home, beautiful."

"Look here, cousin—" Lucas said before Stormy could respond. "You're about two seconds from making Merlee a widow before she becomes a wife. Keep fucking around..." He smiled, pointing his finger in Garret's face. "Yeah boy…just keep fucking around and see what happens."

Garret placed a kiss on Stormy's temple, smiling as if he could dismiss the threat in Lucas's words because they had been uttered amicably. Maybe he believed Merlee's love protected him.

In either case he was wrong.

Lucas snatched Garret away and Stormy stumbled. When she righted herself, Garret's feet were inches from the ground and Lucas had Garret's arms pinned to his side, locking him in a bear hug. By the flexing of the muscles in his upper body, Lucas's hold was constricting tighter and tighter, causing Garret's skin to flush.

"Now it's bad enough that you went and asked my sister to marry you without asking my blessing—"

"Let him go Lucas! This is 2018, not 1818, and he doesn't need your blessing," Merlee said as she tried to pry Garret from Lucas's grip. Her fiancé was turning bright red from the pressure.

"—then you go pressing ya flabby lips against my woman's sienna-red skin as if I'm just gon' stand here and be all right with that too—"

"Lucas, he can't breathe," Stormy said calmly.

"There's only so much a man can stand, Stormy; you know I'm already on edge, got women grinding on you in titty bars, got vibrators being pushed up my ass, and for truth I don't know how I feel about liking it, now I gotta go out to the farm and deal with those rotten motherfuckers when all I want to do is lay in bed and hold you but he—"

Garret's head fell forward.

"Lucas, he's passing out!" Merlee said, punching her brother in the arm.

"I'm right here," Stormy said. "You can continue crushing Garret or you can simply let him go and hold me like you want to." She opened her arms. "I'm right here."

Lucas grunted and side-eyed her. She knew it was coming and shook her head to dissuade him. He smiled and dropped Garret like a sack of sand, stepped over his prone body and lifted her up in a gentler embrace, nuzzling the side of her neck.

Merlee kneeled down and helped sit Garret upright. "You're okay, baby, just breathe slow now."

"I was only trying to love on him, welcome him into the family and such, but sometimes things don't translate how I intend them to."

And there it was. The man lied for no good reason and didn't care that everyone knew. "I wanted to do right by him, Sienna Red, which is more than he can say for me, how was I to know he was weaker than a newborn calf? What he got anyway, Merlee Jean, some kind of wasting disease?"

"This is not funny, Lucas, you could have killed him!" Merlee yelled as she helped Garret stand.

Lucas placed Stormy on her feet and faced the pair.

"I've watched over you your whole life, Merleena Jean Beaumont, let you put pigtails in my hair and makeup on my face when the grands wouldn't get you that Doll-Me-Up doll, took you to the library nearly every weekend for a year straight so you could learn your fill about caring for animals, made Frank Herman eat horseshit when he broke your heart in the eighth grade, taught you to drive a car, taught you how to protect yourself... All I've ever wanted was you to be happy, but as much as you love him, as much as I like him, it's hard for me to respect a man who don't have the balls to come to me and ask for your hand in marriage, prove to me that he's willing to do all that and more for the honor of being your husband."

"He's right," Garret said before Merlee could protest. "I should've asked for his blessing a long time ago, I just didn't want to be told no and lose the chance of spending the rest of my life with the only woman I've ever wanted to make my wife. Lucas, I promise you here and now, it'll be my life's mission to be the best husband your sister could ask for. Do I have your blessing?"

"Shit no, I'll see you in your grave before I let you marry my sister."

Merlee and Garret looked devastated. Stormy couldn't believe Lucas could be so heartless. Then he grinned. "Just fucking with you, cousin. Truth is, you'd 'a been long dead if I thought you couldn't make Merlee happy. It was just the principle of the thing, yeah?"

Garret looked relieved. "Yeah. And thank you."

"Don't thank me just yet," Lucas said. "You betray my sister in any way and death *will* you part, and I'll be death, parting you right down the middle. Now may you both have a lifetime of happiness." He left them standing there to wash his hands and fix his plate.

Stormy felt wrung out and they hadn't even made it to the farm. She prayed that a meal shared with people he loved and who loved him was enough to sustain him through the next family reunion.

In her heart of hearts, she believed that neither of them was truly ready for what was to come.

CHAPTER 11

Inside the sleeves of his newly washed robe, Cornelius gripped the sharp edges of his elbows, fingernails gouging flesh to distract from the way his heart beat in rhythms of fear. Head down to cloak his distress, he took measured steps into the bar, praying that he displayed the same sense of purpose and gratitude he'd felt when Mama had given him permission to move freely about the mountain as long as he didn't attempt to leave. He'd spent the day being out in nature and in his room reading the Bible provided to him, only coming into the bar for meals. He'd been confident in his decision to become the spiritual leader to the people on the mountain, so he'd given his word not to flee.

Now he wished he hadn't.

They all turned to looked at him when he stepped into the room. Unlike earlier in the day when there was only Mama, Terry, Lynx, and the consort Sabrina, now the black-haired and gray-eyed demons were there with the female fallen.

"Now is the *perfect* time to come get me. School goes on break soon and Mrs. Jace has most of my things packed, and I'm ready to go hunting with Zeus and Cizan, and…and, *and* I want to see my new room." A child on the laptop monitor was speaking, unaware of his presence in the room. The child, no more than seven or eight years, was beautiful, a paler-skinned version of Sabrina.

The consort looked down at the screen and shook her head, smiling. "Zeus and I will be there soon, baby girl. Tell Mrs. Jace I'll give her a call in the morning, okay? We love you."

"Love you, too," the precocious child yelled before blowing a kiss.

The consort ended the video transmission.

He could not allow a child to be brought here; he hadn't begun the process of exorcising the demons from their hosts, nor placing the others firmly in the hands of the Lord. To bring an innocent here before his work was completed was to be a party to the corruption of that poor child's soul.

He had communed with grace all day, opening his mind and soul so that he could receive clarity on ways to begin the work of cleansing the mountain of evil and converting those here into warriors for the Lord. Clarity had not come, and now he understood why. It was indeed ego that led him to believe his purpose was to save the fallen, but God had stepped in and shown him that His highest purpose was for Cornelius to save the child.

The demons watched him.

He dug his nails deeper into his flesh, bent his head lower so that the cowl of his robe hid his features and squeezed his eyes shut. No one had saved him all those years ago, but the fate that awaited a child among *actual* demons would be much worse. It was not to be born.

Opening his eyes, he lifted his head and spoke to the consort. She could not welcome such a fate for the child; she just could not.

"You can't allow your daughter to come here, she would not be safe. Allow me to take her away, I'll watch over her, ensure that she lives a *blessed* life."

A menacing oppressive weight pressed him from all sides of the room.

It was as if the demons dwelling inside of the bodies of the fallen had taken control.

A large serrated knife appeared in the right hand of the gray-eyed fallen, twirling through his fingers at an ungodly speed. The black-haired one blended into the shadows, the heavy veil of his hair rippling around him but there was no breeze; there was barely enough air to breathe.

Cornelius would not look at the female fallen; there was ever only hate and the promise of pain in her gaze. He looked at Lynx instead, but was not prepared to see his friend's smile no longer kind but predatory, as if blood and flesh hanging within the spaces could be commonplace.

Humanity remained only in the eyes of Terry and Sabrina.

Mama sat crossed-legged on top of the bar near the back of the room, observing him with detachment. He had begun to count on her support, her tolerance; he'd made the mistake of believing himself high in her esteem, forgetting that first and foremost she was the mother of demons. And he'd just taken a stand in opposition to her children. The older woman pulled the strings…in this case, the invisible umbilical cords that tethered nearly everyone on this godforsaken mountain to her. It was an understanding that came too late. He'd been a fool.

"Terry, I know you're not a man of God, but I would like to confess my sins to you," Cornelius said.

Terry walked toward him and stopped a few feet to Cornelius's right.

"What would you like to confess?"

Cornelius thought of the child, gathered his courage.

"Evil is all around you here. You can't see it but please believe me, you and the consort cannot allow the child to be brought here. If the child is truly the patron's granddaughter as I believe she is, there is a better place for her. I know of a way to get you, the consort, and the child there, but you must trust me."

"Zeus, no!" the consort cried out, but the gray-eyed demon's blade had been released. Terry shoved Cornelius to the ground and he fell with bone-grinding impact as the metal embedded in the door.

Growling filled the space and Cornelius scuttled backward, believing hell hounds had been released upon earth.

The consort stepped in front of the silver-eyed demon and the sound ceased.

Terry walked over and offered Cornelius his hand, lifted him from the floor and steered him toward a stool at the bar before hopping over it and placing a glass of amber-filled liquid in front of Cornelius.

"To steady your nerves, son," Terry said. "So, what do you need to confess, Cornelius?"

Two more blades materialized in the gray-eyed demon's hands.

"He wants to confess," the mother of demons said to the gray-eyed one. "Let him speak."

With shaky hands, Cornelius reached for the glass of alcohol, praying that his first drink wouldn't be his last.

Big Country was sprawled across the living-room sofa with his head in Stormy's lap, feigning sleep as she stroked his hair and talked to his sister. The two women had to be on their second bottle of red wine by now and didn't seem to be slowing down anytime soon.

Garret had gone to his bedroom over twenty minutes ago so the women could have some privacy. Big Country didn't give a damn about their privacy, he was going to listen to every word they said.

He was practically obligated—covert intelligence was literally a part of his job description. Plus, when women got into girl-talk mode, they didn't care about things like boundaries or distinguishing fact from fiction. Nah, he was staying exactly where he was, and if Merlee started sharing stories of his past—like the time his grands took turns chasing after him and whooping him from one side of the farm to the other when he'd glued Merlee's lips together as she slept one night— he'd be right where he needed to be to disrupt any conversation that strayed into uncomfortable territory, especially when it came to his work with the Brood and the other ways he made his money.

"You go your whole life with this curiosity, this wondering," Merlee said, guiding Big Country's attention back to the actual conversation. "I've had a great life with all the love I could ever need, yet I never stopped wondering what they would be like, couldn't understand without better reason than *they are no good*, why our grands wouldn't allow me and Lucas to have any contact with them."

There was an extended pause. "I'm about to be a married woman, Stormy, soon to start my own family. I'd gone a lifetime without knowing my parents and my three other brothers, one of which is already dead. I couldn't imagine going a lifetime without ever seeing the children me and Garret bring into this world; my heart would break every second of the day, that's what I imagined it was like for them, that their hearts were breaking every second of the day without us. When PaPere called me I thought, with my grands having passed, this would be the perfect time to bring what family we have left together. To right all the wrongs, you know." She scoffed. "A child should always make space for forgiveness, I thought, so I told them to come."

Big Country manipulated his breathing, keeping it even as he directed his heart to slow down. He didn't want Stormy to discover his deception and end her conversation with Merlee, he never had an inkling his sister had been so affected by the absence of the rest of their family. Maybe he'd been selfish, should have known, but what could he have done different? Told her the full truth? Nah.

"I betrayed them," Merlee said. Big Country could hear she was crying but he wouldn't get up to comfort her. "I ignored all those years of pain and anger in my grands' eyes when my parents were ever mentioned. I disregarded what I saw in Lucas's eyes when our parents were brought up, didn't understand how it connected to the destruction that followed. I betrayed him for a fantasy, Stormy. I invited them in and for a second, I believed I'd done the right thing, righted the wrong my grands and Lucas had perpetrated by keeping them away. I didn't know…I still don't know all of it, but trust me when I say there is this…I won't say evil, but the feeling when I was around them, it's like this insidious *foulness* in them lying just beneath the surface. Hell, maybe it *is* evil. I don't know if I can forgive myself for putting my brother right in its path. Again."

Stormy shifted, and he heard glass connect with wood.

She must have placed her wine glass on the end table because she leaned over him, one hand stroking the length of his arm as the other swiped his hair from his face. Her lips pressed into his temple and lingered. That connection, that simple connection, gave him a reason to just listen, permission to allow his sister to sit with the depths of her grief instead of trying to save her from it; but it also allowed him to acknowledge his own sadness over the ideal childhoods they'd both lost.

"He needs you," Merlee said. "He's always needed a woman like you, not those money-grubbing bitches who..."

He groaned and shifted, wrapping his arm around Stormy's thighs before settling again. Merlee quieted, likely waiting to see if he'd wake up. When he continued his pretense of sleep, she spoke in quieter tones. "My brother's a good man. And a genius with electronics—"

"So he's told me."

"He puts himself in danger regularly to protect others—all the Brood do—but with Luc's condition, I worry about when the violence of his job will trigger him and he does something he can't undo. Mama says he's more vulnerable right now than she's seen in a long time. Control is his religion and I'm the one whose decisions jeopardized it. I was here worrying about my job when I should have been worrying about the impact of my own choices," Merlee muttered, self-disgust woven within her words.

"It's not foolish, I'd even say it's biological to want to connect with the people that gave you life. There's a lot of things to regret in this world Merlee, and the desire to be connected with those who should love and protect you is not one of them. You're not at fault for your parents' failures or their inability to be decent human beings, and neither is Lucas."

"But he shouldn't have to be the one," Merlee said, her voice tearful again. "They hurt him. They hurt my brother so bad my grands never allowed them to see us again. Our grands were strong, kindhearted folks and they were easy to forgive a wrong, even ones that I thought were unforgivable, but there was no forgiveness in them for my parents. I eavesdropped on a few calls where Belle Mère asked permission to see and talk to Luc—never me—but the grands refused. PaPere would call; they were his parents after all, but he'd only ask them for money, and the grands refused. The last time I know of them calling, I was about nine and I don't know who said what on the other end, but honey…" Merlee began to laugh.

This was all a revelation. He had no idea of the amount of contact his grands had with his parents. He didn't stay in the house much when he was young, he had to be busy and his grandfather made sure he was by working the farm, playing sports, encouraging his love of computers and electronics, allowing him the freedom to break down things so that he could build them up better than before.

"My grandmother got on the phone and began to curse out either one or both of my parents like a foul-mouthed felon. As far as I know, they never called again, until this month."

Big Country was shocked.

"Man, I wish I could have met them," Stormy said, her body vibrating with laughter as she slipped her hand beneath Big Country's shirt and stroked his abdomen. "If only to thank them for loving and protecting you and Lucas so fiercely. Your grands may have helped him in more ways than they know, because yes, there's what he went through and the ways he learned to deal with it, but it's also how they chose to respond that impacted his healing."

"And in one fell swoop I ruined it all."

"No, you didn't, so stop that," Stormy said. "What I know is that life offers us many opportunities to keep on as we've always done, or to grow. Lucas hasn't seen your parents for almost thirty years. You may be the impetus, but ultimately life, the universe, God, has provided him this opportunity to grow, and he's here, showing up to the challenge. And trust me, he didn't have to be here. Mama seemed poised to make you both orphans if Lucas had simply asked her to."

Merlee laughed. "She's so tiny! With those soulful eyes, that ageless black-don't-crack thing y'all got going on, and her long dreadlocks, she looks like a little harmless forest spirit. The woman is deadly, and fiercely protective of those she loves, and so manipulative she could talk sweet into leaving sugar."

Stormy laughed and Big Country wanted to because that was Mama all day long.

He heard movement, as if Merlee was rising from her chair.

"Maybe this situation is providing Lucas more than one opportunity to grow…and maybe it's giving you one, too," Merlee said. "I'll see y'all in the morning. Fair warning; the walls in this house are very thin so please don't traumatize me with sex noises." There was a retching sound. "Sorry, almost threw up just saying that." Merlee laughed; she wasn't even being funny. "Good night, Stormy, glad you've come into our lives."

He heard her give Stormy a smacking kiss before he felt her give him one.

"Goodnight Merlee," Stormy said, then sat in silence drinking her wine. Big Country relaxed with her, almost to the point of truly falling asleep, but the sound of her glass being placed on the table, the feel of her hand smoothing back his hair again, stirred him to wakefulness.

Shifting onto his back, he straightened his legs and crossed his arms over his abdomen, loving how her cushy thighs cradled his head. He opened his eyes and gazed up at her. The longer he was around her, the more facets of her beauty were revealed. Her beauty went beyond looks, it was deeper than that—like watching a dance of veils, and as each layer of gauzy material was stripped away, you were blessed to be caught in the glow of a woman whose naked radiance rivaled the sun and the moon…

"Let me hip you to a fact that maybe you and your sister are not privy to," Stormy said to him. "You are *not* a quiet sleeper…by any means…you rumble like a truck when you doze and when you're sleeping deeply, forget about it."

He grinned. "Maybe I was in a deeply meditative state."

"You were eavesdropping."

"I was, but it's rude of you to throw it in my face."

She shook her head. "I can't with you, Lucas Beaumont." Resting her hand on his chest, her expression turned somber. "You okay with what you heard?"

Am I, he wondered as he mulled over the conversation, then nodded. "I only heard truth, revelation, and you showing you got a little wisdom in you. Learning what you don't know is the best part of listening—which is a much better term than eavesdropping, by the way."

She smacked him on the stomach and began jiggling her legs up and down. "Tomorrow we clean house, let's get you to bed before your big head puts my legs to sleep.

"But I'm not sleepy no more," he drawled, capturing her gaze and drawing it down to Bubba. "Let's traumatize Merlee."

"We're not having sex in your sister's house."

"Of course we ain't! Jesus, woman..."

He hopped up and in two seconds flat, had her on her back with him on top pressing her into the couch cushions. "This ain't my sister's house, though, it's the just-barely-accepted fiancé's house, and you know I don't give a damn about shooting my shot all over this motherfucker's place."

"No."

"Come on, Stormy, we'll be quiet," he promised. "The loudest sound'll be the tearing of the condom wrapper, I swear." He didn't even know where his condoms were.

He dipped his head and kissed her collarbone, licking and sucking his way up along the side of her neck, smiling when he hit that sensitive spot that always seemed to make her thighs clench reflexively around his hips. "Come on, darlin', this'll probably be our last chance to be together before our adventure ends. One last wild ride, yeah?"

"Yeah," she eventually whispered.

He didn't need to hear any more than that.

Rolling to his feet, he lifted her and carried her to their room. They shed their clothes quietly and quickly. Their urgency had an edge of desperation, a finality. Lucas didn't know what tomorrow would bring but he knew it wasn't anything good. He only had tonight; tomorrow held the possibility that Stormy wouldn't even look him in the eye when all was said and done.

She eased onto the bed, lying back on her elbows as he shed the last of his clothing. The way she watched him made him feel like a man capable of burning brighter than the flame that stalked his sanity.

It was a damn shame he'd gone his whole life and hadn't had somebody look at him the way Stormy looked at him. He imprinted her on his retinal memory, because once she left, no matter if his eyes were open or closed, all he'd be able to see was her. All he'd be able to remember was that he had a woman willing to walk with him through the fire.

And poor Bubba…he already believed Stormy's pussy was his forever home, and life was gonna be hard when she was gone.

But she was here now, bending her legs, widening her thighs, calling him and Bubba home. Big Country heeded her call and crept along the length of the bed, navigating the narrow runway of space her thighs permitted until he hovered above her, dominating the room between and around them.

She arched a brow, the edge of her mouth tugged up in a secret smile and he was done; this woman was unadulterated seduction. Lowering his body as if commanded, he felt her body sink further into the bed as he settled his weight on top of her, felt Bubba's head breach the gushy heat of her opening, pushing through her low groan until his tip hit the pliable barrier of her uterine wall. He closed his eyes and blew out a long breath; his sack was already tight and he'd just eased himself through the door. That didn't bode well for his longevity.

Big Country took time to play, easing in and out of her pussy as if he were trying it out for the first time. Stormy dug her heals in the mattress and lifted her demanding hips from the bed, trying to hurry him to his doom.

He lowered his head and whispered in her ear. "Darlin', you got a damn strong back, never knew how much I needed that in a woman until I met you."

She pressed her lips to his ear. "Fuck me right or I'll do it myself; you know I can."

He lifted his head and gazed into her eyes. "That right, darlin'?"

"I'm thinking it ain't wrong," she said, parroting him from earlier.

He nodded, hitched her thighs higher and continued his slow slide in and out of her, hitting her special spot, satisfied with the way her thighs and Bubba glistened with her juices. Stormy tried to roll her hips again and he reared back and slammed into her. She let out a strangled cry, eyes rolling to the back of her head before she squeezed them closed, her throat clicking as she struggled to breathe and swallow.

"Now you play nice, Stormy Sinclair Redmond, and I'll play nice back," he whispered low, for her ears only. He reached down between their bodies and applied a circling pressure to her clit. Her pussy squeezed Bubba—damn near choked the life out of him—but Bubba liked a little strangulation.

Big Country continued to look down as he pumped in and out, mesmerized by the sight and feel of Bubba disappearing into and retreating from her body. He looked up and her head was thrown back, crown pressing into the pillow, the muscles in her throat shifting up and down in a silent scream.

"Oh, you liking the way I'm fucking you now, yeah Stormy? You like how this big-dicked country boy hits this—" He surged. "Spot."

She pressed her lips into his neck, silencing the scream in her throat. She loosened her grip on his shoulders and pressed her palms against the sides of his face, drawing his lips to hers as she consumed him in a heated kiss

Lucas pulled back, shaking his head to clear it. Hungry, he was so hungry for her. Balancing himself on his elbows, hips continuing to move back and forth, he cradled her heavy breasts in his hands, pushing them together, sucking pleasure from one erect nipple then the other as if maddened, starved, feeding until not even that was enough.

He lifted himself away from her torso, balancing on one hand as the other grabbed her knee, angling out and up so he'd have more room to pound into her. The breathy *"Uhn, uhn, unh,"* exploding from her lips every time Bubba's head struck gold. Her ragged exultations were music to his soul as he increased the pace, his thrust was jack-hammer hard. He felt her body tightening, the way her eyes rolled back in her head and he lowered his upper body so he could place his hand over her mouth just in time to mute her ragged cries of release.

He didn't give her a chance to come down. Bubba was on the verge of exploding; Big Country felt the telltale heat and tingle, from the base of his asshole to deep within his tightening ball-sack.

This pace, their pace, was unsustainable, but the mattress didn't make a sound as his hips churned between her thighs. He kept his promise, fucking her hard, fucking her deep, and keeping quiet as he sank into her one last time. Cheeks squeezing, come shot out of his body in a flood, and when she'd emptied his body of its life-giving essence, he collapsed on top of her, stunned. How the hell did it just keep getting better?

Still joined together, he rolled over until Stormy lay on top of him, a glazed look in her eyes as she dipped her head and whispered, "Now that's what I call a good fucking."

They both laughed quietly into each other's necks until Stormy's head settled against his shoulder.

He took a deep breath. "Who-oooooo!" He yelled loud enough to make a dog bark outside.

"Oh *Lord*, Stormy..." he shouted again. She scrambled to sit up, fighting to cover his mouth as he laughed and twisted his head around to avoid her fingers. She shushed him, but Lucas only smiled wider, then shouted as if hurt. "Ow, Stormy *stop*, please! Ah, *ahhhh!* Don't be so rough. Oh my God, you gon' break it!"

"Really, Luc?" Merlee shouted from the other room.

Stormy froze in mortification.

"It's okay, have your fun, Lucas," Garret countered. "Me and Merleena Jean'll just have to get busy and show y'all how it's really done."

Lucas's heart stopped. Shocked and appalled, he looked up at Stormy, then rolled to his side, knocking Stormy off of him as he banged against the shared wall. "Motherfucker, I hear anything besides snoring and cows jumping over the goddamn moon in that bitch, I'll castrate you. Hear me?"

The laughter on the other side of the wall was galling, but he was serious; he'd better not hear…

He was diverted by Stormy's laugher as she worked her way free of him and got beneath the bedcovers. "You are such an *idiot*," she said, shaking her head as she reached over and turned off the bedside lamp. He stared in her direction until his eyes adjusted to the dark, then he slid under the covers, turning to bang his fist against the wall one more time for good measure before settling along Stormy's backside.

Draping his arm over her abdomen, he rested his cheek against the back of her head and settled as Stormy folded her arm over his and interlaced their fingers.

She was asleep within seconds.

Closing his eyes, Lucas tried to stay vigilant to any sex sounds in the other room, but then he remembered that this was the last night he'd get to hold his sienna-red woman, and he tightened his arm around her, breathing her in, imprinting her scent, the feel of her skin, the contour of her body, unable to imagine letting her go.

It burned. The alcohol burned like hellfire.

Cornelius coughed, trying to breathe, to lessen the throat-swelling effect of the alcohol. Gasping, he closed his eyes and reached for the ornate cross that hung from his neck, praying until his body settled.

When he opened his eyes, the demons seemed closer, but he hadn't heard them move. Mama still sat at the far end of the bar, she was looking in her lap, her expression hidden by the ropy locks of hair that obscured it.

"Why are you here, Cornelius? What sins do you need to confess to me?" Terry asked again.

Although he'd received none of the nurturing at Shepherd's Keep that the demons received here, he knew the child would not be safe among them. Her eternal soul would not be safe.

Confess, Cornelius, fulfill your purpose, it's the only way that remains for you to enter the gates of heaven from this dark place.

He pushed the shot glass around with his finger, then shared the Shepherd's edict.

"All members of the order must ascend," he told Terry. "This is my test of ascension. It was to be the antecedent to my awakening or the evidence of my unworthiness." He looked over at the female fallen. "This morning I awakened and believed I had finally discovered God's purpose for me, to live among you and apply God's word and will… but the child, Terry, she's innocent. A home among the fallen would corrupt an innocent, her mind, body, then her soul. I can't let that happen. It's my time to be courageous."

"You're right, of course Cornelius, children must be protected, but —and I don't mean to deride—you don't have the means to protect *yourself*. If I take you off the mountain, I have to know you can keep the girl safe and from what I've deduced from your own words, there is very little safety for an innocent child within your Shepherd's Keep."

He was unable to look Terry in the eye. In good conscious he could never take a female innocent to live among the Shepherd's order, even if females *were* allowed. One had to be broken into the order's ways, and for the ones like him, the breaking never made them stronger, just more at risk for the others' attempts at breaking them. He could not recommend the child be taken there.

The Shepherdssin—she could take the child to the Patron. Cornelius was certain the little one was the child of the consort and the Patron's dead son. In his gratitude, the Patron was sure to allow Cornelius to live with their family and watch over the child's soul.

"I need to contact the Shepherdssin," he informed Terry. "She will help me fulfill my purpose so that I can ascend."

"Thing is, son, Delilah hasn't come back to get your reports or bring you food or anything since we brought you here. For all intents and purposes, she left you there to die, and if you can't contact her, you can't help the child."

Cornelius avoided Terry's gaze again and grazed his thumb over the circular center of the cross. It wasn't that he had no way of contacting her, he simply wasn't supposed to unless his sojourn was completed. He hadn't been honest with them about this; however, one was not obligated to be truthful to those aligned with the world's first and greatest deceiver.

"There is a number I can call," he said to Terry, unable to reconcile the shame he felt at his deception.

Mama stood and walked the length of the bar and squatted down beside him, offering him her phone. "Go ahead and call her, Cornelius," she stated flatly. "Your time for ascension has begun."

He nodded. "And so it has."

He closed his eyes, afraid and confused by Mama's lack of warmth. Why did he still crave it? Because if not for the child, he could have made a home here. He could have…

But in all things, God's will must prevail. Cornelius gave her the number. Terry motioned for the laptop the consort had used to communicate with the child, flipped it back open, and began to type rapidly as Mama dialed Delilah's phone number. Cornelius listened with the others as it rang.

"Cornelius."

"God's blessings be upon you, Shepherdssin."

"Of course they are, Cornelius, what do you have?"

"There is a child—"

Mama wagged her finger at him and placed it against her lips, cutting off any discourse about the child.

"I've found the ones you sought, the killers of the Patron's only son."

"Well, that is a surprise. Perhaps you aren't as unskilled as I was led to believe."

His face heated with embarrassment. "To be honest, they found me."

"No matter, they are the incompetent spawn of demons. The Shepherd was right to choose you for this undertaking, Cornelius, but you're still a disappointment. You know what must be done."

"But God has given me a greater purpose," he whispered. "I must protect the child."

"You must yield to the will of the Good Shepherd," the Shepherdssin said. *"He is the holy redeemer of faith, the mouthpiece of the Lord's will on earth. He is His sword and our salvation. Good Shepherd of the wayward flock continues to guide the unholy, for it is his will and his vision...* You know the rest, Cornelius. Fail and the order will bring His wrath down upon you, make you suffer more than you ever have before. Do what you must, brother. I have my own demon to slay."

Delilah disconnected the call and Cornelius sat there, numb, looking down, tears streaming down his face.

She would not help him.

No one would help him, no one would protect him, no one had ever protected him. There was so much to live for now, but he couldn't live if the Order decreed that he was meant to die. They had killed him in so many ways.

He stood and took a step back from the bar. His death was inevitable, but if the nest of evil was destroyed, the child at least would be safe.

His heart was breaking.

"I'm sorry," he whispered before turning the circular center of the cross and combining the liquid components inside. He gripped the cross with both hands and nodded vigorously. "I'm sorry."

The demons, sensing their time on earth had come to an end, moved as if operating from a hive mind, but they didn't act in aggression toward him. Perhaps they now feared him, feared the light of God that would consume them.

Cornelius looked up when nothing immediately happened.

Perhaps the Lord had found him worthy and stayed this destruction, but no one else seemed to realize this. Terry hit something behind the bar and a sheet of metal descended, covering the rows of alcohol that lined the wall behind the bar.

Mama regarded him with rage-filled eyes. She was no longer Mama, she was the mother of demons, and she leaped off the bar and also struck something near the *Employees Only* door. Tables fell over, as if a piston was sprung at their base, the consort was shoved behind one.

Cornelius felt pain erupt through his chest. Looking down, he saw the demon's blade there, embedded to the hilt. He used one hand to clutch the cross as the other clutched the blade. Overwhelmed by the pain, he fell to his knees, and when he looked up, his gaze was drawn to the metallic glint in the gray-eyed demon's cold glare.

Cornelius fought to stand but his limbs would not obey.

His heart was grinding to a halt, his time winding down, and what did he have to show for it?

Hot tears slid down his face. Nothing. He had nothing.

He wanted the chance to ride a motorcycle, he wished he could have known that kind of freedom just once.

The cross's liquid components ignited and burst through his soul, God's wrath burning the world around him. He cried out, but no longer for God's grace; he just wanted the agony to end.

Anguished, pain-filled screams echoed within the fire as demons were dispatched from this earthly plane and sent back to hell, but there was no comfort for Cornelius, no heavenly intervention for his sacrifice.

Only the pain and the belief that nothing better awaited him in death.

Fate was an impatient bitch screaming for him to get up when all Big Country wanted to do was stay wrapped around Stormy's sleeping body and avoid the clusterfuck that this day was sure to become.

If the clock on the nightstand was to be trusted, it was near on five-fifteen in the morning, still dark but the sun would rise soon. Sighing, Big Country peeled back the covers and exited the bed, careful not to wake Stormy. His grands often preached that when there was important work to be done, it was best to get up and get to it. Let the sun be the one to greet you instead of the other way around. There was nothing to be gained by avoidance.

After retrieving his phone from the jeans he'd left on the floor last night, he pulled on a pair of gray sweatpants and made his way to the kitchen. He went directly to the high-tech coffeepot he'd bought

Merlee two Christmases ago and conjured the strongest, darkest coffee he'd ever made to help get him through this.

"You sure you don't want me to come with you?"

In the process of adding a teaspoon of sugar to his cup, he turned to see Merlee in a nightshirt with her hair like his—all over the place. He reached over and pulled another cup from the cabinet.

"I'm sure," he said, adding a lot of sugar and milk to a cup of coffee for Merlee. She walked over and placed her back against the kitchen sink as he looked out the window on the wall above it. They drank in silence as indigo sky transitioned to a shadowy slate gray. Big Country noticed each furtive glance Merlee threw his way.

"You had a right," he said eventually. "Me and the grands were always so focused on protecting you, we failed to prepare you. If you understood who they were maybe you'd have been ready for their bullshit, so for our oversight, I apologize."

She leaned over and rested her head on his shoulder as he continued. "From day one you were more mine than theirs, you know. Belle Mère had kids, yeah, but she was never one for motherhood, and the ol' man, all he ever cared about was her. They are a kind of sickness to each other. They ruined Thibideux and Wallace early, and because Wallace was the oldest brother, he was most vulnerable to their influence, I truly believed that's why he died so early. By the time I came along, the grands were on alert; they brought me here as often as they could, but I was Belle Mère's special boy. I watched out for Armand even though I was only two years older. I liked to learn, which the ol' man hated, so I learned all I could to spite the bastard. When you were born, I was the one who changed your diapers, fed you, dressed you, put you to sleep, carried you on the hip 'til you was old enough to toddle behind me and Armand."

He placed his empty cup in the sink, noticing the pale blush on the horizon.

"The bad part about it all was that things were not always bad. Me and Armand lived wild in that bayou, you could barely keep us inside." He smiled, remembering. Most times all they wore were cutoff jeans and sneakers, and the cutoffs were more optional than the shoes.

"Belle Mère favored me, and that meant I got the largest dose of the old man's fist whenever she showed me affection."

He felt more than heard Merlee's gasp. "You were a child."

"I was big for my age. Hell, by the time Mama came for us, my flesh was gator tough. For a while I didn't believe I'd ever feel again but when I did..."

"The episodes."

"Yeah."

His phone vibrated, and he reached for it.

"Don't beat yourself up about any of this, Merlee-girl. It's past time I...it's past time."

Merlee hugged him then wiped her eyes and moved toward the fridge. "Go take your call and get out of my kitchen so I can make breakfast before y'all head out."

He opened the sliding glass door that led to the pergola-covered patio and stepped into an atmosphere weighted with moisture. It was warm, a hint of coolness stirring through the breeze, the gathering clouds portending early morning rain.

Looking at his phone, he saw that he'd just missed a message from Lynx simply saying: *I'll c u soon.*

That in and of itself was disturbing, but it was the *not*-so-recent system notifications from his computer system at Mama's House that made him stare at the screen, attempting to control his breathing. Why hadn't anyone called him earlier? Hell, they could have even called Merlee or Stormy if he didn't pick up, but it was obvious they'd never even attempted.

He paused, considered the possibility that maybe they hadn't been able.

It was the fire and detonation protocols that had been activated. He immediately thought of Delilah setting fire to Stormy's home, but none of the external systems had been triggered, so she couldn't have snuck on or off the mountain without Gambit detecting her...hell, anyone.

"Fuck!"

To hell with speculation.

He accessed the video feed in the bar from the moments before the protocol was triggered, heard the saint speaking to Delilah on the phone. The younger man was shattered; Big Country felt his desperation, his hopelessness.

When Cornelius turned the cross's circular center as if setting a cooking timer, Big Country knew...and so did the rest of the Brood. His cross was a detonation device, but it had to be one that held two separate liquids that became combustible when combined. Anything like C4 or gunpowder would never have gotten past the front door. The system scanned for those things.

He should have made a better goddamn system.

Zeus's blade sunk into the saint's chest. Cizan threw himself at Zeus and they went flying as flames engulfed the saint.

Big Country killed the feed and called Mama's House. It was a little before four there, but the call would be answered.

"You safe?" Terry answered, no evidence of being awakened from sleep in his voice. Of course Terry wouldn't sleep, not till he knew the status of every Brood member, no matter where they were in the world.

"I can be on a plane home within the hour," Big Country said.

"You've taken care of your family business?" It was Mama who responded, and he knew he was on speaker because she sounded farther away, her voice gravelly as if she'd just woken from sleep or been crying.

"Y'all okay there?" he asked, maintaining an outward calm.

"Damage to the bar isn't bad, it'll be back up and running in a couple weeks. Your protocols worked with impressive precision, son. No structural damage to the bar. You and Cizan did a good job with building and outfitting our little home fortress," Terry said. "Zeus and Cizan got the worst of the blast, Zeus is bruised up again but Cizan saved him from a hospital visit. Price and Coen have checked in, they're both fine and will be back in the country in a few days. London was off-mountain attending an event in Silicon Valley; he's confirmed that there've been no strikes against him, he'll be back later in the morning."

No one was dead or seriously injured; that should have sufficed, but damn near everyone he cared about could have died in a matter of seconds and he hadn't been there to stop it. He could have stopped it, could have talked Cornelius down, could've offered himself up to Delilah and handled her and whoever else pulled her strings.

He closed his eyes. "I'm on my way back."

"Not until you've settled your family situation," Mama said in the same tone she used when giving mission directives.

"Mama, look—"

"No, it needs to be resolved today. My house is locked and loaded but Merlee needs you to end this thing with your parents. *You* need you to end it."

He paced inside the confines of the patio to keep himself from destroying it. Mama was right, he had to stay focused and in his right mind because there was a more immediate threat and it was less than a fifteen-minute ride away.

A thought drew him up short.

"Why is Lynx coming here?"

"He had a feeling," Mama said. When Lynx had a feeling, it was time to pay attention. "He should be there soon."

"All right, I'll get Stormy up and we'll roll out within thirty. Send me all the info you have on the Shepherd's Keep and I'll get on it when I'm on my way back."

"There's not much," Terry said. "But Bride has given us a possible region in northwestern Ireland to work with. No deeds in the order's name but from what we gather, the Patron may be Kragen III's father and the order may be linked to him, which actually means Zeus and Sabrina are the original targets. Both Delilah's and Cornelius's true identities are still a mystery, but we'll continue to dig. You'll have what we have when you're done on the farm."

"And Lucas, everybody there needs to be ready. Before the explosion, Terry tracked the phone Delilah used to Oklahoma. We didn't pinpoint a location, but I think it's safe to say she's searching for you."

"Well, here's to hoping she finds what she's searching for. I'll call when the farm's been cleared."

He hung up and walked back into the house. Merlee was at the stove scrambling eggs and Stormy sat at the kitchen table fully dressed, face void of makeup, and hair in two freshly done French braids as she sipped coffee from a sturdy mug and watched him.

Just because he couldn't help himself, he walked over and kissed her, then turned back to Merlee. "I'm gonna need the stuff Mama had shipped here."

"It's in Garret's office. Watch the food for a minute and I'll get it."

"I'll get it," Big Country said. "Garret still got the tiny arsenal of guns?"

"I do," Garret said, walking into the kitchen. "Why?"

"'Cause trouble may be coming this way and I'll need Merlee to protect you," Big Country said as he walked toward Garret's office.

"You think your family will try to come here once you force them to leave the farm?" Garret asked when Big Country returned with the package and one of Garret's Glocks.

"Naw, there was a situation on the mountain and it's possible that the folks that caused it will look for me here."

He pulled the tranquilizer gun out of the box and handed it to Stormy.

"Delilah?" she asked.

He nodded.

"I'll be ready to roll out in ten. Eat," he directed Stormy, then headed to the bathroom.

As he cleansed himself, he prayed to anyone and anything that would listen for the ability to keep Stormy, Merlee, and Garret safe.

And if all else failed, he'd just have to survive long enough to do so himself.

CHAPTER 12

"Here's the thing," he said, wheeling the big truck off the highway onto Arlington Avenue, the last public roadway before they hit Beau Lane, the private road leading up to the farm. "I know you want to have my back. I know that, darlin', but it's gonna get bad in there, and I need you to stay in the truck where it's safe."

"Safe for who?" she asked, an underbelly of anger showing beneath her calm. "Definitely not for you; not with at least three people in that house who would rather see you dead before giving up squatter's rights to the farm. If Lynx was here, maybe; but let you go in there alone, I think the fuck not."

Okay, so maybe there was more anger there than he thought. This wasn't the empathic-therapy-mode Stormy, this was the ready-to-fight version.

"Plus," she continued. "I can't imagine it'll be safer for me alone in the truck if your *fiancée* decides to pop up." He glanced over at her and she was looking at him…calmly. "We go in together, just like we agreed."

"Okay, but let me get something straight. You're ain't mad at *me*, right? You ain't planning on shooting me in the ass as payback for all the unsavory shit I may have done to get some lovin', right?"

She threw her head back and laughed, her humor hitting him like brilliant shards of energy, piercing him to the marrow and buoying his spirits. The pressure that had been building since he got out of bed this morning dissipated.

How was he going to hold on to this woman beyond the journey's end, he wondered as he reached out to brush a thumb over her lips to capture the taste of her smile.

She circled her hands around his and kissed his fingers. "Concerned for you," she said. "You want to protect me...and Merlee...and people living on the top of a mountain...and strangers...I just want to protect you, keep you safe. We do this just like we agreed. Right?"

"Well, when you put it like that, darlin', can't imagine how I saw it any other way."

Stormy lowered his hand to her lap and leaned forward as the cream and yellow farmhouse came into view.

"Sienna Red," she said, bemused, making the connection between her nickname and the brownish-red packed earth they rode up on. "Welcome home, Lucas Beaumont."

A chill passed through him. It was as if the ghost of his grandmother had possessed Stormy. Those were his grandmother's words said in the exact timber, cadence, and drawl she used each time she welcomed him home.

Big Country slowed the truck when the road transitioned to gray pavement. Merlee had done their grands justice in her maintenance of the two-story farmhouse. The buttercream exterior, red vaulted roofing, the sturdy porch with sage green railing that wrapped around the whole of the right side of the house, the manicured flowering pots, grass, and aged trees made the house look like it should be featured in some country living magazine.

"It's beautiful."

"Four generations of Beaumonts have lived in this house, and all except for the sorry sack of manhood that poses as my daddy, every generation has added their own piece to the legacy."

"I assume Merlee had her veterinary clinic built. What did you add?"

He shut off the engine and opened his door. The heat and humidity had intensified despite the black and gray clouds churning overhead.

"Just for your own knowing," he said, walking around and opening the door for her. "I helped build and outfit Merlee's little animal hospital. As far as my own contribution…if you're lucky, one day I'll show you."

As they walked up to the front porch, Big Country rolled his shoulders, staying loose and at the ready. Stormy's hand hovered just inside the opening of her bag as Big Country used his key, not bothering to knock.

Opening the door wide, it banged against something and knocked it over. He wouldn't be surprised if that was his family's version of a swamp-rat alarm system. They obviously didn't have the codes or the know-how to use the actual alarm system.

Unlike its exterior, the interior of the house showed blatant signs of abuse, typical of just about everything his kin put their grubby hands on. They didn't care about the hardwood floors or the expensive rugs; grass and dirt and other shit he didn't want to contemplate was tracked over both. Empty bottles littered just about every surface his eyes could see. The smell of cigarette smoke and unwashed bodies stole inside his nostrils, and so far, they'd only walked three feet inside the entryway.

"I'll keep the door open," Stormy muttered. "It smells worse than a stable."

"That's because something worse than animals are living here."

The outdoor air was clean but when the humidity mixed with his family's dissolution, the smells only seemed to fester.

As he walked around the lower level of the house—living room, dining room, kitchen, bathrooms—his anger grew. They had desecrated his grands' home with their debauchery and slovenliness.

"It's only superficial," Stormy said. "With Merlee, Lynx, and Garret, we can have this cleaned up and livable in no time."

He headed toward the back of the house where stairs divided the space between the kitchen and the family room, intending to go up there and...

He froze.

At the top of the stairwell, wearing nothing but a black silk and lace slip that barely hit the middle of her thigh, was the woman who'd birthed him.

He swallowed back his stomach's instinct to void this morning's breakfast.

Maybe it was a trick of the eye, maybe it was a defect of the mind, but she looked exactly like she had that night thirty years ago. Her hair was loose, her mouth was curved in a knowing smile, and she wore what looked like the same damn slip.

It was impossible.

He'd been six, detached from what she was doing, focused on the flickering blue flame of the old electric light designed like a candle on a saucer beside his bed.

It appeared as if she'd walked straight from his nightmares into this very real moment.

But he wasn't the unsuspecting child who loved his Belle Mère more than he loved anyone and anything, he was a grown man who had decades of intrusive memories playing out her betrayal over and over again.

Belle Mère cried out as if she'd been hit, her hand clamping down on her mouth, fingers fluttering against it in agitation. "Oh! *Oh Mon Dieu, ma bon,* my wee beautiful boy. Julian, come see! Our sweet boy has come home to us just like was promised."

Holding onto the railing, she rushed down the stairs.

The closer she got, the further he retreated.

He hadn't been prepared for this. His father, his brothers—that was the battle he was ready to have, that's the vengeance he relished experiencing.

Her—he didn't want to be in touching distance of her, wanted her as far away from him as possible.

Stormy edged in front of him as Belle Mère reached the bottom of the stairs.

The level of aggression Stormy currently displayed was more intense than when they'd fought in the parking lot of Teats and Meat. One thing he knew about Stormy was that she wasn't easily provoked. For all intents and purposes, Belle Mère had done nothing but greet her long-lost son, but Stormy looked ready to lose her license before she'd let Belle Mère embrace him.

When he looked at Belle Mère now, with less than three feet separating them, it was no longer through the filters of the past. She was still beautiful in some ways, but there was a desiccated quality to her. It hung out around her eyes and mouth, in the claw-like nature of her hands.

What was also crystal clear to him was that she was hungover. The stench of alcohol wafting off her let him know that she must have reached for a bottle of whiskey or bourbon moments before coming downstairs. When he was a child, it was her morning ritual. Taking a bite out of the dog that bit you was as routine to her as reaching over to turn off an alarm clock was to a working person.

His mother's gaze sharpened as it swung from Stormy to Big Country. She smiled before laughing softly. "Aw, my poor *bebe*, you still bringing home these dirty untrained bitches, t'inkin' you can turn them into loyal pets? It's a nasty habit life ain't broke you from yet, no?"

Cold rage tunneled his vision, dimming all sensations except the one to reach out, wrap his hand around his mother's throat, throw her...*push her off him, what was she...why was she doing this?* He flinched as the memory transported him back in time. His hand twitched as violence warred with the repulsion of feeling her skin against his. *Choke her, snap her fucking neck, let her feel helpless and numb, let her see how it feels to struggle and know it won't save her,* the buried part of him raged, fighting to break free from its tomb.

Something pressed against his chest, radiating warmth, dispelling the whirlwind of thoughts and emotions that tried to sweep him away. He looked down and saw Stormy's hand splayed across his heart. It could have been the hand of Buddha the way it banished the chaos within him, allowed him to take a breath, allowed the world to take shape again, sharpen into focus.

There was a sweet coolness weaving through the air streaming from the open front door. A steady rain fell outside, dampening the house's entryway.

"Hello, you must be Emilia. My name's Stormy, Stormy Redmond, and I think it's absolutely adorable that you have such fond memories of Lucas caring for untrained bitches. Curious, though; do the only recollections you have of your son date back to when he was a boy?" Stormy tilted her head to the side, her smile polite. "If so, why is that?"

Big Country would've told anybody willing to listen that Belle Mère was born incapable of feeling shame, but right here, right now, that's exactly what he saw, and for the first time he truly got it, understood he wasn't obligated to carry around her discarded shame and make it his simply because she refused to do so. He looked down at his mother and knew he could release it back to its rightful owner, free his younger self from the burden of swaddling it inside his soul.

And true to form, Belle Mère resisted acknowledging the damage she'd done. Instead, her eyes narrowed, and she pointed an accusing finger at Stormy. "This *my* boy, I'm his mama, you don't come in my house—"

"First of all, you're not," Stormy interrupted. "I met the woman he calls Mama and she's a little black woman running things from a mountain top."

"...Second of all, you got a lot of motherfuckin' nerve yeah, bringing ya shabby ass in my grands' home knowing they would've burned it to the ground before they let your perversions through the door," Big Country said.

Belle Mère flinched as if he'd slapped her. "You can't let this one twist ya mind around, *mon fils*, there's a good woman wanting to bring our family back together, you can't let this one twist ya dick and run ya life."

He looked at her for a long time, wondering how such a woman got made. Terry would know, Terry understood the heart of evil; but him, he just understood the effects of it. He eased Stormy to his left, not wanting anything between him and Belle Mère now but truth.

"I was big for my age you used to say, ya special boy, wild, smarter than any man you ever knew. You and PaPere had a knock-down, drag-out fight that night 'cause you caught him flirting with Mrs. Jacobs down at the bait shop. Didn't matter that you regularly spread your legs for profit, power, pettiness, didn't matter what. You never kept it a secret. But let the ol' man look the other way one time and you come to my room and do what you did. With all your crazy, never in a million years would I have thought you capable."

"I was drunk," she said. She'd tried to use that excuse again and again, PaPere accepted it, he and the grands never did.

"I'd seen you drunker." He smiled and raised an eyebrow. "But no worries, I had the grands and Mama. I didn't have to live with you day in and day out, didn't have to see you move through life with no consequence for the pain you caused, didn't have to live with the possibility that you'd hurt me again, though for truth a part of me always feared you'd find a way."

"It couldn't of been so *bad* my darlin' boy, look at you! You got more money and education than all your kin combined, you strong, you...why couldn't y'all see that maybe *I* helped make you into the man you are today."

It was his turn to flinch.

His first night in the hospital he'd told Mama and his grands what had happened but refused to talk about it ever again. His grands had tried to heal him through the church, then therapy but he refused to open up, so his grands let him rage until he exhausted himself, then he would quietly go about trying to clean up any sign of destruction he'd wrought.

By the time he was thirteen, he was bigger than most grown men, and after his grandmother had been injured by the hutch he'd torn from the wall and thrown across the room, his grandfather waited until he'd come back to himself, then took him to the back pasture and told Big Country in no uncertain terms: *Son, I'll forever regret I wasn't there to stop what that woman did to you, what my son did. I love you more than words can convey and thank the Lord daily that Almaya brought you to us, but I'll tell you one time and one time only, never again will the women in our house be hurt or left to pick up the pieces after you let that beast inside of you loose. You don't want to talk about what happened and I respect that, but you'll have to find another way of dealing with that pain or you'll have to go.*

And to a degree Big Country had found a way. He'd go out to the pasture or far from others when the coldness started to take him. He learned to hold tight to calm, he learned to let things roll off his back, to let humor be a kind of therapy, he learned to avoid the drama of relationships, relegating women to the realm of pleasure and release. He engaged his mind, he created, he solved problems, and he got justice for folks who didn't have the power or know-how to fight and win on their own.

"You still don't understand the damage you've done," Stormy said to Belle Mère. "If you cared, if you *truly* cared for Lucas, you wouldn't force him to fight him and Merlee free from you and your husband again."

"Look, you, I know what ya are and what ya not. This *family* business, and your black ass definitely ain't family. My boy got a good woman, now *you* get the fuck out."

She reached for Stormy, but his sienna-red woman was faster.

She grabbed Belle Mère by the upper arm and shoved her backward. Belle Mère yelled out, enraged, and jerked her arm free, balled up her fist and cocked it back to strike Stormy.

"Bitch, I wish you would," Stormy growled, stepping forward, sounding as if she wanted to kill Belle Mère.

Lord, his poor heart swelled. His champion, his woman, his...just *his*.

Big Country shrugged at Belle Mère. "If you feeling froggish and you got them legs, I dare you to jump."

"Yes, 'cause I'm definitely willing to lose my license over this shit," Stormy said.

He couldn't help it, he pulled her to him and kissed her, hard and fast. "Woman, I think you just made me finish falling for you, I mean hitting the ground with meteor-impact hard."

"Oh, dear Lord, I was not prepared for this storm!" Delilah exclaimed as she walked into the house, maneuvering two full grocery bags. She froze when she saw Big Country. "Beloved…you came," she said, dropping the bags. "I knew God would bring you to me, I knew He—"

Big Country reached for the gun holstered at his back and fired.

Screaming, Belle Mère fell to the ground and Delilah simply blinked in confusion, as if struggling to accept that he'd shot at her.

Stormy had kept her alive by pushing Big Country's arm up, making the bullet lodge in the wall above the front door.

"Lucas, what the hell!" Stormy shouted.

"That woman ordered a hit on Mama's House. She doesn't get to live."

"But Mama and Terry said they needed to find out more about the Shepherd and this Patron, she has that information," she said, trying to reason with him.

"She tried to take out *my family*."

"Your family harbors the killers of the Patron's son," Delilah said, no longer hiding her motivation for engaging the Brood. "The death of Zeus and Sabrina is ordained, beloved. The Shepherd has ordered it, God has willed it, and because Cornelius has obviously failed, I will now be the one to execute it."

Heavy feet thumped against the floors upstairs, making the ceiling vibrate…or was that the thunder?

"Emilia, what's dat noise goin' on down there?"

Delilah pulled a phone from her purse and left the house.

He wanted to follow, to stop her from making another move against the Brood, but heavy footsteps moving toward the top of the stairs stopped him.

Three men descended one after the other: Armand, Thibideux, then PaPere.

"Oh shit," Stormy muttered as she looked up to see his father and two brothers come down the stairs, all as big, if not as densely muscled, as Big Country.

Yeah, he thought, securing his gun against his back. Shit was about to go down.

~

Three versions of Lucas, one as imposing as the next, walked down the stairs, temporarily distracting Stormy from the sight of Delilah leaving the house by foot, then by car, neatly avoiding the altercation she undoubtedly played a part in exacerbating.

The first man down the stairs was the youngest, which meant he was Armand. He reminded her most of Lucas and it wasn't just because of his coloring and size; it was in the loose way he wore his faded jeans and gray T-shirt, it was in the appearance of calm assessment, the perceptiveness hiding within his brilliant green gaze.

His eyes roamed over Lucas and there was a residual anger in his gaze. There was also hunger, as if Armand was trying to link the boy he remembered to the man standing in front of him now, as if attempting to detail everything about Lucas in the event that he didn't see him for another three decades.

Stormy was reluctant to trust him anymore than she trusted the others but the grief in Lucas's eyes as he watched Armand settle across from them, to the right of Emilia, made her want to trust him, made her want to ask him to come over to their side. He helped to save the farmhand, helped watch over Merlee's farm—there was no reason he couldn't choose to help Lucas, too.

The next man to step off the stairs was truly frightening.

Initially he looked taller than Lucas's six feet six—the mind wanted to reject how massive Lucas was, as if his proportions were incomprehensible—yet up close all illusions were shattered. Lucas's older brother, Thibideux, was maybe six feet three or six feet four, his bare torso covered in old scars and tattoos. He looked like he lived caged, whether in prison or out. His rage, unlike Lucas's, was wide awake and boiling, appearing as if it never slept.

Of the three men, Stormy decided he was the greatest threat. He would be the one to ease a knife through Lucas's neck, and press his cheek against his younger brother's just to feel the moment Lucas's spirit fled his body in death.

Stepping past Thibideux to take the spot directly in front of Lucas was his father.

Decades older, he was the closest to Lucas in size, but his bulk had gone to paunch and his green eyes were murky as swamp water. Fumes of alcohol and sour sex wafted off his unwashed body, but it was the mockery in his eyes that disgusted Stormy the most. She had the sense that after all these years the man was gloating over his defeat of a six-year-old—as if inhabiting the home of the parents that condemned and rejected his brutality meant he was winning at life.

Lucas's mother stepped around Armand and molded herself against her husband, circling her arm around his waist, daring Stormy to say something now that she was surrounded by her men.

Stormy felt obligated.

"I get it, I do. You've got grown men willing to disregard the fact that you molested a six-year-old boy—your own son—and you think I'm going to do the same just because they're standing beside you. No. You should have gone to jail for what you did; at the very least, anyone with children should've been warned about the level of depravity and sickness that lives in you."

"You got a lot of nerve judging when ya spreadin' ya legs so's to sink ya filthy claws in my boy. I know what you are, you sanctimonious bitch, you no better than me. You think I haven't paid a price? I lost my boy and *ma petite fille* ova *one* indiscretion, ova one night when ma blood was up. I didn't harm the boy, he liked—"

"Stop," Armand said, holding up his hands as if in surrender. Then he clutched his head, rubbing his hands back and forth as to clear his mind. Stormy realized then that Armand hadn't known what led to Lucas and Merlee being taken away.

Armand was the youngest son. Why had he been left there?

Both of Lucas's parents were red in the face.

"Wait now, wait," Armand said, staring at Lucas. "That night when

I woke up and you was just staring off, shaking, it was 'cause…*and they knew?* PaPere, Wallace, and Thibideux, they knew, and they beat ya for it, beat on you near to death because you told 'em she touched you wrong?"

"I *begged* you to come with us," Lucas said, old betrayal lacing his words.

"Reckon I was too young to understand the choice, brotha. We got beat on all the time, yeah, didn't mean I should leave my kin and go with a stranger," he scoffed. "I prayed many a day that you'd come back, come get me, offer again…ya neva did."

"I couldn't," Lucas said. "And I didn't believe you'd want me to."

Armand rubbed a hand over his chest. "Yeah…it's been a rough night and I'm fair needing to sit this little reunion out. I'll be out tending the animals if ya need me."

He took a step and stopped inches from Stormy, looking at her as if she was suddenly the only other person in the room. "It's funny yeah, how you can run from a truth ya whole fuckin' life, and when you stop, thinkin' you've outrun it, ya turn to the side and see it was right there keepin' pace, neva let you outta its sight. Truth is, I ain't shit…but I ain't like them." He continued toward the back door. "Y'all be good."

"Did you touch him?" Lucas asked his mother. He still hadn't acknowledged his father or older brother.

"I neva touched that boy."

"He always was a useless piece of possum shit," Lucas's father muttered.

"You think that evil woman didn't try to keep her foot on our throat the moment she stole you and Merlee away?" Belle Mère asked. "You think anytime the littlest thing happened to that boy—and none of it our doing—we wasn't made to suffer? That bitch tried to ruin us, ya paw couldn't hold a job, T-Bo here always picked on by the law, women in towns always casting they dirty looks, judging me. My oldest boy would still be living if she'd kept her nose out our business. So no, nobody ever touched ya precious brotha." His mother spat out her words, then literally spat. On the floor. *Inside* the house.

Stormy curled her nose in disgust but Lucas didn't react.

"You suffering has nothing to do with Mama," he said. "The way y'all live is the way you've always wanted to live, so don't start making shit up now."

"Watch ya'self now, boy," Lucas's father warned. "That there's still ya Belle Mère, ya give her respect due as ya mama."

Lucas closed his eyes for a moment, his jaw clenched and Stormy knew he was fighting to stay in control. The look of naked hate directed at his father when he opened his eyes made her flinch and instinctively step back.

"Respect her or what?" Lucas smiled.

It wasn't a Lucas smile, it was a wolfish baring of teeth, a sharp-toothed ready-to-rip-flesh-from-bone smile. Stormy slid her hand deeper into her purse and adjusted her fingers so that all she'd have to do is pull out the tranq gun and fire.

"You gon' whoop my ass?" His smile widened.

His father laughed, like real belly laughter, which caused Emilia and Thibideux to snicker. "Boy, you done got all swole and think ya can take ya ol' man on, huh? You been gone a good while, so you don't know but let me tell ya, I still whoop ass like it was my calling. You done had ya moment, now *I'm* telling ya, this hea our home now and I don't reckon we leavin' any time soon."

"Nobody come save ya this time, lil' Luc. Keep on and we'll mourn ya when you dead yeah…maybe," Thibideux said as he squared up.

Stormy's heart was pounding a mile a minute, her body so tense that her breaths came quick and shallow. She forced herself to yawn, a natural relaxant which moved oxygen deep into her lungs, and exhaled slowly, deciding to appeal to whatever sense of decency remained in Lucas's parents. "Don't make him do this; you finally have a chance to do something right for him, leave and let Merlee come home, it's the least you—"

The slap was swift and hard.

Stormy stumbled back and it took a few seconds for her to comprehend that Lucas's father had hit her, and a few seconds more to accept that there wasn't going to be a nonviolent end to this day.

Pressing the tranquilizer gun against her thigh, she reached out with her other hand, pressing it against Lucas's chest, ready to tell him that she was okay, to beg for him not to lose himself, to stay here—

"He hit you."

"Somebody gets out of line with me, I snap 'em back in, long-standing rule that don't go away just 'cause you did, boy," his father said. "Now, unless you wanna get whooped on worse than the last time, I suggest you take this black bitch and run away like you did with the first one who took you."

"Couldn't run. Leg was broke in two places," Lucas said as he reached up and cupped Stormy's stinging cheek. He caressed it with his thumb.

His hand was so cold…

"I'm okay, Lucas," she whispered.

"If I'da done a right and good job I'da broke ya lousy neck," his father taunted.

"It could've ended all right if he hadn't touched you." Lucas's voice was flat, empty. It hurt her heart to lose him this way. "It could have ended…"

She knew the rage was clawing itself free, filling the void that Lucas was falling into.

His hand fell to the side and she reached for it, held it tight, praying the physical connection would anchor him, but he was so cold. She rubbed his hands between hers as if he was going into shock.

"Women can't be left to pick up the pieces," Lucas said. "We take this outside, see who wins the right to stay."

His father's smile turned greedy as he passed them and went to the back door. Shouting into the storm as he stepped out, Thibideux trailing behind him like a trained animal.

"Look at ma *bon bebe*, big and strong, still fighting ova his Belle Mère. I knew ya'd end up a better man than *ton pere*, lil'Luc, I just wish I coulda been there to watch as you grew into your manhood," Lucas's mother said as she walked to the back door, loud enough for her husband to hear.

It was all a manipulation to stoke Julian's anger, and it seemed to be working.

The woman was vile.

"Use the weapon, Stormy," Lucas said before following his mother out of the house, his voice barely human. "Even on me. Especially on me. Don't want to hurt you. Don't let me live knowing I did."

She shook her head. She wouldn't shoot him.

"*Please.*"

The agony in his voice forced her to concede. She was going to lose him. With all her training, there was nothing she could do to stop it. Tears gathered in her eyes, but she wouldn't let them fall. He didn't need to worry about her, he needed to worry about staying alive.

Lifting the strap of her bag off her shoulder, she brought it over her head and placed it diagonally across her chest so she didn't have to worry about it falling. She helped Lucas remove his shirt and placed it inside the bag, pushing it deep so it wouldn't obstruct her access to the tranq gun.

"Okay," she breathed out. "Let him loose. And when you're done, me, you, and Bubba, we're going to start a whole new adventure, all right?"

His gaze was empty as he looked at her, not recognizing who she was or even what she was to him.

He turned and stepped out into the elements. Heavy rainfall obscured Stormy's vision, making Lucas no more than a dark shadow stalking the more distant forms of his father and brother. Stormy walked into the storm, unaffected by the torrential rain soaking her skin, the mud sucking at her feet as she struggled to move forward.

"Lose the gun, boy," Lucas's father called out.

Mud resembling rusted blood splattered up as the gun landed in the space between Emilia and Stormy. Thunder rolled so hard across the heavens, it was as if the earth itself shifted beneath her feet. Jags of bright lightning momentarily blinded Stormy, but she heard the distinct sound of Lucas's roar and knew the battle had begun.

Gripping the tranq gun, she waited for the effects of the lightning to recede. Then she searched through the downpour until she saw the three colossal figures battling viciously fifty feet away.

Witnessing the speed, the savagery, she understood why Lucas was so concerned about her safety. His father, his brother, they carried the same berserker-like rage inside them; they fought with the same kind of unrelenting madness.

Inching forward, she could more clearly see Emilia's black locks plastered against her head, shoulders, and back. The black slip she wore left nothing to the imagination now. As if sensing her, Emilia looked over her shoulder, a twisted smile distorting her features. Dark excitement was alive in her eyes as she turned back to her husband and sons fighting.

No matter how fast the rain fell, that woman will never be washed clean, Stormy thought.

There was another bellow of rage, Lucas's father was on the ground, scrambling to get up as Lucas and Thibideux literally tried to kill each other. There wasn't any attempt at defense, only annihilation. Despite their size, despite the storm, their punches were hard and fast. Fists connected with ribs, jaws, noses, eyes.

Thibideux faltered but Lucas didn't relent. He bellowed again, his moves becoming faster as he pummeled his brother, striking with such impact she feared he would put his fist through the other man.

Rising from the ground covered in grass and mud, Julian punched Lucas in his lower back. The hit would've lifted a normal man off his feet, made him cave on his wounded side, but Lucas grinned and swung his elbow back, cracking his father against the side of his head, sending him back to his knees. Lucas swung around and stomped his father in the chest, propelling him off the ground each time before he kneeled and punched him dead in his face.

Thibideux caught Lucas in a chokehold before he could hit Julian a third time. Stormy couldn't tell what was blood, and what was mud streaming from the older man's face as he struggled to his knees.

Emilia screamed when she saw the state of Julian's face.

Lucas reached up, gripped the back of Thibideux's neck, and flung him overhead. Thibideux was on his feet almost instantly and Lucas lunged, hooked his brother by the waist and drove him back into the ground. Julian rose to his feet, fisted his fingers together and slammed them into the back of Lucas's head.

Lucas toppled over and Stormy took a step forward, but Lucas was up and hitting one man and then the other, taking as many hits as he landed.

The abuse these men endured would have incapacitated a normal human being long ago, but like the undead, the Beaumont men continued to rise, continued to fight.

When Thibideux was down again, Lucas reached out and grabbed his father by the throat, lifting him in the air as Julian tried to claw his way through Lucas's arm to be free. Lucas did not relent or let go, continued to squeeze.

His father's movements became less frenzied, his eyes lost their wildness and turned desperate as the life was slowly being choked out of him.

Emilia screamed and sprinted toward Stormy, stopping midway and kneeling in the mud.

Stormy frowned and looked back at Lucas. Thibideux was on his feet, punching Lucas in the kidney area but Lucas didn't release the father. Instead he reached out and pulled Thibideux close and bit him in the area between shoulder and neck.

Thibideux screamed.

Emilia must have found what she was looking for because she stood and straightened her arms, aiming the gun Lucas had tossed earlier. She fired as Stormy lunged, tackling her.

The rain was weakening in intensity which must have allowed Julian to see Emilia go down and he renewed his struggle to break free of Lucas. Something metallic glinted in Thibideux's hand and Stormy saw him slice Lucas's forearm, saw Julian fall to the ground.

Stormy kicked Emilia in the face and the other woman went still. Stormy prayed she hadn't broken her neck, killed her.

Julian and Thibideux tore into Lucas when he stopped them from getting to their downed matriarch.

They wouldn't stop. They literally would not stop until one or all of them were dead.

Stormy pulled the tranq gun from her bag and aimed it in the direction of the three men still fighting, still trying to annihilate each other.

She fired, and Julian went down.

She shot again and Thibideux crumpled.

She aimed the gun at Lucas, whose gaze swung to her when his combatants fell. His eyes were unnaturally bright when they locked on her, his breaths rapid, his muscles expanding and retracting like a stationary bull sizing up its next victim to gore.

Maddened, he charged.

In that instant, she knew she wouldn't do as he'd requested. She wouldn't be the one to chemically imprison this part of him that destroyed to protect him, the part that contained so much anger, hurt, and innocence within itself.

Stormy lowered her hand and dropped the gun, braced herself as Lucas's footfalls ate up the ground between them. *He doesn't even like to run,* she thought with morose humor, closing her eyes before he struck.

She inhaled deeply, buffeted by the driving wind and rain even as the thunder and lightning died away, becoming more distant, less intense, allowing space for her to hear Lucas stop in front of her.

She felt his body heat, felt his breath lance the side of her face.

Opening her eyes, she saw Lucas's chest and shoulders heaving in front of her. Lifting her gaze, she found herself captured by radiant green eyes still lost to wildness. She reached out and pressed her hand against his jawline.

He bared his teeth, growled low in his throat.

She lifted her other hand, cradled his head in her grasp. He closed his eyes. She felt tremors wrack through his body before he opened them again.

"There you are," she murmured gently swiping a thumb over his brow. "There's my Lucas, my Big Country Beaumont, my Big Luc, wild warrior, safely back in the driver's seat."

"For now," he muttered. "But if another person lays one more hand on you…" He sighed. "I told you to shoot me."

"I know, I was going to, but I chose to take a chance. After all we've been through in this brief moment in time, I chose to trust you, to trust myself with all parts of you." She nodded. "I'm not a mangled mess, I'd say it turned out to be a damned good decision, and now you've got proof that shows you it's okay to trust *yourself* a little more."

He lowered his head to kiss her and she reared back.

"Oh *hell* no. It would be great to kiss you—perfect end to an adventure and all that—but you've got your brother's blood all over your mouth and that's just nasty."

He frowned, swiped his forearm over his mouth and spat out to the side, leaning forward again.

"Yeah, not happening, cousin." She laughed.

"What kind of fucked-up twisted story is this, that a man, a big strapping warrior of a man like me can fight for the very *fabric* of his soul but can't kiss his woman after? That ain't how this is supposed to end, darlin'." He lifted her off the ground and held her tightly against him. "But that just lets me know our little adventure ain't nowhere close to the end. I'm thinking this is just the prologue, yeah, that maybe I got the rest of my days to kiss on you as I see fit."

Stormy wound her arms around his neck. Closing her eyes, she rested her head against his shoulder and finally granted herself the freedom to release her tears of fear, sadness, love, into the steadying stream of rain water washing over them.

"Don't stop loving on me, Sienna Red. My poor heart couldn't survive without its calming storm."

CHAPTER 13

"Come on now, chi, we made it through, yeah? Worst part is over."

Stormy was silent but her double and triple breaths and hot tears flowing onto his shoulder let him know she was still having a good cry.

Big Country tightened his arm around her waist and rubbed her back with his free hand. "All right then, darlin', go ahead and have your cry, but just think, when you're all done, and we've gotten rid of my kin, I'm thinking we have, oh I don't know, at least a couple of weeks of adventure time before you get back to real life."

Her tears quieted. "We let the Brood clean up the Delilah situation, and me and you, we'll start by going to see your relatives in Louisiana, then head on down to New Orleans for a day or two before hopping over to my houseboat on the bayou. You'll see nature's wild beauty. I'll get some knockout pills from Merlee, then we'll hop on a plane to France, pay homage to my ancestry and after we're done fucking, eating, and drinking, we'll make our way back to the Bay." He kissed her forehead. "I'm really gonna blow your mind then."

She looked up and dragged the back of her hand over those pretty whiskey-brown eyes, moisture binding her long lashes together.

"I want beignets," she said, sounding like a child bargaining with an overwhelmed parent over good behavior.

"I'll make you beignets, real ones, not that tourist-trap bullshit."

She wrapped her legs around his hips and leaned back, her hands on his shoulders, her eyes knowing. The game was afoot.

"Toys. I want to bring at least two more toys for us to play with."

"I'm a daring sort, darlin', I think I can handle one or two of your little dick emporium toys," he said, reaching down to pat her ass cheek.

She threw her head back and laughed.

When her eyes grew somber, he held her more securely. She cleaned a spot at the edge of his mouth and pressed her lips there before resting her cheek against his. "I wanted them to do better by you. Not that I believed in a happy-ever-after, but it wasn't unreasonable to want them to own up to hurting you and just move on."

"For them it was highly unreasonable—but I'm fine, Sienna Red, better than fine even."

He placed her on her feet. Despite the rain, he was still covered in mud and blood. "Look at that, I've gone and got you all dirty," he said, rubbing his hand over her breasts.

The edge of her mouth lifted. "Yes, you did, Lucas."

He slowed his swipes down and let his focus and fingers linger on her peaked nipples. "Filthy, even," he murmured, wondering if she'd let him—

"They dead?" He turned to see Armand step over the bodies of their father and brother before coming to a stop beside him.

"Does it matter?" Big Country asked, not wanting to fight his youngest brother.

"It does," Armand answered, looking around. "Back home, I could throw a body in the bayou, food for the gators yeah, but here…" He frowned and rubbed his head. "If Merlee had hogs…but with the fair coming, won't be enough time, I'm thinking." He shrugged. "Maybe I'll find a good spot off the farm to bury 'em. Bad business binding their spirits here, y'all would never get no rest, animals would sicken, land would go to rot. Who shot you anyways?" He asked Big Country.

Stormy searched Lucas, wiped mud away from the slowly seeping gash on his left shoulder.

"That *bitch.*"

"Just flesh wounds, darlin', I don't feel a thing," he said, trying to ease her anger. He'd probably feel this for days to come and not just physically.

"Well, ya forearm is practically shredded," Armand said. "And the place T-bo took his knife to you, yeah, all that's gon' get infected real nasty you don't tend to it."

Big Country glared, trying to will Armand into shutting the fuck up, then he blinked.

He'd forgotten.

Until this moment, he'd forgotten all the times he'd felt and looked at his younger brother with the same exasperation. Forgotten how, from the moment Armand could form sentences, he'd work things through out loud, telling the truth as he understood it, consequences be damned.

"They're not dead," he eventually told his brother. "Load 'em into PaPere's truck with the rest of y'all's stuff and head back to East Orleans parish. Otherwise I'll have Deputy Harlan, the sheriff's soon-to-be replacement, pick 'em up and take all three to jail."

"Best to call the deputy then, 'cause I ain't going back. Merlee and I had an agreement—if I helped take care of the farm, I'd earn room and board, just like Will. I never stopped working, even when they ran her off."

Big Country stared at Armand and Armand stared back. "Merlee don't need you here, what she's offering is a handout. I'm here now asking; you want to come to California with me, make your own way?"

Armand looked at Stormy instead. "Your woman won't mind?"

Stormy's gaze moved from one brother to the other. "I think it would be great for both of you."

"What about your other woman?" Armand asked Big Country.

"Yeah, what about your other woman, Lucas?" Stormy parroted. She was mocking him.

"Delilah's a pretty little thing, but she crazy, yeah?"

"Crazy like a rabid, soulless, deceiving fox," Big Country muttered. He walked over, retrieved his gun and re-holstered it. "Stormy, while you're over there *tee-hee-hee*ing, call Mama, let her know things here are okay. Let her know they'll need to take the lead now that Delilah's on the run again, that we're finishing our adventure. I'll call Harlan, let him know what's about to happen to his boss and see if he's up for dealing with these three. Armand, you call Merlee, tell her to come on home so we can get our house back in order."

"Dude, I did not come all the way out here to clean your nasty-ass house."

Big Country swung around to see Lynx leaning against the back door.

"I came to save my heart," Lynx winked at Stormy before frowning back at Lucas. "Man, you look like shit, like literally. Please tell me that's not shit you're covered in."

Big Country grinned, happy to see his best friend standing there looking like proof that life was getting back on track. "Naw cousin, it ain't shit, it's that glow up from my woman's lovin' mixed with some good ol' country soil," he replied, not surprised Lynx managed to stay untouched by the now-passing storm.

"Oh Stormy, no…don't tell me you've chosen the barbarian over me, you know I can… Jesus *Christ*, it is hot as fuck out here!" Lynx said, wiping sweat from his forehead and pulling off his polo shirt. He had on a sleeveless T-shirt beneath. "What kind of people choose to live inside the ass-crack of hell? This is ridiculous."

Armand pulled up alongside Big Country as Lynx moved back into the house. They all stared at the empty doorway.

"Who's he?" Armand asked.

"Brother from another mother. Bit of a prima donna but don't underestimate him, get on his wrong side and…well, for both our sakes, just don't get on his wrong side."

"Lynx is a sweetheart," Stormy said, walking toward the house.

"But not *your* sweetheart, let's get that clear," Big Country said.

She waved a dismissive hand and kept walking.

Blue sky emerged as the clouds receded. He and his brother remained quiet until they were standing alone among their fallen kin.

"Sorry, for not going back for you. Hope one day you'll see fit to forgive me for it," Big Country said.

"Nothing to forgive, brotha. We make the best choices we can in the moment, and if we're lucky, we live long enough to correct the ones we regret, yeah? I could'a left a long time ago, but I realized when I wasn't there to pay the bills, bad things happened to innocent people. It was just easier to stay."

It was easier to sacrifice himself, Big Country thought, acknowledging the blessing he'd been given when he'd come here. He took in the old red barn washed clean with the storm, the rows and rows of Merle's planter box garden, the veterinary clinic next to the corral, the acres of open space he'd spent years battling himself upon.

He'd been given another chance at life back then, and today, here and now, he was choosing to open his heart up to love the only woman it ever would, the one who knew how to fill it and protect it. The one laughing in the house, the sound of which made him smile, knowing Lynx was in there acting like a fool. He moved toward the sound of his happiness, and Armand kept pace beside him.

"You ever been to California?" he asked his brother.

"Naw, Virginia's the farthest I ever got before I had to come back and deal with some mess they made," Armand said, pointing his thumb toward the unconscious bodies on the ground.

"You're going to love California, brother," Big Country said as they walked inside the house.

Instead of finding Lynx and Stormy engaged in some level of foolishness, they were facing the front door, Stormy's phone moving from her mouth to rest against the side of her thigh.

Big Country frowned and shifted to his left so he could see around the stairwell toward what held their attention as he reached toward his back. The moment Delilah came into view, the polished revolver she had trained on Lynx shifted toward him.

Big Country's hand fell to his side when he saw the gun's twin aimed straight at Stormy's chest. Big Country motioned for Armand not to move and his brother stilled, partially blocked by the stairwell.

The rain had stripped Delilah to her core, but her eyes were fevered in their intensity.

"Nice of you to join us, beloved. Not quite the reunion I'd hoped for, but please have Julian and Emilia join us as well."

Big Country widened his stance, needing to stay grounded because for the first time in life he had something to lose. If he lost it…

"I'd love to do what you ask, sweetness, but it ain't possible right now. Those two tried to take something that didn't belong to them, so they had to pay the price."

"Can't say I'm saddened. It took fortitude to pretend they weren't the disgusting creatures they are. It's good you made them suffer for it, which begs the question, what price should the whore pay for attempting to take what belongs to *me*, hmm?"

Lynx tried to edge closer to Stormy.

"Don't move."

Lynx froze. Neither he nor Big Country seemed willing to challenge the quickness of Delilah's trigger finger.

"I'm right here, darlin'," Big Country said. "Willing to do whatever you ask if it means me and you leave here together."

"So earnest, so charming, but who am I to believe, the man who speaks with sincerity and kindness, or the man who raised his gun and tried to kill me?"

"Yeah…I'd go with the first," Big Country said. "You gotta admit you had it coming though, giving Cornelius the order to destroy Mama's House and all."

"I was fighting for us, I *am* fighting for us but you have to choose something more than pleasure found between a common whore's thighs, beloved. You have to choose *me* because I have done everything asked of me. Everything. The Good Shepherd directs me to seek vengeance for sins done against the order's most generous Patron, Mr. Kragen—because the death of an only son, an *heir*, is apparently a thing which powerful men aren't meant to endure—and I am obligated to punish those who harmed him."

"And you did this on your own?" he asked, needing to know what other players were on the field.

"I'm very good at my job, beloved. The Patron provided some of the support I needed in the states, The Good Shepherd provided an acolyte needing to prove his worth, and me, I harnessed my ability to seek and destroy. But in this process God revealed you, the one man meant to be my joy, my chance at a new beginning."

"God also tell you how to get an explosive in Mama's House?" Big Country asked.

"He certainly was no God, just a man wanting a woman to show him a bit of heaven. He was helpful enough, he shared what he knew about Mama's House, told me that weapons were not allowed in the bar, that there was a security system which detected them. I graced him with a swift death and left it to the Lord to determine if the man was worthy of heaven or not. I'm leaning toward not."

Big Country's gaze darted to Stormy and Lynx standing off to the side with their backs to him. They wouldn't be able to see any signals he might give so he let Delilah talk and waited for an advantage.

"We used liquid chemicals which remained inactive inside the cross until the detonation device was activated. Cornelius was no fighter, we had to arm him in the event an opportunity to kill Zeus and Sabrina arose. Liquids are very hard to predict. It's unfortunate Cornelius had to be the one to lose."

"He didn't have to," Big Country said. "You made that decision. Didn't even stop to think that you *both* could have left the Shepherd and lived new lives. You burned that boy alive."

"So what. He's dead, it makes no sense to concern ourselves over this now. Zeus and Sabrina will die. *She* will die," Delilah said, glancing at Stormy.

His heart hammered. He inhaled deep, allowed his shoulders to drop.

"Nobody else has to die, Delilah. Me and you, we just walk away, yeah, we just start a new life where we'll be happy, just us together."

He took a step forward.

"Don't. Move." Delilah addressed him, but her eyes never left Stormy.

Big Country's fingers twitched. He wouldn't get to his gun in time. He knew this. He didn't know how he was going to save Stormy.

Blue flame flickered somewhere on the periphery of his vision. *No,* he thought. But the cold was spreading, the world fading to mute, his mind's eye turning inward as it waited for the elusive blue flame to land.

If you lose control now, son, you'll lose everything. Stop feeling, just think, just breathe and wait for your moment.

"Delilah," Stormy called out. *Shit.* He couldn't warn her, couldn't convince her Delilah wasn't to be reasoned with. "Delilah, when we first met I told you there was power in your name, and you've proven that it's true. You're a warrior, it's clear. You fight for your God, for your freedom, fight to be loved."

Armand edged toward Lucas when he should have been edging away. What the hell? Were they all trying to get themselves killed, he wondered, but Delilah's gun never moved to Armand; she kept it pointed dead center of his chest.

"God showed you Lucas when you were wanting more from life," Stormy said. "But just as undeniably, She revealed him to me. Had he come into my life even two weeks ago, I wouldn't have been ready, I still had shit to let go, parts I was struggling to reclaim. You have killed innocent people without a drop of remorse, Delilah, you have a *lot* of shit to work through. Being with Lucas won't save you from that, you'd know that within an hour of being with him."

Because Stormy would kill her. Big Country understood her message, even if it escaped Delilah.

"Very noble and insightful words," Delilah said. "But really, how much credence do you expect me to give a whore, especially one as deceitful as you?"

Stormy's hand clenched tighter around her cell phone but she didn't respond.

"I'm gon' say something here, darlin' and you can take it however the hell you gonna take it," Big Country said, angling his body, hoping

Delilah couldn't see Armand's fingers inching toward the gun holstered at his back. "The living truth is, this woman is my heart, and it ain't because of that spark of attraction between us when we first met, it's been everything since. You have no idea who I am or what I need. I'm not saying that as a criticism, I'm just making it clear that if there's any deceiving going on about who we are to one another, it's you, deceiving yourself. Now me and you can walk out of here together, we can work to free you from this Shepherd and I promise you on my life, darlin', I won't leave your side 'til he's dead and his order is destroyed."

"It's what Mama's Brood does," Lynx chimed in. "We make bad people go away."

Delilah ignored him.

"I believed in you, Lucas. You made me believe I could have something more than killing and servitude, *that* was the deception." The gun trained on Stormy, the one aimed at him—neither wavered but there was a gleam of vulnerability in Delilah's eyes. "As tempting as your offer is, it's no longer the Shepherd's order alone we would have to fight. The Patron knows of the child because I relayed the information to his people before erasing my presence from the Inn and returning here. The Patron is a determined man and has never-ending resources, he will have the child as well as the blood of his son's killers." She sighed. "You've defeated me beloved. You are hers, body and soul, I see that, but what do I get, what do I have to hold on to while she's consuming your soul? Nothing. Nothing but the knowledge that though you denied me God's blessing, I contented myself with knowing I destroyed your oh-so-precious heart."

Smoke exploded from both barrels of Delilah's guns.

Big Country roared, thunder reverberating throughout the room as Armand freed his gun and fired. Bullets ripped through Delilah's body, but it was too late.

Sienna Red, his Stormy, lay silent and unmoving on the ground, blood pooling and expanding beneath her and Lynx's fallen bodies.

Armand ran past him, knelt beside the two people he should have given his life to protect.

Armand was shouting at him, and Mama, Mama was calling to him—but that couldn't be real, Mama wasn't there. *She can't save you this time, ol' son, maybe that crazy bitch stole your mind as certainly as she's taken your heart*, he thought.

His heart. He looked at Stormy, at Lynx, and moved to them, the familiar numbness, the pervasive cold, none of it stopped him from recognizing the weighty presence of death stepping into the house.

A terrible force hit her, slamming her into the grimy hardwood floor. Her head bounced against the unyielding surface, rendering her incapable of movement, scrambling her thoughts as an undertow of darkness swept over her. A terrible weight crushed her chest, a fiery pain radiating from her abdomen. She couldn't breathe, she couldn't…

The currents of darkness pulled her further and further from her body's crisis, beckoning her to just let go.

Sleep. A promise of peace lay within the dark entreaty, but a promise of something more compelled her toward the surface of her consciousness. Weight lifted from her chest and she inhaled deeply, filling her lungs. She repeated the process over and over again.

A hand pressed against the side of her face and she opened her eyes. Lucas knelt beside her, and the panic in his gaze nearly stopped her breath again. She reached for him, and the pain burst through the nebula of peace the darkness had provided.

She looked down. Blood…there was so much blood she almost believed she'd been baptized in it. This much blood usually meant death.

She looked to her left and Armand was there, pressing his T-shirt into Lynx's chest. It had been Lynx's body covering hers, making it hard to breathe. He'd launched himself into her as Delilah fired. Now he was on his back, bleeding from his chest and his thigh. Stormy bled from her side, that was where the pain flared the most intensely, but now that she was conscious, she also felt a sharp sting in her left shoulder.

All the blood wasn't from one person. That made her hopeful, but Lynx wasn't moving, wasn't responding to any of Armand's administrations.

"I'm okay, Lucas, I'm okay," Stormy said, trying to sit up. He kissed her hard, and she tasted his terror, breathed in his relief.

"Do it *now*, Lucas!" Mama shouted from the cell phone beside Stormy's knee and Lucas got up and ran out of the room. The call she'd made to Mama before Delilah's arrival hadn't disconnected. She must have heard everything.

Stormy shifted closer to Lynx. His face looked dazed and she wondered if he'd also hit his head. She smoothed the damp hair from his brow and prayed, attempting to ignore the wound in his chest oozing blood as if forced up from an overflowing well. Lynx's skin was sallow, his breathing barely discernible. She reached out and gripped his hand to anchor him to this life even as his eyes closed.

"Please don't go. Please, Lynx..." She sobbed and held tighter, then nodded. "I know it hurts, I know you want to drift away, but hold on to the pain, embrace it, because that's life. Open yourself to all the pain," she begged, held him tighter, gritting her teeth to stem the desire to scream, to find the right words that would hold back death.

"Naw now chi—" Armand said with soft rebuke.

She knew her words bordered on cruel and selfish—sadistic, even —but life lived in Lynx's pain and she had to believe he wanted to live, goddamn it. "Don't let go of the pain, Lynx, let it fill you."

Lucas rushed back into the room, and she scuttled out of the way as he knelt across from Armand. He nodded, and Armand removed the soaked T-shirt from the wound. Lucas packed the wound, then turned Lynx over, stuffing more gauze inside the hole there.

Lucas wrapped some kind of tape around Lynx's torso over each wound site and when Lynx began to seize she stood up and stumbled over to a chair where she watched Lucas and Armand secure Lynx's body. She heard Mama say something about Merlee and EMTs but she continued to retreat.

"Turn him away," she muttered as she watched them. Everything seemed surreal, but she spoke the words again, knowing that she was addressing a force far more powerful than the struggle for life she saw playing out before her.

"Help me…"

Stormy moved toward the plea, no longer feeling her own body, and fell to her hands and knees beside Delilah. So much blood, yet the younger woman was alive, tears running from the corners of her eyes. Her fingers twitched spastically.

"Take me…home." Delilah forced the words out, then sobbed, a cry reminiscent of a child's pain, innocence lost, desperation. The rawness of it reached beyond the shroud of shock surrounding Stormy, shook her to her core.

"Where's home, Delilah?"

"Not…" Delilah shook her head, swallowed repetitively, holding Stormy's gaze. "Abi…gail… Lorne."

Stormy nodded, closing her eyes. "Go home, Abigail. Be at peace."

The other woman didn't respond.

Her silence spoke of death and endings.

A cool breeze brushed against Stormy's cheek and she briefly opened her eyes.

"Let her go home," she prayed. "But please turn Lynx away."

He sacrificed himself to save me, Goddess, please bless him with love and abundant life. Please allow his light to shine for years to come. You brought me back, you didn't abandon me when I'd abandoned myself, so I know it's within your power to turn him away. She breathed deeply as the breeze wrapped itself around her. *Take her home, but turn him away, turn him away.*

EMTs attempted to engage her, shouts erupted as Lynx coded.

Strong arms lifted her, settling her someplace softer than the floor, but she didn't stop praying, not even when Lynx was carried out of the house, escaping with the siren's wail. Stormy focused on sending strengthening energy to Lynx's spirt, not deviating from her now-singular request that he be turned away from the gates of death.

Life moved around her, people pulled at her, but she refused to open her eyes, refused to face a reality where Lynx was no longer a part of it.

It was all just a matter of cold hard reality now.

No emotion, no questions, no more wondering if Stormy, sitting over there not responding to a word anyone said, was going to leave him because he intended to make sure she did.

After what went down, he couldn't ask her to stay with him, not when it meant she'd face loss, death, violence on a regular basis. Stormy hadn't signed up for this life, and just because they shared feelings—intense, soul-adjusting feelings—it didn't mean he wouldn't let the feelings go.

I'm a pro at shutting all that shit down, he thought, pacing back and forth on the front porch and turning to look through the open door each time he passed it.

Nobody seemed to be making headway with getting Stormy to talk to them. The EMTs were walking her through everything they were doing, but they might as well have been talking to an automaton, one that looked as if it had walked off the set of a horror movie. Drying blood and mud were in her hair, crusting on her skin, ruining her dress—yet her face, his Sienna Red woman's face, was serene.

He ran a hand over his head, hoping he hadn't broke her with all this foolishness.

Moving toward the end of the porch, he shifted his focus to the police and emergency medical vehicles in his grands' front yard. The partially-revived bodies of PaPere and Thibideux were handcuffed and placed in the back seats of separate cop cars.

Belle Mère was wide awake and fighting mad. She was cuffed but refusing to get into the back of a third sheriff's car and the deputies seemed real hesitant in the handling of her, likely because of the protections the sheriff had extended to her. They should have knocked her upside the head and tossed her in the car.

When the sheriff's car came rolling up the drive, Belle Mère became a tearful, simpering mess.

"Oh, she's good, Big Luc," Deputy Harlan said, watching the theatrics from the bottom of the steps.

"Yeah boy, she da best," Armand said as he stepped out of the house.

The sheriff parked further down the drive and walked up past his men, glanced at PaPere and T-bo, tipped his head at Belle Mère before scuttling past her which seemed to reignite her anger. She called that poor man names a person shouldn't want to say to another person.

The sheriff was red in the face by the time he reached them, lowering his head in shame and rubbing the back of his neck. "Hell of a morning, ain't it?" the sheriff said, by way of greeting.

Big Country crossed his arms over his chest, remaining silent as he stared the sheriff down.

"Goddamn it, Paul, get her in the goddamn car!" the sheriff shouted at the younger deputy trying to contain Belle Mère. Wiping the back of his hand over his forehead, the sheriff looked at Harlan. "What we got here, fellas?"

Harlan ran down the situation with precision. He'd always been methodical in nature even when they were younger.

"Hey Harlan," a woman's tearful voice said over the CB radio. "We just got a call reporting two dead bodies at the Mollybrook Inn. Floyd and Anna Hutchins were shot in their beds."

Harlan pushed off the porch rail and cursed softly before pressing the button on his shoulder mic. "We're stretched thin here, Gail. Have Hank go over and secure the scene, I'll be there in a bit."

"What the hell is going on? Has everybody forgotten who's sheriff around here?" The sheriff frowned.

"Yeah, we was real sorry to hear about you resigning this morning," Big Country said. "But it makes sense, yeah, given how Merlee had to leave our home because you wouldn't do your *fucking job*. I suspect that spate of poor judgment can also be tied to Will's assault in the barn, and to a number of folks in town being harassed and threatened by the people in the back of those cars. The ones you wouldn't do nothing about because you got caught up in some rancid pussy. It's understandable you'd want to hand the mayor your resignation letter in person by days' end, because if you don't...you know me, sheriff, you know what I can do."

When the sheriff finally gathered his balls, he looked at Big Country. "I'm sorry I caused your family harm, son. Just one foolish choice and…"

"Don't beat yourself up too much. Belle Mère has screwed, and screwed over better men than you," Armand said.

The sheriff turned to Harlan. "I'll head on over to the Inn, help out there." He looked over toward the squad cars again. "You think they killed Floyd and Anna?"

"Naw, that was Delilah, damn near guarantee it," Big Country said.

"She was just unnecessary crazy, yeah," Armand muttered.

The sheriff headed back to his car, and one of the EMTs came to the door, motioning toward the inside of the house.

"Hey Big Luc, your woman's responsive and on the phone talking to her mama or *a* mama. Either way, think you can get her to agree to go to the hospital?"

Big Country nodded, clenching and unclenching his fists as he headed inside to cajole Stormy into leaving. She needed to be away from him and the Brood, live a normal life, but every part of him was fighting the idea of letting her go.

Navigating around Delilah's body, the coroner, and the crime scene investigators, Big Country squatted down in front of Stormy. She reached out and brushed her knuckles across his cheek and he closed his eyes and clenched his jaw.

Lord, he wasn't ready to let her go.

"Mama just got off the phone with Merlee. Lynx is in surgery and she said we shouldn't worry, that Cizan says Lynx won't be dying anytime soon."

He nodded, feeling relief and gratitude.

If Lynx had a bad feeling, something bad was likely to come of it.

By the same token, if Cizan said Lynx would live, Big Country knew his best friend would live.

Flattening Stormy's hand along his jaw, he placed his palm over it, absorbing her warmth, her scent. This woman had been with him every step of this journey, fighting for him, fighting with him, allowing him to show her every angle of his soul, and still, here she was, offering him solace in all the ugliness.

Wrapping his fingers around hers he held on, pressed her deeper into his flesh, fighting off a profound sense of loss.

"Don't we look a sight," Stormy said.

He opened his eyes and smiled. "Like we've been spit from the womb of the earth."

"I was thinking more like the ass of the earth."

He laughed. Unable to stop himself, he leaned in and kissed her. "Thought I'd lost you, beautiful."

"I was praying for Lynx."

"Thank you, darlin', your prayers were answered, but now I'm gonna need you to go to the hospital with these kind folks. Refrain from giving them the trouble you've given me, let them take care of you, yeah."

It had to be something in the way he said it because she frowned and leveled him with a penetrating look.

"You're not coming with me, are you? Not to the hospital, or Louisiana, or France?"

He placed their joined hands against his knee, avoiding her gaze. "I stay breaking our agreements don't I, Sienna Red?" he said, rubbing his thumb over her knuckles. "There's a lot I can live with, Stormy, but you dying and me not being able to protect you is not one of them. If Lynx hadn't been here, you'd be dead. I love you, woman; hard, too much, so damn much. And that means I do whatever it takes to keep you safe. Even if it means letting you go."

Stormy nodded and motioned for him to help her stand. "You're always sacrificing and protecting, aren't you Lucas Beaumont? It's an admirable quality…until it isn't." She reached up and kissed him again. "I love you, too. Hard. But I can't be the only one willing to fight for it; did it before, sweetness, didn't turn out well for me."

She let the EMTs take her from him and place her on the gurney.

"Thanks for the adventure, Big Country Beaumont. I'm going to Louisiana to continue my adventure. Hope life works out for you."

He trailed them out the door, confused, watched them place her in the ambulance.

"Oh!" She called out before they closed the door and he was ready to leap in there and drag her back to him. "Mama wanted you to call her, something about a confession."

The doors closed, and within seconds the ambulance pulled away, taking her away from him at an alarming speed.

What just happened? She just left him like it was nothing.

Wasn't she supposed to fight to get him to change his mind? He would have fought. What kind of fucking love was *that*? It wasn't; her ass didn't love him. If she had, she wouldn't have just walked away, wouldn't have just let him go.

"You kinda stupid, yeah?" Armand said beside him. "But I guess blood will tell. Beaumonts have always been foolish about love."

EPILOGUE

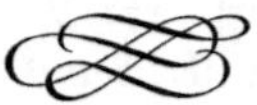

$\mathcal{B}$ig Country sat in his granddaddy's chair watching the chaos around him with forced calm. He'd warned them, told them he needed time, some space; but did they listen, oh no, they descended like a goddamn locust plague.

Merlee and Garret were the first to return, but that was the plan and purpose all along. Mama had arrived less than ten hours later, but he knew Mama would come, of *course* Mama would come, he'd been abandoned, and Lynx had almost died.

Mr. and Mrs. Jung, Lynx's parents, arrived hours after Mama, but they had stayed a few days and left. The bickering between Mama and Mrs. Jung made him want to put a bullet in his own head. Lynx had joined the Brood nearly ten years ago and Mrs. Jung still blamed Mama for ruining Lynx's career as a trauma surgeon. The two women had gone at it nearly every hour on the hour until Lynx asked his parents to return to their home in Canada.

Closing his eyes, he rested his head on the chair. All he wanted was some peace, just a minuscule moment of contentment similar to what he felt when he'd put his head on Stormy's breasts, fill his hands with their bounty…

Not so much as a by your leave, he wanted to shout.

It didn't matter that he'd told her to go; he was being the bigger person. His ass should've known better, should've realized she wouldn't stay if she believed she wasn't wanted. *Damn woman, she should have known I wasn't in my right mind.*

He'd been shot, stabbed, beaten up, thought he'd lost her, had his best friend nearly *killed,* not to mention the fact that he'd faced his worst demons and survived. That was too much shit to go through and be expected to make rational decisions. She was a damn therapist —she should've known that shit. But no, by the time the crime scene had been cleared and he'd gone to the hospital to check on Lynx, ask her to forgive him for his reactivity, she'd left, been released back into the wilds of life to roam without him. She'd been gone almost a week and he was trying, Lord knows he was, but things didn't look good for her future right now.

"Woman, you are crazy!" Mama shouted, as she moved quickly from one side of the house to the other. Lynx's mother shouted something back on speaker phone. "Do you even know your son? The idea of him marrying a good girl is *hysterical,* he needs someone who—"

Big Country refused to open his eyes, and he sure as shit didn't plan on telling Lynx that *his* head was on the chopping block now. Served the bastard right for going behind his back and colluding with Mama. That was a violation that came with consequences.

Footsteps entered the house from the front.

"Boy, you ain't said nothing but a word," he heard Price say, and Armand snort.

Price and Coen, the two Brood members who'd returned from their out-of-country assignment had gone directly to the Jaces' home to watch over Bree until Zeus and Sabrina arrived. After the couple decided to take their niece to France and seek out Zeus's long-lost family, Coen had gone on home to Mama's House and Price had come here.

"This'll be timed," Price, used to giving directions as the Brood's primary team lead, said. "First round, you use a rifle; the targets will be one hundred yards out. Before the second round you'll both drink four shouts of 150-proof rum, wait fifteen minutes and begin the second round, where the targets will be fifty yards out and you'll use the handgun of your choosing."

"Aw man, look at her, lil' bit ain't hardly big enough to hold no gun, no," Armand said, as the trio walked toward the back of the house, Big Country knew *lil' bit* was Bride.

"Man, that's what *I* said, but you know women these days, always trying to prove themselves." Big Country heard Bride snort, which was the equivalent of a normal person laughing their ass off. "Let's make this easy on her pocket, brah, say…loser pays two hundred, cash."

It was a sucker's bet, but Big Country didn't intervene; his brother would have to learn sooner or later.

"I'll take y'all's money…but just in case the impossible happens, ya spot me a hundred?" Armand asked.

"Look at *this* mothafucka," Price muttered as they exited the house.

Big Country heard two pairs of feet coming down the stairs and squeezed his eyes shut. Why wouldn't they all just go away?

"You think we made a baby this time?" Garret whispered.

"Oh baby, I think we made two or three," Merlee said. *His* Merlee.

Lord Jesus help me, Big Country prayed, clenching his fist, trying to stay rooted in the chair's cushions and not lunge for Garret's throat.

He breathed through it, and by the time the screen door toward the rear of the house banged shut again, the house going quiet for the first time in days, Big Country opened his eyes and fished his phone out of his pocket to text Stormy.

BC: Lynx comes home in 2 days

Stormy: I know, talked to him earlier…and Mama…and Merlee lol

BC: U having a good visit?

Stormy: I am. Fam is insane, u'd fit n!

He smiled and rubbed a hand over his chest. He missed his Sienna Red something fierce. Continuing to communicate with her was a study in masochism, more painful than pouring salt vinegar over a gaping wound.

And still that was better than the cavern of emptiness his soul resided in when he didn't.

BC: Hey darlin', do me a favor, wear that red lace set to bed tonight.

It was a full two minutes before she responded.

Stormy: (sad face emoji) I want to Lucas, I do, but it's too hot and humid here baby, I think maybe I'll have to sleep naked tonight.

He sat back as if shoved and let the phone fall to his lap.

Images of her damp and naked and writhing in bed had Bubba waking up as if it was nighttime. Nighttime was their time, his and Bubba's special time with Stormy.

After the first sleepless night without her, Big Country had hacked into her phone's camera and watched her as she prepared for bed. She had to have known he'd do it because her phone was placed on the bedside table each night, providing him with a perfect view of her on the bed.

When she'd began to touch herself, looked at the camera, said his name, Big Bubba had wept like a baby. Every night since, Big Country had come during or after Stormy had masturbated her way to orgasm.

He groaned. This torment had to end and right now he wasn't above groveling if it meant returning his heart back to where she belonged. He stared off into space, using the moment of quiet to imagine how he could entice Stormy back, make her never want to leave him again.

Gunshots rang out and whooping laughter followed. He heard Merlee yell at Bride, Price, and Armand over scaring her animals and chaos ensued.

Rising from his chair, Big Country retrieved his keys and headed out the front door. He intended to go to the hospital, sit with Lynx, and strategize ways to bring Stormy back to them.

Harlan called from the Sheriff's office, so he decided to drop by there first, see what information Harlan had for him.

Two days later, the farmhouse was bursting at the seams and Big Country was totally at peace with it.

Lynx was being released from the hospital today and Mama and

Terry were picking him up after retrieving Stormy from the airport. It had been Lynx's idea to have a Welcome Home celebration for him and invite Stormy to come. The man was fucking brilliant.

Terry had arrived at the farmhouse yesterday evening with Coen and Cizan.

Zeus and Sabrina were in France, and London back in the UK, but the three Brood mates had joined them for a Skype call to discuss what course of action the Brood would take after Lynx's party.

Big Country had shared the information he'd discovered about Kragen, his relationship with the Good Shepherd, and the Shepherd's order. Big Country and Harlan had learned that even though Delilah may have been obsessed with him, she'd also been obsessed with maintaining detailed records, intending to utilize them as leverage for her freedom if she needed to.

Mama and Terry decided it was imperative the Brood strike before either the Shepherd or Kragen had a chance to strike against them again.

Bride and Price would return to Ireland, Bride's place of birth, and find what they could about the order. Cizan and Coen would return to Mama's House with Terry and deal with rebuilding the bar as well as getting all the intel they could on the history of the Shepherd's Order and its leader.

They discovered that Abigail Lorne—Delilah—had been kidnapped when she was five, which meant there was a high likelihood that the Order had been, at the very least, kidnapping children for years to fill their ranks. Like Delilah...like Cornelius.

Sabrina and Zeus would stay in France with Brianna. Once Kragen discovered that he had a grandchild, it was only a matter of time before he took action, legal or illegal, to take Brianna away from them. Depending on how things turned out with Stormy, Big Country planned to meet Zeus and Sabrina in France to provide an added layer of protection.

Lynx, the unlucky bastard, would be staying on the farm with Mama, and Merlee, and possibly his parents if he couldn't talk them into staying up north, until he was ready for action...or until he lost his mind. Poor bastard.

Earlier this morning Stormy's mother and father, along with three of the four women who'd been at Mama's House the night he and Stormy met, had arrived. Her friends Lou and Jules fit right in, but her cousin Reign...somebody was gonna have to sedate her soon, the woman was jumpier than grease on a hot skillet.

The person he held responsible for bringing him and Stormy together, the one who'd negotiated with Mama to have Stormy's party at the bar, Tavi, couldn't come to the celebration because she had finals. Big Country had sent her a gift of gratitude she was sure to enjoy.

Big Country scanned his grands' kitchen, marveling at the massive amounts of food sitting on the counters and dining room table. Mama and Stormy's mother must have thought they were feeding a small army.

His chest tightened as he reached for his homemade barbecue sauce simmering on the stove. His grands would be so proud to see their home overflowing with all this love and laughter. He felt moisture well in his eyes, wishing they were here, wishing they could witness the fruits of their labor and love. He took a moment to extend a prayer of thanks to them; he never would have reached this moment without their love and guidance.

Stormy's father called from the back door, and Big Country walked outside and handed him the barbecue sauce, happy that he'd graduated from *that big-assed white boy* to *son*. It had taken a whole night of drinking and lying, followed by some real talk, before he'd won Stormy's father's approval.

"They're headed up the drive," Stormy's mother shouted as she rushed into the house. She and Merlee had been sitting in the rocking chairs on the front porch talking gardening for the last hour.

Big Country headed outside with Merlee while everyone stayed inside. Stormy didn't know her family and friends were here. He couldn't wait to see her reaction when she walked into the house.

Mama was the first person out of the SUV. She hopped down and opened the rear passenger door for Lynx, fussing over him as he stepped out. Big Country placed a hand over his mouth as Lynx rolled his eyes at Mama's fussing.

Terry was next to get out of the car and he opened the back door for Stormy.

Big Country was sure he stopped breathing for a good thirty seconds as he watched her. She was just that glorious in her sleeveless coral dress that fell to mid-thigh and wrapped delicately around her body. Her hair was in two long French braids and she…she….

He couldn't help it, he walked off the porch, stopping inches away from her. She smiled up at him and his heart beat with a rhythm of love he didn't know it was capable of playing. He bent down and lifted her in his arms, and she reached up with both hands, pressed them along his jawline and pulled his head down, kissing him so softly he couldn't understand why he felt it all the way down to the soles of his feet.

"Beautiful as moonlight on the bayou," he whispered, rubbing his nose against her temple.

"I missed you too, Lucas Beaumont."

He lowered her to the ground and kissed her hard before releasing her.

"Your ass never should have left in the first place. You know I almost died *three* times while you were gone, four if you count how grief led me into a drunken wrestling match with one of Merlee's bulls. Lucky for both of us, I won, and that's the *only* reason we're eating a shit ton of barbecue beef tonight."

"Just for no reason," She smiled, reaching for her purse-bag. "And for the record, I left because I knew what I was willing to do for love; you with your hard head had to find out. I *know* you Lucas—"

"Yeah," he said reaching for her carry-on luggage. "And what do you think you know?" he asked, gently bumping fists with Lynx, mindful of the shoulder brace from his friend's fractured clavicle.

"You stalked me after *one* dance at Mama's House," Stormy said as they walked toward the porch. "You thought you'd be *less* obsessed with me after all we've been through? Like, really?"

Whatever else Stormy was going to say was lost in the loud *Welcome Home!* that erupted as they walked into the house. Events descended into a good hour of hugs, laughter, and out-and-out lying. Everything from the night Big Country and Stormy met to Lynx's rescue was reenvisioned.

Big Country knew he'd taken things too far when Stormy popped him upside the head for claiming he'd begged her to stay and all he'd gotten for his efforts was her derision before she'd stomped away.

After everyone ate, Big Country called them all into the family-room.

"All right y'all, two items need to be dealt with before this celebration continues. First, I'm enacting Brood Law."

Mama began to protest and a few of the Brood mates looked distinctly uncomfortable. Everybody not Brood simply seemed confused by the shift in energy so Big Country explained.

"When a Brood mate betrays another, the offended is awarded the right to exact whatever punishment he sees fit. Then it's settled."

Big Country crossed his arms over his chest, was silent for a good long time as he contemplated Lynx, then shrugged.

"Sorry cousin, a betrayal's a betrayal," he said, and Lynx grimaced and nodded as he stood. Mama began to intervene, but Terry pulled her back.

"Law is law." Lynx nodded, and that was all it took for Mama to settle down. None of the others would interfere.

"Dude," Lynx shrugged. "You gotta admit, it all worked out for you in the end, right?"

"I got no concern for *in the end,* brother, because the end result ain't what this is about, what this is about is you and me. This is about trusting the integrity of our relationship—as brothers." He hung his head. "What has put you above every other man in my life is knowing I could trust you above all others to have my back, that I could take you at your damn word above all others. But you went and threw your lot in with Mama, building one lie on top of another because you thought you knew what was best for me.

"I trusted you with all of me, brother. Everything. And my heart is fair to breaking because I don't know if I'll ever be able to trust you the same way again." Big Country looked toward the ceiling, unable to blink for fear that the moisture gathered would spill out.

Lynx could barely look him in the eye, his shame evident.

"You're right, brother," Lynx said, as his whole demeanor became resolute. "I believed Stormy was the perfect woman for you. That didn't mean I'm free to leverage your trust to get you to see it. Not trusting you to work it out without my interference, that's a betrayal. I apologize, man, I'll do whatever I have to do to atone."

Unfolding his arms, Big Country brought his fists up to chest level, clenching and unclenching his hands as if building power within them.

"You got to take a couple of licks to the face, brother, just as a reminder that if *ever* you take a notion to meddling around in my life like that, there'll be harsh consequences."

Lynx took a deep breath and nodded once, standing firm, a man willing to take whatever was coming to him to prove he was worthy of Big Country's trust.

"If it's not too much to ask," Lynx said. "Could you avoid the pre-existing injuries?"

It was then that the non-Brood members of the group understood that there was going to be a physical price to be paid for Lynx colluding with Mama and manipulating Big Country to get him together with Stormy.

When they realized that, Stormy and Mrs. Redmond had to be physically restrained to stop from interfering.

Big Country rolled his shoulders and shook out his arms like a boxer about to step in the ring to wage war. "Sorry brother, though I don't like to see you in pain, this is how it's got to go to make things right between us."

Big Country stepped to within striking distance of Lynx's rigid six feet one frame, knowing his friend would take his punishment. He was Brood.

Big Country lunged forward, gripped each side of Lynx's head and pressed his lips against Lynx's cheek, giving him the biggest, wettest, cheek-sucking kiss before stepping back and grinning. "I love you brother, you gave me the chance to free my soul, the chance to fall in love, and for that, I'll never be able to repay you—"

Lynx stared at him, golden brown eyes wide, mouth agape in horror, his hand trembling less than an inch from his slobber-drenched cheek. "What did you..." His lips turned down in disgust and his nostrils flared.

"—but I promise, I will make it my life's work to return the favor." Big Country grinned. "That I guarantee."

Lynx touched his hand to his face and gagged as he pulled it back and saw the coating of saliva on his palm. Then he screamed, sending everybody into fits of laughter. Big Country jumped back just as Lynx kicked out at him.

Mama and Mrs. Redmond weren't laughing, they glared at him, fairly accusing him of murder.

"What?" Big Country said innocently, motioning toward Lynx holding his slobbered-down cheek pathetically. "I was just thanking him is all."

Next Big Country walked over to Stormy, reached for her hand, and motioned for Mr. Redmond who returned the envelope Big Country had given him and his family to review.

"Now, it's not that I don't trust you, Stormy, but I have to be sure you understand what you're choosing if you choose to be with me. I can't leave the Brood because they're family and the work we do is needed. I'll cut back if that puts you at ease, but I'll do this job 'til I can't do it anymore."

She started to say something, but he held up his hand. "By the same token, the work you do is important, and I'm living proof that you're damn good at it; But darlin', I'm not gonna lie, you stay with me and you may very well lose that license you've worked so hard for." He took a deep breath. "And that part of me that rages, it's still in there, darlin', but I swear I will never harm you—"

"I know that, Lucas."

"—nor will I ever expect you to be anything other than be who you are, because you Sienna Red, *as you are,* are the only woman I'll ever fallen in love with, you've seen every part of myself and you're still here, so…here."

He handed her the envelope, and held his breath as she took it, then looked back up at him.

"You still have so much to learn about me, Lucas Beaumont."

"And I aim to, sweetness."

"Good, because lesson one in the life and times of Stormy Redmond is that I know life is not guaranteed, Lucas. I would there-fore, have a life of adventure with you than a life of safety without you. I'd choose you over my license, Lucas, because I realized I don't need it to help people. I have a boutique and a pension that provide me enough money to live nicely. Lesson two, I have no doubt you and your family will do all it can to protect me, keep me safe, because you already have. Lynx put his life on the line to protect me because he loves you."

"Love is an awful strong-ass word," Lynx muttered.

"The strongest," she agreed. "I choose you, Lucas, because quite simply, you came into my life and destroyed any notion that there is a better option than us being together. I just needed you to see that."

"She finally stopped punking out," Lou said.

"*Finally*," Jules replied.

"Open the envelope, Stormy," Big Country said, praying for patience.

"You've bumped me up to mangy-bitch status," she told him, before shaking her head at Lucas. "But we don't need another contract—"

"Open. The damn. Envelope."

"You're gonna get enough of cursing at me," she muttered, opening it and pulling out the sheet of paper.

She stared at it for so long he thought she was going to ball it up and throw it at him.

"This is a marriage contract."

"Always knew you were the smartest tool in the shed." He smiled.

"My parents signed this."

"Because unlike he who shall not be named—" He looked at Garret. "—I know how to follow protocol the first goddamn time."

"You've created a contract for marriage."

"Yes, darlin', we've gone over that, it doesn't have to be soon but this says we both agree it will happen."

Her finger skimmed over the articles of the contract.

"You'll be a tester for any new merchandise!" She laughed.

"Woman, if you can stick a vibrating butt plug up my ass and make me come like a bottle rocket, I give you license to experiment however you deem fit."

"*Lord Jesus*," Stormy's mother whispered.

"You're so inappropriate." Stormy smiled, unabashed. "So, we're really going to do this?" she asked, leaning into Lucas as he handed her a pen and kissed her.

"Sign your name on the dotted line, darlin', and let's see where the next adventures take us."

LA FIN

ABOUT THE AUTHOR

Shay Rucker loves to write stories that mash up elements of love, fantasy, action, and horror. Her debut novel, On The Edge of Love, was the 2016 Swirl Awards winner for Romantic Suspense. When she is not writing and working, Shay values spending time with friends and family while plotting ways to go on international adventures.

Join Shay's newsletter at http://eepurl.com/dkteVT

www.ingramcontent.com/pod-product-compliance
Lightning Source LLC
Chambersburg PA
CBHW070429120726
47910CB00003B/703